THE LINEUP

USA TODAY BESTSELLING AUTHOR

MEGHAN QUINN

PROLOGUE

JASON

It isn't in my nature to cry over burnt ham, but here I am, tearing up like a jackass, because the meal I've been reluctantly slaving over for the past four hours is two shades away from charred dust.

I had it all planned out. The timing was right, the recipes perfected, the table decorated with impeccably folded napkins that impersonated angelic swans, and polished silver that I scrubbed for an hour until I could see my balls in the reflection. Nothing says polished silverware like a spoon that gives you a clear upside-down view of your gonads.

But even with countless hours of preparing this feast, naked as the day I was born with only an apron to cover my man-loins, I still ended up with a scorched ham doused in fire extinguisher agent because somehow, the damn thing caught on fire.

Imagine this, a grown-ass man—no, not just a grown-ass man, but a man at the fresh age of twenty-eight, built like a linebacker with buttocks you can bounce rocks off . . . thanks to squatting for a living—dancing around the kitchen on his twinkle toes, arms flailing with pink and white potholders attached to his hands,

1

screaming like a banshee, as flames light up the Jenn-Air double oven where the brown sugar and pineapple ham resided.

Are you seeing it?

Add the imagery of said man naked, dick and balls harmoniously bouncing in panic while the apron his "girlfriend" got him that says *Eat my food, Lick my dick*, unravels in the fit to unleash the fire extinguisher.

That was me . . . a minute ago.

Frantic, screaming, and all in all losing any last shred of my man card I had left.

It's why I'm currently weeping like a nitwit into the flaps of my apron, wondering where I went wrong.

If we're going to be honest with each other—and I would like to establish honesty with you—I'll admit, I've always leaned toward the sensitive side. You know, the cuddly grizzly bear. Big and intimidating but a fucking gooey butterball heart on the inside.

Tell me a love story. I'll listen the crap out of it.

The Bachelor? Why yes, that's one of my favorite shows.

Do I smile when sharing a candlelit dinner with myself, followed by a nice long soak in a bubble bath while Enya—the fucking goddess of all voices—plays in the background? I sure as shit do.

But if some ignorant asswipe gets in my face on the ball field, stirring up trouble, I'm the first to lay a fist across his jaw and the first to be thrown out of a game.

And I'm not even sorry about it.

People are arriving in an hour. I'm vulnerable as fuck with my bare ass resting against the cold white-oak floor of my girl's apartment, while a lonely tear streams down my freshly shaven cheek. I have no main dish, and the apartment smells like burnt rabbit turd.

Why am I in this hopeless predicament?

Because of one person.

One single person who flipped my life upside down.

A bombshell in a suit, a ravenous sex-fiend in the sheets, a classy and sophisticated tight-ass in the boardroom. She's a knockout who's always on my mind. She's the girl you do things for, that you never thought you'd ever do . . .

Like cook a fancy-as-fuck four-course meal for her and her business associates while practicing interesting conversational starters to ensure the night flows smoothly.

Back in college, I might have been referred to as the mother hen of the boys. I might have cooked at least two meals a week for the guys in the loft, and yeah, I was the ironing wizard, the one everyone turned to, to get out the most stubborn wrinkles. The title has carried on over the years, but my creativity in the kitchen has dwindled with the lack of time, my ironing is now done by my apartment keeper once a week, and the fresh flowers scattered around my place? They're more dead now than alive.

My point—I'm not the lady of the house I used to be. But I've been getting back into the swing of it.

So when my girl asked me to perform the impossible feat of an intimate dinner for four, I should have ordered in, tossed everything in serving dishes, and called it a night.

But noooooooooo, I had to attempt to be a goddamn hero and try to cook everything myself.

And all for what?

For one girl?

No. Not just *one girl*. *The* girl who owns my balls, who has a grip so tight on them that if she asked me to bellow out my ABCs in soprano while swirling my finger around my belly button . . . I would.

Who is this girl that has brought me to the brink of boo-boo smush bear insanity and caused me to weep like a schoolgirl in the corner of the apartment?

There's only one lady with more than enough ovaries to buckle the knees of the mighty Jason Orson.

The one and only Dorothy "Dottie" Domico.

CHAPTER ONE

JASON

A *few months earlier...*
There's one sentence every baseball player never wants to hear: you've been traded.

Especially after being drafted by a team you've worked tirelessly through their farm system for, and finally earned a spot on the starting lineup in the big leagues . . . only to be traded after four short years. Not six or eight years. Four. Years. Four years where you've grown relationships, built a fan base, and established all your favorite restaurants within a five-block radius of your apartment.

It's a kick to the crotch . . . for most.

For me, I couldn't be more ecstatic. My agent called me two weeks ago, told me about the trade, and once we ended the phone call, I started looking for apartments.

Don't get me wrong. I'll miss the fans, my teammates, and the gyros with extra tzatziki sauce I've come to rely on, but Tampa has never been my home. It's been a nice temporary place to launch my career, but I'm ready to move on.

So when I got the call that I was being traded to Chicago, I literally whipped my shorts down, yanked out my dick, and shook it to the ceiling out of pure joy.

Bobbies, here I come, right? Going to play with my boys, Carson and Knox. Just like old times, like in college. Maybe they want to share a place, maybe they want me to make them some of my famous potato salad. Maybe they want to rub their loving relationships in my face—fine by me. As long as we're back together, holding each other's nutsacs and singing *Take Me Out to the Ball Game* together, I'm happy.

At least, that's what I thought at first . . . one big happy family.

Until I finally calmed down and stopped shaking my dick enough to hear my agent.

Not the Bobbies, he told me.

The Rebels.

I was traded to the Chicago Rebels.

I'm not going to lie and say my nipples didn't shrivel up from the thought of playing for the rival team of the Bobbies. I grew up in the area, the Bobbies were my team—secretly still are—and as a Bobbie for life, the thought of slipping on a black and red jersey made me want to break out in a cold, dead sweat.

I panicked.

I started to backtrack.

I stuffed my dick back in my pants. No way was I touching that thing while thinking about the Rebels.

Have you ever had a moment of pure rage, where you're about to fly off at someone, spittle ready to shoot past your lips, and arms geared up to flail irrationally? That was me, seconds away from firing off.

How could I possibly even CONSIDER playing for the Rebels?

But then he said five invaluable words.

Annual donations to your charity.

Lump sums.

Lots of cash.

Foundation-changing money.

Damnit all to hell.

That day, I sucked up my pride, smiled, and envisioned myself in red and black, because I would do anything for the benefit of my foundation.

And, the trade wasn't bad. Because I'm near my friends again, living in my home state, and piling on the cash for my charity, The Lineup. I also get to brag to everyone who wants to hear that not only am I catching for the best arm in baseball, Maddox Paige, but I get to play with the one and only . . . Cory Fucking Potter.

Yes, THE Cory Potter. You know, the guy who accomplished more than I could ever dream of by the time he hit thirty. He's a legend. A hero. A goddamn wet dream.

And I get to play ball with him on a regular basis.

I never let a moment go by when talking to my boys about the opportunity. And sure, Cory might be Carson's brother-in-law and he has access to him whenever he wants, but he doesn't get to snuggle up to him in the dugout and nuzzle his shirt while they announce the starting lineup.

Nope. I get that privilege.

Well, technically, I haven't had the opportunity yet since baseball season is freshly over and I was just traded, but this spring, oh boy, Cory Potter better watch out, because there will be some nuzzling.

To bring this full circle, I was traded, I'm happy about it, and because the gods seemed to have lined up with my luck, I'm currently moving into an apartment right across from one of my best friends.

"When do I get a key?" I ask Knox, who sets one of my boxes down on my kitchen counter.

"To my place?" he asks, pointing to his chest.

"Yeah, to your place. We are neighbors, you know."

"Yup. Neighbors, not roommates, therefore no key." He swipes at his forehead just as Carson plops another box on the counter and huffs out in pain.

"What the fuck is in that thing?"

Perfectly labeled with my state-of-the-art label maker, I run my finger over the black typed text and say, "My KitchenAid Pro and attachments. You should be able to carry that without making a stink about it."

Carson slides down the side of the wall, spent. "I threw my back out last night. Milly was adventurous, but that's beside the point. Why the hell do you have a KitchenAid mixer?"

Milly is Carson's wife. They got married a few years ago, right after he made it to the big leagues. It was a small, intimate wedding with family and a few friends, nothing too big, perfect for them.

"Who doesn't have a KitchenAid?" I ask, perplexed. Both Carson and Knox raise their hands. "Well, how the fuck do you make cookies?"

"We don't," Carson answers for both of them. "There are things here in Chicago called bakeries."

I shake my head. "But what about the fresh cookie smell in your apartment?"

"Candles," Knox answers, just as Emory and Milly walk through the door of my new apartment, lunch in hand.

Emory and Knox reconnected this year. *Thank. God.* After being apart for so long, they're finally back together. I'm not going to lie, when I heard the news, my little romantic heart shed a tear of joy. I remember the day they split, because it was the day that a very different Knox was born. He was known for being one of the good guys, the man everyone wanted as their friend, the man who always had a kind word and a quick joke. But when he lost Emory, Knox became a complete bastard. No one wanted to be around him. Carson and I stood by him, but at times, it wasn't easy. But now they're back together, and the world feels right again.

"Wow, looks just like our place," Emory says, setting the food on my table and reaching into her pocket. She hands me a key and says, "In case you need anything."

Smiling wide, I hold up the key to Knox and Emory's apartment and say, "Well, would you look at that. I have a key to the sex den."

8

"Sex den?" Emory's lips curl in disgust.

I thumb toward Knox. "That's what he calls it. Says you're horny all the time."

Eyes wide, Emory spins on her heel just about to pummel Knox with her fist when he says, "I did not fucking say that."

"Yes, you did. When we were lifting the couch into the elevator, you said you guys must have fucked on your couch at least fifteen times since you got back together, so it was good you had a sturdy one."

"Knox." Emory smacks his arm as Knox gives me his *I'm going to kill you* eyes. "If anyone is horny in our apartment it's you. I can't walk by you without you reaching out and trying to graze my breasts."

He stares at her chest. "Can you blame me?"

Milly, the more private of the bunch says to Carson, "We've been together for years. Surely you don't still talk about that stuff, do you?"

"Eh, depends on what you want to hear. If you don't want me talking about our *still* fucking incredible sex life, then nope, I haven't said a damn thing. Stopped years ago." Knox and I both snort. Milly's face turns bright red.

God, he's a lucky fucker, because Milly is the best. Seriously, when we first met her in college, the girl only had to start talking the mechanics of baseball and the guys in the loft got a boner. Throughout the last four years, she's Skyped with me numerous times to offer advice and encouragement, somehow knowing when I needed to *and* was able to hear both. She's one of my best friends.

To ease her embarrassment, I say, "Don't worry, Milly, he was just asking us if it's normal to only last thirty seconds before blowing his load. For the record, it's not. Normal guys can last longer. If you want to see, I can give you a key to my apartment." I wiggle my eyebrows.

"Hey fuckhead, that's my wife," Carson spits at me.

I scratch my chin. "Yeah, I guess wives are different than girlfriends, huh?" I turn to Emory. "I guess that means all my sexual teasing is coming your way."

Knox steps in front of Emory, plucks the key to his apartment out of my hand and sticks it in his pocket. "Or you can get a girl-friend for yourself."

"Yeah, if you had a girlfriend, we wouldn't be moving all your shit for you."

"How do you see that?" I ask.

"Because you would be so busy with her, you wouldn't need us to keep you company," Carson replies. "You would have hired movers instead of being a cheap-ass motherfucker. Dude, we have money, so we shouldn't have to move boxes anymore."

"But then we wouldn't be able to share my first meal in my new place together." I hand out sandwiches with a winning smile. "How nice is this? The gang is together again, minus Holt and Romeo, and Gunner . . ."

Carson takes his sandwich and says, "I still think you need a girl. Did you even date in Tampa?"

I shake my head and pop open the chips bag. We take a seat on the floor, spread out the wrappers of our sandwiches, and pass the chips around, taking a few and placing them on the wrappers while Milly hands out waters.

"Here and there." I shrug. "But nothing serious. Not even sure I'm looking for anything serious at this point."

"But you're such a catch," Knox deadpans with a roll of his eyes.

"Hey," Emory says, defending me. "I think Jason could make any girl happy. He's sensitive—"

"Too sensitive," Knox says.

"Handsome."

I "fluff" my short hair. "Why, thank you."

"And he knows how to cook. That's a win for me," Emory says with a wink in my direction.

Just to piss Knox off, I say, "Well, you're not married yet. Want me to give you a key to my place, you can test things out with me?"

"Keep pushing your luck, man," Knox warns. "See where it gets you. I can get you kicked out of this place. The majority of people who live here are Bobbies fans."

"Yes, but do they get to play baseball with Cory Potter?"

Milly groans and rests her head against the wall. "Please, don't remind me that you're going to be playing baseball with my brother. It haunts me that he is playing for Satan's team."

Born and raised in Chicago, Milly Potter has been a Bobbies fan her entire life. When Carson even joked about playing for the Rebels, she nearly had a heart attack, so to say she took the news hard that her brother was going to be a Rebel is an understatement.

According to Carson, she cried sporadically for a week and refused to acknowledge real life until her other two brothers dragged her back to work.

"Have you worn a Rebels shirt yet?" I ask.

She shakes her head. "No, and I refuse. I can't fathom the idea of even touching one. When Carson and I started dating, they went back and forth with whose jersey I would wear. I thought of making one myself that supported both men in my life, but now"—she shakes her head—"I only support my husband."

Carson kisses the side of her head. "The way it should be."

"Now that you're back in Chicago, do you think you're going to reconnect with any old flames from college or high school?" Emory asks.

"Old flames?" I take a bite of my sandwich and chew for a few seconds before swallowing. "I didn't have any old flames, one-night stands, sure, but nothing I'd consider rekindling."

"Are you open to a relationship?" Milly asks. "I know a few single moms who I'm sure would be interested."

I glance at the two eager matchmakers and motion my finger between the two of them. "Are you guys trying to set me up?"

Emory shrugs. "You're such a catch. It's hard to understand why you don't have a girlfriend."

"Taking a little too much interest in his love life," Knox says from the side of his mouth.

Emory palms his face and pushes him away. "Don't worry, your penis is the last penis I'll ever touch." Knox perks up with a smile. Such a douche. "But wouldn't it be fun to all go out on a date together?"

"The guy just moved here, maybe give him a second to unpack before you start thrusting women at him," Knox says gently. "Unless . . . do you want women thrown at you?"

I grab the bill of my hat and give it a nervous tug. "I don't know. It would have to be the right woman, you know? Someone who'd handle my lifestyle, be understanding, and also despite playing for the Rebels, be able to cheer for me with pride. But I'm not sure if I'm quite ready. This offseason I have a lot to do for my charity, so I'll be focusing a lot of my time on that and training. I might not have time for a woman."

"If you find the right one, she'll help you with your charity," Milly says. "Which reminds me, if you need anything from Division One Athletics, let me know."

That's where Milly works. Did I fail to mention she's a mechanics marvel when it comes to baseball? I would personally say the best in Illinois. She knows her stuff, helped Carson with his swing back in college, and they still work together. She works at one of the top facilities in the country, perfecting the swings of Chicago's youth.

"Thank you, that means a lot to me. Still trying to get everything up and running. There's a lot more to all of this than I thought, but my family has been a huge help."

When I knew I was ready to start a foundation in honor of my brother, I turned to my family to help me. My sister was more than happy to step up, as well as my parents, especially after I told them it was to honor Joseph, who has cerebral palsy.

My twin, my biggest fan, the guy who gives me drive to do better every day. He's the best person I know and because of him, I want to make an inclusion foundation that raises money for those with disabilities to be included in The Lineup by providing them with the right equipment to do so.

In high school, I had the most understanding and caring coach of all time. He saw my talent and saw the way Joseph yearned to be on the field with me, so my junior year, after I sat down with Coach and asked him if Joseph could be the bat boy, he said, "Why don't I do you one better and put him on the team?"

I wasn't sure how that would work given Joseph uses a walker to get around, which requires both of his hands, but Coach Whittaker had another vision: Joseph became a pinch runner.

After sitting our family down, Coach Whittaker asked Joseph, "Have you ever wondered what it felt like to score a run for your team?" When Joseph emphatically shook his head, yes, Coach told him, he was going to get that chance.

And sure enough, Joseph did.

Between our junior and senior year, he scored fifteen runs as a pinch runner.

Let me tell you, standing at home plate, my brother and his walker at third, begging to be able to cross that plate, nothing ever inspired me more to someway, somehow, get my brother to score a run for the team.

Out of those fifteen runs, I hit him in ten times.

That's a feeling I'll never forget, and something I want to be passed on from ballplayer to ballplayer. No matter your limitations, there's always a spot for you in the lineup.

"Don't you have that date thing coming up too?" Carson asks. "I've seen PSA about it all over the damn place."

"Yup, I think people have one more week to enter and then the winner will be announced right away."

"What date thing?" Milly asks while dabbing her mouth with a napkin.

"It's with that group called Charity Hustle. They contacted me a few months ago asking if I wanted to participate. Basically, they set up an exclusive opportunity for fans to have dinner with a celebrity and the way you enter is by donating to the celebrity's charity of choice."

"Oh yeah, I entered a few," Emory says with a blush to her cheeks. "There was one where you could go on a dinner date with Emily Blunt and John Krasinski. I knew it was a long shot but I donated anyway."

"Aren't you cute," Knox says. "I can score you a dinner date with them if you want. Remember, I used to date Mia Ford. I know people." Knox tacks on a smile, but it does nothing to help him from the scowl directed at him. Mia Ford is a well-known celebrity and while Emory and Knox were apart, he dated her. Let's just say, I don't think Mia is a name used often around their apartment.

"Do you want to spend the night in Jason's apartment tonight?"

"I'm a good cuddler," I say. "I'll make sure you feel the love, but I do sleep naked, so it's up to you."

Knox rolls his eyes and pulls Emory into his chest, pressing a kiss to the side of her head. "You know I'm kidding."

"I want to know more about this date," Carson says. "Are you really going to go out with a stranger?"

"Not by myself." I shake my head. "I'm taking Natalie."

"Smart." Carson nods his head.

"For many reasons. First of all, who knows if this person is a psychopath? I need to make sure I have someone with me in case the winner tries to steal me and take me off to their organ harvesting den. And second of all, what if it's a girl? My sister will be my chaperone so she can't pull a fast one on me, like a 'he touched me without my consent' kind of thing."

"Very smart." Carson nods.

Knox asks, "Organ harvesting den? Is that something you're really concerned about?"

"Yep." I bite down on a chip. "I'm always concerned about my organs being harvested. You can never be too sure these days."

"You're insane," Knox says while standing and picking up everyone's garbage.

I clap my hands together. "Okay, who's ready to help me unpack?"

Without another word, my friends stand and quickly make their way out of my apartment, the door shutting with their retreat.

Huh, I'm going to take that as no one.

CHAPTER TWO

DOTTIE

E *mory:* *What are you doing?*
To tell the truth or not.

My best friend isn't here right now. She can't see me, so there's no need to get her mother hen feathers all ruffled by revisiting the rabbit trail of my failed relationships. That's the last thing I want. Picking up my phone, I type out a curt response.

Dottie: *Working.*

Taking a deep breath, I give myself one more look at the memory Facebook decided to share with me today. Happy as can be, I'm smiling at the camera as Nick kisses my cheek. We're standing in front of The Bean, Chicago's iconic Cloud Gate, winter hats decorating our heads, and rosy cheeks from spending the day outside, sightseeing like tourists and enjoying every moment of it.

I thought he was it. I didn't think I'd ever meet a more kind, caring, or empathetic man than Nick. He gave me a sense of confidence to be the killer in the boardroom that I am. He encouraged me, and he made me feel sexy when we were home, sharing a bed. And in those moments when I was weak, didn't think I could stand up to the other tycoons I had to face daily, he stood behind me, rubbed my shoulders, and told me how intelligent I was, how ruthless, and how I could score any deal I put my mind to.

And I believed him.

I fell for him.

Head over heels.

I told my dad I was going to marry Nick one day. One day soon.

And then, I found out the true man he was. I wasn't his love, I didn't matter to him, and I wasn't all the things he told me I was. And he wasn't the things I thought he was. Instead, he was embezzling money from me, using me for my connections, and planning to be with me for a few more months before meeting up with his longtime girlfriend, where they'd ride off into the sunset together . . . rather than be with me.

I've never felt more foolish in my life.

More used.

Not only did I lose my self-confidence, I also jeopardized the biggest deal to date for my dad's company. *He* salvaged that, thank God. Being new in my position as the president of business relations, making such a colossal mistake made every board member doubt my dad's choice to put me in such a prestigious position. It made them question his decision-making and ever since then, it's been an uphill battle to prove that not only do I deserve the position I'm in, but I was meant to hold it.

I stare at the picture, letting it brand my brain, reminding me that I will never let this happen to me again.

Ever.

Once I feel satisfied with the reminder, I close Facebook and turn back to the group text between my two best friends, Emory and Lindsay.

Emory: *You're always working.*

Lindsay: *Why did you even ask? I think we both know what she's doing.*

Leaning back in my white office chair, I glance out the window

17

of my high-rise office, taking in the morning skyline before typing back to them.

Dottie: *It's nine in the morning on a Thursday. I think we all should be working.*

Lindsay: *The kids are taking a spelling test.*

Emory: *Cora is handling story time while I pretend to check in books.*

Lindsay and Emory both work at Cedar Pine Elementary. Lindsay is a third grade teacher with a penchant to slip up with a swear word here and there—how she hasn't been fired yet, I have no idea—and Emory is the librarian who seems to wear inappropriate-length dresses since she's been called into the principal's office a few times for dress code. Despite that, they're the best educators I know, and I would be honored to have either one of them teach my imaginary children.

I say imaginary, because that's as close to children as I'll ever get.

I'm all set on the baby coming out of my vagina thing. Not really interested in that form of torture. Now, if you'd like to tie me to my bedposts and run your tongue over my body for an hour, making me cry out from carnal need, then yes, I'm interested in *that* form of erotic torture.

Dottie: *Your work ethic is impeccable.*

Emory: *Not all of us can run the world like you.*

Dottie: *More like running the infrastructure of Chicago, but we don't have to get technical. What do you two want?*

Lindsay: *I came across something last night and thought you'd like to take a look at it.*

Dottie: *Do not send me naked pictures of giant penises anymore. I'm sick of them.*

Mainly because it's been a dry spell for me for months upon months now. It's scary how long it's been since I've seen a real-life penis in person, and the last thing I want is to get turned on at work because Lindsay has the need to send me dick pics. Women have it bad enough on dating sites; we don't need dick pics from our friends as well.

Lindsay: It's not a dick pic, but that reminds me. You're due for one soon.

Great.

Emory: I can vouch for her that it's not a dick pic. It's even better.

Dottie: Better than a dick pic? *taps chin* Are you sending me a close up of a man's pierced nipple?

Lindsay: No, but do you have one of those?

Dottie: What do you think?

Lindsay: Sarcasm is really hard to read through text messages . . .

Dottie: I don't.

Lindsay: Damn.

Emory: Can we get back to the reason we're ignoring the youth of America and tell Dottie why we're texting her?

Dottie: That would be appreciated since I have a meeting in fifteen minutes.

Lindsay: Right. So I came across this little fundraiser and thought I'd send it to you.

Confused, since my friends never pry me for money even though I have shitloads of it, I type back.

Dottie: What kind of fundraiser?

My computer lights up with a new email from Lindsay. The subject line says: *Be a Rebel with Me.*

What the hell is this?

Lindsay: Just sent you the link. *giggles*

Oh God, whenever Lindsay types "giggles" I know it can't be good.

Dottie: Get to the point.

Emory: Do you remember the giant crush you had in college?

Yes, I do. It was borderline infatuation.

Dottie: I can't recall any crushes.

Lindsay: Puh-lease. I bet you still have a folder in your phone of pictures of him.

Emory: You can't deny this, we both know your weakness for a bubble-butt catcher who stole your attention at baseball parties.

Dottie: Please get to the point.

Emory: Jason Orson, the man you've lusted after for so long, is back in town, and he's having a fundraiser where you can donate money to his charity to enter to win a date with him. We know how much you love donating money . . . and since you refuse to let me set you up with anyone, why don't you put it to chance?

Dottie: Are you daring me?

Lindsay: YES! We dare you to donate to Jason's charity and possibly win a date with him.

Dottie: You both are demented. I fear for the children at Cedar Pine. And if I really wanted a date with the man, I would have asked you to set me up, but I'm not into dating, you know that, especially a guy known to love love. He's hot, yes, and I would love to smack his bare ass, but he's everything I try to avoid. He's a relationship kind of guy.

Emory: It might be nice to settle down. Take a breather from your demanding job.

Lindsay: Or just get your ovaries tickled every once in a while.

And these are my friends. I love them very much, especially since they care about me so much, but this constant badgering to go on a date is starting to get old. They were obviously there for me when Nick picked up and left. They carried me because I was fragile, barely held together by my own body. I gave that man everything in me, and he ripped it apart. Since then, I've focused on work and only work.

Apparently, they have a problem with that.

Dottie: I pray you don't talk to your third graders like that.

Lindsay: They don't even know what ovaries are. If I told them I was about to tickle them, they'd probably cover their armpits.

Emory: Please don't threaten to tickle your students' ovaries. Seriously, Lindsay. What is wrong with you?

Lindsay: I didn't eat a proper breakfast.

Dottie: As much fun as this has been, I'm going to pass. I have to get ready for this meeting. I'll talk to you two later.

I stuff my phone in the drawer of my desk to avoid any more distractions and then pull up the Briar Hurst account folder that's been on my desk all morning—along with a fresh latte and a cut-up apple. I flip open the folder and review the bullet points I need to remember for this morning's meeting.

After I graduated from college, my dad pulled me into the family business, buying and selling buildings throughout the city. First started in California, my dad has grown Domico Industries and expanded it to Chicago, where he's been able to triple the profit margin within a matter of years.

I wasn't handed my position; I earned it, working my way up through the company, but now that I have it, I've helped the business grow even more. My dad credits my tough negotiating skills and ruthless business sense that I learned from him. My mom, on the other hand, wishes I'd soften up more. Wear my hair down occasionally, try on a colorful blouse, as she puts it. And just like Emory and Lindsay, she wishes I'd put myself out there again.

I prefer to stay hardened and closed off, only focusing on business, because even though I miss the touch of a man, I've been burned enough times by men who either can't handle my success, or those looking for a handout. I've found it easier to focus on work, and that's what I plan on doing.

I reach for an apple slice, missing the plate completely. I look up to find the apple in front of my computer and when I do, I spot the email from Lindsay, and even though I try to stay focused, I can't keep my curiosity from spiking.

Jason Orson.

God, the man. My teeth roll over my bottom lip. I remember the first time I saw him in a pair of athletic shorts and a skintight Under Armour shirt. It changed the way I looked at the male physique. Up until that point, I had no idea men could have asses. I thought it was a thing for women to boast about, you know, just like our boobs.

But Jason Orson proved me wrong one sunny day on a walk to class.

I can still see it in my head. It was outside the economics

building, he was standing with a few other baseball players, all wearing workout gear, all with wet heads from recent showers. His backpack was pulled high on his shoulders, giving me the perfect view of his backside.

This was no normal backside. I'm talking firm, high, and shelf-like. His tight and toned back muscles narrowed in and then BAM, his ass poked out unlike anything I'd ever seen. Think Giancarlo Stanton, but better.

I couldn't look away, nor could any other girl who walked by him.

I wasn't alone in the lust department.

Never have been when it came to Jason Orson. Whenever I went to baseball parties, with the goal of finally talking to him, he was always surrounded by an ungodly amount of women.

But that was back in college. I doubt he looks the same, or acts the same for that matter. He's a famous baseball player—which means he's probably hotter.

I look away from my computer just long enough to grab a slice of apple, then back to the email.

My hand itches to open it up, to see what he's been up to.

Maybe he gained a bunch of weight or grew a hideous beard, one of those long horrors baseball players grow for some weird reason. Isn't their face hot? Doesn't it get all sweaty and dirty from long hours on the ball field?

I know one way to kill my libido for the man; one of those beards. Maybe that's what I need to see, a beard on him, and then all will be right with the world. I can get back to the Briar Hurst folder.

Yup, just one peek; that's all.

Come on, beard.

I move the mouse to the email and hover over it.

No, I shouldn't. Opening this email will only result in a rabbit hole of Google searching; I can feel it in my bones.

Step away, Dottie.

Taking a deep breath, I turn back to the folder, giving the bullet points another once-over.

Something, something, something, they're ready to sell . . . something, something . . . wait, what am I reading?

Focus.

Deep breath.

The words swirl on the paper into a terrible version of a bubble butt . . .

"Oh, fuck it," I say out loud while clicking on the email.

In the body, Lindsay wrote, "Mr. Bubble Butt himself, doing good. I dare you to be a rebel with him . . ."

"Jesus," I mutter while clicking on the fundraiser link.

I'm a sucker for a fundraiser. I might seem hard as stone on the outside and keep a safeguard on my heart, but when it comes to raising money for a good cause, I can't help but say yes. Then again, I make more money than I can possibly spend, I have no children, my friends only let me buy them so much, so why not help out those who are trying to do good?

At least that's what I tell myself while Jason's fundraiser home page opens up.

I've heard of Charity Hustle. It's a great company that specializes in helping celebrities raise money while giving their fans a once-in-a-lifetime opportunity. I might have bid on one a while back. It was a dinner date with Emily Blunt and John Krasinski, and the only reason I did it was because I watched Emory bid on it, and I wanted to give her a bigger chance than her fifty-dollar donation. I donated two thousand dollars in hopes she would win, but she didn't . . . clearly. Unfortunately, it's by chance, but the more money you donate, the more entries you're allotted. I thought two thousand would give us the win, but I should have done ten thousand.

You live and you learn.

With a quick glance past my computer to see where my assistant is, I bite into another apple slice and explore the fundraising page.

Front and center is a picture of Jason with his arm around a guy who's holding himself up with a walker. Well, that right there opens the door to the crush I had many years ago. Not to mention the size of his biceps, the span of his chest, and the way his shirt fits tight across his upper torso but tapers and drapes over his hips.

God, look at all those muscles.

I prop my chin on my hand and sigh.

And then his gentle smile accompanied with his kind eyes. From the picture alone, I can tell he's not like the guys I've dated in the past few years. If I lifted his baseball hat off, I know I'd see family man tattooed across his head.

But even so, he's gorgeous. The only thing that's changed about him is his bulk. Everything about him is bigger. Stronger jaw, thicker neck, more powerful chest.

Are there other pictures of him?

I scroll down on the page, skipping over the info about his fundraiser, and scan for more pictures, but I don't see any, just the top one.

Picking up my pen on my desk, I tap it against my chin and then check out the time on my computer. Still ten minutes.

What kind of cyberstalking can I do in ten minutes?

Only one way to find out . . .

I pull up Google and start to type his name when I stop myself.

No. I shouldn't. I'm a serious businesswoman, not a besotted college girl.

I lean back in my chair, eyes fixed on my computer, pen flipping through my fingers.

Maybe . . .

No. I mentally shake my head. Not happening. No good will come of it if you type Jason Orson shirtless into the search bar.

And you know I'll add shirtless in there, because I'm desperate and lonely.

Did I say that out loud? No, I thought it. I'm not lonely, I'm just . . . unprepared for nighttime activities. One can only play solitaire so many times by themselves at night before it starts to become pathetic.

That's all this is, boredom and lack of focus.

Okay. I shake my head and sit tall in my chair. Briar Hurst, let's see what—

Oh, fuck it.

My fingers type out Jason Orson shirtless before I can stop them. I bite down on my pen, sitting at the edge of my seat as the search results load.

It's taking so long. Mental note: ream out IT for faster Internet so I can cyberstalk faster. Although I'll phrase my request a little differently, of course.

Pen lengthwise in my mouth like a horse bit, my fingers tapping at my desk, my excitement ready—just a little glance—I scroll the mouse over the images tab and click.

My . . . oh . . . my.

Would you look at that?

As if someone is lifting the blinds to a window that looks over Narnia, pictures upon pictures of Jason Orson—shirtless—appear in front of me.

I prop my chin in my hand and lean in even closer. Bronze, ripped muscles decorate my computer screen. A variety of "props" are sprinkled throughout every picture. A bat, weights, workout ropes, catching gear . . . backwards hat . . . a smile.

Is that . . .

Is he in . . .

Gulp.

A towel?

The pen falls out of my mouth, clattering to the desk, as my breasts unapologetically heave, sending out a Morse code to my finger.

Click.

Click.

CLICK GODDAMNIT!

The tits have spoken.

My finger hovers over the picture, ready to click. Just one little punch down and the towel glory is all for me to see . . .

"Good Morning, Miss Domico."

"Jesus . . . Christ," I yip while frantically clicking at my screen, doing everything in my power to shut down the almost-naked man gracing every last section of my twenty-four-inch computer screen.

But in my haste to exit out, all I do is make the pictures bigger.

Man nipple covers my screen.

Smooth man chest in full view.

Bulge poking the towel on . . .

Bulge?

I lean in for a better look as my assistant clears her throat. "Am I interrupting something?"

"What?" My head pops up over my screen. I'm thankful she can't see anything I'm looking at. "No." I click the exit button rapidly, but can you believe it, my computer freezes on me. "Not interrupting at all. Nope." I shake my head and clear my throat while adjusting my blouse.

Is it hot in here?

"Just finishing up some uh, research."

My cheeks flame and for a brief moment, I let down my wall, showing an ounce of vulnerability to my assistant. Probably the first time she's ever seen me flustered, which leads me to believe this is exactly why I shouldn't be getting involved with anything when it comes to Jason Orson. Not even donating to his charity, which I'm sure is for a good cause, but staying as far away as possible is smart on my end.

"Okay." Jessica studies me. "Are you feeling all right? You seem a little flushed."

I pat my cheeks, willing my body to cool down. I click on the exit button for the shirtless images again, and this time they go away. Thank God.

"I'm fine, just got a little fired up about an unanswered email." If anything, Jessica knows how much I hate it when people don't answer me.

"Would you like me to send a follow-up for you?"

She's so efficient. Annoying when I'm trying to cover up my obscene work conduct.

"No, I'll send something later." I bring the Briar Hurst file closer and flip through it, acting like I'm making sure everything is in it when in actuality, all I can see on the paper is Jason's taut nipples winking at me.

Damn it.

"Well"—I pat the folder—"looks like everything is ready. Any last things I need to know before heading into the meeting?"

"Yes, actually." She lights up her iPad and with her Apple pencil and scrolls through her checklist. "The meeting with the Carltons next week. They asked if they could move it to eight, rather than seven."

"That's fine. Give them whatever they want, I'm flexible."

"They also requested Italian when I asked what they preferred."

"Great, we'll take them to Piccolo. Make reservations for four."

She winces. "I think it will have to be six."

"Six? Sure, they can bring whoever they want."

"That's the thing." Jessica adjusts her glasses. "They want to bring Heller and Parks with them."

My eyes widen, my jaw growing firm. "They want to bring my competition to the meeting? Why would they want to do that?"

"They said they want to make the same pitch once and then go from there. They're ready to sell, but they want to make it as easy as possible, really get to know the candidates."

"Jesus." I pull on my long black ponytail. "Fine, make it for six. Did you get the tip sheet yet? Do you know what they're looking for when it comes to making a deal?"

The Carltons are selling one of the biggest pieces of real estate in the Chicago area, a ten-acre lot along the lake that's currently used for warehouse storage. Heller and Parks, and of course Domico Industries, have been after the lot for a while. It's now down to our two companies, and I'll be damned if I let Heller and Parks win the bid.

"I wasn't able to dig up too much. They want to know about future plans, how they'll influence the city of Chicago, and then some inside factors that have not been revealed yet. They said they'd talk about it at dinner."

"Great." I stand from my desk and smooth down my pencil skirt. "I love being caught off guard. Ask for the rooftop table for added privacy. Tell them it's for Dottie Domico, and they'll make it happen."

"Got it. Also, got a call from Frankie Lazaro looking for a donation . . ."

"Ugh, Frankie. He won't get off my ass. Yes, it's on my desk, so just fill it out for me."

"Your usual amount?"

"Yeah, he'll call me out if it's anything less." I round my desk, after plucking my phone from the drawer. "When is my dad coming into town?"

"Next week, day before the meeting. He confirmed his attendance for the Carlton dinner."

"And what about the Hanks account, was that finalized?"

She nods. "Papers were signed last night. I sent them to Goldman and Zenlow."

"Perfect." Goldman and Zenlow Law had been handling our legal needs for a long time now. Thank God. They're the best. She hands me a cup of coffee she must have set on the credenza when I was staring intently at the fine circular shape of Jason Orson's nipples.

So symmetrical.

I take a sip from the perfectly tempered coffee and say, "Did you order the catering for lunch today?"

"Yup, and emails went out to all the employees, appreciating them for their hard work during the Hanks acquisition."

"Did you give yourself a raise?"

She smiles. "Just waiting on your signature."

"Remind me later." I tilt my cup of coffee in her direction. "Thank you, Jessica."

I give her a quick goodbye and then head down the bright black and white hallways of our newly renovated offices. Urban chic is what I call it, with exposed piping and brick and soft touches here and there with comfortable couches, lounge areas, and one hell of a break room with free food and drinks, and games to clear your mind. Am I trying to impersonate Google? Maybe, but then again, no one likes to live eight hours of their life in a humdrum cube farm.

My goal for every conference is to not only conduct a meaningful meeting, but to also be the first person to show up. Thanks to my peeping Tom Internet searching, I'm the second person to show up. Matthew, the intern, is already sitting in a chair in the back.

I give him a kind smile and then go to the front of the conference table where I place my notes. My phone lights up with text messages and because I'm a glutton for punishment, I unlock my phone and see what my idiot friends want now.

Lindsay: *You totally checked the link out, didn't you?*

Emory: *You entered to win, didn't you?*

I will take my snooping to the grave with me.

Dottie: *You know I have better things to do with my life than look up pictures of Jason Orson.*

Emory: *⌃⌃⌃ Did you read that, Linds? She said look up pictures . . . we never said anything about pictures.*

Damn it.

Lindsay: *Busted! How's he looking these days? Fine, right? Did you see that towel picture?*

Emory: *Even I studied the towel picture, and I'm utterly devoted to Knox. It's hard to miss the towel picture.*

Lindsay: *Or the obvious bulge. Oh God, I'm getting hot just thinking about it.*

Dottie: *You both are in the presence of children, texting about a man's penis. Don't make me report you.*

Lindsay: You wouldn't.
Emory: Too far, Dottie.
Dottie: Drop the Jason thing and I'll drop my threat.
Lindsay: Where's the fun in that?
Dottie: There is no fun in it. That's exactly the point. Jason is not an option when it comes to my love life, not that I'm looking for an option. So this goes out to the both of you . . . Drop. It.

CHAPTER THREE

DOTTIE

"Jessica, can you come in here for a second?" I call out, looking over my expense sheet and trying to figure out this last charge. This last enormous charge.

"She's out getting dinner," Lindsay says, strutting into my office, Emory tagging closely behind.

I glance at the date on my computer and realize it's our weekly dinner I've been holding at my office lately. With the Carlton dinner a few days away and my dad coming to town shortly, I've spent every waking moment in this office, forcing Jessica to work extra hours so we can make sure we're completely prepared to win over the older couple.

"Let me guess," Emory says, sitting in a chair across from me, "you forgot about our dinner again."

"Things have been crazy around here."

"Same story, different day." Lindsay takes the other seat across from me, moves her satchel to her lap and gives it a good pat. "Don't worry, I brought papers for Emory and me to grade while you do your work. We can call it a working friend-inner."

"I never agreed to helping you grade papers. And what could you possibly grade? They're third graders."

Chin stuck up in the air, Lindsay says, "I'll have you know, I run a tight ship in my classroom. I make those kids work. I have spelling tests, math tests, and stories about what they want to be when they grow up to grade."

Emory waves her hand at Lindsay. "Throw a smiley face sticker on them and call it a day. It's not like you're actually going to fail any of these kids."

Chuckling, I say, "Look at the librarian being lazy."

"I'm not lazy, I just don't want to have to decipher third grade handwriting all night. I had a second grader spit in my face today, so I'm done with children for now."

"You're cranky," I say, which is abnormal for my usually very positive friend.

She sighs heavily. "Knox has been holding out on me lately. We got in a disagreement and now he said he's going to withhold the goods until I agree with him."

"Still wants you to get rid of the lease on your apartment?"

"Yeah. He said keeping it is insulting to him, as if I don't think we'll be together forever. What he doesn't realize is that the apartment meant something to me before he came back into my life. It was my place of solace during the rough times."

Growing serious, I say, "But don't you think it's time you build a new place where you can find peace? Knox means everything to you. I don't think you need an apartment to remind you of what you went through. You need a place that will remind you of where you're going."

Lindsay touches her heart. "Good God, Dottie, that was really fucking touching."

"It was," Emory agrees, tearing up.

"Are you okay?" I ask, motioning to her eyes. "It looks like you're going to cry."

Emory waves her hand in front of her eyes. "I think I'm just hard up. All these pent-up orgasms are really getting to me."

"If that's the case, Dottie and I should be bawling every day of our lives from lack of sex."

Jessica takes that moment to walk into my office, two to-go bags in hand from one of our favorite Greek restaurants.

"I seem to have bad timing every time you guys have dinner here," she says with a blush.

"Oh, we're besties by now." Lindsay motions to another seat. "Please, Jessica, sit down, talk about our sex lives with us."

"That's not necessary," I say. "Don't really want to get HR involved."

"You're such a tight-ass," Lindsay says. "It's not like you're hitting on Jessica; we're just gabbing like good friends."

Jessica pushes her glasses on her nose and folds her hands together. "With all due respect, I think I should leave the gabbing to you ladies. I don't want to make Miss Domico uncomfortable."

"Why?" Lindsay asks, leaning in like a rabid beast, looking for nourishment. "Is your sex life insane? You're a fresh twenty-three, right? What's it like to be young?"

"You're young, you idiot," I say to Lindsay. "Twenty-nine is not old."

"It's not twenty-three," she mutters.

Before Lindsay can get into the fine details of Jessica's personal life, I say, "Jessica, before you take off, can you please look at this charge? I have no idea what it's for. It's a ten-thousand-dollar charge."

Emory's mouth falls open. "You don't know about a ten-thousand-dollar charge on your credit card? I'm pretty sure I'd know what I was wearing, what I smelled like, and the exact time I charged ten thousand dollars to my credit card."

Smelled like? Eww.

Lindsay nods her thumb in my direction with a smart-ass smile. "Rich girl problems."

Ignoring them, I point to the charge with my mouse when Jessica rounds my desk. "The Lineup, what is that?"

Lindsay and Emory both snort at the same time, covering their faces in tandem.

Uh, am I missing something? Oh shit, is it some weird porn website? I'm not an avid watcher, but after a few glasses of wine, sometimes I like to jump online and have a little fun. Did I buy some baller subscription without remembering?

Immediately a trickle of sweat starts to stream down my back from the thought of Jessica knowing about my "extracurricular activities" outside of work.

"Uh, you know what, never mind, I think I remember."

"Do you?" Lindsay asks, a full-on grin spread across her face.

"Ten thousand dollars? Damn, Dottie, I didn't know you were that adamant about winning a date."

"Winning a date? What are you talking about?"

Please don't say it's a dating website, a dating website I spent ten thousand dollars on. If that doesn't read desperately single, I don't know what does.

"Miss Domico, it was for the fundraiser you told me to donate to."

Ohh . . . thank God.

Wait . . . what fundraiser?

Twirling the end of my ponytail with my index finger, I casually say, "Remind me which one again?"

"Frankie's I believe? You said it was on your desk. The day of the Briar Hurst meeting." My stomach drops, recalling that morning and what I did. "I couldn't quite find anything on your desk, but then I saw your computer screen."

Oh.

God.

Nipples.

Winking fucking nipples.

My vision starts to tunnel, and my skin feels like it's shrinking as both Emory and Lindsay laugh in front of me.

No.

Please don't tell me I donated ten thousand dollars to go on a date with Jason Orson.

"I assumed it was what you were talking about. Was I wrong?"

Lindsay wipes her eyes. "Oh no, Jessica. You were so, so right."

"I don't think you could have been more right," Emory adds.

Confused, Jessica looks between us. "Am I . . . missing something?"

Unable to comprehend what happened, I place my head in my hands and take deep breaths. Ten thousand dollars, how many entries did *that* gain me? I'm guessing a whole fucking lot.

"Miss Domico?" Jessica's worried voice pulls me back into the present.

I give her a curt smile. "Wrong charity, but that's okay, Jessica. It's fine. I wasn't clear."

Mortification falls over her features. "Oh my gosh, Miss Domico. I'm so sorry. I can't believe"—she sucks in a short breath, her eyes watering—"I can't believe I made such a horrible mistake. I . . . I can pay it off. Take it out of my paycheck."

Ten thousand dollars to Jessica is not pocket change. It's probably half her rent for the year.

"No, it's really okay. I planned on donating anyway. That's why I had the tab up."

"I think you're being kind to me right now for an awful mistake." Her lip quivers.

With anyone else, I probably would have fired them over such a thing. They don't say I'm ruthless for no reason, but Jessica? No way can I lose her. She's the reason I haven't lost my mind working this job. God, she must be mortified to not only have made this mistake, but in front of two of my friends. I know what that's like, trying to impress women senior to you.

I look her in the eyes and say, "It was a mistake, poor communication, and something that won't happen again, right?"

"Yes, of course. Never. I'm so sorry. I feel awful." A tear slips down her cheek and she quickly wipes it away. "I'm so sorry. Please let me make it up to you. I'll stay late for as long as you want with no overtime."

"Don't be ridiculous. You've worked more hours than anyone in this office besides me. I won't take away your pay for your hard work. But next time, if something isn't where I've said it should be, please clarify before you act."

"Of course." She steps back and takes a deep breath. Clasping her hands together, she asks, "Is there anything else I can get you ladies?"

"We're good. Take the night off, Jessica."

She shakes her head. "No, I'll be at my desk if you need anything." She gives me a small smile, one that barely reaches her eyes, and then shuts the door to my office quietly.

"Jesus," Lindsay says, pulling food out of the bags. "That was awkward as shit."

Leaning forward, in a whisper, Emory says, "My ass cheeks were nervously clenched that whole time. Poor Jessica."

"Poor Jessica?" I whisper back, not wanting her to hear me. "What about me? She fucking donated ten thousand dollars to Jason's charity under my name."

"Yeah, that part was great. I think you need to make Jessica employee of the month. I feel bad for her screwup," Lindsay says, "but I don't think it could have worked out more perfectly."

"Now we just have to hope she gets picked," Emory says with glee.

"That's true." Lindsay hands me my steak kabobs with a side of grilled veggies. "His date was a hot commodity. Every teacher at Cedar Pine donated twenty-five dollars for a chance, even the married ones."

"My spin class was very enthusiastic about the opportunity," Emory says. "I think your chances of winning are slim."

"You think?" I ask, the dread building in my chest finally easing.

"Total long shot." Lindsay dips a pita in some hummus. "There is probably a one percent chance you'll win."

"I can live with one percent," I say, feeling much better.

She's right. Thousands upon thousands of people most likely entered to win, so just because my donation was large, doesn't mean I'll actually win. Who knows, maybe there's a mega fan who donated even more, giving them more entries to the contest.

I'm fine.

One percent chance.

I can't be mad with those odds.

~

Bang. Bang. Bang.

No answer.

Bang. Bang. Bang. BANG.

"Open up, I know you're in there," I call through the metal door that leads to Emory and Knox's apartment. "I have all night. I'll wait. It's not like I have a big meeting to prepare for. Nope, I don't have to entertain my father or anything, I have all freaking—"

The door swings open, Emory stands on the other side with a robe wrapped around her body, her hair a complete mess.

"Dottie," she breathes. "What are you doing here?"

"Sure, I would love to come in," I say, plowing right past my friend and into her kitchen where I know Knox keeps a few beers chilled.

I'm normally not a beer person, but right now, it doesn't matter what goes into my body, as long as it's alcohol.

"Is everything okay? You seem like you're on the verge of a mental breakdown."

I give my friend a slow once-over and ask, "Were you having sex?"

Emory smooths her hair down. "Foreplay. We weren't quite at the penetration part yet."

"Yeah, thanks for that," Knox says as he walks into the kitchen wearing nothing but a pair of sweats.

I'm not one to gawk at my friends' boyfriends, but it's hard to keep my eyes off Knox as he makes his way to the fridge and pulls out a beer for himself. He takes mine from my hands, cracks the top open, then his, and follows it up with a clink of our bottlenecks. He leans against the wall of the kitchen, his fine body on fire with every move he makes.

As starting shortstop for the Bobbies, his body is fucking amazing.

Really, really hot. Emory is one lucky girl.

"This better be good, Dottie," he says between sips.

"Need I remind you, I'm the reason you got Emory's phone number in the first place?" Back in college, when Emory was on a boy hiatus, Knox turned to me for a little help, and I had no problem handing him the information he wanted, as long as he took good care of my friend.

He eyes me from over his beer bottle. "Damn, how long have you been holding on to that one?"

"Thought it would come in handy one day."

"Fine." He chuckles. "You're forgiven."

I look between the two of them. "So I guess the sex ban has been lifted?"

"All it took was one brush of my bare breast against his naked chest and he was mine."

"Don't try to be cool in front of your friend." Knox walks up behind her and wraps his arm around her waist, placing a sweet kiss to her temple. "She terminated her lease, and then rubbed her bare breast on my chest."

"She doesn't need to know the details." Addressing me, Emory asks, "Why are you pounding on our door as if you're about to be hounded by a pack of zombies?"

"Oh, you know . . ." I casually pull a piece of paper out of my purse and lay it flat on the table. "Because of this."

As a couple, they lean forward and take in the printed congratulations email.

Yeah, fucking congratulations!

"Oh. My. God." Emory covers her mouth right before she starts laughing.

"It's not funny," I yell, snapping the paper away.

"Wait, what's going on?" Knox asks, a pinch between his brow.

"Your girlfriend, my now former friend, sent me the link to Jason Orson's Charity Hustle fundraiser, my assistant accidentally donated to it on my behalf, and according to this email, I won."

Emory laughs some more, at least giving me the respect of turning to Knox's chest so I don't see the pure joy written all over her face.

"You mean you won a date with Jason and his sister?"

"It's with his sister?" I ask, not realizing that little tidbit of information. "That makes it even worse."

"Yeah, he didn't want to be accused of anything inappropriate, so he signed on a witness. But wait, how on earth did you win? I heard thousands of people entered. He raised over two hundred thousand dollars for his charity."

"She donated . . ." Emory's voice dies off from being pressed against Knox's chest.

"She donated how much?" Knox asks.

"Ten thousand dollars." His eyes widen and his mouth drops.

"Damn, girl. Are you crushing on my boy?"

"What? No," I say with outrage, even though, yes, there has been crushing in the past. Now it's more like an appreciation for the male form. For the most gorgeous, muscle-upon-muscle, delectable, drool-worthy male form of Jason Orson to be specific . . .

No crushing.

No lusting.

Did I say lusting? I mean, there has been absolutely no lusting. And before you even ask, NO, I have not looked at the towel pic since that first day, or any picture for that matter. I have better things to be doing with my life.

Okay . . . maybe the other night, I perused the shirtless

pictures again, but just because I couldn't remember if I saw a birthmark near his armpit or not and it was driving me crazy.

For the record, no birthmark.

And no tattoos. I found that out last night when I wanted to clarify that as well.

And then this morning, when I was wondering if he was really bulging or not in that towel . . . okay, FINE. I've looked at pictures of him every day since Lindsay and Emory sent that damn link. Are you happy? *Well, you may be happy, but I was more . . . delirious after my battery-driven-while-imagining-licking-Jason-Orson's-abs orgasm. Or two.*

"I have not been crushing on him. Ten thousand is my normal donation amount. It was a mistake, a miscommunication, and because of it, I'm stuck in the middle of one giant clusterfuck."

Emory shakes her head in disbelief. "I can't believe you won. It's meant to be."

"No. Stop that. I'm not going to go on the date."

Knox shakes his head. "Man, if you don't show up, Jason will take it personally."

"What do you mean?"

"I mean, he's a sensitive guy." Knox sips his beer, acting so casual while an inner war of nerves is in an epic battle in the pit of my stomach. "He prides himself on being honest and true and keeping his word. If he promised someone a date, he's going to make it happen."

And that's exactly why I can't get mixed up with this guy. Words like honest and true and sensitive . . . I have a feeling I could easily eat him up and spit him out.

I've been known to do the rare dishonest thing, especially when it comes to work.

You're thinking, wow, what an upstanding lady, aren't you?

Well, you don't get to where I am in business without taking advantage of every situation you can. And before you get on your high horse to lecture me about being a good person, I will say this:

I never cheat or steal. I just twist the truth at times to get what I want. But what businessman doesn't?

Yeah, businessman, because that's what this world is full of, alpha businessmen with high-rise offices and large desks they fuck their wenches on—well, some are wenches, most are probably really nice ladies. Either way, no one is judging these "ruthless" men and their tactics. Instead, they're praised. *Rewarded*. Women are rewarded with the moniker of *bitch*. Even today. Ridiculous.

So to wrap up this rant, picture me with a dick.

Wait, no, don't picture me with a dick, that's weird. Just realize, I've done what every other guy in my position would have done, but at least I have the common sense to realize even though Jason Orson checks off every box in the looks department—that ass, *sigh* —I know better than to get anywhere near him.

"I'll just send someone else on a date with him."

Knox studies me, his eyes peeling off a piece of my shield, making me feel vulnerable. "Do you like him or something?"

"No," I say as Emory says, "Yes."

"Emory," I whisper, trying to give her a hint. Girl code. Let's not talk about this in front of one of Jason's best friends.

"What?" She shrugs. "It's true. In college he was all you ever talked about when we discussed baseball players. Jason this and Jason that." She turns to Knox and says, "She had the biggest obsession with his ass."

"You know"—I tap the kitchen counter—"there's a special place in hell for people like you, Emory."

She laughs out loud and Knox, apparently loving the maniacal sound, presses kisses along her neck. "Is it or is it not true?"

"You know, I don't have to take this kind of abuse." I down a big gulp of beer and set the bottle on the counter. "I hope Knox has limp dick for the rest of the night."

I start to walk away when Knox calls out, "Hey, what the hell did I do?"

"You're attached to her." I point at Emory. "And you listen up,

Knox Gentry, you better not tell Jason about any of this, or else I'll wish worse things than limp dick on you."

"What's worse than limp dick?"

"A one-fifty batting average."

His brows sharpen, his eyes narrowing. "Don't you fucking dare."

"Then keep your lips sealed. Don't forget, I know people around this city."

With that, I begin to leave their apartment when Emory says, "Careful, Jason lives in the same building now, right across the hall actually."

I still, my body rigid, my hand about to open the door as I spin around. Swallowing hard, I ask, "Can I use your fire escape?"

CHAPTER FOUR

JASON

"Did you hear?" I ask Natalie, who sits at my kitchen bar, setting her purse down on the other seat while I grab her a drink.

"That you're in contention for best butt in baseball?"

I pause, mid-pour of the fresh iced tea I brewed this morning. "Excuse me? What's this? Best butt in baseball?"

She laughs, a little too uncontrollably. "Oh God, I'm sorry, I didn't realize you were actually going to be really excited about that." I know that laugh, I've heard it almost my whole life. That's my sister's laugh that tells me once again, she's joking around.

"You know I'm fucking sensitive about my ass, so why would you joke about it?"

"Because I'm your sister and I have to keep you grounded."

I finish filling her cup and hand it to her. "Don't joke about possibly winning one of the best awards I could possibly think of."

She shakes her head. "You have problems."

Because I always strive to be a good host, I reach for the food I prepared earlier: a vegetable crudité from the fridge, and home-made pita chips, which I place in the toaster oven to heat up.

Cut-up veggies, check.

Pitas, check.

Homemade hummus, check.

I lay it out all in front of Natalie who takes in the impressive spread. "Are you sure you're a ballplayer? Looks like you could be a home chef."

"Presentation is everything," I say, adjusting a little dish of olives. "But let's get back to the topic at hand; did you see they picked a winner for my Charity Hustle fundraiser?"

Mouthful of my garlic hummus, she shakes her head and swallows. "I didn't. That's exciting. Is it a boy or a girl?"

"Girl." I wiggle my eyebrows. "Her name is Dorothy Domico and get this, she donated ten thousand dollars."

"Shut up." Natalie's eyes widen. "Holy crap, she must really want to go on a date with you."

I turn around, showing off my backside. "Must be the ass, it brings all the ladies in."

"Yeah, I'm sure," Natalie deadpans. "That's why you're single and making homemade hummus for your sister because you have nothing better to do."

"You know, if you're going to make fun of my hummus, I can take it away." I reach for the bowl, but she swats at my hand, deflecting it.

"If you want to be known as a terrible host, then yeah, take it away."

"You know how to strike me where it hurts." I clutch my chest.

"Always a flair for the dramatic." Natalie rolls her eyes and dips a carrot stick in the hummus. "So, do we know anything about Dorothy other than she was very anxious to win?"

"Nothing. But my PR team sent over the date information. Next Friday night. She lives here in Chicago, so it makes things super easy."

"She could be a stalker. Do you have security on standby?"

"Or," I say, pulling the pita slices out of the toaster oven, "she could be a really nice woman and this could be a meet cute."

Natalie perks up. "You mean . . . you would date this woman?"

I shrug. "You never know. People are brought into your life for a reason, and maybe Dorothy is supposed to be my forever."

"You know"—Natalie takes a sip of her iced tea—"it's concerning that you're looking to actually date through this fundraiser. Are you really that desperate to be with someone that you're going to make them pay to go on a date with you?"

"Jesus," I mutter. My sister doesn't ever beat around the bush. "You don't have to be so goddamn negative all the time. I was just thinking hypothetically."

Natalie pats my hand. "I'm not being negative, I'm just trying to keep your head out of the clouds since that's where you like to live most of the time. Just be cautious with this girl. She could be bad news. After all, she did donate a lot of money." *Or she could be someone after my own heart who likes to give generously to a good cause.* There is always a silver lining . . . at least in my mind.

"You're going to be there, so you can look out for me, give me the nod if you think she's a stalker or not."

"Should we have a code word that means abort?"

"That's a great idea." I lean against the counter, tapping my chin with a slice of a red pepper. "What could it be?"

"A word that wouldn't come up in everyday conversation."

"Precisely." I spin toward her. "How about gallbladder?"

"Why did that even come into your head?"

I bite the red pepper slice. "It's a mystery what goes on in my brain."

"Well, since I don't think I ever say gallbladder, I think we have a winner. Finding a way to bring it up should be fun."

"Hey, you might not have to, she could be pretty awesome."

Natalie eyes me. "I have my doubts."

"Because of what happened in the minors?"

"How could you not be jaded after Melissa? She used you."

"That she did," I murmur, staring at my feet, my mind falling back to my first year in the minor leagues. "She's why I haven't invested any time into a relationship."

Fresh out of college and into the minors, I was lonely, separated from my normal support system, and I filled that void with the wrong person. Melissa used me in every way possible. I didn't realize it until about four months in when she'd drained my signing bonus, taken all my energy trying to keep her happy, and the worst part? She'd been fucking other guys on the team. Why no one said anything was beyond comprehension, as I would have thought the same level of bro code slash loyalty I'd had with my friends in college carried over into the minors. Yes, she was hot, but man, if you know a girl is taken, you don't cross that line. Before that experience, I'd been easygoing and quick to make friends. But I learned very quickly that trust took time to earn. I also learned that doubling up on protection was a must. No doubt there were other girls out there like Melissa, whose long-term goal included using whoever's sperm as her future paycheck.

Yeah, she was a real catch. And I'd been the first fool, but not the last, thank God.

"I understand what you went through with her wasn't easy, but that doesn't mean you shouldn't date."

"You're sending mixed signals here, Natalie. You want me to date, but you don't want me to date, what is it?" I chuckle, shaking off the feeling of Melissa. I don't talk about her. Being that stupid jock who didn't see the signs from a mile away, took a hit to my pride. You live and learn.

Growing serious, Natalie says, "I want you to find love, the kind of love I share with Ansel, the kind of love Mom and Dad have. You deserve it, because you're a kind and giving soul, but because of that, you need to make sure the girl you go out with is in it for you, not for the jersey you wear. I just want you to be cautious, that's all."

"Yeah, I get that." I lean against the counter, my forearms propping me up. "But you never know, maybe this Dorothy Domico is someone special."

"Or she's an eighty-year-old grandma who used all her social security to buy a date with you."

Smiling, I say, "I can get into the granny thing. Wrinkles are a turn-on."

"You're so fucked up." She laughs and throws a carrot at my head, nailing me between the eyes.

I rub the offended spot and say, "You know, we might need you on the Rebels with an accurate arm like that if the general manager doesn't pick up some strong arms for next season."

"More time with my big brother? I think I'll pass."

"Such a punk." I chuckle and bite into another carrot.

I slam the door to Knox's apartment and stand there, anger rolling through my body like a tidal wave. Carson and Knox are both sitting on the couch, playing MLB The Show 19, PlayStation's sanctioned professional baseball game. When the slam of the door cuts through the surround sound of their game—they like to play as themselves, such idiots—they turn toward me, the game put on pause.

"Dude, why are you slamming doors?" Knox asks.

I stomp toward them and flop on one of the armchairs perpendicular to the couch. "Because I'm pissed."

"This seems like it's going to be a moment," Carson whispers, but not quiet enough. "Should I get beers?"

"Get them for everyone," I say, flailing my arm in the air. "I have wings being delivered shortly."

"And mozzarella sticks?" Carson asks, desperate for his stupid cheese sticks.

"You know I ordered them," I huff. "Because I'm a considerate fuck."

"That you are." Knox leans back on the couch and takes a beer from Carson. I do the same. He's a good man and has popped open the tops already. "So . . . do you want to talk about it?"

"Of course I do. That's why I'm here."

"Oh, I thought you were just being dramatic for no fucking reason," Knox replies sarcastically.

"I get the need to be snarky, that's how we are with each other." I set my feet on the coffee table in front of me, stretching out. "But please, not in my time of need."

"Jesus Christ," Carson murmurs, resting his arm on the side of the couch and getting comfortable. "Just get on with it. We're two innings away from killing the Rebels in the World Series."

Of course that's who they'd be playing. At least I'm not on the team since I was just traded, or else they'd have me doing stupid shit. They did that when I was in Tampa and sent videos of me running in circles on the field. They're really fucking mature.

"So you know how I did that Charity Hustle thing?"

"Yeah," they both reply.

"Well, a winner was picked and we were supposed to meet tomorrow night, but the girl cancelled and according to the PR team, she doesn't want to set up another date."

Knox looks away while Carson snorts to himself.

"This isn't funny. Why the hell do you think she'd do that? She has me questioning every last thing I've done over the past week. Did I post something wrong on my Instagram? I know I'm a little braggy when it comes to my potato salad, but my presentation with the potato skins was on point, so how could I not post about that?" I mean, I could have posted sweaty, post-workout pics of my muscles, but I showed self-control. You'd think any female would be happy I was bragging about food and not my ripped bod. Can you see my eye-roll here?

"I don't know about you"—Carson holds his chest—"but personally, I found the potato salad to be incredibly offensive."

"Shut the fuck up," I say, slouching more in my chair. "I don't get it. Why would she cancel when she donated so much money?"

"Do you know anything about her?" Carson asks while Knox stays strangely silent.

"Just that her name is Dorothy Domico, and she donated ten thousand dollars."

"Domico, Domico," Carson repeats, putting emphasis behind the last name. "Why is that name so familiar?"

Knox coughs into his hand, muttering something with it, but I can't quite understand him.

"Hey, what's Dottie's last name?" Carson pokes Knox in the side.

"Anyone need more beer?" Knox asks, standing abruptly.

"I'm nursing mine," I say.

"I swear it's Dottie Domico. Right?" Carson is still trying to decipher this poor girl's name. "Have you ever met Dottie?" Carson asks me.

"Uh, no. Pretty sure I'd remember that name. Is she a cleat chaser?"

"Nah, she's cool. One of Emory's best friends. She was in my grade, so a year ahead of you. I swear you've met her before. Hey, Knox, what's Dottie's last name?"

"When are those wings showing up?" Knox calls from the kitchen.

"Ten minutes," I call out before dragging my hand over my face. "I don't know, man. I feel like a dipshit, like this girl goes and donates a crap ton of money but doesn't want to go on a date with me. I feel like I owe it to her. Ten thousand dollars is a lot of money to just throw away."

"Maybe she really liked the cause but is too nervous to cash in on the date," Knox says from the kitchen.

Carson snaps his fingers. "It is Dottie Domico, because I remember saying, *like the sugar*? And she said, 'No, that's Domino.'" Carson twists his body over the couch. "It's Dottie Domico, right, Knox?"

"Want me to cut up some vegetables to go with the wings?"

"Sure," I call out, scratching my chin. "I don't know, should I at least send her some flowers and signed gear as a thank you?"

"I think I'm friends with Dottie on Instagram," Carson continues. *Christ, why won't he get a clue? When he goes down a rabbit trail, he can't seem to come out of it.* "Did you get a picture of her?"

"No," I answer. "Natalie suggested she's an old woman who doesn't really want to show her face or has the energy to go on a date. If she's old, I'll go to her. The elderly love me, as I'm an entertaining dickhead when I want to be."

"Yeah, I was right, Dottie Domico," Carson says.

"What do you think, Knox?" I call out as he busies himself in the kitchen. "Think she's old?"

"Dottie is always donating to shit," Carson says. "Hey Knox, did Emory say anything about Dottie donating?"

"Why are you so hung up on Emory's friend?" I finally ask. "Like a twenty-nine-year-old could really drop ten thousand dollars on a fundraiser. Use your fucking head, man."

"She's rich, dude. She's a VP or something. Right, Knox?"

We both turn toward him to find him buried into the chopping of celery. It is not like him to remain mute on *any* occasion or subject, so what's his deal tonight?

"Hey, we're talking to you," Carson calls out.

"I know, and I chose not to answer."

What the hell?

He knows something . . .

Obvious, I know, but I might have been hit in the head with foul balls for far too many years, so it takes me a few more minutes to catch up.

"What are you not telling us?" I say, hopping onto the arm of my chair.

"I think I'll go meet the wing person in the lobby instead of having the concierge bring up our food." Knox wipes off his hands and beelines for the door despite not having a shirt or shoes on.

But Carson is quicker, hurdling over the couch and straight to the door where he blocks Knox. "Oh no, you don't, you have some explaining to do."

I join them at the door. What is Knox hiding?

Arms crossed over my chest, I say, "Do you know Dorothy Domico?"

He pulls on the back of his neck with both hands. *Guilty* is written all over him. "Doesn't everyone know her?" he asks.

I reach out and snag his nipple with my index finger and thumb. He yelps, smacks my hand away, and steps backward. "What the fuck, dude?"

"Stop avoiding the question and tell us what you know."

"She threatened to wish a one-fifty batting average on me," Knox says, looking pathetic and panicked all at once. "One fucking fifty."

Carson leans against the door, arms crossed as well. "You are the least superstitious person I know."

It's true, when every other Brentwood baseball player believed in the power of the locker room and how if you took your girl back there to do the deed, you'd end up together forever, Knox pushed it off as a bunch of bullshit.

"You don't know Dottie, she's powerful." He whispers, "She *knows people*."

"Well, Christ, if she *knows* people, then we shouldn't touch her with a ten-foot pole." Carson rolls his eyes. "Fine, if you don't want to say anything because one of Emory's friends seems like a threat to you, then just nod or shake your head to our questions, and that way you're not actually saying anything."

Finger poised to make a point, I say, "Body language counts as a universal—"

"Dude, shut the fuck up," Carson says to me. "Don't you want to know more about Dottie?"

He has a point.

"Sorry. Proceed."

"Thank you." Turning back to Knox, Carson asks, "Did Dottie donate to Jason's fundraiser?"

He nods yes.

"Is she the Dorothy Domico that won the date?"

Yes.

"Did you know she was cancelling the date?"

Yes.

"Do you know why?"

No.

"Are you lying to us?"

No.

Carson taps his chin and then asks, "Why did she donate the money?"

"That's not a yes or no question," Knox says.

"I'm sick of this shit. Be a man and tell us what you know."

"Was it from my potato salad post?"

"No one cares about your potato salad," Knox groans and walks back to the living room where we follow him.

"I'll have you know, that post got me a lot of DMs. I was fielding recipe questions for hours."

"Congratulations," Carson says, annoyed. "You have the attention of every seventy-five-year-old woman." He scrubs his face. "I don't know why I insist on helping you fools."

"I'm not going to tell you guys anything. I made a promise to Emory and Dottie that I wouldn't."

"That's shit and you know it," I say, pointing at Knox. "What ever happened to balls before booty calls?"

"First of all," Knox says, voice stern, "Emory is anything but a booty call. Second, when you're in a serious and committed relationship, you'll know what it means to keep a secret. Back me up, Carson."

He groans and then nods. "Hate to admit it, but the missus is the same way. I would die with her secrets. I think you might be out of luck."

"Great." I throw up my arms. "So you're telling me one of Emory's friends who we went to college with donated ten thousand dollars to my charity but refuses to go on a date with me? What was the point even of donating?"

They both shrug their shoulders, annoying the shit out of me.

"You're both useless. Looks like I might just have to take matters into my own hands."

"Sorry, man," Knox mumbles. At least he looks marginally contrite.

"There's still wings, beer, and PlayStation," Carson says. Like that will fix my dilemma. Although, wings, beer, and PlayStation have worked before.

That night, after sharing three dozen wings with the boys and playing PlayStation, I scooted across to my apartment and pulled up my good friend, Google, where I spent the next hour searching out every piece of information I could find on Dottie.

Normally, I'm not this invested in creeping on someone, but ten thousand dollars? No one donates that much money without a reason.

And I'm going to find out what it is.

CHAPTER FIVE

DOTTIE

K nock. *Knock.*
I don't have to look up from my computer to know my dad is standing in the doorway of my office. If I hadn't heard him chatting up my employees on the way in, I could have smelled his cool aftershave from the moment he walked down the hall. It's not overpowering, but instead, has a surprising light air about it that carries throughout the halls. It matches his persona—charismatic and powerful.

"Aren't you going to come give your dad a hug?" I smile. I've missed hearing his rich and calming voice.

"Let me finish this email."

"Ah, always working. I should have taught you to have some fun too." He rounds my desk and leans over to give me a hug. I know his eyes are fixed on my computer while he does it, because even though he trusts me in this position, he's still very much invested in the company. Looking over my shoulder has never been something he's hidden. And in many ways, it's given me confidence over the years. He's often had words of encouragement and well-timed suggestions.

I return the hug and finish my email quickly, while he takes a seat across from me. I save it in my drafts so I can review it one more time before pressing send and then direct my attention to my dad.

"How are you?" I smile at him. I've been a daddy's girl for as long as I can remember, and even though I have a strong relationship with my mom, my father and I have a more dynamic bond. I love my dad more than anything. "Enjoying your time in Chicago?"

"Always. I love it here. I can see why you wanted to stay and establish roots. It has a New York City quality to it but not as dirty."

"Plus the food is amazing."

He pats his stomach. "I think I've put on a few pounds since I've been here. Your mother keeps dragging me to all these places on her Yelp approved list."

"Mom just loves finding holes-in-the-wall, doesn't she?"

"You could say that. She found this place the other day that didn't have one window in it. I thought we were done, that was until we snuck into a basement and had some of the best dim sum I've ever put in my mouth."

"Better than the dim sum you had in San Francisco in Chinatown?"

"Dare I say, yes?" He chuckles, a good hearty sound. "Although, don't tell your mother that. She'd divorce me. We still make trips to San Francisco so she can have that dim sum a few times a year."

"She knows what she likes, and you can't fault her for that."

My dad shakes his head. "I never would. She's an angel, and I plan on keeping her as happy as can be."

What I wouldn't give for a relationship like what my parents have. They met before my dad started making a ton of money, before his company really boomed. Growing up, they told me stories about their humble beginnings, in the small studio apartment in Los Angeles they lived in for two years, the bed working as a dining room table, a place to sleep, and my dad's home office. I don't know how they did it, but they still tell me to this day, it was some of the best times they had together. They struggled through occasional disagreements and frustrations, and sometimes found the four walls a little . . . cramped . . . to say the least. But the perseverance it took to keep the company and their marriage together—*and the learned knowledge that humor was often required in spades*—was what grew their relationship from friends to lovers to best friends and more.

Unfortunately, I don't think I'll ever share the same experience with a man.

"Tell me, how did you think dinner went the other night with the Carltons? We haven't had a chance to deconstruct it."

I fold my hands on my lap and lean back in my chair. "I think it went well. Heller and Parks tried to blatantly stick their noses up the Carltons' asses, it was almost sickening to be in the presence of them."

Dad chuckles. "They've always been like that. Nothing I haven't seen before. I enjoy going to dinner with them because it feels like a circus show. Quite entertaining. I was proud of you though, you held your cool, spoke about the Carltons and their interests rather than the acreage we're trying to accrue. You showed interest in them as humans and asked intelligent questions, thought-provoking but nothing that would spark a debate. I was very impressed."

"Yeah?" I can't contain my smile. "I worked hard to prepare myself. They value a strong family bond, so I made sure to focus on that."

"They do. It's one of the reasons they started speaking with us, because they know our family dynamic is strong."

"I think we can use that to our advantage."

"I agree. Let's keep it in our back pocket for now." He checks his Cartier watch and winces. "I spent a little too much time laughing it up with your employees. If I don't leave now, I'll be late to dinner with your mom, and you know how she feels about being late."

"Don't let me keep you."

He stands but then pauses and points his finger at me. "I almost forgot. Did I see you won a date with Jason Orson, the catcher for the Rebels?"

Where the hell did he hear about that?

"Uh . . . what now?"

I pick up my pen and scratch the side of my head, trying to look as casual as possible, which only makes my dad tilt his head back and laugh wholeheartedly.

"Dorothy Domico, you are a titan when it comes to business, but your personal life is a shitshow."

"I don't know what you're talking about."

He shakes his head. "It was in our company newsletter. *Domico's very own wins date with new Rebel*. Quite an interesting read. Ten thousand dollars, huh?"

"It was a miscommunication." I sigh and rub my temple. "But don't worry, I cancelled the date."

"Why?" My dad's brow pulls together. "Jason Orson is nothing to sneeze at. His stats alone will give the Rebels a shot at the play-offs next season. It was a huge acquisition for them."

"Yes, he's great. He was amazing in college. But I'm not into dating right now, as I just want to focus on work."

He nods, his short silence startling. I know that look in his eyes. He's mulling over something and I don't think I'm going to like it.

"I love you, Dottie."

"But . . ."

He shakes his head and buttons his suit jacket. "No but. Just wanted to tell you I love you."

"I don't believe you." I laugh. "You always have a hidden agenda."

"Not this time. You're a grown woman and can handle things on your own. I will tell you this though, I would hate for you to go through life without a partner in crime, someone to keep you grounded. Even though I thank God every day for you, your mother has been the biggest blessing in my life."

"It was easier for you back then to meet someone. I'm in a different position."

"How so?"

"Uh . . . most of Chicago knows who I am."

"So?" He shrugs. "You're a good judge of character and know how to filter out the losers from the good ones. Go on that date with Orson; you never know what will come of it." That's the thing, though. I'm not a good judge of character. If I was, I never would have fallen for Nick, and I never would have allowed him to take advantage of me.

My dad walks out of my office with a quick wave and a parting smile.

I'm not surprised that he came in here, laid down a pool of thought for me to wade through, and then left. I don't think there's been a time when he hasn't done that. I should know by now what's coming.

But go on a date with Jason Orson?

I mentally shake my head.

No way. He would be amazing to look at, but I know we wouldn't work.

~

Nooooooo.
My head falls in my hand.
Fuck.

I stare at my screen, reading the email one of my on-site managers sent me about an infrastructure we're working on downtown.

Water main break is the subject. Flooding is in the body. Estimated total cost in repairs: over two hundred thousand.

I lean back in my chair and bounce my foot up and down, trying to steady my breath.

I take a deep breath and stare at the email again.
Shit.

Dad is not going to be happy. I told him about this property, saw it myself, told him to take a chance on it. He was concerned with the structural integrity. I told him it was old, but holding up well. Now with this . . . God, he's going to give me the look. The disapproving look. The *I told you so* look.

And just like that, I feel my emotions start to build up and my throat grow tight. My eyes begin to water but before I let the tears fall, I take a deep breath, sip some water, and attempt to compose myself.

It's okay. Accidents happen all the time in projects like these. It's why we have a cushion of money, but two hundred thousand dollars eats up that cushion pretty fast.

My lip trembles again and I inwardly curse myself as embarrassment washes over me. I swore I would never make another mistake while working under my dad, not after the last time, not after letting him down. And here I am again, putting myself out on the line for a project I believed in.

I quickly pull up the account file and look over the numbers. I factor in the two hundred thousand dollars in repairs and quickly do the math. We will be cutting it close, but we could do it.

I quickly type out a response to the project manager about an emergency meeting tomorrow. I can take care of this. I don't need to tell my dad. I can do this on my own.

Shaken with my anxiety on full alert, I send the email and try to calm myself.

"Miss Domico." Jessica appears at my door, a nervous look on her face, startling me.

I quickly wipe at my cheek, just in case a tear escaped and I say, "Jessica, what are you still doing here? I told you to leave at six. That was five minutes ago."

"Yes, well, there's a visitor for you."

"A visitor?" I try to peek around to the outside of my office, but I don't see anyone. "Did my dad come back?" *Please, no, please don't let him still be here.*

"No, not quite. Um"—Jessica bites her bottom lip—"I've been told not to announce who it is."

I groan, tossing my pen to my desk. People have stress balls, I have pens. I click them, flick them, chew on them, they are my go-to when I'm stressed out, need to think, or I'm just flat-out bored. Jessica keeps a bin full of the pen I like so I never run out.

This isn't the first time I've had a visitor not want to be announced and guess who it always is?

Lindsay and Emory. And when they don't want to be announced, it's because they have some elaborate game or dinner or plan to "help me escape" my workweek. I've been putting in the hours this week after the Carlton dinner, which means I've been ignoring both of them, so I'm not surprised they're here. After that email, it might be nice to see my friends.

"Send them in," I say. I'm hoping they at least have brownies or something. I could really go for a dessert despite not having dinner yet. Never eat your feelings, that's what my chef says. Whoever doesn't eat their feelings isn't dealing with mishaps and pain correctly.

"Are you sure?"

"Yes, it's fine."

Jessica leaves my office and while I wait for Emory and Lindsay to come barging in, I reach up to my hair and pull out the pen I have stuffed back there. Just as my hair floats around my shoulders, a tall, broad figure walks into my office.

Starting at his feet, I work my way up past his jean-clad thighs, to the narrow of his waist, to the taut fabric of his button-up shirt that stretches across his chest, to his strong jaw, to . . .

Oh . . .

Mother . . .

Fucker . . .

"Dorothy Domico," he says with a smile.

My stomach bottoms out. What is he doing here?

Nerves bloom in the pit of my stomach as I try to pick my

mouth up off the floor. Standing in the doorway of my office is the one and only Jason Orson.

I swallow hard, digging deep within my soul to find my inner businesswoman and put on a strong face, to not be intimidated by his handsome features or sucked in by his kind eyes. My staff know I'm not a walkover, and this man before me needs to know too.

Pushing my chair away from my desk, I stand tall, and clasp my hands together. "Yes, how can I help you?"

Straight-faced, stiff back, firm set in my shoulders, I don't show one ounce of insecurity or nervousness, even though I feel like throwing up inside.

Can you believe he's even more good-looking in person?

The way he just stands there with confidence . . . it's both enticing and annoying. The sleeves of his button-up shirt are folded to his elbows, showing off the sinew in his forearms that ripples when he moves. His ruggedly handsome face, with a sprinkle of five o'clock shadow, his compelling green eyes, and the firm set in his jaw, it quickens my pulse, speeding up my breath.

He steps farther into my office and shuts the door. From behind his back, he holds out a small bouquet of flowers—daises to be precise—and says, "These are for you."

Oh God, what is happening?

Flowers?

He's here in my office?

He's smiling?

What the hell did Knox and Emory tell him?

"I'm confused, why are you here?"

He steps even closer, but approaches slowly, as if I'm a scared animal, ready to flee any second. He's right. I'm not above scurrying out of this office when the opportunity presents itself.

"For our date, of course. It's Friday."

"That was cancelled. No need to be here. Jessica can show you out." A firm brush-off, just what he needs.

"Ah, but I don't work like that, you see." He takes another step closer, his cologne filtering into my personal space, making me feel dizzy with lust.

Yes, lust.

I'm lusting. I've lusted after this man for so long that seeing him here, in the flesh, it's doing all sorts of weird things to my body, like heating it up inappropriately for the workplace.

"Mr. Orson—"

"You can call me Jason."

Exhaling, I fold my hands together. "Jason, thank you for stopping by, but I have work to get done." I motion to the door. "Jessica will see you out."

"I heard you the first time about Jessica, but I'm in no hurry to leave. You paid for a date with me, so I'm here. Let's date."

"First of all"—I hold up my finger, my irritation of him not listening starting to grate on my nerves—"I did not pay for a date with you. My assistant accidentally donated money to your Charity Hustle fundraiser that was supposed to be donated to a different charity. I, by no means, was looking for a date with you, nor do I care to go on one either. So, please leave."

His face falls and for a brief moment, I feel guilty for telling him the truth. I'm sure no one wants to know a donation to a foundation that's close to your heart was a mistake. I should clarify that I was impressed with *his* charity, but hadn't chosen to donate at this time. But of course, out of my depth, I remain mute.

With a brief nod, he sets the flowers on my desk and then backs away, making my conscience take over my emotions.

Man, I feel like a dick.

And I wasn't even that bad. I've said worse, more harsh things to people, but the way he's walking out of here like I just told him he has the worst swing in baseball, it cuts me deep. Which is EXACTLY why I need to stay true to my decision. I don't need someone cutting me deep with emotions.

Emotions can destroy your demeanor in the boardroom, it can throw you off your ability to make a deal. They can affect your head, play games with you, making it impossible to be the stiff-armed, businesswoman I've trained myself to be.

One of the biggest things I've learned about being in this position of power, one that's usually held by a person with a penis, is there's a stigma; women are too emotional. They base their decisions off emotions rather than facts, making them weak. At least that's what I've heard from many chauvinistic assholes—thankfully, none of them have been my dad—and I've made it a point to never be that woman they speak of.

I've become strong, inflexible when necessary, and I go after what I want with no shame.

That's not going to change because the boy from college, who I deemed the perfect man, just came waltzing into my office with flowers and the idea of taking me out on a date.

He leaves, and I keep my chin held high when I sit back in my chair and pull myself closer to my desk. That was the right decision.

Sending him on his way so I don't spend another second soaking in his masculine scent or the smooth, alpha-like movements of his body.

Yup, the right—

"I hope you like burgers," his booming voice declares. Instead of flowers, he's carrying a cardboard tray of food and two drinks . . . into my office.

What on earth . . .

Without even asking, he moves some of my papers to the side, along with my jar of pens, and makes room for the food. He unfolds a few napkins and lays them across the cool glass of my desk. Next, he goes back outside and then brings in a canvas bag. Like Mary Poppins, he starts extracting plates, cups, silverware, and a vase for the flowers, which he expertly shuffles the daisies into followed by a dash of water from a water bottle.

"What are you doing?"

"Setting up our date. I know what you said about me leaving.

Don't think I didn't hear you." He pulls on his ear. "Because I did, I heard you loud and clear, but I chose to ignore it."

I fold my arms across my chest. "What did Knox tell you?" I ask, cutting to the chase.

"Nothing actually. So, no wishing one-fifty batting averages on him."

Okay, sure, Knox didn't say anything.

"He clearly told you something if he let you know about the threat."

"Nothing gets by you." He looks up and smiles, and brilliant white teeth flash at me. Damn it. "But he told me he wasn't telling me shit because of your threat. Carson was the one who figured everything out."

Crap, how could I forget about Carson?

I don't hang out with him as much, it's quite rare actually when we're in the same room, but if I wasn't so bogged down with staring at the bulge in the "towel picture" then I might have sent him a quick message to keep his mouth shut too.

See what happens when I'm distracted? I lose my ability to think clearly.

"Honestly, I was offended that you cancelled the date. After spending so much money, I thought it was because I posted something you didn't agree with on social media. I was scrolling through my feed trying to figure it out. I knew it wasn't my potato salad."

What the hell is he talking about?

"I don't follow you on social media." I unfollowed him after I graduated, because I realized following him was once again, another distraction.

"What? You don't?" He looks hurt. I'm sure he'll get over it. "Then how did you find out about the fundraiser?"

"Amazingly enough, I don't get all my information from Instagram posts."

"Snarky, okay. Then how did you find out about it?"

He unwraps the burgers and fries and sets them carefully on the plate, making an entire presentation out of it by making a swirl across the white surface with ketchup and mustard. Uh, is he a baseball player or is he competing for a spot on Top Chef?

"Lindsay and Emory," I answer, not even thinking about it as I stare at the way his fingers delicately place the fries to resemble a teepee.

"And why would they send it to you?"

His thumb rubs against the plate, smooth and with pressure as he spins it around. What else could that thumb do?

"Because they were teasing me." The moment the words slip past my lips, I instantly regret them.

"Teasing you, huh? What were they teasing you about? Do you have some kind of crush on me?" He wiggles his eyebrows, and I nearly throw up on the elegantly displayed burger and fries.

"What? No." I shake my head. "No." I flatten my palm against the surface of my desk. "No."

Go ahead, say no one more time, Dottie, you can't be more obvious at this point.

"Uh-huh." He eyes me suspiciously and then stands from his chair, leans over my desk, and unfolds a napkin, only to slip it into my exposed neckline. And for some weird reason, I want more than a napkin dipping into my exposed neckline. I want his fingers. Maybe his tongue.

What the hell, Domico? Get it together.

Which I will . . . once he stops standing so close, being a gentleman, pandering to my needs . . .

He tips my chin up with a smile and says, "Bon appétit."

CHAPTER SIX

JASON

T hanks to Carson and some "research," these are the things I
know about Dorothy "Dottie" Domico:

She went to school with us.

She was a year ahead of me.

She doesn't have much of a life outside of work.

She's a bigwig for one of the biggest real estate companies in
the country—yeah, the fucking country.

She's best friends with Lindsay and Emory.

And she likes burgers and fries—thanks, Emory, for that small
tidbit.

But what I wasn't prepared for was how goddamn gorgeous
she is.

Yeah, I saw a few pictures of her, but they were nothing
compared to the real thing. Because sitting in front of me is by far
the most beautiful woman I've ever fucking seen. We're talking, *I
can't take my eyes off her* beautiful.

She went to fucking college with me, partied at the baseball
house, so how did I not *see* her?

Long black hair, straight and luscious, with ocean-blue eyes, and the longest eyelashes I've ever seen. And don't get me started on her lips . . . full and enticing, just looking for trouble.

I was expecting Dottie to be attractive, but a bombshell? She has me feeling all nervous and fumbly. I spent extra time arranging her plate so I didn't show how shaky my hands were. My hands. Shaky. I get paid a hella lot of money because my hands are *never* shaky.

Besides her obvious *smack me in the dick* good looks, she's also a powerhouse, from the firm set in her jaw, the assertive tone of her voice, and the way she carries herself. There's no denying she has a shield up and prefers to keep it that way.

Too bad for her, I can look past shields.

"Normally I'd cook something for a date, but since this was for a fundraiser and I'm not good with traveling with homecooked meals, I thought ordering out would be easier." When she doesn't touch her food, I say, "Emory told me you like this burger, that it's your favorite out of all the burgers in the world, which means you have no reason not to eat it."

"I'm on a diet," she says with a monotone voice.

"Liar. Now eat, unless you plan on hurting my feelings twice in one night."

"I have no problem hurting people's feelings."

"Ah, a tight-ass with no awareness for the people around them. Pretty sure I've seen your type before."

"Are you calling me unoriginal?"

"Nope." I smile. "I'm calling your current attitude unoriginal. Try unclenching your ass cheeks for a second to take a deep breath."

Her jaw works side to side, her arms tightening, giving off a *don't approach me* vibe. I'm thinking I should have asked Emory for more information about her friend, because I don't think this date is off to a good start.

"I'm going to ask you nicely one more time to leave, and if you don't, I will call security."

"No, you won't. You would never toss one of Knox's friends to the curb."

She leans forward, legs crossed under her desk, but from the glass desk, I can see how smooth and tan they are. "Knox is currently on my shit list so I have zero reservations about getting rid of you."

I take a bite of a fry and give her an effortless once-over. "Why don't we start over?" I reach out my hand to her, which she makes no attempt to shake. "Jason Orson, thank you for donating to my charity; it meant a lot to me."

She stares at my hand for an achingly long ten seconds before taking my hand with hers and giving it a firm, not dainty shake. Okay . . .

"You thanked me. You can leave now."

"I think you're forgetting how a typical conversation works. You see, I said thank you, you should say you're welcome."

Groaning, she picks up a fry and bites into it. "Let me guess, you're one of those annoying people who charms with quick wit and then gets their way."

I raise my hand. "Guilty."

"So you're just like Knox. Will keep wearing you down until you give in."

"Glad you're seeing it now, saving me the hassle of having to chip away at that cold exterior of yours." I whisper and say, "P.S. I knew you wouldn't call security on me."

She picks up her burger and before taking a big bite, she says, "Twelve-year-old girls say P.S. and security is only a quick phone call away. Don't test me."

"Does that mean we're on a date?"

She squints in mocked anger. "It means I'm hungry, and I can only have this burger in front of me untouched for so long."

"Please tell me you're about to own that piece of meat."

Slyly, she glances at me and says, "I own every piece of meat that's put in front of me."

Good.

Fuck.

My dick just twitched. Not sure if it was out of excitement or pure terror, but I guess there's only one way to find out.

Have you ever eaten a meal by yourself? The peaceful silence, the thought-provoking conversations you have in your head, the inside jokes you tell yourself. A winning experience every person should have at least once.

But when you have it, make sure you're actually alone, not sitting across from a burger-annihilating woman with a pinch in her brow and a snarl in her lip.

First, I'd like to preface what I'm about to say with this: I find it super sexy when a woman eats in front of a man. I love it when they're not embarrassed and just act themselves. Now, don't kill me when I say, watching Dottie Domico take down her burger is one of the most terrifying things I've ever experienced.

I don't think she stopped to take a breath.

It was as if her burger were a pair of ripe tits and she motorboated them until there was nothing left. At one point, I looked up to see her cheeks puffed out like a chipmunk, ketchup hanging off her chin, chomping down like she had one minute left to eat the whole thing.

I've never seen anything like it.

It's clearly why we sat there in silence the whole time, not a word passing between us. Every time I went to ask her a question, it was as if she had a sixth sense—knowing exactly when I was going to speak—and she shoved another big bite in her mouth, followed by a fry chaser.

After my fifth attempt to say something, I stopped trying for the mere chance that if she kept going at the rate she was, she could die from asphyxiation by burger meat.

So instead, I sat there, ate my burger at a normal human rate, and tried to think of things to talk about after we were done with our meal.

Because I'm a good guy, I feel this need to make right on this date, to really give her the full experience, even if she accidentally donated to my charity. Which, can we pause for a second and talk about that? A little bit of a gut check happened when she claimed to want to donate to something else. That kind of realization never feels good, but what I did find interesting is somehow she was looking at my fundraiser, especially if Lindsay and Emory sent it, so there was some interest there. Who knows if it was interest in me or interest in my charity. Either way, I'm still in the picture.

Interest is all I need. If there was no interest, I'd probably think of an escape route, but something tells me there's more to Dottie. It's like I've seen the incredible, fearsome, and fucking amazing surface . . . her façade. What she gives to those she doesn't yet trust. But she's Emory's best friend, so I know she must be good people. I want to know the next level. Who is she away from her desk? Who is she when she's not a bigwig of a major company? And why hasn't she asked anything about me? I'm still confused how we didn't know each other in college. And I'm extremely curious why she denied four times that she had a crush on me. *That* little tidbit has been filed away in the *I'll explore that later* box. Right now, I'm determined to find the friend. The girl I'm sure I'll like.

Plus, I'm that guy who needs everyone to like them. It's why I cook for my teammates. I want them to know I can nourish them, that I'm the key to pleasing their taste buds. It's general knowledge that chefs are always loved the most in the group of friends, because who doesn't want to be fed properly?

Dottie is putting up a front, acting like she doesn't like me, like she doesn't want me near her, but I'm going to peel back that defensive layer and let her true personality shine.

She'll want to be friends by the end of this night, I just know it.

"Enjoy your burger?" From the back of her throat, she burps, the sound muffled by her closed mouth but I still heard it, so I say, "I'm going to take that as a yes."

She presses her napkin to her mouth, her cheeks turning a light shade of pink. "It was fine."

"Fine?" I ask, unable to control myself. "No one takes a burger down like you just did if it was only fine."

Her cheeks flush even more. It's interesting that a strong, put-together woman who doesn't care to shred an ounce of emotion can actually blush. Maybe there's a living being inside her after all.

"You know, I wasn't judging the way you ate one fry at a time, your pinky finger reaching to the sky, so why don't you lay off the way I eat a burger?"

"Oh, so you were paying attention to me. Huh, I thought you were just trying to tongue your burger the whole time. I almost put a *do not disturb* sign on your office door."

She folds her arms over her chest as she leans back in her chair, a look of disapproval on her face. "Explain to me how being an asshole is saving you from me calling security?"

"Threats are like assholes; they're pointless." Huh, is that what I wanted to say?

"That makes no sense at all, and I don't know about you, but my asshole is impeccably clean."

I motion for her to stand with my fingers and whistle as my fingers twist, indicating her to turn around as well. "I'll be the judge of that. Whip them off, Domico."

Her eyes narrow, her face contorting to one of pure hatred.

Yikes.

Looks like my teasing approach is a no-go.

"We're not friends, so don't talk to me like one. If I ever 'whipped' my skirt off, it wouldn't be for you. And, security is here."

"What?" I turn around in my chair to see two large men, dressed in all black making a beeline for me. They both grab one of my arms and lift me out of my chair. "Unhand me at once," I say, struggling to get out of their grasps. I'm a large, strong man who's spent many hours in the weight room, but I'm no match for the two men dragging me out of Dottie Domico's office, my heels dragging in her plush rug.

"Thanks for the burger." She waves and then turns back to her computer.

"You eat like a savage," I call out. "And you have a piece of pepper in your teeth." Her office door slams as I mutter, "Ungrateful wench."

In the elevator, I find out the names of her security guards—Edgar and Harry—and that they've been working with Miss Domico for two years now, and I'm the first one to be dragged out of her office. By the time we reached the lobby, we're good friends. I signed a few autographs for them, took a picture for my IG—it's always about the gram—told them I would tag them, and then I took off.

To say I'm confused is an understatement.

What the hell just happened?

~

"I knew telling you about the empty space across from my apartment was a bad idea," Knox groans while I file into his living room wearing nothing but a pair of my favorite silk pajama pants, midnight black. They feel so smooth on my ass and balls that I love wearing them around the house, only to slip into my bed completely naked. It's like a pre-game of relaxation for my most private areas.

I take a seat on his couch and set down a plate of freshly baked brownies. I'm a sucker for a deliciously rich brownie, especially if they have walnuts and marshmallows in them. *Kisses fingers* Perfection.

"Don't yell at him, he brought goodies," Emory says. Wrapped up in a robe, she sits next to me and takes two brownies off the plate. "Oh, they're still warm. Hey Knox, grab us some milk." Emory takes a giant bite and moans before taking one more.

"Double fisting. Nice," I say to her as she reaches for one more. "Hey, they're not going anywhere." I laugh as she whips her head toward me and stares venomously.

Jesus.

What's with women today?

"I can take as many as I want," she hisses.

I put my hands up, one clutching a brownie. "I'm not going to stop you, so by all means, eat the whole plate."

Knox brings over three glasses of milk and says, "She's been temperamental all day. She threw an empty can of peanuts at me this morning because she was mad they were all gone."

"Who puts the empty can back in the pantry? Get rid of it, don't trick a hungry person looking for peanuts into thinking there are still peanuts left," she says, her voice growing angrier. "There were NO PEANUTS left, Knox. No goddamn peanuts!"

Ehhh . . .

I scoot a few inches away, feeling the boiling heat popping off Emory, afraid she might lash out on me over the lack of peanuts.

"Um, I have some peanuts over at my place, if you want some."

"You do, do you? Aren't you super helpful? Especially since I wanted them at six this morning. How do you think your peanuts are going to help me now? Huh, Jason? How the hell are they supposed to HELP ME NOW?" She rips into a brownie and chomps at me, snapping her teeth like a motherfucking lobster coming at me with its claws. Brownie seeps into the cracks of her teeth as she snarls and I swear to Christ himself, if I lose my face skin over peanuts, I'm going to be super pissed.

Just when she leans in closer, teeth bared and brownies held tightly in her clutches, the doorbell rings.

Knox hops to his feet. "That would be the test."

"The test?" I ask, scooting farther away.

Knox answers the door, thanks the concierge, and then shuts the door. He thrusts a brown bag at Emory and points down the hall. "Go. Now."

She stands tall, brownies still in one hand. "Don't you dare talk to me like that."

"I'll talk to you however I please, woman. Now go to the bathroom and tell me if there is a demon growing inside you or not."

Demon? Inside her?

"If there is, it's yours, which means this is all your fault. All of this." She motions up and down her body. "If anything is sadistic in this house"—she pats Knox's junk, causing him to buckle over—"it's your sperm."

Ahhh . . . She's pregnant. I don't need to see the results of that test to know. Emory is the coolest, sweetest girl I know, but right now, she looks like she's two seconds away from morphing in an ogre and shitting on everyone's dinner with a giant green plop.

After she stomps down the hallway, I ask, "Uh, maybe I should go. This seems like a private matter."

Knox shakes his head. "No, you have to stay now because I'm afraid what will happen if the test is positive. I'm not sure if she'll be happy or ready to rip my balls off and stuff them down my throat."

"Valid concern." I look down the hallway where Emory disappeared. "She was straight-up terrifying back there."

"Tell me about it. She's been like that for the last week. I have no idea what to do. One minute she's laughing, then she's crying, and then she's laughing again . . . between sobs. Dude, it's some freaky shit."

"Yeah, she sounds pregnant. Are you excited?"

"I mean"—he scratches the back of his head—"it's a little out of order than how I would want things to go, but yeah, I'm excited. I want babies with Emory, I just hope she's okay with it."

"I'm sure she will be. She would be an awesome mom and you would be a subpar dad."

"Wow, thanks."

We both laugh and I adjust myself on the couch, turning more toward Knox. "So, I uh . . . went to see Dottie at her office today."

"Jesus, fuck. Why?" Knox groans, slouching.

"Because, I owed her a date and if anything, I keep my word. I took her food."

"How did she react to seeing you? Did she mention me?"

"Umm." I look away. "You know, she might have mentioned your name."

"Jason. Fucking hell, man."

"Before you start throwing up everywhere—"

"Why would I throw up?"

I shrug. "Nerves?" Knox rolls his eyes so I continue. "I told her you didn't tell me anything, that you wouldn't. I blamed it all on Carson."

That makes Knox chuckle. "Okay, I can get on board with that. So what did she say? Was she into the date?"

"Well, at first, she threatened security on me, but I coerced my way into her office along with food and quite the spread of dinnerware. I set up our food and we ate . . . in silence."

"Oh fuck." He chuckles. "She silenced you?"

"Yup." Shifting, I get closer. "Have you ever seen her eat before?" I bring my hand up to my mouth and impersonate her rather robust way of eating, going to town on my hand. Knox throws his head back and laughs while shaking it yes.

"Oh shit, yes. When she's into something she's eating, it's like she can't focus on anything else. It's a sight to behold."

"You could say that," I say, draping my arm over the couch. "Frankly, I was impressed, and maybe a little turned on. If she can eat a burger like that, how good would she eat my dick?"

Knox punches my side. He does it so fast I have no way of protecting myself.

"Dude," I moan, falling into the couch. "What the hell was that for?"

"Don't talk about Emory's friends eating dick. Jesus, man."

"Touchy," I grunt out.

"Get back to what happened. She ate her burger and then what?"

"Like I said, it was kind of a turn-on, seeing her devour her meat like that. Oh fuck, and she made this offhand comment about being able to handle any meat that comes her way. I got hard immediately."

"You're so fucking horny."

"It's been a while, so don't dick shame me." I take a bite of my brownie, letting the chocolate soothe my aching loins. It's been a loooong time since I've been in the presence of a naked woman and even though she was a snarly beast of a woman, there was something about Dottie that piqued my interest. Until she sent me on my way.

"Just get on with it."

"After we were finished eating, I tried to strike up a conversation, but I probably took the wrong approach by commenting on how she downed her burger."

Knox winces. "Not smart."

"Yeah, I realize that now, but before I knew it, I was being dragged out of her office by security."

"Oh fuck, seriously?" Knox laughs.

"Yup, arm in arm, dragged right out of there. But don't worry, by the time we made it to the lobby, I was best friends with the guys."

"I wasn't worried." Such a dick. "Dottie is a tough one. She's hardened over the years. Back in college, she was warmer, more welcoming, but over the last few years, she's really become more closed off. Emory was saying it's because—"

"I'M PREGNANT," Emory yells as she sprints down the hallway, right into Knox's arms.

"What? Are you serious?"

"Yes, we're having a baby."

"Holy shit, babe."

Emory cries.

Knox cries.

Hell, I get teary eyed. And as I watch them kiss and talk quietly about the little bundle of joy they created, it hits me how fast things are changing. My best friend is going to be a dad. *A dad.* But that kid? He'll be the luckiest kid on the planet . . . but I can't help wondering . . . what was the end to Knox's sentence?

CHAPTER SEVEN

DOTTIE

"WHY did you bring booze?" I ask Lindsay as we ride up to Knox and Emory's apartment in the elevator.

She looks at the bottle of champagne in her hand and says, "Because we're celebrating. Bubbly is always needed when celebrating."

"She's pregnant; she can't drink."

"Who cares about her? I have a babysitter and I plan on drinking."

"How thoughtful," I say sarcastically.

"You're a little more irritable than usual, what's your deal?"

I have yet to tell my friends about the impromptu "date" I had Friday night. I considered it, but when Emory called us Saturday morning to tell us the news, I knew talking about Jason's sudden appearance wasn't necessary. And I plan on keeping it that way. No one needs to know. I took care of it. It's all done.

"Just tense. Work stuff," I answer as the doors part and we filter into the hall. Knox and Emory have their door open, already greeting Carson and Milly.

When Emory sees us, her eyes get all watery, and I can't help but feel the same way. She has loved Knox for so long, and to see her finally happy with the man of her dreams, it lightens up my walled heart I've worked so hard at turning dark.

"You guys, I'm pregnant." Emory greets us once Carson and Milly make their way into the house.

Lindsay is the first to pull Emory to a hug, so I turn to Knox who has a weird look on his face. I give him a hug and say, "Congrats, Knox."

"Uh, thank you." He looks into his apartment and then gives me a half-smile.

Okay, that's weird.

I swap with Lindsay and give Emory a big hug. Friends since we were kids, it feels like yesterday we were huddling in her room, going through our high school yearbook, putting hearts next to all the guys we thought were hot.

Grown-up, with adult jobs, and apartments . . . it's crazy how time flies.

"I'm so happy for you two," I say into her ear while my arms are wrapped around her. "You guys are going to be amazing parents."

"Thank you." She pulls away, but she keeps her hand on my arm when she says, "And thank you for coming today. I know it's going to be weird."

She walks me into her apartment. "Why would it be—?"

My words are cut off the minute I see Jason standing by the window, a smile on his face, a drink in his hand, and his eyes trained on me.

Oh crap.

I've been so caught up in work and Emory's news that I completely forgot that not only does Jason live across from Knox and Emory, but he's really good friends with them too.

From the side of my mouth, I ask, "What did he say to you?"

Emory continues to smile and holds her non-existent belly. "Just that you had security drag him out."

I press my hand to my forehead. "Jesus. Did he say that he

came unannounced and was bothering me? He commented on my eating."

"Yes, we heard all of that, but it was also sweet what he was trying to do, so you didn't need to throw him out."

No, that's exactly what I needed to do. He is sweet, too sweet. And the problem with sweet is that he'd tire of my barbs. I'd have to change my world to be with someone like him. So, nipping any attraction in the bud was crucial. I needed him to see me as someone who's emotionally unattractive, so there was no chance to make a proper connection with me. Did I enjoy being so dismissive and cold when it came to my college crush, the man I've lusted after for so long? No, it was painful. It hurt to see him be dragged out by security. It wounded me to hear the things he mumbled as he made his way out of my office. It was embarrassing to see the looks on my security staff the next day as I arrived for work. They're professionals, so they were careful not to show bewilderment, but it was there. Subtle. What Jason did was unlike anything I'd ever experienced and that right there was a warning sign. Stay away, heart could be broken . . . easily. Just like Nick.

"Poor timing. I was very busy," I say, even though it isn't the truth. But they don't need the truth; they might not understand my hesitation, and I don't want to be convinced otherwise. I glance around, feeling my body start to retreat but Emory has a firm hold on my arm.

Sheesh, for a pregnant woman, she's surprisingly strong.

"I will remind you, this day is about me and Knox and you are one of my best friends, so I expect you to be here celebrating for a long time with all of us. And there will be no drama."

I hear what she's saying, and even though I want nothing more than to sprint back to my apartment and enjoy a nice bubble bath where I can attempt to forget this is happening, I know Emory's right. I'm here for a reason, and I'm just going to have to strap on my big girl panties and work through it.

"You don't even need to mention it." I kiss her cheek. "Let's show this baby what it has to look forward to."

∼

"Are you just going to avoid me the entire party?"

My back tenses as Jason's body presses against me, his shoulder rubbing mine as I stare at the skyline. It's been ten minutes.

Ten minutes of pure torture.

Little glances here and there, smirks from the man who I had extracted from my office only days ago, and winks . . . God, can he stop with the winking? It's weird, and it keeps heating up my body with every dip of his long eyelashes.

But deep down, despite my *don't come near me* vibes, I knew he'd make his way toward me eventually. He's the guy who doesn't let things go, but rather he builds on them and builds on them. Looks like we're about to have our first layer.

"Not avoiding you," I say, keeping my eyes trained on the city outside. "Just don't have anything to say to you, therefore, I haven't spoken to you."

"Nothing to say to me? Really? You had me carried out of your office by two men who happen to be great friends of mine now and you have nothing to say?"

Of course they are. There's no doubt Jason won them over with his charm. At least that explains the looks I received.

"No, nothing. And I had security come and get you for good reason; you were bothering me when I was trying to get work done."

"Bothering you?" he asks, his voice rising.

I shush him quickly. "Don't make a scene. This is a party for our friends. Let's keep it that way and not turn it into whatever dramatic affair you're about to make it."

"Dramatic affair?"

"Are you just going to repeat everything I say?"

"Repeat everything you say? Pishh."

Oh my God, he's annoying. Really freaking annoying.

Hot, with the best butt on a man I've ever seen, but beyond

annoying. But I also can't blame him, because despite the façade he's trying to mimic—if the hurt in his eyes is any indication—he's a man who wears his emotions on his sleeve. It must have bruised his pride to not be fawned over, or even appreciated for his kind gesture. I know I would be if I were in his shoes.

Keeping calm, I say, "Unless you have anything of substance to say to me, I suggest you move it along."

He pauses and I can feel his eyes blaze a trail up and down my body before saying, "Damn, girl, how long has that stick been shoved up your ass?"

No, he didn't.

Calm breaths. He's hurt, he's mad. You are better than this . . .

I turn to face him with a smile on my face. "Just because I don't want to talk to you, means I have a stick up my ass? Are you being sexist?"

He smiles back and pats my arm. "No, if I was being sexist, I would have said women as a whole have sticks up their asses. As far as I can tell, you're the only one who's bent over and begging for a flagpole to be shoved up there."

"Wow, you're offensive."

"Hmm."

"Hmm?"

He shrugs, then gives me another once-over. Motioning to my purple turtleneck dress that covers my entire upper torso and hits me just above my knees, he leans in and asks, "Are they in hiding?"

"In hiding? What on earth—?"

"Dottie, you've got great tits. Why are you hiding them?"

Okay, I am trying to work out if that was a compliment or a dig. I still have no clue why he's talking to me, especially now that I know he thinks a stick is up my ass. I lean forward and press my hand to his chest, still keeping a smile on my face. "Maybe I don't have to show off my tits to be friendly. I don't see you hanging your balls out of your zipper."

Of course, he smiles at that. "Want me to?"

Argh. I give up.

"You're disgusting. Stay away from me."

"Fine by me." He gives me a quick pat to my arm and takes off.

The fucking nerve of that man. *Are they in hiding?* What was he even thinking coming over here? *Let's see how much I can push Dottie to her limits?*

Well, he got me there, because I'm fired up and ready to do some damage.

~

"D id you try the potato salad? I heard it's amazing."
Seriously?

I look over my shoulder to find Jason hovering over me, plate in hand, ready to dig into the buffet of food Emory and Knox had catered.

"You're breathing on my neck."

"Want me to lick it too while I'm this close?"

Is he mad? Is he flirting? Is he trying to annoy me into submission? What is it? Pick a lane, man.

"I'd rather stab my eye with my fork," I answer, putting some potato salad on my plate and moving out of the way.

Lindsay is busy talking to Carson and Milly. Emory and Knox are speaking with a few of his teammates, which leaves me to myself. It's for the best, as I'm not feeling very conversational right now.

But as I'm about to stick a forkful of potato salad in my mouth, Jason takes a seat next to me and sets his drink on the side table between us.

This man has a death wish; it's the only explanation why he's coming for round two . . . or would this be three if we're counting my office?

Ignoring him, I take a bite and—oh my God . . . this *has to be* the best potato salad I've ever had. Without even thinking, I scoop up another forkful and stuff it in my mouth. Barely chewing, just swallowing because damn, this is so good, I hear Jason clear his throat as I'm about to stick the last bite in my mouth.

"Enjoying that, aren't you?" His smile is so wide, I want to flick it back in place with my middle finger. I felt bad for him earlier, now I'm just irritated.

"Yes," I answer curtly as I put the last forkful in my mouth.

"Good to know, because I made it."

My mouth pauses, the beautiful dill and sage flavoring immediately turning sour and before I can stop myself, I lean my mouth over my plate and let my half chewed-up potato salad fall past my lips and back onto my plate.

"What the—?"

I set my plate on top of his, stand from my chair, and go back to the buffet where I serve myself again, this time, avoiding the potato salad altogether.

~

"You look tense," Lindsay says, carrying a glass of champagne in her hand and when I say glass, I mean a pint glass filled to the top.

Class doesn't exist within her.

"You think?" I look around, spotting Jason talking to Carson and Knox. They all laugh at the same time, three perfect smiles gracing all their handsome faces.

"Does this have to do with Jason? Is it because you're so overwhelmed with his hotness? Tell me about it. It's hard being in this apartment right now with all these athletes. I mean, just look at the way they all grip their beer bottles. By the neck, like they're choking the bitch for some nectar."

"What the hell is wrong with you?" I take her pint glass away. "You need to start drinking water before you embarrass yourself."

She retrieves her pint glass and takes a big gulp. "Embarrassing myself is in my nature. Why are you trying to change me, Dottie? Let me live."

"Yeah, let her live, Dottie." Jason stands in front of us, "choking" his beer while the other hand is casually tucked in his pocket.

Where the hell did he just come from? It's as if he floated across the hardwood floor and appeared out of nowhere.

Why is he talking to me? I'm sure he doesn't find me pleasant at this point, I don't even find myself pleasant. Have you ever gotten yourself in a mood and have to go to bed in order to press the reset button? It's the only way out. That's where I'm at.

I'm mad at myself for being rude when I shouldn't be. I'm mad at myself for allowing one single man to ruin future interactions with men to the point that I'm quick to defend and retaliate rather than befriend. And I'm mad at myself for not being able to actually be normal around someone who I've actually thought very highly of for quite a long time.

But for some awful reason, even though I can calculate those thoughts and feelings in my head, it's as if I can't translate them for my body so it will act like a normal person. And I'm sad that he probably thinks I'm a horrible human now, most definitely not worth his time. And that is not what I want, not deep down.

"Oh, Jason." Lindsay giggles uncontrollably. "Look at you standing there with all those muscles."

Great, Loose Lips Lindsay just made it to the party.

Like the cute doofus he is, Jason flexes his bicep and says, "Thank you."

I pretend not to look, but who am I kidding? The man is a walking sex machine, and seeing him flex, his bicep popping up like a second head, makes me want to claw at his shirt to see the rest.

I've seen the rest with all my cyberstalking, but in person is a whole other beast.

I bet he's a beast in bed.

An animal.

An animal with a really good tongue.

"Tongue," I mutter, startling myself.

"What?" Jason asks.

Eyes wide and panicked, I stand there mute. Umm . . .

Lindsay thankfully says, "You've met Dottie, right?"

"Yup, we've met." He smiles at me. "She loves my potato salad."

Lindsay laughs, and then slides her hand unapologetically down Jason's arm, giving his bicep a squeeze with a giggle. "Oh, there's a lot more Dottie loves about you than just your potato salad."

You know . . .

I should have seen that coming.

I've known Lindsay long enough to recognize what stage of drunk she's in, and Loose Lips Lindsay never holds back, meaning, she's about to unravel all of my secrets.

"Is that so?" Jason's brows lift as he faces me.

"She's drunk; she has no idea what she's talking about. I need to get her some water." I pull on Lindsay's arm, but she doesn't budge. "Come on, time to sober up."

"I'm not drunk and I do know what I'm talking about." Shit, we're about to have a confession in three . . . two . . . "She thinks you have the best ass in all of baseball." In all the world technically, but we don't have to go there.

"The best ass?" The smile that crosses his face makes me want to crawl in a hole and die, literally keel over from sheer embarrassment.

But because tonight I'm the stiff wench who can't control my tongue from self-destruct mode, I shake my head. "Lindsay, you have it wrong. I said Walker Rockwell on the Bobbies has the best ass. Remember that picture I sent to you last week of him on deck?" I did send her a picture, and I'm hoping she's just drunk enough to get confused.

"Huh, you did send me that picture." See, piece of cake.

Jason's face grows stern as he says, "Walker Rockwell? You think he has the best ass in baseball? No fucking way."

"Easily. No competition and believe me, being a Bobbies fan, I've had plenty of time to stare at it, especially when I'm sitting first row, right next to the dugout."

His jaw works back and forth, irritation evident in his eyes.

"You're lying."

"Afraid not. Walker is what dreams are made of."

"He is so hot," Lindsay says, leaning into me. I take that as my cue to take her to the kitchen for some water.

"Walker is an ass," Jason says as I start to walk away, Lindsay in tow.

"Did you say he's an ass, or that he has the best ass? Don't be jealous, Orson; it's not pretty on you."

~

"D ottie, why are you ruining this party for me?" Emory asks, sitting next to me on the couch.

"What?" I sit taller. "How am I ruining it?

"Well," she huffs out, "technically you're not ruining it, Jason is, but you started it."

"What did I start?" I glance over to where Jason is standing next to Carson and Knox, showing his ass off to them. He's insufferable.

"All Jason can talk about is who has a better butt, him or Walker. Why did you find it necessary to turn him into a neurotic mess?"

In a calm voice, I say, "I had no idea he was going to be such a whine-baby about it. And," I whisper, "Lindsay was spouting off facts I didn't want Jason knowing."

"Ahh." Emory nods her head. "Loose Lips Lindsay."

"Exactly. I had to distract both of them and get the hell out of there."

Biting her lip, Emory looks around and then says, "He really is a nice guy. You should give him a chance."

"A chance? At what? He brought dinner to my office to fulfil our charity date, because he was worried he'd offended me. About his potato salad, I think. And as an aside, he makes . . . from scratch . . . the best potato salad I've ever had in my life. And I know how he used to cook for the boys in the loft. He's been a total jerk tonight—so have I—but you've told me how *nice* he is, and you and both know I don't do *nice*. That man has boyfriend potential written all over him. He's not someone I would date."

"Who's not someone you would date?"

I jump to the sound of his voice as the couch dips next to me, indicating his arrival. I swear he has a super sense and knows when I'm talking about him. What I want to know is why he keeps coming back for more. He can't possibly see anything in me that he likes. Not many people do, unless they're looking at my bank statement.

"You," I say, without being discreet anymore. "I would not date you."

"Who's asking?"

I thumb toward Emory. "This girl. She seems to have it in her head that you're not a bad guy and that I should give you a chance."

Jason laughs . . . loud.

Loud and hard.

Even slaps his knee.

Okay, it's not that freaking funny.

"You and me?" He motions between us with two of his fingers and then laughs again, this time buckling over. "Oh, that's just rich."

Who says rich? What is he, an eighty-year-old man? From the way he's coughing from laughter, I'm going to guess yes.

"That's great. Oh man, good one, Em. Wow, yup, me and Dottie, suurrrre," he drawls out.

I was okay with a little bit of laughter. I would even let the knee slap pass, but now he's just being rude. What's so funny on the off chance that we would date? It's not like I'm a bad catch. I have a fun personality when I want it to show, and I have amazing boobs. Any man would be lucky to have me.

"It's not that funny," I say through clenched teeth as he continues to laugh, drawing the attention of everyone else in the room.

"Oh, but it is. You and me." More laughter as tears fall down his face.

Actual tears.

"Dorothy Domico and Jason Orson. Keep wishing, you witty wench."

"Witty wench." Emory bursts out as well, joining Jason in the humor parade. "Oh, that fits her to a T. She's such a witty wench."

"Hey," I snap at my friend. "That's not true."

"Did I hear witty wench over here?" Lindsay asks, walking over with Milly.

Emory nods. "It's what he called Dottie."

The drunkard in front of me claps her hands obnoxiously while saying, "You. Are. Such. A. Witty. Wench."

It's official, I hate my friends. The only person I possibly like at this minute is Milly—

Wait, hold that thought. She's smirking, so nope, she's dead to me too.

"Well, I'm glad I can give you all a good laugh." I stand from the couch and step away just as Jason calls out.

"Wait, Dottie." I turn around and he holds his hand out to me, as if he's clutching something.

"This pole just fell out of your ass. Don't want you to forget it."

I HATE him.

~

"Are you leaving because you really have work, or because you're a little butt hurt?" Emory asks, walking me out to the elevator of her apartment.

Did she have to use the term *butt hurt* after the whole flagpole comment?

"I'm not butt hurt, so get that out of your head. I don't get butt hurt. I'm leaving because I have work to do and to be honest, if I have to hear that man's voice one more time, I might stab one of your cushions with a knife."

"Well, we don't want that," Emory says with a resounding sigh. "This is about the witty wench thing, isn't it?"

"Not at all. I love that nickname. I'm going to have it tattooed on my ass later this week."

"Your sarcasm is ringing through."

I let out a pent-up breath and give my pregnant friend a hug. "Listen, I love you dearly. I'm so happy for you, but I think I've had my fill of Jason Orson for the day."

"Fair enough. He can be a bit much."

"Just a little," I say while lifting my fingers up and showing off a small space between my forefinger and thumb.

"Before you leave, can I ask you a favor?" She clutches my hand.

"If it's go on a date with Jason, the answer is no."

She chuckles and shakes her head. "No, I wouldn't do that to you. But I was wondering if you could apartment sit for us. You know how I am about my plants, they need love every day and repositioning."

"Are you serious? Where are you going?"

"We decided last night to surprise our parents and fly to them to tell them the good news. I would ask Lindsay, but she has to stick close to her son's school and activities. Carson and Milly are headed to the Bahamas for a week—"

"And what about Jason? He lives across the hall. There's no way I'm going to be here when he is."

Emory shakes his head. "He'll be out of town too. It's after baseball season, so all the guys are going on vacation. I know it's asking a lot but I would be super appreciative."

"What about my plants?" I ask, folding my arms.

"You have a fake cactus."

"It still needs friendship and company."

Emory pulls me into a hug. "You can bring it with you. I'm sure your fake cactus would love a vacation to Auntie Emory's. Please, I would love you forever."

"You should already love me forever."

We pull away, and she says, "Forever and ever."

"Ugh, fine. But Jason won't be here?"

She shakes her head. "Nope, he'll be gone. It will be a nice, easy stay for you. And we'll use the fancy sheets for your bed. And you know how Knox feels about having strangers in the house. He doesn't want to ask the concierge to do it."

"Yeah, I get that. It's no biggie. My mom and dad are in town. I'll convince them to stay longer and have them ditch the hotel and stay at my place. It will be nice to have them here but not on top of me."

"Oh perfect. This means a lot to me. Thank you so much."

"Of course." With a resigned sigh, I pull my friend into another hug. "I really am happy for you."

"I know. Thank you so much for coming today."

"Wouldn't miss it for the world." But how I wish I'd found the ability to withdraw my claws and interacted with Jason with less . . . aggression. That's just not me. Or rather, *it didn't used to be me . . .*

CHAPTER EIGHT

JASON

"Natalie, don't do this to me," I beg.

Sitting across from me in our favorite booth at our favorite bar, Natalie smiles wickedly. "What's done is done."

"Why would you cancel my vacation? You know I don't get to do nice things during the season. I want to feel the sand in my toes." I'm bloody exhausted. Finishing out the season and then moving was way more tiring than I thought it would be. The whole Dottie debacle didn't help either. But knowing I was getting away for a total break kept me going. *And now this.*

She rolls her eyes. "I didn't cancel it, I just moved it. I didn't have a choice. There are quite a few things we need to get done before the end of the year for The Lineup. You'll still get your vacation, but for now, you're stuck here."

I slump over the table. "But I packed my Speedos. I was going to rock the shit out of them."

"Speedos? With the size of your ass?" She shakes her head. "You would be showing crack the whole time."

"I had them custom-made," I say through clenched teeth.

"Well, the tailored Speedos can wait. Especially since I got the photographer you wanted. She can only shoot next week. I already set everything up with Joseph, so you're the only one who needs to adjust his schedule."

"She better be worth it," I say, my voice full of sadness. Although playing baseball for a living is fun, it's also a long-ass season during the summer, meaning we never really get to enjoy the summer. It's very common for professional baseball players to vacation in the tropics after the season is finished, and I was going to the Bahamas with Carson and Milly, ready to proudly wear the third-wheel badge. But now I'll have to go by myself. Not a bad thing, but company is always nice to have.

Personally, I was excited to clink cocktails decked in umbrellas and pineapple together. Think of all the possible Boomerangs we could have made.

Such a lost opportunity.

A thought comes to my head. "Are you pushing back my vacation so it works better with your schedule?"

She smiles. "It just so happens and Ansel and I can go with you now."

I point my finger at her. "You're an asshole."

"I'm okay with that. Now, let's get down to business. We have a lot to cover, and I want to know your ideas for the photoshoot. Joseph only had one requirement, that you don't force him to match what you're wearing."

"What are you talking about? We look good matching." Ever since I can remember, my mom dressed Joseph and me together, matching like two goddamn angels. When I was young, I remember being jealous of his walker, asking my mom if I could have one too. Joseph still makes fun of me for that.

"He made it known he doesn't want to have to match with his little brother anymore. He's a grown-ass man."

"Little brother? He's two minutes older than I am."

"Are you really going to cry about matching with your brother?"

I fold my arms over my chest. "Maybe."

"You're impossible."

So I've been told.

~

C **arson:** *It's beautiful here. All you can drink piña coladas.*
Jason: *I'm going to puke, I'm so upset.*
Carson: *Why do you always have to go to the extreme?*
Jason: *I have emotions, let me feel them.*
Carson: *You feel them too hard.*
Jason: *My dick is hard just seeing your feet in the sand.*
Carson: *^^^ and that's why you have two friends.*

I laugh to myself and turn the corner to my apartment, dinner dangling in a bag off my forearm as I text Carson back. One of the things I love about my "two friends" is that I can be a dick to the extreme, over-dramatic, and effeminate just to get a reaction from them—because I'm that guy—and they're still friends with me.

Jason: *You know you love it when my dick gets hard.*
Carson: *This might shock you but I really don't.*

I look up and catch George, holding the door open for me. I give him a tip of my cap. "Thanks, man."

"Any time, Mr. Orson. Have a good night."

"You too."

I spot the open doors of the elevator and jog toward them as they start to close. "Hold the elevator." A small hand blocks the doors, giving me enough time to make it inside.

"Tha—"

My voice falls short when I almost collide with Dottie in the elevator. The look on her face tells me she wasn't expecting to see me, and I'm sure I'm mirroring the same shock, because she's the last person I expected to see after our interaction a few days ago.

"What are you doing here?" she sneers as the doors shut behind me.

"Nice to see you too. I'm doing great, thanks."

She folds her arms across her chest, and that's when I take her in. Pressed wide-legged black pants that crawl up her hips and button above her belly button. A tight red and black shirt that covers her arms is tucked into her waistline, framing perfectly how small she is. Thin suspenders connect from her pants over her shoulders, and she's paired the whole ensemble with black heels.

Business sexy . . . really sexy.

I want to play with those suspenders.

I want to snap them over her tits to see if I can make her nipples hard.

Bet her nipples are like fucking torpedoes.

"What are you staring at?"

"Your boobs," I answer honestly. "Want me to stare at something else?"

"Yes, for God's sake, have some class."

"Eh, having class is boring."

"You didn't answer my question. What are you doing here?"

I look from side to side and then whisper, "I live here."

Groaning in frustration, she clenches her fists at her side and says, "I'm aware, but you're supposed to be on vacation."

"Keeping track of me, sweet cheeks? That's cute."

"Don't call me that, and no, I'm watching Emory's plants while they're away."

"Plant-sitting?" I scoff. "People are so weird."

"Why aren't you on vacation?"

Persistent. I wonder if she's as relentless in the boardroom. For some reason, that pulls up an image in my head: Dottie naked, bent over her desk, demanding to be fucked from behind until the task is complete. My fingers digging into her hips, smashing back into me until she cries out my name in sweet surrender.

Huh. Being fucking horny around this woman is dangerous. At least her caustic façade is enough to settle the ol' dong down. It has been a long-ass time since I last got laid though, and I'm not really sure what I can do about fixing that. Random hookups haven't been my thing for a while now.

I chuckle to myself, which only pisses off the woman next to me.

"Why are you laughing?"

"Whoa." I pretend to tamp her down with my hand. "Easy there, killer. If you get any more tense you might snap."

"Whatever," she answers like the mature woman she is. "Now that you're here, I don't have to watch the stupid plants. You can do it."

"Oh, no can do." I shake my head. "Plants aren't my thing."

"What do you mean plants aren't your thing? They're easier than a dog. You just water them."

"Yeahhh." I cringe. "All those leaves? Nah, I'm good."

"Are you serious right now? You're not going to water their plants because of, and I quote, 'all those leaves'?"

"Yup. I'm good."

"You have got to be—"

Her sentence is cut short when the elevator makes an abrupt stop, jostling both of us into the walls of the small carrier.

"Huh, would you look at that?" I glance around the small room, wondering what's wrong.

"No, no, no," Dottie says over and over again, as she rushes to the panel and presses the emergency button.

When nothing happens, she presses all the other buttons.

"That's intelligent," I say, arms crossed and observing her from behind. "Confuse the damn thing so it has no idea what to do."

She doesn't answer, but instead pulls her phone out from her purse and starts holding it up in the air, searching for a signal.

"It's cute that you think raising the phone higher will grant you service. We're in a metal box surrounded by concrete, sweetheart. I never get reception in here."

"Damn it," she mutters, stuffing her phone back in her purse.

"Looks like you're stuck here with me until someone figures out the elevator broke, so it's best you get comfortable." I sit on the floor and then pat my lap. "You can sit right here."

"I'd rather lick the elevator floor."

"There's a disgusting visual. Suit yourself."

I get comfortable and start rifling through my bag of food.

Thank God I grabbed dinner before this, because I'm starving, and if I was stuck in this elevator with no food, I'd be a raging bastard, bashing his head against the metal door from pure hunger.

Low blood sugar does crazy things to me.

I bring the term hangry to a new level.

There's only—

"Why are you smiling like that?"

I look up at her. "Smiling like what? I'm just being normal."

"No, you're smiling like you're having a conversation inside your head and you think you're funny."

How would she know that?

"Well, I am funny." I pop open my to-go box filled to the brim with a Philly cheesesteak sandwich and tons of fries. Staring at it, I say, "Oh yes, come to papa."

I lift half of the sandwich and bring it to my mouth just as Dottie says, "It's rude to eat in front of someone who doesn't have food."

"Are you calling me rude?"

"Yes, I am." She folds her arms over her chest, staring at me as if I'm minced meat.

"That's funny. Isn't that the pot calling the kettle black?"

Her eyes narrow. "Are you saying I'm rude?"

I laugh. Does she really have no clue? She has been mean and ill-tempered every time we've spoken. In fact, there hasn't been a moment where she's been . . . nice. Although my teasing hasn't helped her surly attitude, I'm sure. "Babe, you've been rude to me since the minute I walked into your office."

"Because I needed to work and couldn't afford the distraction."

I shake my head. "No, because someone was doing something nice for you and instead of saying thank you, you ignored them, took their food, and then kicked them out."

Her lips work to the side and I can see her mulling it over. Huh, maybe I actually got through to her and penetrated that thick, leathery exterior and truly made her consider the way she treats people.

"You were rude by not adhering to my wish of leaving, therefore, I had to be rude to get my point across. I didn't want you there."

Fucking businesswoman, what a spin. I've got to hand it to her —mentally claps—she really dug deep for that one.

"Yeah, okay, I was rude first. Sure." I roll my eyes and then take a giant bite of my sandwich. The cheese seeps into my taste buds, and if Dottie wasn't here right now, I'd be eating this sandwich naked . . . while gripping my cock. That's how good it is.

This is a cock-gripping sandwich—or pussy-cupping sandwich if you're a lady. I'm an equal opportunist, after all.

"Are you really not going to share that?"

I look up, sandwich halfway to my mouth. "Are you kidding me?"

"No. I'm hungry too; who knows how long we'll be stuck in here."

"After everything that has happened between us, you really think I'm going to share my sandwich with you?"

"If you are the decent man you claim to be, then yes, you will."

Isn't she just a joy to be around?

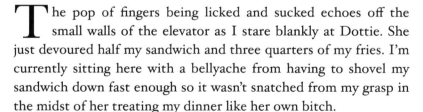

The pop of fingers being licked and sucked echoes off the small walls of the elevator as I stare blankly at Dottie. She just devoured half my sandwich and three quarters of my fries. I'm currently sitting here with a bellyache from having to shovel my sandwich down fast enough so it wasn't snatched from my grasp in the midst of her treating my dinner like her own bitch.

And despite seeing cheese drip from her chin, and watching her carnivorous teeth break apart the cheesesteak meat as if it was dust, I still got hard taking in what I can only describe as a spectacle—Dottie eating a meal.

With a dainty lift of her napkin, she pats the corners of her mouth and sighs.

"Was that good?"

"Yes." She glances at me. "Thank you."

Well, would you look at that, a thank you. I'm not sure I'll ever hear those words drip from her lips and be directed at me again, so I'm going to savor them.

"What are you doing? Why are you holding your chest like that?"

"Just committing your 'thank you' to memory, as I'm not sure I'll ever hear it again."

"Doubt that you will," she says, her surly attitude resurfacing.

I set the empty to-go container in the bag and off to the side. I take a sip from my water and watch as she surveys it like a hawk, eyes trained and focused on snatching away my drink.

Groaning, I hand it over to her.

"Thanks," she says with a smile, looking like a completely different woman. She downs the rest of my water and then smacks her lips together. "Now I can pass out."

"You're going to pass out in the elevator?"

"What else am I going to do?"

"I don't know." I shrug. "Talk to me?"

She gives me a slow once-over and then rests her head against the wall of the elevator. "Think I'll pass out."

Look who's rude now.

"You'd be much more comfortable if you used my lap as a pillow," I say, after five minutes of her shifting from side to side. There's no passing out in here if you're unwilling to spread across the floor, which she is.

"I'm not into tiny pillows." She gives up her attempt to sleep and stares straight ahead instead, resting her hands on her lap.

"Clearly you haven't seen the towel bulge picture."

From the corner of my eye, I see the smallest of smirks pull up the corner of her lip. Or maybe she has seen it . . . interesting.

When silence falls between us, I try to think of things I can talk to her about, but anything that pops up into my head is quickly turned down, because they're questions about her life and I'm pretty sure she's not going to answer them. She's pretty closed off, so I have to warm her up first.

And yeah, maybe I should just not talk to her since she does seem to have a protective wall erected all around her, but I've never been that guy to give up.

So . . .

(Are you cringing? Hold on to your tits, I'm going in.)

"So, you're cranky most of the time."

You're cringing now, aren't you? It's all about causing a reaction to get her to start talking. Don't worry, I know what I'm doing.

"You sure know how to win over people, don't you?" she says with a disdainful side-eye. God, there is something about a woman with hard edges that really gets to me. Because I suspect, deep down, they were hurt somehow and they deserve happiness. They deserve someone to be nice to them, to help smooth out those rough edges. Most men would label her as a bitch and walk away, but I see past that façade. I want to get to know her, what has made her so brash and hard, and I want to see if I can unlock her sensitive side. I know it's in there, I just need to find it.

"Were you like this in college?"

"Like what?" she asks, lulling her head to the side to look at me.

See . . . it's working.

"Easily ignitable." I tack on a smile to the end of my sentence.

"Are you saying I have a short fuse?"

"Well, you sure as hell aren't easygoing and relaxed." I chuckle, really trying to lighten the mood and when she responds, I think it might work.

"It's hard to relax with a job like mine," she admits, shocking me with her sullen voice.

"Why's that?"

She plays with the fabric of her shirt. "Everyone needs and

wants something from you. There's no stopping, and one slip-up can cost you a multi-million-dollar deal." Her voice fades and right there, I see it. The vulnerability. It's small, but it's there. From what I learned about her from Google—and from Emory—she wasn't given her position on a silver platter. She's fought her way to the top. Well, it's her family's company, so she's more than likely worked hard to get where she is, and that's commendable. But that sense of sadness makes me think she's disappointed people along the way. Unintentionally. And she's judged herself more harshly for it than she would others. *Perfectionist.* "I have to be tense and rigid for a reason, because the second I let go, I could mess up a lot of jobs for a lot of people."

I nod and gently say, "I can understand not relaxing when you're at work, or in the conference room, or at a business dinner, but when you're alone, in your apartment, you're telling me you don't let loose a little?"

"Never."

I laugh. "You're such a bullshitter."

She chuckles and I whip my head to the side, catching the humor in her face. "Holy shit, you just laughed. Wait." I hold my arms out as if to still the air. "Are you . . . relaxing right now? Right this very minute?" I cup my hands around my mouth and shout with my booming voice in the small space. "Ladies and gentleman, Dorothy Domico is relaxing."

"You're obnoxious," she says when I lower my hands.

"Obnoxious in a good way?" I ask while batting my eyelashes.

She stares at me for a few seconds and then answers, "No."

Sheesh, tough crowd.

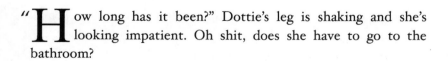

"How long has it been?" Dottie's leg is shaking and she's looking impatient. Oh shit, does she have to go to the bathroom?

"Thirty-six minutes," I answer, looking at the time on my phone.

"Only thirty-six minutes?" She groans. "Feels like three hours."

"Time sure does fly by when you're having fun, huh?" I say sarcastically, eyes trained on her leg that doesn't seem to be able to sit still. "Do you have to pee or something?"

"What? No. Why?"

"Because you're bouncing your leg, and it's annoying."

"Oh, I'm annoying?" She points to her chest. "This coming from the guy who doesn't seem to get a hint."

"Oh, I get them, I just choose not to accept them." I nod at her leg. "So why the bouncing? Are you claustrophobic?"

"Not really, but I don't like being suspended in the air by cables, wondering if we're going to plummet to our death."

"Now that you put it like that, you have me slightly shaking in my skivvies. Can you hold me?" I stretch out my arms, giving her easy access.

"You're pathetic. If you want a piece of me, you're going to have to try harder than that."

"You think I want a piece of you?"

"It's so obvious, Jason."

There's a light air about her right now, as if she's forgotten that she hates me. And it's funny, watching her almost . . . flirt. There's still a stiff set to her shoulders and robotic movements with her hands, but there's a smile that wants to peek through and I'll be honest, I'm here for it.

Also, yeah, I want a piece of her. She's confident, sexy, and even though she prefers to keep the fun side of her away from the public eye as much as possible, I see it in her, and I want to expose it.

"And if I asked you out on a date? What would you say?"

"No."

Oof. If she didn't follow that comment with a tiny glint in her eye, I would be taking a beating to my ego.

"What if I asked you out with my shirt off, would that change your mind?"

She glances at my stomach and then back up at my eyes. "I'm not really into beer guts."

Oh, she's fucking fresh.

"I know what you're doing." I wag my finger at her. "You think you're clever, don't you? But I see right through you, Dot Dot."

"Call me that again and I will kick your dick off."

"Yikes, woman." I laugh and she smiles back at me. "No nick-names, I get it, but your off-color threat doesn't distract me from finding you out."

"What are you talking about?" she asks, exasperated.

"Saying I have a beer gut. You and I both know that's not true. You're just trying to rile me up so I take my shirt off. Oh yes, I see right through you, lady."

"I really couldn't care less if you take your shirt off."

"See?" I point at her. "There you go again. Reverse psychology. It's not going to work on me. I'm smarter than you think. I might be a jock, but I'm not a dumb jock. I was an engineering major."

"Okay, whatever."

"You know what?" I stab the floor with my finger. "I'm going to prove you wrong. I'm going to take my shirt off because I want to, not because you told me not to. I'm reversing your reverse psychology."

She looks puzzled. "Uh, I don't think that's a thing."

"It is. Watch." From behind, I reach and pull my shirt up and over my head then neatly fold it and set it on my lap. I turn more toward her and give her a good flex.

But when I catch her facial expression, it's completely blank. No googly eyes, no shocked expression, no admiration. Just blank.

Well, shit.

CHAPTER NINE

DOTTIE

I f I had cell service, I would be texting Emory right now telling her we're no longer friends.

Oh, don't worry, Dottie, Jason won't be there. He'll be on vacation.

Lies. All lies.

And now I'm stuck in an elevator with the man, the guy who hasn't left my mind since that godforsaken email Lindsay sent. Two weeks. Yup. Two weeks of me thinking about Jason Orson in inappropriate ways, of searching his name on the Internet and envisioning what it would feel like to run my fingers up and down his rigid abs. Two weeks of wondering what his voice sounds like in bed. Two weeks of trying to hold back the smile that crosses my face when I see him.

It's been draining, to say the least. I'm a tough girl, I know that, but I've never been . . . nasty. And honestly, some of the things that have come out of my mouth when talking to Jason would horrify my parents. Hell, they've horrified me when they've come out. They didn't raise me to be sharp-tongued and vindictive. Quite the opposite if I'm honest. But this man? He pushes my buttons, and not always in a bad way like my behavior would indicate.

So why don't I just give in and go out with him? Because we are all kinds of wrong for each other. Jason always had a harem of girls around him in college, but he wasn't one of those assholes that led girls on and then fucked and dumped. As I've thought about him— *a little obsessively*—I recall how kind he was. Funny, idiotic, but not conceited. I mean, I had a crush on him for a reason. He's a romancer, a gift giver, the type of man you cling on to and never let go.

You know what I'm talking about . . . the kind of man you take home to your parents.

Sounds great, right?

Well, I had that with Nick.

And he screwed me over, broke my heart, and left me in pieces I've had to pick up and tape everything back together.

I'm not going to do that to myself. So even though Jason is tempting, I'm not going for it.

But I will say this, Jason with his shirt off in a broken elevator? It's not a bad end to my day. He's a vision to behold with his shirt off: tan, not a jersey line in sight somehow, chiseled and sculpted like a marble monument with a tiny splattering of clipped hair in the middle of his chest.

If I did let myself go and give in to temptation, I would start with that chest hair, letting my fingertips glide over the incredibly short strands, then travel over his thick pecs and down his torso where I would spend an almost indecent amount of time fingering his abs. I would glide my digits through the ridges, coming close to his waistline but never close enough. I would enjoy seeing him squirm, watching him ache with need. It would be such a turn-on that I would straddle him and, without a second thought, begin to ride his lap, letting our centers collide and—

"Are you okay?"

"What?" I ask, snapping out of my thoughts.

"It didn't seem like you were breathing. Are you breathing? Oh wait, I get it." He dramatically shakes his head. "You want me to give you mouth-to-mouth. Once again, very clever."

He's ridiculously cute, and it's frustrating.

"Yup, that's it." In a begging voice that is entirely fake, I clasp my hands together and say, "Please, Jason, will you please, please give me mouth-to-mouth? I can't seem to find my breath anywhere; I need yours to replenish my depleted lungs."

"Damn, girl, I had no idea." He lunges toward me, lips puckered. "Open up."

Before he can close in on my lips, I halt his head with my palm, just as a wave of his fresh cologne surrounds me. Ugh, why does he have to smell so masculine? It's unfair that men's cologne can induce an orgasm, or at least get pretty close to it.

"I was kidding."

"I'm not," he says, his lips brushing against my palm as he speaks. "You're turning purple. Quick, lie down; I got you, babe."

I give him a shove and he laughs, sitting back against the elevator door and putting his shirt back on.

Damn it, he could have kept that off.

"You know, the attraction you're feeling for me is too strong, so it's best we just stay as friends. I don't want you falling in love with me so hard that I can't catch up to your feelings. Friends is really where we should stay."

"Friends aren't necessary."

"Oh, now you're just trying to protect your heart. I get it, Dottie. I really do. So after we're let out of this tin box, I say we go our separate ways, our hearts intact."

"I think that's the most intelligent thing you've said since I met you."

"Well, I'm just full of surprises, aren't I?"

He really is, surprises that are starting to eat away at my cold exterior. And that's a problem. Because that's what I'll never allow to happen . . . again.

Cute, sexy, crazy baseball player be damned.

~

"Albert, Bart, Chris, Darrel . . . Emmitt, Uh, Franklyn, George, Harrison, Ichabod . . . umm . . ." I wince. "Jake?"

"No," Jason groans. "Jesus Christ, woman. Jorge, it was Jorge." Jason throws his arms in the air, clearly distressed over the stupid ABC game we're playing. "We are never going to make it all the way to Z with the kind of gnat brain you have."

"Hey, you screwed up once too."

"Because you said the most abstract girl name I've ever heard and I couldn't remember it for the life of me."

"Abstract means you remember it better."

"Abstract means I'm going to forget how to pronounce it in seconds."

"Oh, I forgot, you get hit in the head with balls for a living."

He scoffs. "No, I don't. If I did, I wouldn't be a damn good catcher, one of the best in the league, thank you very much." He sighs and shifts his body so he's lying completely on the floor, his shirt as a pillow. Yes, he's removed his shirt again, and I'm not complaining one bit. "What kind of name is Euphemia anyway?"

"Oh, now you get it right."

"Well, you screamed it at me five times in a row as your spittle smacked me in the face, drilling it in my brain."

"There was no spittle."

"Oh . . . there was spittle," he says, his voice full of humor.

Damn him for making me smile again. That's what the last twenty minutes have been—him being ridiculous, me trying not to smile. I've finally resolved to laying my head on my purse so I don't have to look directly at him.

Smacking his hands together, he rubs them and says, "Okay, let's go for actor last names now. I'll start. Aniston."

This is what my life has come to.

"Aniston, Bullock."

"Aniston, Bullock, Cox," he replies.

I lift up to look at him. "Are you just going to list off cast members from Friends?"

"Shh." He waves his hand at me and then presses his fingers to his temples, massaging his skull. "I'm trying to concentrate."

Good . . . God.

~

"**H**."

"Nooope," Jason drags out, a smart-ass look on his face. "One more leg and you've been hanged, milady."

I can NOT believe I'm losing to Jason at hangman. Not just losing but losing terribly. We're talking ten games deep, and he's won every single one of them. When he initially suggested the game, I thought, sure, why not? This will be easy. He acts like an immature frat boy with the IQ of a pigeon despite majoring in engineering, so all I'll have to do is guess different sexual organs and it will be money in the bag.

But here I am, one leg away from losing *once again*, which means if he wins all ten games, I have to take my shirt off as well.

Stupid bet, but I really didn't think he could sweep me.

Think, Domico, think.

Blank, U, M, blank, S, blank, U, blank, blank.

Yup.

I'm screwed.

I tap my chin, really pretending to put some though into it. "Let's go with Y."

"I'm sorry to do this because you're pretty, but the noose is coming for you." He adds the last leg and then draws two X's where the eyes should be and a squiggle mouth, indicating death.

"Ugh, what is it?"

He fills in the blanks and I read the word out loud, "Numbskull."

"Yup." He bops my nose with the pen and says, "That's exactly what you are, a numbskull." His laugh does nothing but make me madder. He motions to my shirt. "Show me the goods. A bet is a bet."

"You realize when I take my shirt off, you're going to regret it, right?"

"Pretty sure I won't."

"You will when I start playing with my tits and jiggling them. Pinching my nipples, moaning from the sensation . . ."

"Yeah, I won't regret that."

"You will when you get hard and you can't do anything about it."

He laughs and motions with the pen to take my shirt off. "It's funny how you think I have no issue jacking off right here, right now. I have zero modesty, Dorothy, so I would watch what you do with those tits."

I should have expected that. With a resigned sigh, I take my shirt off and watch Jason nod in appreciation. He takes my breasts in, long and hard, never blinking, just observing until he gives me one curt nod and says, "They'll do."

He's such an ass.

～

"Heads."

"Tails. Ha HA!" Jason clasps the quarter in his fist and raises it to the elevator. "Pants, Domico."

"You didn't flip it right," I counter, not wanting to lose my pants. I'm wearing a thong and sitting in an elevator in only a thong and bra doesn't really scream good time to me.

I also didn't think I'd be this terrible at heads or tails. Who loses twelve times in a row? It's like there is some magnetic force controlling the elevator, blocking me from winning any ridiculous game I play with Jason.

"What do you mean I didn't flip it right? I flipped it in the air, it turned multiple times, I caught it and then flipped it on the back of my hand. Standard heads or tails rules."

"You have a trick quarter."

"It was from your purse."

Valid point.

"Ugh, fine. But I'm warning you, don't consider this an invitation to gawk at me."

"Oh, like you haven't been gawking at me this entire time. And don't you even try to deny it. I see the way you look at my stomach, lust and desire swimming in your eyes."

"Oh, get over yourself. You're delirious and exhausted."

"Either way, you want me," he says with a pant-load of confidence.

Grumbling to myself, I take off my pants and sit on top of them so my bare ass isn't on the elevator floor. Thank God this is a really, really nice building because if Emory and Knox lived in a pit of an apartment, there is no way I'd follow through on my bet.

Jason scans my side and then the other, observing my choice of underwear. "Are you wearing a thong?"

"Yes."

"Stand up so I can make the final assessment on that."

"It's a thong," I say through clenched teeth.

"Yeah, but I should still see."

"Bite me," I answer back.

"Where?" He wickedly grins.

"Oh, you would love that, wouldn't you, getting a chance to bite me wherever you want?"

"Sure." He shrugs. "I'm bored. Let's make things interesting." He rubs his hands together. "Where do you want my mouth?"

If he wants to bite me, he can bite me all right.

I lift up my shoeless right foot and wiggle my toes at him. "Mr. Big Toe wants some attention."

"*Mr.* Big Toe?" He quirks a brow.

"Yup. He's lonely. Make your teeth his new best friend."

"Fine." Before I can stop him, he grabs my ankle and chomps down on my big toe, pressing hard, just hard enough that I yelp and retract my foot quickly.

"What the hell was that?" I ask, scanning my toe where I spot definite teeth marks.

"You told me to bite you, so I did."

"Not really. Are you insane?" I rub my toe. "If anything, I thought you'd be stupid sensual about it, not actually try to eat Mr. Big Toe."

"You can never tell what I'm going to do. Let that be a lesson to you."

CHAPTER TEN

JASON

I'm. In. Hell. HELL!

Yes, it was my idea to lose clothes, but I really didn't think she'd be that terrible at hangman and heads or tails. Who loses that many times? Just embarrassing.

When she took off her shirt, I had to suck in my tongue from falling out of my mouth.

Sure, I made it seem like I wasn't interested in the goods with my casual response of "they'll do." But I've never told such a bold-faced lie before in my entire life.

They won't *just do*. Dottie's tits will be the star of my dreams for weeks to come.

Plump, almost spilling out of the tops of her bra and firm, but also look like they would be heaven to rest my head on. And because it's a cool temperature in here, her nipples are poking against the thin, lace fabric of her bra and they're nipples I could see myself getting along with. Not quite the torpedoes I hoped for, but not pint-sized peas either.

I caught myself leaning toward her a few times, lips pursed, ready to suckle. Thank God, she's been clueless or else I'm sure I would have heard about it.

After a while, I started to get used to her topless, but now that she doesn't have pants on, yup, my jeans are feeling tight in the crotch and I'm doing everything in my power to keep myself in check.

"Do you always wear thongs?"

"Why is that a question you're asking?"

Because all I can think about is you, in a thong, sitting on the luckiest pair of pants ever. I wonder what she would say if I offered her to sit on my face instead of the cold hard floor . . .

"Just trying to get to know you."

"How about this, do you always wear thongs?" She crosses her arms over her chest which only lifts her breasts up more. I swear she's doing that on purpose.

Clearing my throat, I say, "Only on long runs."

"Yeah." She rolls her eyes. "Okay."

"I do," I answer honestly. "My friend Holt introduced me to the man thong in college, said it held his junk close to him while running, but he also had the added benefit of his shorts brushing against his bare ass. So I decided to give it a try and I've never looked back."

"Wait." She blinks a few times. "You mean to tell me, if I went into your apartment, pulled open your dresser drawer, I'd find a collection of male thongs?"

"Yup. My favorite ones are leopard print."

"Stop it. You do not have a leopard print thong."

"Want to bet?"

"No," she answers immediately and with finality. "No more bets."

"Okay, then how about we just agree that I have one and we start making out?"

We're both sitting up, facing each other, and if any time is the perfect time to make out with someone, it's when you're stuck in an elevator.

"We are not making out."

"Scared?"

"No. You're not my type, and I don't waste kisses on boys not my type."

"Oh damn." I smile and lean back on my hands. "For some odd reason, even though it denies me your lips, I really liked that response."

"We're never getting out of here. Emory's plants are going to die," Dottie says, after the two-hour mark hits.

"I wonder what floor we're on," I say, looking at the ceiling as if that will tell me.

"It felt like we were pretty high, but who knows. I blacked out from rage being stuck in an elevator with you."

"Rage seems like a strong word."

"Rage is accurate. You're supposed to be on vacation."

"So you said." I poke her leg. "But aren't you glad I'm here?"

"Why do you make me be mean to you? You know what my answer is going to be."

"Hey." I stand tall so she has to take all of me in. "I've been entertaining, I shared my dinner with you, and I've only stared at your boobs a few times." *Because they are fucking sexy and if I looked more than a few times, I'd seriously need to fuck you senseless. Talk about self-control, people.* "I think you should be grateful I was the one you got stuck in an elevator with."

She stands as well, in all her almost naked glory. Hands on her hips, she goes to say something just as the door to the elevator opens and Mr. Trigger at the end of the hallway stands there, mouth agape, staring at the both of us.

Dottie squeals and covers up, holding her clothes over her body as I, like the chivalrous man I am, stand in front of her.

"Mr. Trigger," I say in a cool, even tone, "you're looking handsome tonight. Dinner plans?"

He narrows his eyes at me and points his cane. "You youngins have no class. Keep it in your pants."

I chuckle. "It's not what you think. We were stuck in the elevator. You actually saved us. Thank you."

"You were stuck? Doesn't seem like it since you're on your apartment floor. You're going to have to come up with something more creative than that." He motions to our bodies as I feel Dottie getting dressed behind me. "Why are you naked?"

"Technically, Mr. Trigger, naked means being completely devoid of clothes, and as you can see, we aren't bare ass and chest, winging our willies around—"

"Your friend has a willy?" Mr. Trigger leans to the side, trying to get a look at Dottie.

I chuckle and shake my head as Dottie elbows my back. "No, I think she wishes she had one at times, but no. She has lady parts." I lean forward and say, "A vagina."

"Can you not?" Dottie asks, storming past me fully clothed, with her bag at her side. She gives Mr. Trigger a curt wave and then takes off down the hall.

Gathering my shirt, I salute Mr. Trigger and as I pass, I whisper, "She's sensitive about her vagina, so it's nothing against you. Have a good night, sir."

I walk down the hallway, watching Dottie struggle with her purse the entire time. She sets it on the ground and starts digging around by the time I reach her. I pull my key out of my pocket and unlock my door only to lean against it and ask, "Looking for something?"

She groans and sits on her heels, frustrated and exhausted. "I forgot the key to their apartment at my office." She pulls on her silky raven hair. "Could this night get any worse?"

"I think it started off pretty well if you ask me. Shared dinner with a devastatingly handsome man, played a few nostalgic games, aired out a bit . . . I think your night is just getting started."

Her eyes snap at me and her finger points, a slight shake to it. "This is all your fault."

"Me?" I point to my chest. "How is this my fault? I didn't tell the elevator to stop. You're the one who started pressing all the buttons. If you didn't press them, the doors might have opened instead of you confusing it. Ever think about that?" I tap my temple. "This has elevator confusion written all over it."

"That's not even a thing." She stands, tosses her purse over her shoulder, and starts marching down the hallway.

"Where you going?"

"Back to my office to get the key. What does it look like?"

"Oh okay, but if you don't want to go all the way back to your office, I have a spare in my apartment if you want to use that. Up to you."

She pauses and spins on her heel, charging right back to me. I open my door, giving her plenty of space to come in. When she steps inside, she immediately crosses her arms and stands as close to the door as possible.

"Make yourself at home. You don't have to stick yourself to the wall."

"I'm just here for the key."

"Okay, that might be a few minutes." I toss my shirt on the back of the couch, near the pile of laundry I've yet to fold, and then I put our dinner trash in the kitchen.

"Why will it be a few minutes? Just hand it to me."

"Yeah, about that." I scratch the side of my cheek. "I can't remember where I put it. Emory brought it over here before they left *in case of emergency* and I'll be honest, I was a tad drunk."

"You're a moron." She huffs in frustration.

She goes to leave, but I stop her by saying, "I think it's in my bedroom. Give me a second."

"Oh, let me guess, you want me to help you look for it, and

then oh look, we fall into your bed, and our clothes just happen to come off—"

"I mean . . . you said it, not me."

"You are going to make me drink," she mutters, stomping back to my bedroom. I let her lead the way, loving the way her pert ass sways with determination.

"Do you want to get naked first or should I? We could do it at the same time. That might be fun."

"Shut up. My God, Jason. I'm helping you look for the key. Two eyes are better than one."

"Ahh, yup, I knew that's what was happening this whole time." I truly think teasing her is becoming my new favorite hobby. Talk about a short fuse. Yeesh. This girl is strung tight, but I like that about her. It's like she's seconds away from either ripping all our clothes off and letting out her frustration or screaming and giving my junk a good old one-two punch. Either way, the uncertainty is thrilling.

When I get to my bedroom, she's already rummaging through my dresser, plucking through my underwear drawer.

"Looking for keys, or looking for those man thongs I was talking about?"

"Get over yourself, I couldn't care—" She lifts up my black thong with embroidered roses on it up in the air. "Where on earth did you get this? And why is it so big?"

I chuckle and walk up to her, taking the thong away. I stretch it and say, "Grammy Q made this for me. She wasn't sure what size I was, so she went with the largest size. She said if I was anything like her hubby, I was going to need the extra crotch room." I whisper, "Crotch room is greatly needed."

"For the socks I'm sure you like to stuff in there." She brushes past me, her hair floating over my bare shoulder. Damn, she smells good, like a goddamn flower. Being stuck in that elevator with our dinner, I couldn't really catch a whiff of her, but now we're out in the open, her scent pings me right in the chest.

"Just like you stuff your pants too, right?"

"What?" She stops her pursuit to my nightstand.

I point at her crotch and say, "You stuff too, don't you? Camel toe is in, right?"

She tilts to the side and stares . . . hard. "What the hell is wrong with you? Did your mom drop you on your head when you were young?"

"Possibly." I cup my hand over my mouth. "But as if she would really tell the truth, am I right?"

Ignoring me, she pulls on the handle of my nightstand, yanking it harder than I think she expected, flinging the drawer off its track. It hits the ground with a splash, spreading the collection of condoms I have stashed inside.

As a hopeful male, moving to a new city with possible potential to meet the love of his life, I found an amazing deal on condoms on Amazon. Buy in bulk; it's how I roll.

I have yet to use one, but . . . fingers crossed.

"Oh my God." Dottie stands straight, staring at the drawerful of foil wrappers. The XL on the packaging clear. She blushes and takes a step back, as if she gets too close, she might get sucked into my sex den. "Why . . ." She swallows hard. "Why do you have so many?"

"I like to buy in bulk," I answer, hands stuffed in my pockets.

"I see." She clears her throat and turns away, her eyes scanning my crotch before she heads back down the hallway.

I follow, a smile pulling at my lips the entire time. Just that little glance tells me she's interested, even if she'll deny it till the day she dies, I know there's interest.

When we're in the living room, she starts shuffling through my laundry. "Did you wash it—?" She holds up her hands, thongs dangling off her fingers. "How many of these do you have? Are you wearing one right now?"

"With jeans? No, thank you. I run a lot. I never want to run out because I've been too lazy to do laundry."

She drops them back in the pile and pushes her hands through her hair. "I should have gone to my office instead. All I've come to find here is that you have a need to collect man thongs, have an excessive bin of condoms, and your decorating style is less than desirable."

"What does that mean?" I take in my homey surroundings, pictures of baseball bats and gloves haphazardly hung around the apartment. "I like baseball gear."

"Yes, that's evident."

"It's better than naked women on the walls. Is that what you'd prefer to see?"

"I don't prefer to see anything. I just want the key so I can go."

"And I'll have you know, I just replenished on condoms, and I'm holding out for the right woman so when I do have sex, it means something. In the interim, I will occasionally jack off with a condom on to help build my endurance and to avoid a mess. I'm afraid to admit it, but I'm a cum shooter. I've been known to shoot it so hard up the vagina, the girl can taste it."

Blinks.

Blinks again.

Shakes her head and takes off toward the door. "I'll be here all week. For the love of God, please leave me alone."

"What about the key?" I call out, laughing at the same time.

"I'll go back to my office."

She opens the door, just as I spot the shiny red keychain Emory attached the key on.

"Oh wait, I found it."

She pauses and I walk to the door, so close that my chest presses against her back. I reach over her shoulder to the hooks where I hang my keys.

"Here it is." I smile when her eyes turn murderous. "Look at that, even when I'm drunk, I'm mindful of organization."

She snatches the key from my hand without another word and walks out of my apartment.

"I'm going to need that back—"

She unlocks the door to Emory and Knox's apartment in record time and tosses the key back to me before I can finish.

"Have a good night."

The door slams behind her with a resounding boom.

"Sure, yup." I wave at the door. "I'll have a good night too. Why thank you, I do believe I look spectacular without a shirt on. That's so kind. Oh, you're going to think of me tonight when you touch yourself, you're so—"

The door flings open and a shoe flies from one end of the hallway to the other, hitting me directly in the chest with a thump.

Oof.

The door slams again and I'm left there, chuckling to myself. I hold up the shoe and call out, "If you want this back, you're going to have to come and get it."

Teach her to throw a damn shoe at me.

With a smile that won't quit, I shut the door to my apartment and go to my laundry where I start to fold it. God, that woman. I can see now why she and Emory are such good friends. And even though I'm not completely sure what she's thinking right now about me, the sparring has made me feel . . . alive.

Like me again.

Glancing around my bare-bones bachelor pad, I start thinking about her comment. I haven't been here long enough to make it mine yet—I still have some unpacking to do—but maybe there are things I can do to it to make the place more inviting. Dating has been on the backburner, once bitten and all that, but if I'm going to possibly consider *looking* for my someone, this place needs to feel like home.

CHAPTER ELEVEN

DOTTIE

Even though it's seven in the morning and I'm pretty sure Jason is still sleeping, given he has nowhere to be this morning, I still look out the peephole to make sure he's not outside waiting for me.

Last night was . . . God, I don't even know what last night was.

Irritating.

Annoying.

Educational?

And I hate to admit it, but just a tiny bit fun.

Okay maybe a lot of fun.

But I will say this, it will be a cold day in hell before I go back to his apartment and retrieve my tossed shoe. At this point, I'm considering it a loss. Or maybe, when Emory gets back, I'll be sure to force her to grab it for me as payment for watching her stupid plants. It's the least she can do for me. If I didn't know Knox was very protective about their apartment and who enters it—rightfully so—I'd hire a plant-sitter so I wouldn't have to deal with seeing Jason, but I think my escape plan will work perfectly.

With the coast clear, I sling my purse over my shoulder, slip my feet in my heels, and swing the door open, ready to make my—

"Goooooooooooood morning," Jason says, louder than necessary, probably waking up the floors above and below ours. Where the hell did he come from? Was he just waiting there? "Don't you look ravishing. That blouse really brings out the blue of your eyes."

I couldn't agree more, but I won't let him know that.

Holding my hand over my racing heart, calming myself from being startled and running into his handsome face so early in the morning. Putting on the best front I can, I say, "What do you want?"

From behind his back, he brings my shoe forward with a coffee tucked inside.

"Shoe drink." He smiles boldly, chest puffed. "Cute, right?"

Oh my God.

Why is he such a moron?

An adorably sweet moron.

A moron that keeps tempting me to laugh.

Hold it in, Dottie, hold it in.

But . . . shoe drink. I mentally chuckle. So stupid.

I sigh and take the shoe, pulling the drink from it and tossing the shoe behind me. I already locked the door from the inside, so I close it and give him a once-over.

Drenched in sweat, wearing slate-gray athletic shorts with a skintight Lycra shirt and a backward baseball cap, he looks all kinds of sexy—especially with his five o'clock shadow and cheery eyes.

"Were you waiting out there for me?"

"Yup." He reaches to the ground and pulls up a water. He takes a quick gulp and says, "I'm friends with the door staff, who told me you hadn't left yet, so I grabbed this drink for you because I'm a nice guy."

He is. He's too nice.

"Were you running?"

He wipes his brow with his forearm. "Is it that obvious? I told

121

my glands to try to hold in the sweat but looks like they ignored me." He stretches out his arms. "Give Jason Boo Boo a hug for the coffee." I pin myself against the door, hand held out.

"Don't come near me."

He chuckles and falls forward, his arms propping him up on either side of my body. The heat coming off him suffocates me, making it hard to breathe. I can feel my pulse in my throat. His gorgeous eyes study me, and all I can think is how delicious he smells despite being a sweaty mess. He has an amazing deodorant and laundry detergent, because I could make a candle out of his scent, it's that good.

"I think we got off on the wrong foot," he says in a deep, rough voice. "You seem to not like me and I don't think I can handle that." He glances at my lips and then back up to my eyes. "You see, I don't like it when people don't like me for no reason, so I'm going to need a valid reason why."

If only he knew how wrong he really was. It's not that I don't like him, it's that I'm too afraid to allow myself to like him. He's so magnetic I fear I would fall for him and fall hard.

"I don't need to tell you anything," I answer, clutching the coffee to my chest.

"Fine, then come to my place tonight for dinner. I'll make you something."

"Why?"

"Because I don't have anyone to eat with and I like to cook. You're going to be alone over there, so we might as well eat together."

"I'm good." I try to move past him but he doesn't budge, and there's no way I'm going to touch his sweaty body.

"Then give me a reason."

"A reason for what?"

"For why you don't like me and I'll leave you alone."

"Why would I do that?" I answer, my breath catching in my throat.

"Because I don't really believe you don't like me." He tugs

lightly on my ponytail and then drags his fingers down my neck, sending a wave of goosebumps to cover my arms. "I think you do, but you're too scared to admit."

"Don't be ridiculous. I have better things to do with my time than hold a grudge against random guys." I nervously laugh and look to the side.

"Then dinner tonight, so you can get to know me better."

"I'm busy."

He moves in, his body so close, and my skin starts to crawl with anticipation.

"Let's get one thing straight," he says, dropping the humor in his voice and becoming completely serious. The raspy sound of his voice, the way it cuts through my defenses, I don't think I've ever heard anything sexier. "Lying to me is not going to fly."

My face tingles; that's how aware I am of his energy and power.

"How do you know I'm lying?" I ask, head over tits turned on by this switch in attitude. Yes, I enjoy his teasing and ridiculous self, but this alpha side, the one I guessed would surface in the bedroom, is making my nipples hard. His chest is a breath away from rubbing against them.

"There's a waver in your voice. If you weren't lying, you'd be confident with your answer." Damn it. "So, tonight, my place, eight sharp. If you're not here, I'm banging on your door until you show up."

"How pleasant, being forced into your company."

"That's me, Mr. Pleasant." He leans in closer, his mouth against my ear. "So, you'll . . . *come?*"

Oh my God, my thighs just clenched together. *God, to think I missed out on this in college because I was too reserved to approach him.* How I wish I got him out of my system then . . . when things were . . . simpler. *Before I understood the black-hearted side of men.*

"Only to avoid"—I swallow, letting my breath catch up —"verbal assassination in the hallway."

"Smart." He lifts a little so now we're looking each other in the eyes. "I'll see you tonight. Be a proper guest and bring wine."

I might need something stronger than wine to get through the night.

"Are you going to let me leave now?"

He pushes off the door and steps away. Eyes on mine, he reaches behind him and yanks his shirt over his head, along with his hat, revealing his impeccably chiseled chest, sweat dripping down each contour and curve.

His lips curve up. "Time to hit the showers. I'll see you tonight."

He turns around and damn my betraying eyes, they fall straight to his ass, his tight, rounded, and delicious ass.

That's it, I'm not going tonight. I don't care how long he pounds on the door, I'm far too infatuated, and honestly, with my shrinking willpower, who knows what might happen.

Jason Orson will be eating dinner alone tonight.

∾

"Miss Domico?"

Shit.

I quickly exit out of my Jason Orson's Butt Google search—yes, it has its own search title—feeling a blush creep up my cheeks from being caught once again. What's that, the third time in a week? How humiliating.

"Yes, Jessica." I smile up at her.

"Mr. Domico is here. He wanted to talk with you before the Carltons arrive."

"Sure, yeah, let him in."

I check the time and realize we're six minutes away from the meeting. Good God, this is exactly why I need to stay away from Jason; he is a giant distraction. I guess technically, I'm staying away from him but still getting distracted.

I curse the day Lindsay sent me that stupid email, as that's what started all of this. The obsession with looking at pictures of him, secretly ogling him behind my computer screen, the daydreaming of what it would be like to run my fingers along his abs. I wasn't like this before. I didn't even think of the man before the email. Occasionally, I'd hear something about him and maybe look him up, but it never got as extreme as it is right now. The obsession is borderline stalkerish.

Looks like there'll be no dinner tonight.

There's a knock on my door right before my dad steps in. Dressed impeccably in a finely tailored grey suit with black shirt and tie, his salt-and-pepper hair and charming eyes, he doesn't look a day over fifty.

"Hey there, killer. Are you ready to kiss some Carlton ass?"

"Applied a good layer of ChapStick five minutes ago."

He laughs and pulls me into a hug. "You've got this, girl."

"So you're not here to tell me how you want me to run the meeting?"

"Those days are over. I'm just here to tell you how proud of you I am. You're the best person to close this deal, and I have the utmost confidence that you will."

"Thank you."

I take a deep breath. He has confidence in me. This is something he tells me every time he sees me and I know why, because he's trying to build me up after what happened with Nick. On the outside, I might seem confident and powerful, but on the inside, I'm the little girl always looking to impress her dad. And I can't stop myself from trying incredibly hard every chance I get, because even though I know he has so much trust in me, there's that seed of doubt in the back of my head that tells me I'm not good enough. Maybe it's from Nick, maybe it's from being the owner's daughter, but whatever it is, it's there. And even days later, after we fixed everything with the water main break and leveled the budget, I still feel sick about it, about almost letting my dad down again. I never want to do that . . . ever again.

He steps away and motions to my shirt. "But button up, these people are conservative."

MEGHAN QUINN

"It's not bad." I look down at my shirt. "You want me going in there like a nun?"

"Yes. Now hide those bosoms."

Can't hear that enough from my dad.

I take a second to button my shirt all the way up, until my neck feels like it's being choked. What's a lack of breath going to do to me? Better to be covered than able to breathe.

Together, we walk down the hallway to the conference room where the Carltons are being escorted in by our receptionist. There are a variety of drinks on the conference table as well as a Mediterranean charcuterie I had Jessica put together.

"Mr. and Mrs. Carlton, thank you so much for making it to our office. Was your ride comfortable?"

"Yes," Mr. Carlton says, shaking my hand. "It was so nice of you to send a car to get us. The driver was very pleasant. From Georgia. He used to be in the CIA but is now retired, enjoying driving around his hometown of Chicago. Very fascinating fellow."

"Yes, Mark Sandberg, he's a wonderful man. If you ever get a chance to get stuck in traffic with him, he'll tell you some really good stories."

"Well, I'll be wishing for some holdups after this."

I lean over and give Mrs. Carlton a handshake as my dad talks to her husband. "Mrs. Carlton, so glad you could make it. This dress is stunning."

"Thank you. My friend Patricia Freeman from Free Designs made it for me. Isn't she talented?"

It's the ugliest garment I've ever seen. Looks like she rolled around in her tapestries and called it a day.

"You're going to have to give me her contact information because I need an original in my closet."

"I'll have Marjorie send over the information in an email from me." She touches my arm kindly and we both take a seat along with my dad and Mr. Carlton.

I offer some drinks for the table, hand out plates, and once everyone is settled, I take a seat. We spend some time talking

126

about the weather and the run the Bobbies had in the playoffs, short-lived but at least they made it . . . unlike the Rebels. But once my dad clears his throat, it's time to get down to business.

"Again, thank you so much for taking the time to talk to us about your property. We couldn't be more excited about this opportunity."

Mr. Carlton steeples his fingers. "It's really between Domico and Heller and Parks. The proposals submitted are comparable, so it comes down to who we want to do business with."

"Yes, I can understand that. Working with like-minded people is of utmost importance," I say, sounding as heartfelt as I can.

This moment right here, where a deal is in the balance, this is what I was made for. I think on the spot, I'm quick to please, and I have no problem throwing down more on the deal to win it. I'm great at living in this moment. Anxiety and nerves don't affect me; instead, adrenaline pumps through my veins as I use my ability to please and be unrelenting to my advantage.

"That's why we're leaning more toward Heller and Parks right now."

Uhh . . . say what?

Keeping a smile on my face even though it feels entirely forced now, I say, "Thank you for being so upfront, Mr. Carlton. May I ask what is swaying you in their direction?"

He leans back in his chair and looks at his wife. "I must admit, this might sound a bit caddy, but when we started this business, we started it on the foundation of our morals and beliefs."

"Which is incredibly admirable of you."

"Thank you." Mr. Carlton shifts in his seat, looking uncomfortable and I realize in that moment, this isn't about what Mr. Carlton wants, this isn't about pleasing him . . . this is about pleasing his wife.

He looks to her and she steps in, hands folded in her lap, her pearls shining like a bright beacon of hope. "You see, dear, I find the dynamic between you and your father inspiring. You have raised a fine daughter, intelligent, kind, a go-getter." My dad nods his head in appreciation. "And passing the family business down to the next generation is what we've always dreamed of. Unfortunately, we were never able to have children."

"Oh, Mrs. Carlton, I'm so sorry to hear that. I can't imagine how that must feel."

She nods solemnly and Mr. Carlton picks it up from there. "It's been hard, building this business with no one to pass it on to, but it's something we've come to terms with." He clears his throat and takes a sip of his water. "Which brings us to this uncomfortable topic, but one we figured we should be open and honest with you about."

"Which we truly appreciate," I say, my ass cheeks clenched. What the hell could we possibly not have that Heller and Parks has? Hello, father-daughter duo, that is exactly what the Carltons want.

"As you know, Heller and Parks is a family operated business like yours. We've been working closely with Kate Heller, and we've gotten to know her quite well." Fucking Kate Heller, talk about mean girl at her finest. She's two-faced and has a mole the size of Texas on her ass. I saw it once when she was drunk and stumbling in the bathroom at a charity event. She puts on a good appearance for clients, but she's as awful as they come.

"Kate is an . . . interesting woman," I say with a smile even though it's painful.

"Yes, and we recently found out that she's engaged to Emmet Parks. They're growing a family within the family with potential to pass down the business one day. It's a beautiful story."

You've got to be freaking kidding me. *How gullible is this woman?*

Mrs. Carlton cuts in. "We adore you, Dottie. We get along with you better and prefer your proposal, but this is important to us, and since you don't have a significant other—"

"I have a boyfriend."

I don't know what comes over me. Desperation maybe?

But I lie out of my ass so fast that as the words fall past my lips, I even shock myself.

I laugh like a crazy woman trying to show off her teeth. Deep breaths. "Sorry for interrupting, but I have a boyfriend." From the corner of my eye, I watch my dad slowly turn in his chair to look at me. Yup, I know what he's doing. He's chastising me with his eyes because he knows fully well there's no special man in my life.

"You do?"

I nod. "Yup. He uh, he's a professional baseball player, which is why I rarely talk about him. You know how people are . . . free tickets." I catch myself and say, "Oh, but if you want free tickets, they're all yours. I can get you the best seats. Just name it, they're yours." My dad coughs, and I gain my composure. "Anyway, yes, I don't talk about him much to afford him privacy, but we're very much in love. I can hear wedding bells in the future." Oh God, I hate myself so much right now. Wedding bells? If Jason could hear me now.

"Really?" Mrs. Carlton leans forward. "I'm sorry to pry, but can I ask who?"

I gulp. "Yup, of course. He uh, just got traded back to Chicago. Jason Orson."

Very softly I can hear my dad mutter, "Christ."

"Jason Orson?" Mr. Carlton whistles. "He's incredible. Where did you meet him?"

"College." I nod. "Yeah, college. I used to frequent the baseball loft with my best friend, Emory, who is dating Knox Gentry." Mrs. Carlton's eyes light up. "Jason and I hit it off back then, stayed in touch, and during the off-season four years ago, we reconnected. When he was traded at the end of the season, it felt like everything was meant to be. Albeit, he's playing for the Rebels, but I've been able to get over that quickly, especially since my man is finally in the same city as me."

Mrs. Carlton clasps her hand to her heart, a sigh exiting her. "Oh, that's so sweet. I'm so happy for you, honey."

"Thank you. We're happy and keeping things traditional. He has his own place, and we're courting each other, building that foundation you and Mr. Carlton have talked about."

I can see the brownie points racking up. I might need a wheelbarrow to help me carry them out of here at the end of this conversation.

"Well." Mr. Carlton leans back and strokes his goatee. "You sure have given us a lot to think about. Four years with a long-distance relationship in the midst of a hectic profession. Looks like you've grown a very strong bond."

"We have. I'm truly blessed."

Did you just hear that? It was the devil punching my ticket straight to hell.

After we talk more business, we shake hands again and send the Carltons on their way, promising to be in touch. Once they're out of earshot, my dad turns to me, arms crossed over his brawny chest and stares me down with those intimidating eyebrows of his.

"For the love of God, Dorothy, please tell me you know Jason Orson."

"Come on, Dad, do you really think—?"

"Yes, I do. I think you're like me and would say anything to make a deal. But please don't tell me you just pulled a rookie mistake and said something you can't follow through on."

"Pshh, what little you trust me." I walk back to my office, my dad at my side. "I'm seeing him tonight. Don't worry, Dad." I swallow hard, my nerves finally appearing. "I got this in the bag."

Shit. Shit. Shit. I got nothing in no bag . . .

Looks like I'll be going to dinner tonight.

What kind of wine should I bring that says, hey, I just lied about us dating for four years and said we're madly in love, you on board?

Merlot . . . definitely a merlot.

CHAPTER TWELVE

JASON

D inner in the oven, check.
    Apartment cleaned, check.
Apartment *decorated*, check.

Hair styled, smelling good, looking dapper, wearing a thong, check, check, check . . . *check*.

I'm ready for tonight.

I debated on whether I should wear a thong because I have jeans on, and we all know how I feel about that combo, but I couldn't get past the idea of snapping my thong strap at her for pure reaction.

While making my homemade enchiladas with green chili sauce, I went back and forth between wearing it and not wearing it. I finally decided on my lime-green thong. It looks great against my tan and is just bright enough for an impact.

Dottie. This girl invented the word *challenge.* I'd like to get through that tough shell and have her open up more, but she constantly surprises me, so only time will tell. But I'm up for the challenge, because it's not like me to back away from one.

I rub my hands together, giving my apartment one last once-over as my phone buzzes in my pocket.

There are two text messages: one from the doorman advising Dottie just arrived at the building—those guys are awesome. And a text from Carson, checking in.

Carson: *Have you fallen into an ice cream-induced coma from depression?*

I text back as I wait for Dottie to arrive.

Jason: *I've only had two pints since you left.*

Carson: *I expected more, so that's good. Still going on your runs?*

Jason: *Six miles this morning.*

Carson: *Only six? I guess that's all your body can handle, carrying around that giant ass.*

Jason: *First of all, six is really good, you run shamer. Second of all, baseball players aren't marathon runners. Third of all, it is a challenge carrying around such a fine butt, as people stop me all over just so they can stare at it.*

Carson: *~~~ reasons why I'm glad you're still in Chicago.*

Jason: *You don't mean that. You wish I was in the Bahamas with you and the wifey so I could bother you with annoying questions and gush over the fine cuisine.*

Carson: *I have to admit, I do miss your orgasm face when you eat something so good, you get happy in your pants.*

Jason: *Pervert.*

Carson: *LOL. But you're good?*

Jason: *Yup, I have company tonight . . . lady company.*

Carson: *Oh yeah? Who is it? Dottie? LOL*

Jason: *Why did you LOL at that?*

Carson: *Because she's the last person I'd expect you to have dinner with.*

I'm about to tell him like it is but there's a knock at the door. Stuffing my phone back in my pocket, I try to contain my excitement that she decided to show up. I was ready to tear her door down and extract her from Knox and Emory's apartment. I had no issues with it.

But she's here . . . willingly. Looks like my "chat" this morning got through to her.

On a deep breath, I open the door to find Dottie with a smile on her face, a wine bottle in her hand, and a pretty red dress draped over her body. Did I mention a smile?

Like . . . a real smile.

Something's not right.

I take a step back.

Confusion crosses her brow.

I point at her, taking another step back.

Her confusion increases.

"You look . . . weird."

Her eyes widen. Blink. "Uh, wow. That's one way to greet someone."

"It's the smile. Why are you smiling? You don't smile at me."

"Well, I never will again," she says, charging into the apartment, bumping my shoulder in the process. "Did you decorate?"

I shut the door and ignore her question. "Why were you smiling? Did you just fart or something? Was that really a smile or a side effect from releasing wind?"

"Do I look like someone who would 'release wind' right before the door is answered?"

I shrug. "I don't know, maybe. Could be a party trick."

She presses her hand to her forehead. "I don't know why I came here. I knew I should have stayed home. You tell me I look weird and blame me for farting the first ten seconds of being here. You act like a twenty-two-year-old boy at times. How is that a wise way to spend my night?"

"Uh, what about me? You smiled at me. Talk about throwing the entire night into a tailspin."

Expressionless, she asks, "And how did you want me to greet you?"

"A scowl, like the one you have right now." I sigh in relief. "There, that's better. Just keep scowling like that, then we'll be okay."

"Keep acting like a moron and I will."

"Oh, an insult, now we're getting warmed up." I rub my hands together. "By the way, you do look nice, sexy as shit actually. I like that dress on you."

The smallest of smiles peeks past her lips before she turns around to survey my apartment. I took down the pictures of baseball bats and gloves and replaced them with some tasteful art. I put up some curtains, even ironed the wrinkles out. Got a few throw pillows and bought a coffee table book of all the ballparks in the United States. It's not much, but the place does look better.

"I like what you've done with your place."

"Thanks. Feels more like a sex den, right?"

She shakes her head and walks to the kitchen where she sets the wine down. "I'm going to need you to open this so I can get through the night."

"Fair enough." I join her in the kitchen and retrieve my corkscrew. "How was your day, sweet cheeks?"

She leans her hip against the counter, her demeanor different. I can't quite put my finger on what's changed, but there's an air about her that doesn't give me the *get away from me* vibe. Like right now, we're a good distance away, but she's leaning in toward me. And when I pour us both a glass and hand her one, her fingers brush mine.

That's different.

Plus . . . when she doesn't tell me not to call her sweet cheeks, I know something's really different. What is she up to?

"It was fine. Meetings and all that crap. Had lunch with my dad, who's currently staying at my place with my mom while I watch Emory and Knox's apartment."

"Do you have plants that need to be watered and moved as well?"

"No, I'm not insane."

"Did you know she names them too?"

"Oh yes, you should see the binder that has a picture of each plant, its name, and caring instructions. I think Knox needs to be careful with who he's having a baby with."

"Well, there's no turning back now," I say. "He already planted his seed." She rolls her eyes. "Get it, it's a play on the whole plant thing."

"Yeah." She takes a big gulp of wine. "I get it." She looks at the oven. "Dinner ready?"

"Ten minutes. We can sit on the couch until it's ready." I guide her with my hand on the small of her back to the living room, and I'm surprised when she doesn't move away. *What the hell has gotten into her tonight?* Smiling, not super critical within thirty seconds, allowing me to touch her without a nipple twist in sight. Who is this Dottie?

We both take a seat and face each other, both of us propping a leg up on the couch.

I observe her, the sleek line of her neck, the smooth sheen of her raven-black hair, her impossibly long eyelashes. She's an absolute bombshell and must have men propositioning her all the time. It does beg the question why she's here. I might be a catch—who clearly loves puns—but Dottie Domico could have anyone. *Anyone.* Yet, she's alone. I've always had a vague picture in my head about who I'd want as my forever, but she's never resembled the stunning woman in front of me. So polished. Refined. Fiercely independent. Self-sufficient, without the need for anyone by her side. *I want someone who wants and needs me in her life.* And yet, she's someone I can't seem to stop thinking about.

"Tell me about college."

"What about it?" she asks.

"Why didn't you ever come say hi to me? Emory was dating Knox, and you two are best friends. We could be married by now."

"Well"—she draws her finger over the back of the couch—"it was hard getting close to you in college because you were always surrounded by groupies."

"No, I wasn't."

"At baseball parties you were."

"Because that's where they all congregated. But I'm sure you saw me on campus, right? You could have set up a double date with Knox and Emory."

"Who's to say I would have wanted a double date in the first place? Yeah, I knew you in college, but you were also a year younger, and I had better things to do than try to please a younger man."

I laugh, the sound heavy in my chest. "You were scared."

"I wasn't interested."

"What did I say about lying to me?" I stare at her, challenging her statement. "Tell me the truth, did you like me in college?"

"I didn't know you in college." She sips her wine carefully, keeping her gaze on me.

"Then let me rephrase. Did you think I was hot?"

She looks away, and there's my answer.

"I think you know the answer to that." She twists a finger in her hair.

"I want to hear it from your lips."

For a second, I see a change in demeanor, as if she really has to consider what she's about to say to me. It isn't an easy answer or confession, something that almost looks like it pains her to admit.

But despite the pain and reluctance I see in her eyes, she swallows hard, as if telling herself "here we go" and says, "I saw you for the first time in the quad. You were talking to some of the other guys on the team. Your ass was the first thing I saw, and I had a hard time forgetting about it."

Well, well, well, would you look at that?

I wasn't expecting such an easy admission. Given our night in the elevator followed by the race around my apartment and her pure discomfort this morning, I was looking forward to some repartee this evening, but it seems I won't be getting that.

What is it that's so different tonight? It's like something's flipped a switch.

I don't want to look too much into it right now, because I have her opening up, but I am a man who notes these things.

"When you say hard time forgetting about it, what does that mean exactly? How long have you been thinking about my ass?"

She looks away and downs the rest of her drink. If I didn't know better, I'd think she's trying to get drunk to make it through this night.

After smacking her lips, she says, "I've thought about your ass ever since college. Ever since I laid eyes on it." No teasing tone, her eyes are dead set on mine, and not even the slightest twitch in her lips. "I've wanted you for as long as I can remember." She leans forward, the neckline of her dress falling forward, giving me a perfect view down the top. I remember those tits, still as voluptuous as last night. Her hand falls to my thigh and she says, "I'm tired of playing this cat and mouse game, Jason."

Eh, what's happening right now?

She scoots even closer, setting her empty wineglass on the table, her body tipping toward me. "I'm tired of denying what I feel for you." Her hand slides up my thigh, right to my hip.

Hey-o, watch it there, lady.

"Let's drop the act."

I nervously laugh. "What act?"

"This chase. This repartee. Let's just give in to what we want . . . each other."

Her other hand falls to my chest and then glides up my neck to my jaw as she starts to climb on top of my lap. My body is saying yes, my mind is saying *what the fuck is happening right now* just as the oven timer goes off.

Not even giving it a second thought, I fly off the couch, knocking her on her ass, and sprint toward the kitchen.

Her thump on the floor seems to echo through the apartment as I strap on oven mitts and pull the perfectly cooked enchiladas out of the oven. Slightly browned on the top with bubbling cheese. My mouth waters at that sight, causing me to temporarily forget about the woman I just knocked to the floor. That's until I see her hobbling toward me, her hand on her hip.

Trying to make the most of it, I say, "Just got the rug. Was it plush?"

Her eyes narrow. "No."

"Hmm, I knew I should have gotten that extra cushion mat."

She rubs her side and steps into the kitchen, right next to me, her proximity concerning.

The anger from dropping her to the floor subsides as she says, "You know, those oven mitts look really sexy on you."

"These old things?" I show off the stained and food-coated mitts right before I cup my pecs and give them a good squeeze. "Honk, honk," I add nervously, using my muscular man breasts as sound-making devices.

Her brow lifts, but she doesn't let my awkwardness interfere with her . . . whatever she's doing right now. She runs her hand up my chest, playing with the divot in the middle—man cleavage— and leaves but only a few inches between us.

"You know, we can skip dinner if you want? Go straight to dessert."

She's drunk.

Or high.

Or both.

Either way, I need to put an end to this.

"You know"—I grip her by her shoulders with my oven mitts and push her a foot away—"I think you're hungry, maybe your blood sugar is low, because you seem to be acting a little strange. Why don't we get you some—?"

She swats my arms away and plasters her body against mine. Fuck, her tits feel incredible against my chest and if I didn't know any better, I'd swear her nipples are hard . . . Oh wait, maybe those are mine that are hard. Either way, with her this close, something else is getting hard, and fast.

"I thought you wanted me. Come on, let's date. Let's do this."

"Heh." I laugh, a little terrified. I back up, my ass hitting the oven. I place my hands behind me, trying to get as far away as possible. But she doesn't let me get very far. No, she pins me against the oven. "What, uh, what has gotten into you?"

"I know who *hasn't* gotten into me." She dances her fingers up my chest until they reach my face, with one bop to the nose. I'm rearing back, my hand connecting directly with the enchiladas, startling me so much I fling the dish forward. And we both watch in slow motion as the Williams Sonoma glass nine-by-thirteen dish floats through the air, smacks against the island, and falls to the ground in a mighty crash as waves of tortillas, chicken, and cheese splatter my kitchen.

"My masterpiece." I fall to the floor, gathering the cheese and sauce in my oven mitts, scooping it back into the broken and shattered dish.

"Oh my God, what did you do?" Dottie asks, standing above me, hand to her heart.

I look over my shoulder. "What did I do? What did *you* do?"

"Are you saying that I was the one who ruined dinner?"

I stand tall, enchilada sauce dripping off my oven mitts. "Yes, that's exactly what I'm saying."

"How dare you blame me for your clumsiness." She folds her arms over her chest. "I would hate to see how you perform in bed after this fiasco."

Eh, what? Come again. Fiasco? Does she not realize she's the reason all this happened? Because she apparently can't keep her panties on long enough to enjoy a homecooked meal.

"Excuse me, but you're the one trying to stroke my dick before dinner is served. I was just trying to give you a chance to sober up."

"Sober up?"

"Yeah." I motion to her body. "Isn't that why you're acting weird? You're high or drunk. One of the two." I wince. "Both?"

"I am not drunk or high."

"Oh." I pat her on the shoulder. "Stressed then. I get it, when I'm stressed I do weird things too."

"How am I being weird?" she asks, growing angry.

"Well, for one, you wouldn't touch me with a ten-foot pole about ten hours ago, but now you're ready to shove your hand down my pants. Seems odd. Also, you're being nice to me, offering up smiles and hitting on me. You just don't flip a switch like that. So tell me, what's this all really about?"

Her eyes search mine as she takes a step back, her teeth gnawing on her bottom lip. "This was a bad idea. I'm going to go."

"So you're just going to leave me like this?" I call out, dinner dripping down my jeans.

"The plants need me. Keep the wine." Without another word, she sprints to the door and lets herself out.

The plants need me?

Can someone explain to me what the hell occurred tonight? Because I'm confused as fuck.

"A re you alone?" I whisper into the phone, even though I don't need to.

"Why are you whispering?" Knox asks.

"I don't know," I continue to whisper. "I just need to talk to you, and I can't have your baby mama listening in."

"Dude, I told you, it's okay to use KY Jelly when jacking off."

"It's not about that." For fuck's sake, one drunk conversation about lube and he's never let me live it down. "Just tell me you're alone."

"I'm alone. Emory's in town with my mom right now. What's up?"

Sighing, I fling my body back on my bed, ready to gab. "I had the weirdest fucking night last night."

"Okay, what happened?"

Tugging on the short strands of my hair, I try to explain everything from the beginning. "Long story short, I've been trying to get to know Dottie."

"Ah, good luck with that. Dottie is very particular about every aspect of her life. Not warm and fuzzy when you first meet her, that one."

"Yeah, tell me about it. I'm still surprised we didn't hang out in college."

"She was around. We often hung with her."

"Yeah, that's what she said." *Weird.* "Anyway. So yesterday morning, I told her in a not so subtle way that she was having dinner with me."

Knox roars with laughter. "And how did she take that?"

"Not well at the time, but I convinced her with my passionate ways."

"Jesus," he mutters softly.

"And I honestly didn't think she was going to show up, but when she did, she was . . . different."

"Different how?"

"Well, other times I've been around her, she's had this constant sneer toward me."

"Ah, yes, I feel the same way, but continue."

Such a jackass.

"There was no sneer, not even close to one. She smiled at me and then . . . she touched me."

"Oh my God, no. Don't tell me that. My ears are virginal. She touched you. Wait while I fan myself."

I pause.

"Your sarcasm isn't needed right now. I'm feeling odd and I need someone to talk to about it."

"You know I hate this feelings shit."

"And you know I need it, so be a goddamn friend and let me unload." He groans but stays silent, letting me continue. "She was up in my business. Telling me she wanted me. Gripping my inner thigh, almost a graze to my dick, and then in the kitchen when I was taking the enchiladas out of the oven, she started mauling my chest with her hands. I was so caught off guard that I ended up spilling the entire dinner all over the floor."

"Oh shit, did you cry?"

"No, I didn't cry." Internally I did. "But she was acting so strange that I asked if she was high or drunk."

"I'm going to guess that didn't go over well."

"Nope, after that she told me your plants needed her and bolted."

Knox chuckles and then exhales. "Yeah, that doesn't sound like Dottie at all. She's usually calm and collected. Maybe you've messed with her head a bit. She has a big deal she's trying to close right now, so maybe that's where all this is coming from. I don't know, man, maybe lay off for a bit, at least until the deal is closed."

"See, I offered up the suggestion that maybe she was stressed, and she didn't seem to care for that."

"Because Dottie is a unique one. She's strong-willed, a killer when it comes to business, and an alpha in many ways. Emory says she doesn't need a man to simply *take care of her*, but rather someone who would step up for her, someone who will put her in her place when she needs it but also lift her up when she's on the warpath to take over the world. A strong man is what she deserves. Well, that's what Emory says anyway. Personally, I think she's a little scary." *I can definitely relate to the scary part.*

"Yeah, I could see that in her. I just don't understand what took over her last night."

"Could be stress, could be wanting to scare you away. She does that, puts up a shield when she starts to feel something. Emory has said that many times. I think you two could be great together, but I would also be hesitant. She's been hurt in the past by men who have taken advantage of her. She seems to have a lot going on, and if she feels like she's losing control, she'll lash out. Maybe that's what happened last night."

I think about it and start to feel guilty. "Shit," I groan. "I wonder if I pushed her too hard. I really hope not because I would hate to stress her out more."

"Who knows? The best thing I think you can do right now is lie low. Let her have some space and if she's interested, she'll come around. My bet is the deal is making her crazy because it's a big one, and having a new factor enter in her life—that factor being you—it's too much for her to handle."

"Yeah, okay." I blow out a sharp breath of air. "Damn, that sucks, because her tits are really nice."

"Really, man?"

I chuckle. "You know I'm kidding. It's her nipples I was really looking forward to meeting."

Click.

The phone goes dead, and I laugh out loud.

I toss it to the side and stare at the ceiling. Give her space. I can do that. I don't want to, but I can. Right after I apologize for *my* behavior.

CHAPTER THIRTEEN

DOTTIE

"Can I tell you something that you promise you won't tell anyone, and I mean anyone?"

Lindsay looks over her glass of iced tea that's poised at her mouth and then slowly sets it down. "Are you pregnant too?" she gasps out loud. "Oh my God, with Knox's baby as well?"

I roll my eyes, wishing my friend wasn't such an idiot. "Can you not say stupid things?"

"I'm sorry, but that would be such a twist in all of our lives. It would be kind of cool if it were true because, you know"—she puts on an Orpah-like voice when she drags out—"drama!"

"As much fun as that sounds, no, I'm not pregnant with our best friend's boyfriend's baby."

"Ooo, what a book title." She scrolls her hand through the air. "I'm Having My Best Friend's Boyfriend's Baby. Or wait, Baby Daddy: Best Friend's Boyfriend. It could be a series. Baby Daddy: Daddy's Best Friend. Baby Daddy: Brother's Best Friend. Baby Daddy—"

"I get it." I take a calming breath and say, "This is big and I really need you to focus."

"Oh, crap, okay." Lindsay sets her drink down. "What happened?"

"And you promise this stays between us?"

"Of course. What's going on?"

I play with the silverware next to my drink, a quiet breeze picking up the edge of the tablecloth of our outdoor table. We're taking advantage of the warm fall day by sitting outside, especially since we're both hauled up inside all day every day.

"So you know how I'm in the midst of a big deal with the Carlton acreage?"

"Yeah, is everything okay with that?"

"Sort of, they basically told me yesterday they might have to go with Heller and Parks because Kate Heller is engaged to the Parks kid and they like the idea of passing the family business down to family."

"Uh, that's been the whole structure with you and your dad."

I hold up my hand. "Don't even get me started. But they began to say since I wasn't even dating anyone . . ."

Lindsay's eyes widen. "Oh, no . . . you didn't."

I bite my bottom lip, feeling ashamed. "I did."

"Who?"

"Well, you know, I've been in correspondence with this guy lately."

"Oh, Dottie. Please tell me you didn't say Jason." There's no understanding in Lindsay's eyes; it's pure judgment, and I don't even blame her.

"I couldn't stop myself even if I wanted to. I was on a mission not to lose the deal."

Lindsay subtly shakes her head. "Did you tell him?"

"No. How on earth could I tell him? He thinks I hate him, when I don't. I mean, he's really annoying at times, but he is also a good guy, too good if anything."

"And yet, you're dragging him into your crazy."

"I know. I know." I lean back in my chair and cross one leg over the other while pulling on my high ponytail. "That's not even the worst part."

"Please tell me you didn't say you were engaged."

"No, thank God." Hinted at being madly in love, but I don't need to relay that information to Lindsay. "Knowing that the Carltons are probably going to want to meet him at some point, I decided last night to make a move on him." I pick up my glass of water and take a sip. "Let's just say it went horribly wrong."

"How wrong?"

"It ended with the enchiladas he'd cooked for dinner, smashed on the floor because I startled him so much with my advances."

Lindsay covers her mouth and laughs, while apologizing at the same time. "Sorry, but, what were you doing? Poking him with torpedo tits or something?"

"No." I brush my hand over my slicked-back hair. "I was, you know, not being myself. Apparently, he's used to me being a bitch to him. So he kept asking if I was drunk or high. That morning I was mean to him, so he noticed the difference. I bolted out of the apartment after the dinner went crashing to the floor. The whole thing was a giant mess."

"It makes sense though. You needed to ease into it, not go full force 'Let's be boyfriend girlfriend.'"

"Yeah, I totally tried to label us as a couple last night. Good God, what was I thinking?"

"You weren't. I think for the first time since I've known you, you actually weren't thinking. But it's understandable, because you are the type that will say yes to make a deal, even if the answer is no, and then you'll find a way to make it a yes."

"That's exactly what I did, and now I'm at a loss for what to do. The Carltons think I'm dating Jason Orson, Jason thinks I'm psycho, and my dad is relying on me to close this deal."

"So why don't you just tell Jason what's going on? He seems like an understanding guy, and he'd probably go through with pretending."

I shake my head. "Not only would that be humiliating, but I'm afraid he would be hurt by it since I tried to attack him last night. I'm afraid he'll think I was only hitting on him because of what I said during the meeting."

"Well, that is the only reason you were hitting on him, so yeah, he'll probably be hurt by it. He's sensitive, it seems."

"Very," I say, thinking back to last night and how scared he looked at my advances. "God, what do I do?"

"Well, you have two options." Lindsay casually takes a sip from her iced tea. "You can either tell the Carltons you just broke up with Jason Orson and risk the deal, or you can actually try to pursue the man on a less crazy scale."

"I don't want to date him," I say, groaning.

"Why not? He's so perfect."

"Exactly," I say, my patience wearing thin. "He's perfect. He's kind and sweet, and extremely good-looking. He has a weird sense of humor and makes me smile with most of the stupid things he says."

Lindsay looks at me as if I'm crazy. And right then, I decide that I really am crazy, because I just described the type of man I'd want *if* I was wanting to date. I no longer think that what I'm feeling is simply leftover lust from college. The guy is a dork, such a goof, but there are so many qualities I actually like about him. He made me dinner last night, for fuck's sake. Didn't order take-out. Didn't grab a meal from the freezer. He cooked. A whole meal. For me. Even though I was so rude to him the night before and then in the morning. *Who does that? Why would he do that . . . for me?* Because that's the man Jason Orson is. He goes the extra mile for a friend . . . or in my case, a friend of a friend. And then it hits me. My very real concern.

"I'm scared, Lindsay. I'm scared I'm going to fall hard for this guy, really hard and then what, the season starts up again, he's surrounded by all these opportunities with women, and he goes off and finds someone with a softer personality, someone who won't spend late hours in their office, someone who can be at his beck and call. I can't take that. My heart can't take that."

Lindsay softens and leans forward, placing her hand on mine. "Sweetie, I know you've had a rough go of it in the dating world, but I truly think Jason is different."

"I don't know." I shake my head.

"Well, just think about it, okay? It's not like you have many options. You put yourself in a really tough spot. Maybe next time when you're making up a fake boyfriend, don't say someone who's famous. Maybe try a classic John Smith."

Advice I wish I'd heard a little earlier.

fter lunch with Lindsay, I spent the rest of my day in my office, doing God knows what. I'm on autopilot, getting work done even when I don't think about it. I hate working on the weekends, but my neighbor isn't someone I prefer to look in the eyes at this moment, so I've stayed as far away as possible.

Now that it's eight, my brain is fried, and I can barely hold my eyes open—and all I want is to climb into my silk pajamas—I find myself climbing the floors in the elevator I was stuck in with Jason. The space is pretty big, but when he was in it, shirt off, it felt exponentially smaller.

If I really concentrate, and take a big whiff, I feel like I can smell him . . . that or it's my imagination.

The elevator dings, the doors part, and there he is, standing in front of my door, about to knock on it.

Ugh, this is exactly why I wanted to stay at my office. The easy access is killing me.

"Oh, hey." He smiles sheepishly and I want to die inside as humiliation from last night consumes me. But like always, I put on a strong face and give him a small wave.

"Hey."

He steps away from my door, allowing me to unlock it.

"I uh, was hoping I could apologize."

The door to the apartment is halfway open when I turn around to stare at him, confused. *He* wants to apologize?

"Why?" I ask, completely questioning this man's sanity. "You didn't do anything wrong."

"Yes, I did." His hands are in his pockets, his hair styled to the side, his beautiful green eyes reflect sincerity and remorse. I have no idea why. He's positively gorgeous. Just standing in front of him is putting my stomach into knots and making my heart pound faster. "I shouldn't have asked if you were high or drunk. That wasn't cool on my part."

I shake my head. "It was a valid concern. I was a little weird last night." Dropping my head, I stare at the keys in my hand. "I'm sorry. I don't know what I was thinking."

He lifts his hand to my chin and gently encourages me to look him in the eyes. When I do, everything around us fades to black and all I can see is this strong, confident man who should not be talking to me right now.

In that moment, with his eyes locked with mine, his expression soft and concerned, I realize, even though I'm terrified and nervous of what might happen, I don't think I have any other option than to want Jason Orson.

"Don't apologize, I was in the wrong. I pushed you and I shouldn't have." *But I like when you push me.* "I shouldn't have invited you over for dinner or forced you to come over." *But it made my day when you pinned me against the door.* "I shouldn't have forced the date on you for your donation." *But seeing you in my office, with food, made me happier than I've ever been.* "I'm sorry for everything and I hope we can be friends." *What? No. I know now that I want so much more than that.* He nods into the apartment. "I can take care of the plants so you can go back home. No need for you to stay here." *I don't want to go back home, not now that I want to see you when I arrive home from work.* He takes the key from my hand. "I'll water—"

I take the key right back. "It's okay, my parents are at my place anyway, so I'll just stay here and finish up the job." I give him a weak smile.

He nods and takes a step back. "Okay, well, guess I'll see you around." He waves and backs up to his apartment.

The word "wait" is on the tip of my tongue, urging me to shout it out, to stop him, to ask him to dinner, but I stay quiet as he ducks into his apartment and shuts the door.

He apologized to me? After everything I did last night, breaking his dish, ruining his dinner, not helping clean up, ditching when I should have stayed, he was the one who apologized?

There's something extremely different about that man, and even though my mind is hearing warning bells, my heart is exploding with ideas on how to slowly—and I mean slowly—get Jason Orson to date me. Because the alternative—*staying friends*—isn't right. All I can hope is the interest he seemed to display initially was real, and not him pretending. I'm terrified, but it might be time for me to be brave and open up my heart to some-one. *If I'm not too late. Because a man like Jason Orson doesn't stay single for long.*

CHAPTER FOURTEEN

JASON

"Thanks so much for meeting with me," I say to Walker Rockwell, the catcher for the Bobbies.

I felt intimidated reaching out to him, because Rockwell isn't known as a touchy-feely guy. *cue montage clips of him beating the ever-living shit out of water coolers with his bat* He has been known to have an attitude, to be tossed out of games for mouthing off to umpires about strike zone consistency, and he's the first one off the bench when a fight breaks out. Basically, he's the devil to my angel.

But despite the rage he seems to have on simmer at all hours of the day, I knew he would be a great ally to have when it comes to my charity because through careful research, I discovered he had a sister with special needs. I don't truly know what happened when she passed, but I do know he hasn't been the same since.

Walker takes my hand and gives it a firm shake. "Sure."

We both situate ourselves at the table and put in a quick order for some drinks and apps—I'm going to have to control myself around the pretzel bites, though, as I don't want Walker thinking I'm a glutton.

He looks around the restaurant and then asks, "How you liking Chicago?"

"I grew up here, so being back home is amazing."

"Oh yeah, I think I saw that somewhere." His jaw works to the side. "Have you seen what they're already saying about us?"

Another reason why I decided to call up Walker, because the media has been having a field day with the both of us. There's no doubt the rivalry between the Bobbies and the Rebels is thick in the city, potent, so heavy in the air that you have to use a machete to walk around during baseball season.

You're either a diehard Bobbie for life or you're a Rebel at heart. There's no bouncing between the two, there's no rooting for both. It's either or, which the media loves sensationalizing, increasing the rivalry between fans with propaganda-filled articles that show feuds, and include the differences between the hell-bent Rebels and the hometown heroes, the Bobbies.

I laugh. "Yeah, they're ridiculous, saying we're playing for the wrong teams."

He looks off to the side. "Yeah, we might be."

There's no doubt Walker has had his ups and downs with the Bobbies. He's been with them from the beginning, but trade rumors have been circulating, and they always seem to circle around Walker. I can't imagine what it feels like to never feel safe with your job, to continually wonder if this year is the year you're traded. He has one year left on his contract and then he's a free agent. From what I've heard from Knox and Carson, he wants to retire as a Bobbie, but the front office isn't too sure.

Knowing the type of personality Walker has—closed off and not very talkative—I take the lead. "I know we play for different teams, but I figured I'd call you because I thought it would be a good idea to bring the city together for a good cause."

"The Lineup, right?" he asks, shifting in his seat and finally making eye contact.

"Yes. My brother has cerebral palsy. He's the reason I started it. In high school, because my coach was awesome, he was included in our games. But there are a lot of kids out there who don't have the resources, the transportation, or the equipment, and this charity's goal is to help those individuals. To help educate coaches, to sponsor teams who include a diverse group of kids on the teams."

"You played with your brother?"

I nod. "In high school. He was a part of the team, pinch runner. He used his walker, and I swear, watching him score runs is still one of the best experiences of my life. Now he's an assistant coach at our high school."

"Wow." He pushes his hand through his hair. "Your coach is a good man."

"He is. I spoke with Coach Whittaker, and he's going to be a spokesperson for the charity, along with Joseph, my brother. We're doing a video montage of them to help encourage other coaches and athletes to be inclusive. That's where I was hoping you would come in. I know you had a sister with special needs."

He nods solemnly. "Yeah." He clears his throat. "What can I do?"

I smile to myself, understanding how amazing having Walker Rockwell on board will be. Not only is it going to boost The Lineup, but I also think it will boost his image as well. A win-win for everyone. This man needs someone who gets him. If it helps him heal? Even better.

∼

*A*re *you home?*

I stare at the text message, confused. What stranger has my number and is asking if I'm home?

Standing outside my building, sweat dripping down the front of my chest, my shirt tucked into the back of my shorts, I jog in place, trying to calm my already racing heart from my eight-mile run—*suck my ass, Carson.*

Contemplating what I should do, I slowly text back.

Jason: *Not to be a complete asshole . . . but who is this?*

I hit send and the dots appear right away.

I slow down to a sidestep, allowing my muscles to cool down as the text comes through.

Unknown: *Sorry, it's Dottie.*

Oh . . . how did she get my number?

Duh, that was a stupid question. *Emory.* I send her a text back.

Jason: *Glad you're not a murderer. I'm headed up right now.*

Dottie: *Okay, I'm outside the apartment.*

I take off toward the elevator wondering what she wants. I'm still surprised how shocked she was by my apology. I don't know what kind of men she's been hanging out with, but I was raised to believe that even if both parties were to blame for a disastrous night, you own up to it and apologize. It's called being a man. Didn't mean I wasn't disappointed that she hadn't wanted to talk more about us being *friends* though. Am I interested in Dottie? Hell, yeah. I'm putting that weird behavior down to whatever's stressing her at work, and not a direct hit to me. But, still . . . I had begun hoping we could be more than friends. I like what I see in Dottie Domico, strange behavior aside.

When the elevator reaches my floor, I walk out the doors and spot Dottie immediately. She's holding a wrapped present in her hand and seems to be struggling with it. I quickly walk up to her and help her with the box.

"What are you doing?" I ask.

She shakes out her arms. "I got you something."

I hold up the box. "This is for me?"

"Yeah. Go ahead, open it."

"I love presents, especially if they're wrapped." Like a kid on Christmas, I tear open the wrapping paper and pop open the box. I push the tissue paper to the side to reveal a brand-new Williams Sonoma baking dish with ingredients to make enchiladas.

Fucking thoughtful shit right there.

"The chicken and cheese are in that mini cooler. Not sure if this is how you make them, but I thought it's a start. Sorry about ruining your dinner."

"Hey, I told you it was cool. You didn't have to do this."

She points to the box. "There are new oven mitts in there too."

I push a few things to the side only to find two pink and white mitts at the bottom. I pull them out and slip them on my hands.

"Wow, these are comfortable."

"They're the same ones I have in my apartment. They're top of the line. Unfortunately, it was the only color they had but if anyone could rock them, it's you."

When I look up at her, I see a spark of vulnerability. Dottie rarely shows her emotions. She doesn't flinch when things go wrong, nor does she tend to smile when things go right, but in this moment, it's as if she's lowered the shield and is letting me see a small, well-hidden piece of her.

"I'm really sorry about the other night. I'm hoping the invitation to be friends is still open."

I smile at her. "Hell yeah."

"Okay, good." She backs away. "I have some dry cleaning to pick up and some errands to run. I'll see you around."

"Thanks again." I hold the box up to her and she nods, giving me a quick once-over with her eyes. A small blush creeps over her cheeks.

"You're welcome."

With a small wave, she walks back to the elevators, leaving me in a state of wonderment.

Friends sounds nice. Maybe if we're friends, she'll start to melt that icicle surface of hers.

$\rightsquigarrow$

Dottie: *I won't be back to the apartment until really late. Do you think you can water the plants for me? I promise it's the only time I'll ask.*

Jason: *Yeah, sure. Anything special I need to do?*

Dottie: *Instructions are on the counter.*

Jason: *Holy shit, why are things laminated in here?*

Dottie: *She's intense about her plants. Thanks, I owe you.*
Jason: *Nah, you don't owe me anything. What are friends for?*
Dottie: *Thank you.*

~

D ***ottie:*** *Are you still awake?*
        I look at the clock, ten thirty. Is she really just getting back to the apartment?
Jason: *Yup. What's up?*
Dottie: *I'm outside your apartment. Open the door.*
Jason: *One second, I sleep naked.*

I slip out of bed, throw some clothes on—not bothering with underwear because *why* at this point—and open the door to my apartment where Dottie is standing on the other side, holding a Dairy Queen Blizzard in each of her hands.

"Do you like ice cream?" she asks.

"I'm lactose intolerant."

"Oh." Her face falls, and I laugh, pulling her into my apartment.

"I'm only kidding. Ice cream is my jam. What flavor did you get?"

She sets her purse down in the entryway and follows me to my living room where I take a seat on the couch and she stands awkwardly at the edge of the rug.

"You can come in, you know. Make yourself comfortable."

"Just dropping off ice cream."

"Dottie. Sit."

After staring at the couch for a few seconds, she finally gives in and takes a seat. She holds the blizzards out to me and says, "Strawberry cheesecake or double chocolate brownie?"

"Brownie. Brownie every time." She hands me the little cup of ice cream and in seconds chocolate is searing my tongue, making me one happy man. "This is fucking perfect. Thank you."

"The least I could do for your help today."

I nudge her with my foot. "I told you it was no problem. I can seriously take care of the plants from now on if you want."

She shakes her head. "No, the distance from my parents is nice."

"Oh yeah, I keep forgetting they're at your place. When I was reading the instructions, I saw that you're not to water them past nine? What's that about?"

"I have no idea. I just do what the instructions tell me to do. I swear she treats them like animals. She was never like this in college. It wasn't until she was living alone that she developed a green thumb. I think it's because she missed Knox and poured her love into greenery."

"Better than pouring her love into a bottle."

"I guess so." She scoops a spoonful of ice cream in her mouth and looks around the place. "You really did do a nice job decorating."

"Thank you. I hate decorating, because I really only care about the kitchen."

"So you actually like to cook?"

"Love it," I answer, ice cream sloshing around in my mouth. "It soothes me. I spend a lot of hours getting beat up behind home plate, and it's a nice getaway from all of that."

"What's your favorite thing to make?"

"Potato salad of course." I wink. "Which I still have not forgiven you for spitting that out in front of my face."

"You were annoying me. I don't feel bad."

"Didn't think you did." I laugh and study her, while still shoveling ice cream in my mouth. "So why the change of heart?"

"What do you mean?" she asks, even though I know she knows what I mean. I can tell from the way she looks away, no doubt her mind spinning to find an appropriate answer. Whatever she says probably won't be the full truth and that's fine, because if she's had trust issues in the past, it's going to take a while to know I'm trustworthy.

"You want to be friends. But a few days ago, I think you would

157

have rather stuck your head in my jockstrap and worn it as an eyepatch than be friends with me."

"That's revolting."

"Exactly my point."

She sets her cup down and says, "Emory and Knox are going through some big things. There are going to be parties and cele- brations coming up, and I want to make sure it's comfortable for everyone, which means we should get along."

That does make sense, but I still don't believe that's the full truth.

"Think they'll have one of those gender reveal parties?"

Dottie nods. "Oh yeah. I bet Knox hits one of those color balls with a bat to reveal it."

"That is so him." I devoured my ice cream, so I take the last bite and set my empty cup down. Dottie still has half of hers left. "Are you going to finish that?"

"Go ahead." She hands it to me and I don't even bother switching spoons. I take big scoops while smiling at her.

"Told you ice cream was my lover. Do you have one . . . a lover?"

"What? No. I haven't dated in a really long time."

"Not a person. But a thing that you attach yourself to during the good times and bad. A comfort food."

"Oh." Her shoulders are stiff as she talks. What's it going to take to see her actually loosen up—but not in a weird *I'm trying to slip my hands down your pants for no reason* way. "Um, comfort food, well, I guess guacamole."

"Really?" I ask, slightly stunned. For Knox, it's Oreos, for Carson it's M&M's now—used to be brownies—I guess I just assumed she'd pick something sweet as well.

"Why is that such a shock?"

"I've never heard anyone say guacamole before. Do you have an accompanying chip with that? Scoops, black bean tortillas, a regular old Lay? Maybe a pretzel or pita chips?"

"Carrots."

I blink . . . a few times. "Your go-to *I need comfort* meal is carrots dipped in guacamole."

"Have you ever tried it?"

I finish the last spoonful and set the empty cup down. I lick my lips thoroughly, soaking up every last drip of ice cream. "I'm a healthy man, Dottie. I work out every day, I eat like a champion most of the time, kale being consumed daily, but I can tell you right now, carrots dipped in guacamole holds no appeal to me whatsoever."

"You say that now. Just wait, one of these days I'll make you try it. Maybe I'll bring a guacamole platter over whenever Emory and Knox have another celebration."

"Or, you can prove me wrong and bring it over this week. Show me what this comfort food is all about."

She thoughtfully nods. "You know what, I will."

"I don't think I've ever seen anything more beautiful in my life," I say, taking in the beautiful plating and artistic cuts of carrots, displayed on a wooden charcuterie board. Yellow and orange carrots decorate a wooden bowl of guacamole—sans tomatoes, smart woman—while sliced bell peppers border the outside. "You did this?"

She chuckles. It's quiet, but it's still there. "No, my chef made it for me. I don't cook."

"You don't cook?" I ask, not understanding that concept. "Why not?"

"Never been good at it, never had the time to learn. My personal chef is amazing, so I just rely on him and his husband to feed me."

"You don't cook at all? Not even a little?"

"Does heating things up in the microwave count?"

"Not even," I say, picking up a carrot in the shape of a flower. Who has time to do something like this?

I guess a personal chef.

"I'm afraid to eat these," I admit. "They're too fancy."

"I have no problem with it." Still in her suit jacket and matching skirt with light blue blouse, she takes a carrot flower, scoops up a chunk of guacamole, and pops it in her mouth, tearing the flower apart with her teeth. She closes her eyes and makes a yummy noise in the back of her throat. "So good, and better than your ice cream."

I laugh at that and dip my carrot into the guac as well. "I can promise you one thing, this might taste good, but it's not going to be anywhere near ice cream level." I pop the carrot in my mouth and chew.

Yeah, it's good. It's a carrot with guac on it, but would I lean on this if I had a bad day? If I needed a pick-me-up? If I was trying to apologize to someone? Nope. This I'd eat during the season as a snack to stay healthy.

"What do you think? Amazing, right?"

I chew and swallow and then choose my words wisely.

On a steady breath, I clasp my hands together and say, "I've had better."

"What?" Her eyes widen, playful insult taking over. "How on earth could you say that? This is clearly amazing, and your taste buds are lacking in sophistication."

"Whoa, whoa, whoa." I shake my head and hands, trying to erase her statement from the air. "You did not just say that."

When I look up at her, she has a small smile playing against her lips. The light tug, that tiny hint of amusement, fuck, it turns my stomach upside down and unleashes all sorts of butterflies. I'm not sure if I've ever seen anything more beautiful than the smallest of smirks from Dorothy Domico.

She casually picks up another carrot, dips it, and says, "You haven't proven me wrong yet."

"Are you challenging my palate?"

"Maybe."

"Oh . . . It. IS. ON." I push her platter away. "Take that somewhere else, I have some planning to do." I grab a pen and a piece of paper from one of my drawers.

"Planning?" she asks, confused.

"Yeah, this Friday, you're about to get schooled."

"Schooled in what? Good food?"

"No." I hold up the pen. "Not just good food, but how to make good food."

She shakes her head and picks up her platter off the counter. "Oh, no. You're not getting me in the kitchen. Nice try." She flashes one hand. "These fingers don't go near knives."

"They will Friday." I dab the pen tip on my tongue and pretend to write something down.

"You're ridiculous. It's not happening."

"Oh, okay, sure . . . it's not happening." I stare her dead in the eyes. "It is so fucking happening."

∽

Dottie: *I have to work late on Friday, sorry.*
    Jason: I'll wait up. I'll snack on some carrots and guac.
    Dottie: *Why do I feel like you're being sarcastic?*
    Jason: I am. I don't think I want that flavor combo in my mouth again.
    Dottie: *Just like I don't ever want your potato salad in my mouth again.*
    Jason: DON'T. YOU. DARE. SAY. THAT.
    Dottie: *Why are you so dramatic?*
    Jason: Why are you so wretched?
    Dottie: *Wretched . . . or right?*
    Jason: Wretched, most definitely wretched.

∽

Dottie: *Just learned I have to go north for the weekend, so I really can't make it Friday. I'm leaving Thursday night.*
Jason: *Who's making you go?*
Dottie: *My inner self.*
Jason: *It's not a work thing?*
Dottie: *No, it's a sanity thing.*
Jason: *Great, I'll pack my bags. We can make the cooking lesson an all-weekend thing.*
Dottie: *I'll pass.*
Jason: *I can drive, but that means it's my playlist.*
Dottie: *You're not going.*
Jason: *Can you give me the address? I like to plan the trip.*
Dottie: *Why don't you ever listen?*

~

Jason: *Picking you up in twenty. I have your suitcase. Lindsay is all set with the plants for the weekend.*
Dottie: *I still can't believe you forced your way into this trip.*
Jason: *See what consistent nagging and selfies in flannel can do?*
Dottie: *If you send me one more picture of you looking down at the camera to see how many chins you can form, I'm going to physically hurt you.*
Jason: *Those are classic. You should be saving them.*
Dottie: *Yes, to remind me how annoying you are.*
Jason: *I like that we're back to our old repartee, I missed it. Can't wait to squeeze your cheek when you get in the car.*
Dottie: *Why the hell would you do that?*
Jason: *Seems like the thing to do. You get in the car, I squeeze your cheeks, ask how your day was, and then hand you one of the many snacks I packed for our trip.*
Dottie: *You packed snacks?*
Jason: *What kind of lady of the house would I be if I didn't?*

CHAPTER FIFTEEN

DOTTIE

"Going somewhere?"

"Dad." I startle, turning around to see him leaning against my doorjamb. It's past seven, the office is cleared out, I let Jessica leave early today, and I was just finishing some work. I changed into a pair of leggings and a loose-fitting sweater so I'm comfortable on the drive. "I thought you were already home."

"Nope. I had some phone calls to make." He points at my outfit. "You weren't wearing that earlier, were you?"

"No. I changed. Heading to the cabin for the weekend. Need a little R and R."

"Good. I'm glad to hear it. One of the things I wish I did more when I was younger was take a breather. I don't want you running yourself ragged."

"Yeah, I've been feeling it lately."

Having worked until eight or nine at night all this week, I'm starting to drag, and it's showing in my work, in my meetings, in my whole life. I made the decision quickly and was going to ask Jason to watch the plants for me, but of course, he found a way to include himself in the trip. When Lindsay started texting me like a madwoman, asking me what was happening and why she's uprooting her child so I can go north with Jason Orson, I knew his ticket to the cabin was stamped.

I told her we're friends, and we are . . . we're friends who like to annoy each other. I've been trying to find an easy way to start dating this man, maybe ask him out to dinner, but for the life of me I can't get up the nerve. How reminiscent of college days when I couldn't find the courage to even talk to him. Plus, odd as it might sound, I like how things are right now. I have some time with the Carltons while they're away on vacation.

I got an email from them Tuesday night saying they were going to take a small trip to Vermont. They wanted to sit down, relax, and consider their options now that they're aware I have someone serious in *my* life—but when did business deals revolve around personal lives? And I can't help but wonder, if I were a guy, would this be a factor?

Either way, after I got their email I started wondering when I last went to our cabin. It had been a mini vacation after an intense infrastructure summit in California. Considering how overworked I felt, and also how hard I'd been working Jessica, I knew getting a small rest away from the office was a wise choice. *Although, it won't be as quiet as I'd anticipated . . .*

"Did you have Anderson clear out the cabin and stock it up?"

"Yes. He was very sweet and even sent pictures to make sure everything was in order."

"He's a good man." My dad steps away from the door and walks over to me. He pulls me into a hug and presses a kiss to my forehead. "You sure you know what you're doing? I'm afraid you got yourself into a pickle with this Jason thing."

I can understand his nerves over the situation, because I'm feeling the same concern. Not only because I lied to the Carltons, but because I like Jason.

"I know, but if it makes you feel better, he's about to pick me up... we're going to the cabin together."

My dad steps back. "Really? Well, who says I want my daughter going to a cabin with a man for the weekend? I don't even know him. He's coming to pick you up?"

"Yes, but—"

"Perfect." He buttons up his suit coat. "I'll go down and meet him."

"Dad, no. That's not necessary."

"The hell it isn't. I need to make sure he's a man of integrity."

"Dad, I promise you—"

But before I can finish, he's headed out of my office and toward the elevators just as I get a text from Jason.

Jason: *Honk, honk. I'm here, sweet cheeks. I'm parked where you told me to park. Luggage is in the back, snacks are ready, playlist is warmed up, time for a road trip.*

Oh God.

~

"He's parked in your spot?" my dad asks, walking faster than I've ever seen him walk.

"Yes, I had Mark pick me up this morning." I catch up to him, thankful for my tennis shoes, rather than my heels I went to work in. "Dad, please be nice. He's just a friend right now, has no idea—"

"He has no idea you told the Carltons that you two had been in a relationship for four years?" he huffed.

I shrugged, something I never did, especially with my father. He then rolled his eyes and said, "My middle name is cool."

Somehow, I don't believe that.

We round the corner to my parking spot where a black SUV is parked. From our approach, Jason hops out of the car wearing a pair of jeans and one of the stupid flannel shirts he sent me a picture of. This one is forest green and black and despite hating everything about it, it fits him like a glove. Sleeves rolled up to his elbows, brawny chest filling out the top . . . he's totally got the sexy mountain man look going on, and I approve, especially the scruff he didn't seem to shave off.

Like the respectable man that he is, he lifts his hand in a wave when he sees both me and my dad and walks over, lending it out for a greeting.

My dad takes it and gives Jason a good shake. "From the same blue eyes you two share, I'm going to assume this is your dad, sweet cheeks." He winks at me then turns back to my dad. "Jason Orson. It's a pleasure to meet you, Mr. Domico."

A small twitch forms at my dad's lips, and I know he's just about dying inside right now.

Let me let you in on a little secret. I think Jason is the first man to ever come up and confidently shake my dad's hand. My dad can be a very intimidating man and has been to any past boy or man who has met him—there aren't many. They cowered, they never stood tall, and they were a big no on my dad's end.

But from the twitch at the corner of my dad's mouth alone, I know he already appreciates Jason and his strength of character.

"Jason, it's a pleasure." Instead of being in awe or "fangirling" over one of the best catchers in the country, my dad acts normal and doesn't even mention the fact that Jason is a major league baseball player. "Going up north with my daughter?"

"Yes, sir." Jason sticks his hands in his back pockets and all I can focus on is the way his pecs press against the soft fabric of his shirt. "A-plus driver here in case you were wondering. No tickets, I enjoy a comfortable position of ten and two on the steering wheel, and I already established the rule in the car that it's my playlist we're listening to so there's no fighting over music. Also, since it's my off season, I took a siesta earlier today so I was fresh and alive for the drive tonight. I packed snacks, the tank is full, and there is water in reusable water bottles in the center console for each of us. Oh, and gum, in case I need something to chew if this one falls asleep." He thumbs toward me. "I know how to use my fists if a bear comes near us, but I'm also not an idiot and know if it's brown, hit the ground, if it's black, fight that bastard back." Oh my God, why is he so adorable? "I plan on teaching your daughter how to cook a proper meal this weekend, something she can make for you and your wife when you're in town."

"Now this I like." My dad chuckles. *Chuckles. At Jason.* I think I'm in an alternate universe.

"I saw this great place that serves apparently the best pancakes in Illinois, so Sunday morning, I'd like to go there. I'd also like to hike, and when it comes to the sleeping arrangements, I was informed there are two bedrooms, and I plan on using one of them alone. No worries there."

Oh, I'm worried . . . that he plans on using the other one.

"Well, looks like you've covered everything. This is a solid gentleman, Dottie."

I know. I really know.

"Are you good? Am I allowed to leave now?"

"I don't know." My dad scratches the side of his jaw. "Just from how charismatic this man is and his plans, I'm thinking I should take your place instead."

"I'm up for a bro weekend," Jason says, his banter and decorum so easy. No wonder he's loved so much. "Then I wouldn't have to see the deep eye-roll your daughter gives me on a constant basis."

My dad leans in and says, "She gets that from me, but I will say this, I can't possibly see myself eye-rolling with you. Do you have extra clothes packed for me?"

"Do you mind sharing underwear with another man? Because I'm game."

My dad's head falls back as he laughs. "I've never rubbed another man's underwear on my junk, but never say never."

"Ohhh-kay, you two are done." I reach up and press a kiss to my dad's cheek. "We are leaving." I take Jason by the arm and direct him back to the car. From over his shoulder, he mouths to my dad to call him, which my dad replies with a thumbs up.

Ridiculous. *Hilarious.*

When we're saddled up in the car, I let out a long breath and shift my head to the side so I can look at him. Sincerely I say, "Sorry about that."

With the biggest smile on his face, his hand lands on my thigh. He gives it a good squeeze and says, "Don't apologize, that was fucking awesome."

~

T he two-hour drive to the house was . . . fun.
Oh my God, was it fun.

I tried to hold back, but there were times that Jason had me laughing hard, and every time he heard my laugh, it was like he was spurred to make me laugh even harder. We played stupid car games that he packed, like car Bingo, which was difficult to play since it was dark—a miss on his end that he admitted it—we played would you rather, the alphabet game again, and even jammed out to some old school songs from the sixties. He found the playlist on Spotify and it was called Dancing Songs for Toddlers. I was skeptical at first, but surprisingly, I was the one begging for more. They were perfect songs for him to sing to. And he sang, boy, did he sing. *Terribly*.

I can't remember the last time I had that much fun, especially with just one person.

"This place is beautiful," Jason says, taking in the front of the cabin. "How can you not live here full-time?"

"I know. I love it here." I observe the much-loved family cabin with its wraparound porch and rustic-looking windows. With lush evergreens surrounding the beautifully renovated home on all sides, it's calming and one of my favorite places of all time. I wish I had more spare moments to come up here. I make a mental note to put it into my calendar: more time at the cabin.

"Let me carry that for you." Jason takes my suitcase from me and then motions to the house. "Lead the way."

Leaves rustle in the wind as we make our way to the cabin, and then I unlock the front door and push it open for him. "The house has been prepped. There's food and the power is on so we won't be bumping over everything to find our way. The house is split into two sides, each side has its own master suite. I'll take the west, and you can take the east."

"Fancy." He smiles. "Want me to take your suitcase to the west room?"

"No, I can roll it over there, but thank you. The living quarters, kitchen, and dining are all in the middle. The back porch looks over a beautiful lake and there are books, games, and a few movies in the closet over there to help with your time here."

"Any naughty books in there? I love a good sex scene to put me to bed."

I stare at him, not answering, which makes him shake my shoulder and laugh.

"Kidding. I don't read. I watch porn, so how's the Internet here?" *Of course. He cooks, but doesn't read.*

"There is none."

"Wait . . . no Internet? How am I supposed to watch porn?"

I know he's kidding, but still I answer. "Looks like you're going to have to read one of those naughty books."

"Wait, you have some?"

"No. I think my mom would faint if we did. You're going to have to let the sway of the trees and the sounds of crickets put you to sleep."

"God, it's like we're mere peasants, being one with Mother Nature."

"That's the point. You're supposed to relax here."

He looks around, a big smile on his face. "That I can do."

F ire flickering in front of us, we both have a cup of hot apple cider in hand, and it's pitch black all around us besides the light from the fire and one side lamp next to me. We're sitting in comfortable silence, absorbing the quiet peace of nature surrounding us.

"Thank you for not kicking me out of this trip," Jason says, shifting his large body on the brown leather couch we're sharing. "I was bummed when I had to move my vacation, so this is a nice getaway for me."

"Oh, I forgot you had to move that. I don't know, the Bahamas seem more fun than this."

"Nah, I'd take the woods over the beach any day. No sharks."

"Yes, but murderers can lurk in the trees."

"A chance I'm willing to take." Growing serious he says, "Seriously though, thank you."

"You don't have to thank me. It was nice to have the company on the drive, despite the wretched pitch in your voice when you sing."

"Excuse me? Wretched?" He sits a little taller. "I've been told by many that my singing voice is beautiful."

"Who told you? Your mother?"

"She's one."

I chuckle and take a sip of my apple cider, the spices doing all sorts of things for my belly . . . or is it the man sitting next to me? Maybe a combination of both. We changed into our pajamas, prepared our bedrooms, and met back out here for a relaxing hot cider before bed. Jason is wearing a full-on flannel pajama set, and if I wasn't so intrigued by the flap at the top he left unbuttoned where I catch glimpses of his ripped chest, I'd think he was ridiculous.

"You said you sleep naked," I say, remembering that little tidbit.

"I do. Would you like me to change into what I actually wear to bed? Because that can be arranged. It's a quick lift up of a shirt and a push down of pants."

"Are you saying you're not wearing underwear?"

"Psh, no. Free balling; feels good against the flannel."

Why do I find that answer erotic? Him not wearing underwear, only one layer of fabric blocking me from the view. I try to convince my eyes to stay on his face, to not glance down, but they betray me and fall to his crotch but quickly divert to my cider. I didn't get a good enough look, of what, I don't really know, couldn't tell you, but whatever I was trying to look at, I barely got a glance.

Clearing my throat, I ask, "Did you get those pajamas for this weekend?"

"I did, but I will admit, I might make them an every-other-Friday thing. My nether regions feel like a king."

I shake my head. "Seriously, what is wrong with you?"

"What?" he asks, as if he doesn't understand what's wrong. "I talk to my friends all the time about my balls. We share products and such to help each other feel more comfortable. Try having two dangling balls hanging off your body. It's very uncomfortable, so if something makes them feel good, I'm going to let everyone know."

"I have boobs."

He looks at them and back up at me. "That you do, sweet cheeks."

"I mean, I have dangling things hanging off my body as well but mine weigh heavier than yours and they can cause backpain, plus they're attached to very sensitive nipples."

I watch him slowly swallow while his eyes fall to my breasts again. When he talks, his voice is a little squeaky. "Sensitive nipples, huh? Like what kind of sensitive? If I blew on them, would you have an orgasm?"

"Do you really believe that's a thing?"

"I mean . . . yeah. Picture this." He sets his apple cider down and shifts so he's closer. His arm is draped over the back of the couch, and he sits close enough where he can pick up a strand of my hair and start twisting it in his finger, which he does. It's a small move, my scalp barely registers the touch, but it causes my whole body to break out into goosebumps. "You're tied up, wait . . . have you ever been tied up?"

"Umm, no," I answer, my body starting to heat from the mention of being tied up. Is that something Jason does? Why can I easily see it, him in control in the bedroom, using that deep, unwavering voice of his to direct me how he wants me to sit, lie down, where to put my hands, what to touch, what not to touch, what to suck . . .

"Christ, okay, I'm going to ignore that answer." He pushes his hand through his hair. "So, let's say you're tied up, you're completely naked, legs spread, and arms above your head. You have no control in what happens to you next, and you're at the mercy of your lover. He comes down on the bed and hovers over you but never touches you. He's naked as well, his cock raging hard, because all he can focus on are your tight, tender nipples. They're hard, aching, begging to be touched, but he doesn't lift a hand to ease the pressure building inside of you. He can smell how aroused you are, and on top of wanting to suck your nipples into his mouth —*hard*—he wants to tongue your needy and delectable pussy and clit. Instead, he slowly lowers his head so he's a whisper away from your nipples and he ever-so-lightly blows. It's small, a featherlike wind that caresses you, but it starts to build, and build, and build, until the pressure that's been coiling in your wet pussy starts to unfold. Your hips rub against the sheets, your body heaves, your spine straightens, and with one small flick of his tongue over your right breast, you tumble over into ecstasy, your orgasm plummeting you into a high, the kind of pleasure you haven't felt in such a long time that you're calling out his name, begging him to make it last longer . . ."

Fuck.

Breathless.

Throbbing.

And seconds away from straddling the man in front of me, ready to make him ease the ache he just put inside me.

"What do you think? Orgasm?" he asks, tugging on the strand of hair he's been twirling.

Uhhhhh . . .

Yeah.

Parched mouth, I gulp my cider and then say, "I guess it would depend on the man."

But I can tell you right now, the man sitting in front of me could probably speak a few more naughty words and I'd come from that. *God, I want everything he just said. Now.*

"I guess that's true." He leans back. "Okay, I should be getting to bed, I'm exhausted." He holds his hand out for a high five and a part of me dies when I return it, wishing it was a hug, a kiss, a slip of his hand down my pants, something other than a high five only friends would share.

"Yeah, I'm tired too." And turned on. "Are you good? Do you need anything?" *A blow job? Something warm and tight to sink into? A boob in your mouth?*

He stands and stretches his arms over his head. His shirt rolls up showing off his low-hanging pants and . . .

Oh.

My.

God.

His bulge.

It's huge. I hold back the tears that want to fall from that small sneak peek. The towel picture has nothing on the in-person angle.

"I'm good," he says, releasing his hands. "Want me to put your cup in the sink?"

"Yes." I stand abruptly and hand him the half-drunk apple cider. "I, uh, yeah, I'm going to my room. Have a good night."

"You too," he calls out casually.

I quickly walk back to my bedroom, hearing dishes clattering in the sink in the distance. *Get as far away from him as possible.*

When I reach my room, I shut the door and lock it, as if that will stop me from attacking the man across the house. I make quick work of brushing my teeth and going to the bathroom, the whole time thinking about Jason and his laugh, his lighthearted smile, the way he casually touches me, but not in a sexual way, just a friendly way, the deep tone of his voice, the way he delivered his erotic speech like it was second nature.

By the time I reach my bed, I'm so worked up that I reach down and slip my hand under my nightgown where my legs are spread. I press my finger along my slit and good God, I'm so wet.

173

Biting my bottom lip, I sink deeper into my mattress, run my other hand up my stomach to my breasts, and start playing with my nipples. I can feel him above me. Watching me. Breathing rapid breaths. Turned on. My hand down my panties brings the pleasure roaring in my body to a full-on inferno. God, I want him. I want his lips and tongue on my pussy, my clit. I want his fingers tugging my hair, pulling it hard as he sucks me in. I want him to lean down and blow breaths over my nipples, then suck them into his hot mouth. And then it hits, one of the strongest orgasms of my life. *All because of the sexy-as-sin man on the other side of the house.*

CHAPTER SIXTEEN

JASON

J**ason:** *I've jacked off twice since I arrived at the cabin last night.*
    ***Knox:** Dude, self-control.*
    ***Jason:** I have zero. You have no idea what this woman is doing to me. She wore a camisole last night with no fucking bra. What am I supposed to do with that? Oh, and then she goes and tells me her nipples are really sensitive. I'm trying to be cool here, but I can feel myself unraveling.*

    ***Knox:** What's holding you back from making a move? You're in a cabin together, a romantic setting, so this should be a dream come true to you.*

    ***Jason:** Your last conversation with me about her scared me away. At least, made me move into ultra-slow mode, which was ramped up to hyper speed last night. Fuck, dude, I heard her laugh, and it was, hell, it was perfect.*

    ***Knox:** Whoa, you really like her?*

    ***Jason:** Yeah, I think so. The more time I spend with her, the more I realize I like her surly attitude and the way she rolls her eyes at me. Oh, and get this, met her dad last night and we hit it off.*

    ***Knox:** Then go for it. Just be gentle, and don't attack her full-on with your neediness.*

Jason: Fuck you. I'm not needy.

Knox: Sure, okay, man. You're not needy.

Jason: There was sarcasm in that statement.

Knox: Yup. Now stop talking to me and go make her breakfast. That's a good way to start.

Jason: Shit, you're right. So I'm doing this? I'm going to make a move this weekend?

Knox: If you don't, I'm going to punch you in the balls when I get home just to make sure you still have them.

Jason: Believe me, I do. They've excreted a lot of my sperm in the last twelve hours.

Knox: Jesus fuck.

I laugh to myself and set my phone back on the nightstand. I stretch from side to side, warming up my spine and then hop out of bed. I take a quick piss, brush my teeth, because I'd rather eat minty pancakes than have morning breath, slip on my flannel pants but leave it at that. If I'm going to make a move, I have to entice her somehow, and I don't just work out to be good at baseball. I want to look good for the girl I plan on dating as well.

Before I step out of my room, I check myself in the mirror near the door and toss my hand through my hair a few times, trying to even out the messiness, but when it goes back in place, I figure, nothing like some good rumpled hair. Girls like that shit.

When I leave my room, I'm greeted by the smell of coffee. She's awake.

But when I reach the kitchen and don't see her, I wonder if I'm wrong, until I see her head peeking past a chair on the deck. There's a misty fog settling through the trees, casting a dream-like view out the windows.

I pour myself a cup of coffee, add some sugar, because Daddy needs a little sweet in his coffee, and then open the door to the deck. The fresh morning air is a shock to my lungs as well as the chilly temperature.

No worries about boners here. Well, the only hard things are my freezing nipples.

"Good morning," I say, taking the seat next to hers, but instead of facing the trees, I face her.

She's wrapped up in a blanket, her silky hair piled into a bun on top of her head, and she's wearing round, thick-rimmed black glasses.

So fucking adorable. It takes everything in me not to cuddle her ass.

"Hey, good morning." She lightly smiles at me, her eyes roaming my chest for a brief second. Look all you want, sweet cheeks. "How did you sleep?"

After I jacked off to you in my head? Amazingly.

"Good. That mattress is comfortable. I don't think I could ever go back to my own."

"My dad is all about maximum comfort when sleeping. It's why I'm so well rested after staying a few nights here."

"Yeah, sleep like an angel?" I sip my coffee.

"You could say that." She looks out at the trees and the calm water. "One of my favorite things to do in the morning is watch the fog lift off the lake; it's breathtaking."

I can name a few other things that are breathtaking . . . like her eyes and the way they shine when she wants to smile but holds back, or her laugh, how it's throaty and only earned, or the way she carries herself in a suit, with confidence and power.

Jesus Christ, I'm a fucking goner.

"Are you hungry?" I ask.

"Are you going to make me cook?"

I chuckle. "Nah, not breakfast. But dinner, you're mine, got it?"

Her eyes flash an emotion I can't quite decipher, and she doesn't give me enough time to work it out before she says, "Fine, dinner it is. What's for breakfast?"

"Pancakes? I saw the ingredients in the cupboards last night. Does that work for you?"

"With raspberries?" She bats her eyelashes.

I point my finger at her. "Only if you say please."

"Please, Jason?"

Oh fuck, that sounded good. Why did she have to add my name at the end? Now all I can hear is her saying that while I'm playing with her clit, massaging it to the point of her release but then pulling back before she falls over.

"Yup, sure." I stand abruptly. "Pancakes with raspberries it is."

"Thank you, I'll be right in to keep you company."

I tug on her ponytail. "No, just sit back and relax. I'll let you know when they're done."

And when my libido has calmed down, because it seems that Dottie Domico can defeat the chill in the air and cause my dick to harden regardless. As I said, breathtaking.

~

Breakfast was good but uneventful. I made pancakes peacefully in the kitchen while Dottie hung outside. She looked so calm, so relaxed, that I didn't bother her when I saw her head lull to the side and she fell asleep for a few short minutes.

We shared breakfast on the deck, staring at the lake, not really saying anything to each other. It was a comfortable silence I haven't shared with many people. After breakfast, she cleaned the kitchen and I took a shower where I took matters into my own hands again, because the minute we were back in the house, Dottie dropped her blanket and showed off that little nightgown she packed for the trip. I swear she did it with pure torture—for me—in mind.

After a nice long shower and a rather quick release—*I apparently transformed into a teenager the minute we hit the woods*—I spent time catching up on some reading for the foundation. Thanks to no Internet, I can't tackle any of the emails Natalie sent, but I did draft some things for later.

I close my computer as Dottie appears from her side of the house looking like a mountain goddess. Skinny jeans with hiking socks halfway up her shins, denim long-sleeved shirt, fresh face, and hair in high ponytail.

"Want to go for a hike?" she asks, sitting down on the couch with some hiking boots that she starts to strap on.

"Hell yeah. Let me grab my shoes and a jacket." I take off toward my room, snag the things I need, and meet Dottie in the foyer. She has on a jacket as well and a backpack strapped to her back.

"What's in the bag?"

"Snacks, water, a box cutter."

"Box cutter?" I lift a brow.

"You know, self-defense."

I hold up my fists. "That's what these are for, sweet cheeks."

"Oh, okay." She rolls her eyes and opens the door.

"What?" We walk out of the cabin and lock up. "You don't think I can do damage with these?"

"Oh, I've seen you do some damage on the playing field."

She leads the way to a trail that flanks the side of the cabin. I fall in step with her, loving the still air and quiet sounds of nature still waking up. It's stunning, and I get to experience it all with an equally stunning woman.

"You have, have you? Keeping track of me? Let me guess, you know my stats by heart."

"No, not even close. Are you even good?" she asks, joking around.

I pull her in by the shoulder and give her a squeeze. "You know I'm fucking good, so don't even pretend." She pushes me away playfully.

"You're all right. But I did see that one fight you got into with the Catamounts. That punch was all over the Internet."

I chuckle to myself, thinking about that day. "I think that was the one and only time I actually blacked out from rage. I'm a pretty easygoing guy and can take a lot of shit, but that pitcher was asking to get punched. He'd pegged our players left and right all season, and when he tattooed my ribs with seams, I was over it."

"You tossed your bat like a boss. I've seen the look on your face in slow motion. I'm pretty sure you were ready to eat that pitcher's head off his shoulders."

I casually shrug. "Don't fuck with my team and don't be a bitch on the mound."

"You don't seem like a fighter, you know. The footage surprised me."

"You don't think I'm tough?" I ask, flexing both arms for her, but she doesn't give me the appreciation I was looking for. Instead, she shakes her head at me and keeps walking forward.

"You're tough when you want to be, but most of the time, I think you're just a giant teddy bear. Super sensitive, but also knows how to take a joke."

"Sensitive isn't a bad thing."

"Never said it was. I think I need to work on my sensitivity a little."

"Nooo, I would never say that about you," I say sarcastically. "You're the most sensitive person I know."

She pushes me but barely makes me budge. "I can be sensitive. I just don't cry over everything."

"I don't cry."

"Puh-lease. You probably wept yourself to sleep last night over how beautiful the night sky was."

No, I wept myself to sleep while jacking off to the image of you in that nightgown.

"You have me pegged all wrong. I don't boo-hoo just for the hell of it. Something has to really get my emotions working for me to start up the waterworks."

"Like what?" She pushes a branch to the side so it doesn't whack me in the face. The farther we walk, the farther we dive into the woods, the dirt trail shrinking, making it a tight fit for the both of us to walk side by side, but we still maintain the position, even if our shoulders are now brushing against each other. I'm tempted to reach down and take her hand in mine. What would she do if I did? Rip her hand away? Snuggle closer? Give me a *what the hell* look?

I'm thinking maybe the third option, so I refrain, even though I feel the need deep within my bones, this almost uncontrollable urge. We need a few more flirty moments before I pull a stunt like holding her hand.

"What makes me weep?" I ask, loving that this is what we're talking about. Any other man would probably puff his chest and clutch his balls, stating he doesn't weep.

Well guess what, ladies? I've been known to blubber into my shirt, cry on a shoulder, burst out in an ugly Kim Kardashian-like sob over something that cuts deep.

I'm not ashamed. I know who I am, and I own that.

"Yes, weep." She grins up at me but then focuses back on the trail.

"It has to be something that really tugs on my heartstrings, like animals. They're so innocent and when I see them get hurt, abused, or taken from their home, you can bet your pretty little ass my head will be buried in a box of tissues. Or . . . oh fuck, you know those videos of dogs being rescued from a sewer drain, given a makeover, and then they're bouncing around, full of life, in a goddamn Hawaiian shirt at their new home? I'm drenched in tears."

"Animals get me too. What about soldiers coming home?"

"No, I just feel happy for them, but not that gut-wrenching happiness that makes me buckle over. I'll also weep if someone accomplishes their goals."

"Really?" she asks, seemingly stunned.

"Oh yeah, big time. Any time one of my guys got the call up and started in the big leagues, fuck, I bawled like a baby."

"Bawled? I could understand being happy, but bawling?"

I nod. "Yes, cried like a goddamn baby. But there's a reason." I duck under a branch and push back another for her, using the other hand to guide her by the small of her back. She leans into the touch for a second before pulling away. It feels like a glimpse of what could be.

"Are you going to say the reason?" She chuckles.

"Yes, give me a second. It's nice to be dramatic, really make you feel the consuming passion when talking about this."

"Oh my God, just get on with it."

"You just sounded like Knox. *Just get on with it.* You make it hard to set the mood." I clear my throat. "From middle school on, I knew one thing: I wanted to play baseball professionally. I geared my entire life around accomplishing this goal. I would practice constantly, every day, sometimes twice a day. I worked out, lifted weights, ate healthy even as a teen. I never wanted to see that goal slip from my fingers, so I held on to it tight and worked toward it, always reminding myself when I was sore and tired and exhausted why I was doing it. I had a reason. I've held that goal, that feeling close to my heart, waiting for the moment for me to accomplish it and knowing the joy it brought me when I did. When I see someone else accomplish their dream, I know the long hours and dedication that got them there. There is no such thing as an easy ride for elite athletes. They feel the burn in every training session or they're doing it wrong. So, for me, it's like I feel their emotions in that moment and it hits me hard." *I clearly remember my own tears when I was called up. Nothing has ever compared to that, and probably nothing will.*

Dottie pauses to look up at me, wonderment in her eyes. "That's really sweet. You have a good heart, Jason."

"That's a wonderful compliment. Thank you, sweet cheeks."

I give her a quick side hug and then continue to move forward with our hike, a smile on my face.

"I really like your version of a hike snack. You could have brought some fruit, or trail mix, or a protein bar, but no, you went straight-up savage with nutrition and packed us puppy chow, Chips Ahoy, and chocolate-covered raisins. What happened to my carrot and guac girl?"

"Your girl?" she asks, nudging my shoulder.

"Yeah, you're sucked into my world now, which means I claim you."

"Fair enough." *Say what? Fair enough? Does that mean she thinks she's my girl too?* We chose a spot out on a giant boulder that over-looks the lake. It's serene, birds chirping in the background, and a few twigs snapping here and there, nothing that would cause alarm. "When I hike, I always end up famished and don't want anything healthy. I want the bad stuff. When I was young and went on hikes at Lake Skinner with my dad, we stopped at the local 7-Eleven and bought the worst junk food possible, things my mom never allowed at home. We'd park in front of the lake, pretend to fish, and eat our snacks. Then I started bringing Emory and Lindsay with me and it became a smorgasbord."

"You guys have been friends for a long time."

"Yes, they're my girls. We had a small falling out with Emory after high school, but we quickly made up for lost time. I can't see my life without them. They've really helped me through some tough times."

"Yeah? Like—" A low grumble followed by a twig snapping echoes behind us. Holding still, I ask Dottie, "What was that?" She doesn't move either.

"That wasn't your stomach?"

"I'm kind of wishing it was at this point." I swallow hard. "I think you should turn around and look."

"Me? You're the man," she says from the corner of her mouth.

"I'm also an equal opportunist."

"Just look."

"I'm too scared," I answer as another twig snaps, this one even closer.

"I thought you said your fists are—"

Snap, snap, snap.

"Oh . . . shit." I grip her hand, but not in the way I want to and slowly turn my head.

Standing about ten feet away is a black bear, sniffing his way to our snacks, having zero concern that there are two humans sitting like dead ducks in front of him.

"Oh Jesus. Oh God. Oh, I might shit myself," I cry hysterically.

At that moment, Dottie turns her head as well. She stifles a screech and then starts digging around her bag, pulling out the box cutter with a shaky hand.

"Wh-what do we do?" she asks, looking terrified, almost as terrified as me, while holding the box cutter the wrong way.

"Scream bloody murder?"

"What about what you said to my dad? If the bear is black, fight back?"

I sarcastically laugh. "Okay, that was a fun rhyme to spout off to your dad, but never once did I mean it." I slowly stand and pull Dottie up with me. I clutch her backpack in my hand like a metal shield, hold it out arm distance, and grasp her hand with mine, holding on tight.

"Are you gearing up to do something?" she asks, sounding panicked. "I feel like you're building up for an attack. Is that what you're doing? Jason, I need you to talk to me. Please don't do anything rash—"

"Ahhhhhhhhhhhh, ya ya ya ya, eeeeeeeeeee," I cry, my nerves so shocked by my high-pitched squeal, that I actually feel my penis crawl inside my balls, praying we don't get attacked by this enormously large, teeth-baring, sharply clawed beast of a bear. I charge forward, swinging the backpack back and forth like a death-wielding machete. *Holy shit. Holy shit. Holy shit.*

My vision tunnels in on itself as I make a beeline for safety. My legs move fast, hopping over logs, pushing past low-hanging branches with the backpack, all the while towing Dottie behind me. At some point, I'm moving so fast—my deathly cry still ringing in my ears—that I'm sure Dottie's flapping in the wind like a flag behind me, holding on for dear life.

It isn't until I can see the cabin—and I don't feel like the bear has followed us—that I slow down to a steady walk. Dottie lets go of my hand and pauses to bend at the waist, her hands falling to her thighs.

"Jesus Christ, Jason. What the hell was that?"

"That was called saving your life. Did you see the look in that beast's eyes? We were sitting ducks, his lunch. He was ready to bat around our bodies looking for the good meat. And trust me, my penis is good meat."

"The bear barely reached my hips. It wasn't big once we stood up. And it went scampering the other way the minute it heard your ear-piercing scream. You would have heard me telling you to stop if you'd turned down your vocal cords for one second."

I shake my head. "No way was he hip height. I saw him point at me and make a chomping sound with his jowls. We were his dinner."

"Bears don't point."

I thumb toward the woods. "That sadistic bastard back there did. Fucking singled me out. I had no choice but to save both of us with the sprint of our lives. Mind you, I'm incredibly slow, but I've never felt such wind below my feet before." I jump a few times, adrenaline pumping through me. "Did you see my moves back there?" I wield the backpack like nunchaku and do some fancy footwork and end it on a spin. "That bear had no idea what to do with itself."

"That bear ran off to get a hearing aid from your lady shriek." Dottie pulls on her ear. "Dogs for miles heard your screaming."

"More like war cry." I cross my arms over my chest.

"More like your balls crawled up inside of you to hit such a high octave."

More like balls shriveled up from pure terror.

"Are you saying you weren't impressed with my display of hero-ism? I was a goddamn white knight back there."

She looks back at me as she heads toward the cabin. "You were a petrified clown, but it was . . . cute."

She turns away, continuing to the cabin.

Cute?

I'll take cute. It's a start. At least, it will be once my heart rate returns to normal. *Fuck.*

CHAPTER SEVENTEEN

DOTTIE

Hours later, I still have Jason's high-pitched squeal stuck in my head. It's as if it's on replay, constantly playing over and over again, and every time I hear it, I chuckle.

His attack on the bear and attempt to get us out of there unscathed was one of the most comical things I've ever seen.

The flail of his arms.

The use of the backpack as a sword.

The ear-piercing sound of an adolescent screeching for their life.

It was almost too much to handle.

When we got back to the house, I went to my room and laughed for a good five minutes, then I took a nap, but even at that, I dreamt of Jason running and screaming through the woods, his hand firmly gripping mine.

I can still feel the imprint of his hand, the way it clutched tightly, the way his fingers easily looped around mine.

I can't remember the last time I held a man's hand. Even though he was doing it to be my hero against a three-foot bear cub

—yes, three feet, maybe—it still made me feel wild with excitement.

Now, we're about to make dinner and instead of feeling that excitement, I'm feeling nervous, really nervous. Being close to him, cutting things—yes, I'm really good at cheffing—and mixing things, I'm not sure I'll be able to hold it together. I've thought of at least twenty *beary* punny one-liners that I'm struggling to stop smiling about using. And I want . . . I want him to see me as more than a friend, but I'm not sure of the right time. *Is there such a thing?*

Before leaving my room, I take one last look at myself in the mirror. I chose a simple pair of leggings and a shirt that hangs off my right shoulder, showing off the strap of my bralette. I left my hair in a high ponytail to keep it away from the food. And even though it seemed like Jason liked my glasses, I leave my contacts in because I don't want to be fumbling around with glasses if we so happen to progress things further. That's positive thinking though, who knows what will happen tonight?

On a deep breath, I exit my room and walk into the main living space. That's where I spot Jason hunched over the counter, looking at his phone. When he hears me approach, he turns and his face lights up when he takes me in.

God, that's a look that will never get old.

"Hey, you look comfy."

"I am. Thanks."

He claps his hands together. "Are you ready for this?"

"As much as I can be." He takes me by the shoulders and directs me into the kitchen. Wearing nothing but a pair of jeans and a plain, dark green shirt, he looks amazing, especially with the no shoes and socks.

Barefoot and in the kitchen; doesn't get better than that. *What on earth am I thinking?* If he took off his shirt, it would get better. Not sure how I can make that happen . . .

"All right. I chose something easy for us to make, something that wouldn't be too hard for you to replicate."

I look at the ingredients, trying to decipher what it is. "Uhh, what are we making?"

"Gnocchi. I thought about making my homemade spaghetti sauce but figured that would be too much for you in one go, but we will be making our own garlic bread."

"You want to make pasta? Are you insane?"

He chuckles. "It's not as hard as you think. I already have the potatoes cooked and softened. We need to start shaving them down and then we can make the dough."

He brings a plate of potatoes over to the main island along with a cheese grater. "Do you expect me to do this?"

"It's not hard. Have you ever grated cheese?"

"No."

He sighs but laughs at the same time. "Okay, so we're at a real basic level then."

"If I can't microwave it, I can't do it."

"Good to know." Stepping up behind me, he wraps his arms around me and brings his hands to mine. His chest is flush against my back while his head hangs forward over my shoulder. God, he smells so good, and he feels so good. This is exactly what I wanted. This kind of close proximity. I just didn't think it was going to happen this fast.

Talking softly, he says, "Okay, hold the grater with this hand, and then move the potato up and down over those ridges, like this." He demonstrates and I nod, the whole time wishing we would stay in this position the whole night or at least a version of it. "Yeah, just like that. Good job, Dottie. You continue to shave down the potatoes while I measure out the rest of the ingredients."

He pulls away and I instantly feel like messing up so he can return to his previous position, arms wrapped around me, his scent filling the air around us. But I also don't want to look completely incompetent, so I continue to shred.

"Who taught you how to cook this meal?"

"My grandpa. He was the chef in the house. Owned his own

restaurant for quite some time. He would always tell me the best way to a woman's heart was knowing your way around the kitchen. We would spend hours cooking together. When I wasn't training."

"That's sweet. So is this one of his famous recipes?"

"Yeah, he was known for his pasta, which was funny since he's not Italian. He's Irish. Ireland gets a bad reputation for not having the best food. One of my grandpa's favorite things to say was he was an Irishman who knew how to cook better pasta than his Italian friends."

"I'm sure that chapped their asses."

He pauses, mid scoop with his flour. "Chapped their asses?" A low rumble of a laugh rolls through his chest, the sound positively delicious. "I've never heard that phrase before."

"Seriously? My dad says it all the time. He always asked me if I intended on chapping his ass whenever I did something wrong."

"Did you ever offer him up ChapStick? I could totally see you doing that, the smart-ass in you."

"Not ChapStick," I answer. "But petroleum jelly. I gave it to him the Christmas of my senior year in high school with a card that said, for all the times I chapped your ass."

"Oh, that's fucking perfect." Jason laughs some more. "Please tell me he loved it."

"I think it was the hardest I ever saw him laugh. Then he cried, of course, because I was going off to college. I assured him I'd still be able to chap his ass long distance . . . and I did."

"Oh, I'm sure you did."

I move on to the next potato, picking up my pace. "What about you, are you close with your parents?"

"Yup, my whole family actually. Natalie is my sister, she helps me run my foundation, The Lineup. She's actually the CEO, and I'm just the pretty face." He flashes me his best smile. Pretty face indeed. "And of course, Joseph, my twin brother who has cerebral palsy, is my best friend. We're really tight-knit, and I think it all stems from wanting to give Joseph the best life possible. Natalie and I became super protective of him and my parents encouraged it."

"That's really amazing. I admire that. Other people could have been resentful about having to take care of a sibling their whole life, catering to their daily activities, but you weren't. You embraced it."

Jason shrugs. "He's my brother. We shared a womb together. I would do anything for him."

He sets the measured-out ingredients to the side and props his hip on the counter, facing me.

"Can I tell you something?"

"Of course."

"You know how you said I was a sob baby?"

"Yes, how you cry about everything."

"Yup." He chuckles. "Well, the last time I full-on bawled was when I finally realized that Joseph would be able to go to all my games again. Well, at least all my home games. In my contract, I made a stipulation that he would have a permanent handicap seat dedicated to him and his guest so no matter what, he always had a seat at my game. When they said yes to it and made it happen, I lost it."

I finish up the last potato and then turn to Jason. Talk about one of the biggest hearts I've ever seen, ever met. Jason is the winner. He has a heart you don't see very often, one that's genuine, positive, and so addicting that all you want to do is be surrounded by it.

And I not only want to be surrounded by his heart and his personality, I want to be consumed by it, and quite frankly? That fucking terrifies me. I feel this pull within me, warning me about getting too close, not to trust his pretty façade, not to fall for possible hypocrisy. To deny my want. But then I consider how he stepped back when he believed he'd pushed me too far. How he squeezed himself into my life despite my often-bitchy charade, content to be my friend. Because what man does that voluntarily? It's not him that has a hidden agenda, although I know without a doubt now that it's not the stupid deal that's driving my actions. *My heart.* After being very anti-relationship, very cynical that men had something I wanted, my heart is being lured in. Jason Orson is hypnotic. And I'm not sure I can deny that for myself. *I want him to know how incredible I believe he is.*

I reach out and take his hand in mine. Staring into his eyes, I say with full conviction and not an ounce of sarcasm, "You are one of the best men I know."

"Thank you." He smiles sheepishly. "Uh, we kind of got off course. Want to continue with this gnocchi?"

"Of course." I pull my hand away and face the counter. Jason moves the ingredients closer and then stands behind me again, his chest to my back, his arms wrapped around me, his head next to mine.

Talking softly he says, "Okay, we're going to mix all these ingredients together with our hands." He takes mine in his and starts pouring the ingredients together directly onto the countertop. His lips practically kissing my ear, he continues, "Now we don't want to overmix, just enough, and then we form a hole, a little nest for our egg."

"Like this?" I ask, forming a "nest" like he said.

"Perfect," he answers, his breath sending goosebumps down my body. "Mix it all together until it's a dough-like consistency." Together, we mix, and mix, and mix. Clumps form on our fingers, then fall off in disgusting chunks, but I'm comforted from the closeness of Jason and the way he seems to not back away but rather keeps his body as close to mine as possible. "Clumping is the worst," he says, pulling at the dough clumps on my fingers. "But look, see how it's forming a good consistency?" He picks up a pinch of flour and dusts the countertop, making it less sticky.

Once the dough is formed, he says, "Here comes the fun part. We have to roll it out and cut it up."

He slides his dough-covered fingers up my forearms and spreads them out with a slight suggestion. He picks up a piece of dough and starts rolling it on the counter. Once it resembles a snake, he takes my hands and I roll with him.

"Isn't this fun?"

I turn to look at him, his body covering mine, his head inches from mine. "It's a lot of fun." Before I turn back to the gnocchi, I give myself a second to stare at him, to hopefully portray in my eyes how quickly he makes my heart beat, how with one flash of his grin, he lights me up inside.

I swipe my lips with my tongue and he watches, so I do it again, but slower this time, just letting the tip of my tongue peek out. His eyes follow, darkening, narrowing.

From behind, I can feel his chest grow tighter, thicker with his breath.

His arms tighten around me and for a split second, when he leans a few inches closer, I think he's going to kiss me, that he might actually want me. But before I can catch another breath, he clears his throat and steps away, leaving me cold and wanting.

Embarrassed, I go back to rolling while I hear him digging around in the drawers.

This is ridiculous. I've hit on men before. I've made the first move before. Hell, I've flashed men just to get them to take me to their room before. I'm no innocent. I've been around the block, and yet, for some reason, trying to make something happen with Jason seems next to impossible.

Is it because he's too good for me? Subconsciously, I don't think I deserve him?

Is it because if he lets me down, hurts me, I'll lose all faith in men?

Probably a combination of all three.

"Sorry," he says, coming back to the island. This time, he doesn't get behind me to help, but stands to my side. Well, if that isn't a clear-cut sign of disinterest, I don't know what is. After all, it's exactly what I did to him when we first met. *Probably gave him too many lessons in how to give the perfect cold shoulder.* Okay. "I was trying to find a knife." He sets it on the counter. "This one should do. Just start cutting the roll into one-inch chunks and then we'll set them to the side."

"Okay," I say, cutting up the long dough snake into the signature shape of gnocchi. "Hey, if I forget to say this later, after all is said and done, thank you for teaching me this. You really didn't have to."

"And you really didn't have to bring me here with you."

"It wouldn't have been the same without you." I give him a curt smile and then start chopping the dough again, him helping with every piece . . . but from far away.

Dinner was amazing, some of the best pasta I've ever eaten. Jason complained about the pasta sauce, wishing he made his own, but I said it was tasty and was very pleased with it.

Making gnocchi wasn't too hard. The tricky part was boiling the little pieces and then frying them right after. It took a lot of concentration and timing, but Jason was a huge help. And the garlic bread, there was no burning it. It came out a perfect golden brown and was crispy and buttery and so, so delicious. I may have had a few too many pieces.

After dinner, I cleaned up the kitchen and made Jason sit at the counter and talk to me while I did the dishes.

We talked about stupid things like our favorite places to eat in Chicago, who has the best deep-dish pizza, and what our favorite place to visit in the city is. We joked, teased each other, and we undoubtedly kept stealing glances. I would catch him looking at my butt and he would catch me scanning his chest and the way his muscles pulled against the fabric.

A thick air started to form between us, the desire in our eyes evident, or at least that's what I thought. Once the dishes were done, Jason retired to the couch and started reading a book.

That's where we are now, both on the couch, both with a book in our hand, but unlike him, who keeps flipping through his pages completely captivated by the Stephen King novel perched in his hands, I've read the same two sentences for the past thirty minutes. My concentration is shot and my nerves have unraveled.

Our legs are stretched out on the couch together, his in the front, mine in the back and the only light in the room is coming from the two side tables with tall lights on them. I have this pulsing itch to drop my book to the side and climb on top of his lap; it's so bold and vibrant in my head I can't think of anything else. All I can envision is the way he'd grab my hips and hold me still as I situated myself on top of him. I'd quickly remove my shirt with my bra following close behind. I'd show him with my hands how I like my tits to be played with, how I love for my nipples to be pinched. I'd encourage him to touch me, holding my breath the entire time . . .

"Mmm," I moan, just in time for my eyes to widen and notice that I said that out loud.

I look past my book to where Jason lifts his head to take me in. "Are you okay?"

"Mm-hmm, yup. Just uh, thinking about that dinner again, it was really good."

"It was." He smiles and goes back to reading.

Jesus.

Get it together, Dottie.

Focus on this book. This . . .

What the hell am I reading?

Jason shifts on the couch, his leg brushing against mine, the friction heating me from the tips of my toes to my core as an aching sensation starts to build between my legs.

It's been so long since I've been with a man, so long since I've had that sweet release only a talented guy can give.

Just looking at Jason, I know he'd be a good lover. Not just good, but exceptional. Probably world-altering. His caring demeanor would make him a giving lover, but the alpha side I've seen here and there persuades me that he wouldn't be polite in the bedroom.

His toe brushes against mine and I peek over my book to look at him, but all I can see is the book in front of his face. Damn it.

But then his foot rubs against mine.

One stroke.

Two.

Oh fuck . . . three. Every last nerve ending in my body is starting to tingle from the thought that this could be it, this is the open invitation I've been looking for, the—

"Holy shit." Jason sits straight up and lowers his book.

"What?" I ask, being knocked from my fantasies.

"This book, it's fucking scary."

"Oh." I chuckle. "Do you need me to hold you?"

"Yeah, I fucking do." He shifts on the couch so he leans against the back and he props his feet up on the coffee table in front of him, then he takes my arm and swings me around as well until I'm plastered against his side, his arm draped over my shoulder holding me tight. "There," he says, while letting out a deep breath. "Are you comfortable?"

No.

I'm horny.

And being next to you, this close, taking in your cologne and being wrapped up by your beefy arm, it's not helping my libido.

"Very comfortable, thanks."

"Are you liking your book?"

"Sure, yup. It's great," I answer, not knowing one thing about it.

"Good." He turns back to his book. The fire crackles in front of us, the mood set for romance, but there isn't one ounce of romance stirring in this cabin. Just gnocchi-making, high-fiving friends.

What would he do if I stole his book away from him, tossed it to the side, and straddled his lap? Welcome me? Stick his hand up my shirt? Motorboat me?

God, I'd love a good motorboating. Scruff rubbing back and

forth between my breasts, marring my skin with beard burn. What I wouldn't give for that right now.

I guess I can't be mad, because even though we don't have our tongues down each other's throats, at least he's holding me. I've never simply sat like this with a guy, enjoying the quiet, content in his arms. It makes me feel . . . safe. *Adored.* And that right there should be good enough for me.

Right?

$\sim$

"I'm tired," Jason says, startling me from staring at my page. "I'm going to bed."

He strokes my arm lightly with his fingers, once again skyrocketing my pulse.

"What about you? Are you going to stay up a little longer?"

I shake my head and lift myself out of his embrace, feeling incredibly hot all of a sudden. I stand from the couch and release the straps of the robe I'm wearing, revealing one of the silk night-gowns I brought with me.

Jason looks up at me, his eyes quickly traveling down my body before he clears his throat and stands as well.

"I'm going to bed."

"Yeah . . . me too," he says awkwardly, setting his book down on the coffee table. He grabs the back of his neck, looking me in the eyes for a brief second before his eyes travel down my body once again, taking longer to observe my breasts. I know my nipples are hard, I can feel them press against the silk of the fabric, and it's obvious Jason sees them too from the way he tries *not* to look at them.

Maybe I was going about this seduction thing entirely the wrong way.

I let my robe drop all the way off my arms and then toss it over the back of the couch. I run my hand over my chest and say, "I didn't realize how hot I was until just now. You're like a furnace."

"Yeah, it did get pretty hot in here, huh?" He pulls at his shirt, wafting air inside. "Should I put water on the fire?"

I shake my head. "It's just embers, and they'll die down soon."

"Yeah, okay." He glances at my breasts again.

I step forward and press my hand against his chest as one of the straps to my nightgown falls down my shoulder. His eyes travel with its descent and then find mine again.

"Thank you for tonight. For today, saving us from the bear, the dinner. It was a lot of fun."

"You're welcome," he says, his voice growing soft. He lifts his arm and with the slightest touch, he slowly brings the strap of my nightgown back up my shoulder and then he leaves his hand there, in the crook of my shoulder and neck. His thumb travels along my collarbone, back and forth, back and forth as he stares into my eyes. "You did a good job in the kitchen."

"You think?" I ask, stepping in a little closer, the moment intensifying, sparking with awareness.

"Yeah, I do. A few more lessons and you'll be inviting me over for dinner."

"You might be pushing your luck." I smile at him.

He smiles back.

And then we stare.

Our breaths heavy, our needs evident in our body language, in the grip we have on each other.

Just do it. Just lean down and kiss me. Please take away this ache I feel in my bones.

His thumb moves tantalizingly over my collarbone, slower, more deliberate.

His eyes burn with heat, quietly communicating.

His chest leans in, brushing against my hard nipples.

And when my hand climbs to his neck, he sucks in a sharp breath right before stepping away, putting a good two feet between us, and draining all the air from my lungs in defeat.

"Uh, yeah, bed. I'm going to go to bed." He walks backward and trips over a side table, falling flat on his ass.

Thunk.

The cabin floors shake from the massive male that just fell to the floor, the vibration rocking center.

He quickly scrambles up, pulling on the table for assistance, only for it to start to tip over, sending the table lamp careening to the floor with a crash.

"Shit," he mumbles, while gathering the lamp and its cord. Haphazardly he attempts to wrap the cord around the trunk of the lamp but fails miserably as the trunk is thin, and he has to wrap it multiple times. Finally he gives up, sets it on the table on its side, and then stands.

With a loud laugh, too loud of a laugh, like he's trying to use his laugh to erase the memory of him fumbling around from my memory, he claps his hands, points at me with playful finger guns, and then takes off without another word.

What the hell was that?

I'll tell you what it wasn't.

It wasn't a good-night kiss. Nor was it an invitation back to his room. Instead, his pride is probably bruised and his libido is shot from embarrassment. Perfect.

But what really is starting to *chap my ass*, is why he didn't kiss me in that moment. What held him back? I saw it in his eyes. I saw it in his body. So why the hesitation?

Maybe because he doesn't want to start anything with me.

I don't sleep well. My mind whirls with what I could have possibly done wrong. What could have turned him off. But the more I think about it, the more I know I did nothing wrong. I was clear in my intentions. I did everything but jump his bones . . . and he still turned away.

Which only means one thing: he's not interested.

I'm totally screwed with this deal.

And now I'm mad.

CHAPTER EIGHTEEN

JASON

"I need help," I whisper, keeping a look out for Dottie through the car window.

"Jesus . . . Christ," Knox says through the phone. "What now? I thought I told you to make a move."

"Yeah, well, I didn't initiate anything." *I was nervous.*

"Will you grow a goddamn pair? Fuck, man. It's not hard; say, 'Will you go out with me?' "

"But she's different. She's so cold, emotionless at times, and she's hard to read. And we had a moment last night."

"Yeah, please, tell me about this moment. I'm just waiting on pins and needles," Knox says sarcastically.

"You know, I could call Carson instead. I don't have to share my intimate life with you."

"I'd prefer it that way."

"Well, you're going to hear it, you insensitive prick," I seethe, ducking to keep my eye out the window, the phone pressed tightly against my ear. Fuck, the hours I spent listening to his whiny ass over Emory. Years' worth. Now it's my turn.

"Joy," he deadpans. "Okay, so the moment."

Even though he acts like this is painful, I know no matter what, Knox would be there for me. He's there for every one of us because he's always been the glue that held us together. The guy we all turned to. Our captain.

"We were about to go to bed and we had this odd embrace before we took off, not a hug, but more of a touching of sorts."

"You touched her boobs?"

"No."

"Her side boob?"

"No."

"Her ass?"

"No."

"Her . . . pussy?"

"No, for fuck's sake."

"Then where did you touch her?"

I take a deep breath and think back to how smooth her skin was, how beautiful it was to see her chest rise and fall with her breath so close. On a dreamy sigh, I answer, "Her collarbone."

Silence.

More silence.

"Did you hear me? I said collar—"

"I fucking heard you. You touched her collarbone, and you're acting like you had access to her nipples? What the fuck is wrong with you?"

I scoff. "You wouldn't know what romance was if it tapped at your dick and asked you to fuck it."

"That makes zero sense, and I'm two seconds from hanging up. So you touched her *collarbone*," he says in a girly voice. "And?"

"I was going in, man, I was prepping to kiss her but then, I froze. I fucking froze. I wasn't sure if she wanted me to kiss her or what, but when it came down to it, I put distance between us, stumbled over a goddamn table, and then ran away with my tail tucked between my legs." I drag my hand down my face. "What is wrong with me? She's so goddamn beautiful and funny, and a force, but when it comes to actually committing the last two inches, I can't seem to make it happen. I don't know, I really think I'm nervous."

"I can't handle you right now."

"That's not helpful. What do I do?" I whine.

"I don't know, maybe stop acting like a ball-less asshole and actually take what you want? Stop being all talk, and actually take some action."

Dottie takes that moment to appear from the gas station.

"Oh shit, I have to go."

"Don't call me until you've done something. We're back in two days, and you better be at least kissing by then."

He hangs up before I can reply. I stuff my phone in my pocket, look straight out the window with both my hands on the steering wheel, holding them at ten and two. The door opens and she takes a seat, going straight to her seatbelt to strap herself in.

This entire car ride has been uncomfortable. We haven't really spoken, we haven't played music, we've just sat there in silence. Every time I try to talk to her, she shuts me down quickly. I know how to read a room—or car for that matter—and she's pissed.

Yup, really fucking mad.

She's tense, she has a pinch in her brow, and she's curt with me. To say the water is icy over on her side is an understatement. So I've stayed far away.

I clear my throat. "Go pee?"

"Yeah."

"Did you wash your hands?"

Her head tilts to the side. "What kind of question is that?"

"A valid one. No one wants public restroom hands all over their car." Not the way to win her heart, saying she has piss hands, but then again, at least she's talking . . . right?

"I washed my hands, and I don't need reminding from you about it either."

"Sheesh," I say, pushing my luck. "Sorr—eee for asking." Because I'm curious, I ask, "Did they have the beef jerky I wanted?"

She glances at me and then lifts her bundled-up sweatshirt to the window and rests her head against it, closing her eyes immediately and shutting me out.

"I'm going to take that as a no."

~

W hat was supposed to be a relaxing weekend full of fresh air and the sounds of nature flittering in and out of my ears has turned into a tension-filled mess.

Car is parked. Bags have been removed from the back. And we're currently exiting the elevator to our respective apartments, Dottie leading the way in an almost all-out sprint.

Fine my me. I get to watch her ass jiggle in those leggings.

Might be the last time I get the chance after how uncomfortable things are between us.

I'm soaking up that jiggle as much as I can.

When we reach our doors, she's already unlocked hers and halfway in when I say, "Great weekend, thanks for the—"

Her door slams.

"—invite," I finish to myself. Well, that couldn't have gone any better.

I consider knocking on her door, asking her how I could make things better, but I'm pretty sure she wants to be alone right now and honestly, I think I would be a dead man walking if I knocked on her door.

Kicked in the crotch by her words no doubt.

Not in the mood, so I unlock my door and start to settle in my apartment. I leave my suitcase in the entryway because even though I might be quite the lady of the house, I can also be a slob occasionally and taking care of a suitcase is never the first thing I do when I get home.

Nope, I need comfort food.

I head straight to the kitchen where I pull out a beer, pop the top off, and take a long swig. Pretzel bites, Daddy needs some pretzel bites.

With queso.

I rummage through my freezer, grateful I have some, splash them on a baking sheet, and stick them in the oven. I then look through my pantry and spot an unopen jar of queso. Bingo, bango!

It might have been a shitty last twelve hours, but things are about to be in my favor.

When everything starts to heat up, I go to my TV and start scrolling through the On Demand movies.

GASP! *Isn't it Romantic* is available. I've heard great things about the rom-com starring Rebel Wilson and Adam Devine. Don't mind if I do.

Now I just need to get into my flannel jam-jams and this will be—

Knock. Knock.

Actually it was more of a *POUND. POUND.*

There is only one person who could make such a threatening sound with their fist, and I'm pretty sure they're a five-foot-six force of nature with black hair and clear blue eyes.

I stand there, in my living room, contemplating if I should answer in a high-pitched voice, "No one's here," or if I should answer.

I take a step forward toward the door.

POUND, POUND.

My balls hug each other, collectively protecting my unfertilized children.

Another step forward.

POUND, POUND.

My dick turtles in on itself, *un*circumcising its own length.

One more step.

POUND. POUND. POUND.

My nipples shrivel up into dust, leaving a note behind that says "You're on your own, buddy."

One last step.

POUND. POUND. POUND. POUND

My sphincter swallows in on itself, soldering my ass cheeks together, making it so there's no entrance or exit available.

Swallowing hard, I say, "N-no one's h-here," in my best ladylike voice.

"Open the goddamn door, Jason."

I yelp and leap back, feeling the hiss of her tongue lick the side of my neck through the door.

Demon possessed, it's the only way one could possibly make an entire body recoil with fear. If I wasn't so worried about her seeping through the crack under my door and attacking me with her serpent tongue, I'd slowly back away, but a slithering Dottie does not seem appealing, so I open the door to an irate woman, hand on her hip, irritation heavy in her eyes.

"Oh, hey, didn't know that was you."

She steps up, points her manicured finger at me and says, "Cut the crap, Jason."

I hold my hands up. "Whoa, whoa, whoa. Where's all this hostility coming from?"

She pokes my chest, her finger feeling like an ice pick trying to pierce my skin. "You know what it's from."

"Mind reading seems like one hell of a super power, unfortunately, I haven't been able to obtain such an anomaly."

And then, after that snarky comment, the top of her head pops right off, hair and all. Her eyebrows turn into flames, her eyes morph into green slits with a red ring of death around them, and her mouth hinges wide open, her canines turning into straight-up fangs.

Hissing and spitting, steam pouring from her ears, her fingers change into death-defying claws. In the matter of seconds, she transforms into a mythical creature that has yet to be discovered in the land of fantasy. A new species, one that's sole purpose is to destroy any and all men with the name Jason Orson.

World, it's been nice knowing you. Please remember me for the following:

Baseball's finest ass—firm and tight.

THE towel picture.

Perfectly proportioned balls to dick ratio.

Sensitive man-bear with an uppercut that can rip open a jaw.

And of course, the most important accomplishment of my entire life, the ability to razzle-dazzle my peers with a combination of mayo, dill, and potatoes. #BestDamnTatoSaladEver

Through clenched teeth, her jaw so tight, I can see every vein in her once elegant, now scaly neck, she seethes, "Why . . . didn't . . . you"—her jaw juts out, and I really am terrified for the next few words that take their time to form in her mouth—"kiss . . . ME . . . IN THE CABIN?" She enunciates every word with evil precision.

Why didn't I kiss her? Maybe because I knew secretly she had it within her to morph into the *thing* she is right now.

I gulp and bump into my doorway as I try to gain some distance, but it's useless because she follows me. At least when I die, I'll be in the comfort of my own dwelling. It's small miracles like this that make me feel at ease with my impending doom.

"Why didn't I kiss you? Well, I mean, you're just so lovely, and look at you—"

"Jason," she booms, her voice a combination of James Earl Jones and an unhinged woman on the verge of an all-out mental breakdown. I've never heard anything like it, let alone my name spoken with such baritone and hysteria at the same time.

Kind of wish I could make her say it again, just to study the pitch—

"Are you paying attention?"

"What? Of course. You want to know why I didn't kiss you. Well, you know"—I dig my hands in my pockets, backing up again—"it's kind of funny." Her eyes narrow and I swear, I might be delirious, but I swear I just saw her serpent tongue flash before me. "Uh, about the kissing. Well, there's kissing and then there's no kissing, you know?"

"What?"

"Man and woman, wow, what a combination. The things they

can do with their mouths. But also, man with man, woman with woman, man, man woman. Then there's woman, woman—"

"I swear to God—"

"You know." I tap her shoulder and she nearly bites my hand off. *Oh God, don't touch her, man.* "I was just going to say swearing to God could be offensive, but I think I'll keep that one to myself." I tap my temple, quick learner. "So, about the kissing. Yes, lips and mouths, they do those things you know. Quite a spectacle." I lean forward. "Have you ever kissed anyone?"

"Arghhh," she shouts, tossing her arms to the sky and charging back to her apartment, slamming my door in the process.

Well . . . that wasn't so bad after all.

~

J *ason: That conversation was weird, huh?*

Jason: *For what it's worth, you truly held your composure.*

Jason: *I wasn't frightened at all.*

Jason: *Okay, throwing down some honesty. I was a little frightened.*

Jason: *Just a little, nothing like pissing my pants or anything like that.*

Jason: *Did you know you have a pulsing vein in your forehead when you're angry?*

Jason: *I counted its pulse rate and I think you might have high blood pressure.*

Jason: *I'm not a nurse, I don't know about blood pressure, but CVS has one of those arm-pressure-checker things. Want me to take you? #WorriedAboutYourHealth*

Jason: *#PulsingVein*

Jason: *#SerpentTongue*

Jason: *^ Oh shit that was for Knox.*

Jason: *I wasn't saying you have a serpent tongue. I'm sure your tongue is normal. Not one ounce of evil in it.*

Jason: *Okay, I was talking about your tongue.*

Jason: *I feel like since you're not texting back I might be digging myself an even bigger hole than before. Am I right?*

Jason: *I'm going to take your silence as a yes, which in that case, you don't have a serpent tongue. Love that pulsing vein, and not once was I frightened. There. *Wipes forehead* Glad we cleared that up. Have a good night. #GodBless*

Jason: *P.S. Don't know why I said God bless, just go with it. #PrayerHands*

Jason: *P.S.S. I'm wearing my flannel jam-jams. I like when they ride up in my crack. #FeelsNice*

CHAPTER NINETEEN

DOTTIE

Sitting in a third grader's seat, my lunch spread out over a desk that belongs to Juniper apparently, I watch as one of my best friends laughs hysterically to the point of tears streaming down her face, her head buried in the desk across from mine, her shoulders shaking so hard and so fast that I'm afraid she might hurt herself.

I'm unamused.

So I sit back in the tiny chair, arms crossed, and wait for Lindsay to catch her breath.

It takes a while because every time she starts to talk, she lets out another roar of a laugh, denying her ability to talk through her hysterics. There's no point even trying to understand her so I reach out, dip a carrot into my guac, and chew.

And chew.

And chew.

"Enough, Lindsay, it's not that funny."

She waves her hand in front of her face, her other hand clutched to my phone. "Oh . . . my . . . God . . . I'm"—hiccup —"dying."

That's obvious; she didn't need to announce it to the empty classroom.

After last night's mental crisis—that's what I'm calling it now—I decided to have an emergency lunch with Lindsay to find out what I should do with the barrage of texts I received from Jason last night.

I was surprised to even get anything from him after his mumbling about mouths and lips and men and women. What the hell was that? For a minor second, I thought he was having a stroke but then realized, it's just him.

So far, coming here to ask Lindsay for advice has been pointless.

"If you're just going to sit there and laugh, I'm leaving. Hand me my phone."

She shakes her head and clutches the phone to her chest. "I need to screenshot these and send them to me." She laughs even harder, a tear slipping down her cheek. "Hashtag God bless."

"Fine, I'll just buy a new phone." I stand but she snags my hand.

"Pull the stick out, Dottie, and sit down." She tugs on me just enough that I'm forced to take a seat.

"Can you stop laughing? This is serious. I have no idea what to do. This guy is unlike anyone I've ever met. I don't know what to do with him."

She wipes her tears away and sobers up. "It's clear he doesn't know what to do with you either. So no reason why he didn't kiss you?"

"None." I sigh.

On the way home from the cabin, I was texting Lindsay, telling her everything that happened, well, everything that *didn't* happen. She was as confused as I was, and then when I filled her in on last night and showed her the texts, she lost it—clearly.

"It seems so"—she pauses, her mouth falling open—"oh my God, Dottie."

"What?" I ask, sitting a little taller. I know that look on Lindsay's face; that's the look of understanding.

"He's gay."

"What? No, he's not gay. Emory would have said something."

"Yes, he is. Why else would he recoil after being so close to you? Moments from kissing?"

"But I saw him staring at my breasts."

"Of course he did." She slides my phone to me. "He was probably curious since he usually sees man pecs all the time." She whispers, "He's gay, sweetie, which oh boy does that put a kink in your plans for dating him. Deeply and passionately in love, if he comes out, the Carltons are going to call bullshit."

"No." I shake my head. "He's not gay . . ."

Is he?

No . . .

But . . . no.

"He's not," I say, trying to convince myself even though Lindsay planted a seed of doubt.

She shrugs and takes a bite of her bologna sandwich. "Suit yourself, but he's gay." *What? She cannot be serious. Jason Orson . . . gay.* No, I can't go there, especially when I consider his words in the cabin, and how they turned me on more than anything else in my life.

"Your body heaves, your spine straightens and with one small flick of his tongue over your right breast, you tumble over into ecstasy . . . you're calling out his name, begging him to make it last longer." It was so hot. But . . . he had ample times to touch me, kiss me. I felt his body hard against my back. He leaned into my neck while helping me make gnocchi. I offered him my body. *But . . . he didn't kiss me. He didn't take what I offered him.* Hell, is he gay?

Huh, that would explain the obsession with his potato salad.

～

P lants are watered.
Sweats have replaced my pencil skirt.
And my hair is knotted on the top of my head.

On a deep breath, I push up my glasses and raise my hand, knocking twice on the door across from mine.

I told myself I wasn't going to do this. That I was going to drop the entire façade of trying to date Jason and get him to be in a relationship with me. It's become such a big mess, and honestly, is the Carlton account really worth it?

But then I got an update on the plans we've been mapping out for the acreage and hope and excitement bloomed inside of me.

So, here I am. At the threshold of Jason's apartment, with one question on my mind . . .

The door swings open, Jason's torso covered in a boring red apron. He's wearing a tank that shows off his sculpted shoulders, and on top of his head, he's wearing a white chef's hat.

Good God. *What on earth am I to do with this paradoxical man?*

"Dottie." He bows with a wooden spoon in his hand. "To what do I owe the pleasure?"

"Are you gay?" I don't even beat around the bush. I get right to the point because frankly, I'm just tired. Tired of it all.

He blinks a few times. "Gay? What do you mean? Like . . . happy?"

Jesus.

Christ.

"No, like gay. Do you like men?"

"They're the best kind of friends. Girls are good friends too, but I really only have guy friends. They're so chill and—"

"Do you like penis in your mouth?" I shout, wishing this man knew how to answer a simple question.

"Ohhh . . . I see what you're asking here. Am I *gay?*"

"Yes," I answer exasperated. "I didn't think I needed to spell it out any other way. Are you?"

"Gay?" He shakes his head. "No."

Well, that solves that. I spin on my heel and head back to my apartment, slamming the door behind me.

Back to square one.

~

"He's secretly married for a green card."

"Are you insane?" I ask Lindsay through the phone. "He's from Chicago."

"Or so you think he is. People will say pretty much anything to stay in the country. Bet you he has a green card marriage. Ask him."

"I'm not asking him," I say, biting on my bottom lip.

"Suit yourself."

~

Knock. Knock.

I tap the ground impatiently, my arms crossed over my chest.

He answers the door, still in his apron and white hat.

"Two visits in one night, how did I become so—"

"Do you have a green card marriage?"

He scratches his unshaven scruff with his wooden spoon. "Huh, not that I know of."

"Ugh," I groan, walking back to my apartment and slamming the door.

~

"He's a virgin."

"Will you stop?" I groan.

"It's the only other explanation. He stares at your boobs, rubs your collarbone, but when push comes to shove, he fumbles and stumbles away. Total virgin."

"Jason Orson is not a virgin."

~

K nock. *Knock.*
Tap, tap, tap.
Door unlocks, Jason appears. "I knew it was going to be you."
He smiles charmingly and asks, "Okay, I'm ready, what's your next
question?"

I hate him.

I really, really hate . . . hell, who am I kidding? There's no way I
could hate this man, no matter how hard I tried.

Succumbing to my last inquiry of the night, I ask, "Are you a
virgin?"

"Well, depends." I perk up, is he? "Some might consider me a
born-again virgin given my lack of sex life lately, but actual virgin,
no. Lost the V-card at fifteen to a lovely girl named Mindy. Poor
girl."

Yeah, I didn't think he was a virgin.

"Was that it? Anything else you want to know?"

I stare for a few seconds, at a complete loss. I could ask him
why he didn't kiss me, but it just seems like I'll never get the
answer at this point.

Maybe it's simple . . . maybe he just didn't want to and that's a
reality I'll have to face.

Feeling sad, I shake my head, turn to my apartment, and shut
the door behind me. It's official. I'm unwantable. *Is that even a
word?* The one thing I didn't believe when I was betrayed was that
I'd never know the true love of a man, that I was simply unwanted.
I hadn't doubted me. My self-confidence never took a hit with . . .
him, because I blamed their deceit on his own vapid and selfish
ways. But maybe, just maybe, I've been wrong. One of the best
straight men I know doesn't find me attractive. I'd been a game to
him initially, but once I showed interest, albeit ingenuine . . . kind

of . . . he backed off. Fuck. What a stupid, stupid night, I could have been—

Knock. Knock.

I slowly turn around and look through the peephole, not that I need to. I know who it is, but I look anyway.

I open the door and the minute he's fully in view—sans apron and hat—I catch the determination in his eyes as his large frame swoops into my apartment, snags my body, and presses me against the wall. His hands immediately grip my jaw and before I can give it a thought, his lips descend onto mine, claiming my mouth the way I've always dreamed of.

There's no humor in his kiss. No fumbling. It's as if this has been the kiss I've been waiting for my whole life, the one that would alter my world forever.

Shaking, I allow my hands to fall to his waist as I part my mouth for him. Desire rips through me when his tongue glides across mine and lightly explores. His grip powerful, his kisses soft, just what I would expect from this strong and sure man.

Giving myself freely to the surprise of his kiss, I allow myself to relax, to enjoy the moment as the determined hardness of his lips take control. Sweeping, exploring, tantalizing.

God . . .

It's everything. He's everything.

His mouth starts to slow, his lips press against mine, and then he gently covers my mouth before he pulls away.

Hands still griping my jaw, all I can see is determination. "I didn't kiss you in the cabin because I was a goddamn idiot. Forgive me, Dottie."

Lips stained with passion, I slowly bring my fingertips to them and nod, in shock.

"Good." He leans forward and presses a kiss to my forehead. "Have a good night."

With a parting smile, he departs my apartment leaving me unsatisfied, confused . . . but utterly happy.

CHAPTER TWENTY

DOTTIE

W hat's this? I've never seen this picture before.
I lean in closer to my computer, observing the treasure I've come across during my daily cyberstalking of the man who kissed me last night. Backward baseball hat, shirtless, bat in hand, him staring at the camera as his muscles ripple like a beast.

This picture is deliriously hot.

This one's being saved to my personal file.

Yup, that's right, Dorothy Domico, the power-suit princess, the ruthless boardroom ball-buster, has a file on her computer under the name "Eggplant" with pictures of Jason Orson. A variety of photos at that. Some shirtless, some not, some casual, some in a suit, and then of course, the picture of them all, the center of the collage, THE towel picture.

I'm in the midst of saving when there's a knock at my door. Hunched over, I quickly pop my head over my computer screen to see Jessica standing there with a smile. Must have had a good night's sleep, as her smile is rare.

"Miss Domico."

This time I don't fumble to close out of the screen, I just open up Outlook to cover up my obsession. "Yes, Jessica?"

"Two things. Madison in finance asked if you could push her meeting to tomorrow. She got a call from her son's school. He's throwing up and she needs to get him."

I cringe. Gross. Details I didn't need. "Yes, that's fine. Tell her to work from home for the next few days and we can do a conference call tomorrow same time."

"Will do. And you have a visitor."

"A visitor?" I ask, perking up.

Jessica smiles even wider, causing a wave of butterflies to erupt in my stomach. Is he visiting me at work?

I swear to God if this is Lindsay or my dad, I'm going to scream.

"Okay, send them in."

Jessica practically giggles on her way out my door and I stand from my desk, flatten my skirt out, and fold my hands together in front of me, then release, then fold, then—

A bouquet of flowers enters my office, red roses—red, *eep*—held by a very tall, very strong, and very beautiful man. My heart soars as I mentally thank Cupid himself for sending this man right now.

I spent the entire night reliving his kiss, letting my lips marvel in the feel of his mouth on mine, his possessive grip on my face, the way he was soft and rough all at the same time. Searing and passionate, it was the best kiss I've ever had.

And then he left.

I labored over why last night—why he just disappeared—and by two in the morning, I finally let my mind relax. *Maybe* it will come in time. *Maybe* this is the pace he likes. And then, as I recalled his words—"*I didn't kiss you in the cabin because I was a goddamn idiot. Forgive me, Dottie.*"—I fell asleep. *Yes, Jason Orson, I will forgive you.* I woke this morning with an extra pep in my step. It was incredible.

I curled my hair rather than put it up in a ponytail or bun, giving me a much softer appearance. And instead of a suit, I wore a pencil skirt, but paired it with an ice-blue blouse that has a deeper neckline than I normally wear at work. In the off chance I ran into Jason in the hallway, I wanted to make sure I looked how I felt . . . beautiful.

Unfortunately, I didn't meet him in the hallway, I didn't hear from him all morning, and when lunch rolled around with no surprise or text or call, I started to worry. Three o'clock hit, and I succumbed to filling my soul with pictures of him instead of the real thing.

So you can imagine how giddy and excited I feel right now with Jason standing in front of me, dressed casually in a pair of jeans and a black button-up shirt, holding a bouquet of flowers.

"I hope this is okay," he says, stepping forward. "I know you're busy with work, but I thought I'd stop by and give you these."

I move around my desk and meet him in the middle of my office. I gratefully take the flowers and give them a sniff.

"Of course, this is okay. Thank you."

And then we just stare at each other like two besotted idiots not knowing what to do next. We kissed last night, so do we kiss again? Do I hug him? Do I ask him to sit down?

Should I ask him out?

I'm so bad at this, so out of practice, and from the looks of it, so is Jason.

"Do you want to sit down?" I ask, gesturing to a chair.

He sticks his hands in his back pockets and shakes his head. "I can't. I'm off to another meeting but wanted to swing by your office this afternoon to give you these and to, uh"—he grips the back of his neck—"to see if you wanted to go out to dinner with me tonight?"

I can't contain the giant smile that pulls at my lips. "I would love that."

"Yeah?" he asks, almost looking surprised.

"Yeah."

"Awesome." He nods and backs away. "Cool, yeah, so uh, pick you up tonight? How about seven?"

"That works."

"Cool," he answers looking adorably awkward. He checks behind him and laughs. "Just want to make sure I don't stumble over any furniture again."

"Smart."

"Okay, I'll see you at seven. Bye, Dottie."

"Bye, Jason."

He shuts my door behind him and I sigh out loud while clutching the flowers to my chest. I have a date with Jason Orson. Maybe I'm not unwantable.

He likes me.

Jason Orson likes me.

Finally.

~

I'd like to say I knew exactly what to wear tonight and that I spent the last hour relaxing and making sure my legs were lotioned and as silky as possible, but that would be a lie.

A giant lie.

I got home from work late, leaving me forty-five minutes to get ready. During the drive home I had an idea what I was going to wear but when I put it on, it looked terrible. From there, it was like a tornado hit the bedroom. Nothing looked right, everything felt ill-fitting, or made me look washed out. There are clothes flung all over the room, and in this very moment, I wished I was at my place rather than Knox and Emory's. If I was in my apartment, I would have so many more options.

With five minutes left, I throw on a simple black dress that I normally wear a blazer with, slip on some pumps, put on a bright red lipstick, and call it a night. Thankfully my hair is still curled from this morning and my makeup is decent. I lotion quickly, spray some perfume, brush my teeth and just as I finish, a knock comes at the door.

Clutch in hand, I give myself one more look in the mirror. The dress really is flattering with its sweetheart neckline and tight-fitting bodice. I just wish I had some jewelry or something to pair it with.

It's fine, he won't notice.

I say that now but knowing Jason and how detail oriented—read *quirky*—he is, he'll make some offhand comment about not having the right accessories for my outfit.

Nervous and excited, I open the door and there's Jason on the other side looking beyond yummy. He makes jeans and a blazer look hot, especially when he's sporting that wicked smile of his.

"Damn, Dottie," he says, taking my hand in his and making me spin. "You look gorgeous."

A blush creep over my cheeks. "Thank you. You look very handsome yourself."

"Oh, I know. I took at least ten selfies in the mirror before coming over here."

He's so ridiculous, but I'm grateful for the lightheartedness, because it's felt like our last interactions have either been awkward or intense. I've missed this side of him, the fun side that I quickly started to become obsessed with.

"Ten seems excessive."

"Five were with my shirt unbuttoned."

The thought of Jason wearing his button-up and blazer with his jeans, but his shirt unbuttoned, staring into a mirror . . . good Lord, my legs tremble. I can see it, the ripple of his abs, the way his pants hang off his hips, only held up by his belt, the deep V in his sides.

I'm going to need to see those pictures and it must be written all over my face because Jason says, "Want me to send you one for the wallpaper of your phone?"

"Yes, I do." *Eager much?*

"Damn right," he says, snagging me by the waist and pulling me into his body. I shut the door and start to walk down the hallway but not before Jason tugs on me again, bringing me back into his reach. "Where's my kiss?"

"Who's to say you should get one right now? This is a date, after all."

"You're going to make me wait?" His brow lifts.

"Yeah, I am."

"I can respect that. At least give me a hug."

"That I can do." He pulls me in and wraps his strong arms around me. Being held by this man is slowly becoming one of my favorite things. Who knew I loved hugs so much? Or maybe it's just him.

"Thanks for saying yes to tonight," he whispers. "I was nervous as shit to ask you."

I pull away slightly so I can look him in the eyes. "I've been waiting, so I'm glad you asked."

"Waiting? For how long?"

"Does it matter?"

He nods. "Yup, I want to know how long I've been blowing this."

I stand on my toes and press a kiss to his jaw. "You haven't been blowing this at all."

"Do we need to review the texts from the other night?"

I chuckle and shake my head, placing my hand in his and walking toward the elevators.

"That won't be necessary . . . I already reviewed them with Lindsay."

"Come *on*." He laughs and hugs me at the same time. This is only the start of our date and I already feel like I'm at the capacity of happiness. Can it really get any better than this?

I t can.
It can get so much better.

Food in front of us, seated in a romantic booth, sitting across from each other, I can't stop laughing.

I laugh so hard that I almost choke on my food.

I cough a few times and down some water before laughing again.

Jason just told me a story from his freshman year in college, his initiation. Let's just say it required him dressing up in drag and trying to catch a chicken. You can fill in the rest. And because he's the best date ever, he brought visuals with him, meaning, I saw him dressed in drag and despite being super muscular, he made for a very beautiful lady. Who knew his pecs could double as breasts, or that he would look better in a mini skirt than I do? It's the ass . . . it made that skirt pop.

"I don't know if I'll ever get that visual out of my head, just so you know."

"Uh-oh, did I just ruin my chances at bedding you?"

I pause, my glass of water halfway to my mouth. "Bedding? Are you an eighty-year-old? You can say fucking."

"Bedding makes more of an impact." In an English accent, he says, "I'm going to bed you, you witty wench."

"You're really not if you call me wench."

"Have you or have you not been wench-like over the past week?"

"Excuse me?" I chuckle. "I have not been wenchy."

"Oh, you've been wenchy." He takes a bite of bread. "You've been really wenchy ever since I barged in on you trying to be romantic with a date. If a date is all you wanted, why didn't you take it to begin with?"

"Honestly, because I didn't think you were right for me despite having a crush on you." Yes, I told him. And was suitably embarrassed for my stupid revelation. Although, it was really cute watching his face once he knew I'd crushed on him at college.

"Right for you?" He grows serious. "Why?"

"Because, there have been men in my life who've been just like you, fun and sweet, made me laugh." I move my food around on my plate with my fork. "Very charismatic, but in the end, they were only trying to win me over because of my title, because of my family name, and because of what was in the bank. It had nothing to do with me and everything to do with the credit card I carried in my purse. You reminded me of those guys and learning from my mistakes, I decided to stay away."

"So why the change of heart?"

I bite my bottom lip, contemplating if I should tell him about the Carltons, and the stupid things I said to them to save a deal. The truth is on the tip of my tongue, but then again, I really don't want to ruin the night. It wasn't really the Carltons that changed my mind. Yes, they gave me the push to pursue him, but it was his personality I couldn't stay away from.

"You wore me down," I answer, giving him the half-truth. "Your kind gestures, your apology to *me* after I lost it on you during the night of the broken enchiladas. You apologized to me when it should have been the other way around. You've been patient and kind with my mood swings. You don't ever complain about my working late, but rather understand the hustle it takes to make something of yourself. Yes, your fun and outgoing attitude might have resembled those other men, but your character, your personality, your heart, they seem to be one of a kind. Plus"—I smile wickedly—"if you ever tried to screw me over, I know Knox would have a word with you."

"Yeah, he would have more than a word with me. By the way, have you told Emory about this?"

"No."

"Well, she probably knows."

"Why?" I ask, staring him down.

"You see, I might have gone to Knox for advice on how to handle you."

"How to handle me?" I ask, feeling slightly like a piece of meat.

He pacifies me with a pat to my hand. "Before you get in a tizzy, please consider what you just said, how you were hot and cold and weren't sure if you wanted to date me. I got that sense too, and I needed advice. Knox knows you better than Carson, so I leaned on him. He told me to take things slow and be cautious. Given his advice, I'd assume he told Emory about us."

"He's a gossip and thrives off it. Of course, he told Emory, which only means one thing . . . Lindsay and Emory are probably talking about us as well." Although, their radio silence is totally . . . not them. Hmm.

"Wow, isn't that special? So many people talking about the beautiful connection we have. Touches your heart, doesn't it?"

"Is that how this is going to be? Me being negative and you putting your Jason spin on it?"

"Doesn't have to be. I can be grouchy too, especially when I have to buy toilet paper."

"What?" I laugh. "Why does that make you grouchy?"

"Because there should be an endless supply coming from my wall. It's a life necessity and when it's not available to me, I get upset."

"I guess that's valid. Let me know when you run out of toilet paper so I can be positive that day."

"That's a fair deal."

∽

"I have some important questions to ask you," Jason says while we wait for our dessert. We ordered the molten chocolate lava cake. Jason's eyes lit up when he saw it on the menu, and I couldn't help thinking how adorable he was, getting excited over a chocolate dessert. He admitted once we ordered that other than ice cream, chocolate is one of his favorite things to indulge in. Any kind of chocolate. Doesn't matter how it comes to him, as long as there's chocolate in it, he'll eat it.

"Should I be scared?"

"I think you should get ready for quite an inquiry, but they're necessary questions that must be answered if I want to ask you out on a second date."

"What if I don't want to go on a second date?"

"Hmm." He taps his chin with his fork, ready to dig in the minute the plate arrives at our table. "That's a good point. All right. If the question arose, would you go on a second date with me?"

"Well, now I feel pressured to say yes just so I can hear the inquiry."

"You're going to have to deal with the pressure, sweet cheeks."

"Fine. Hypothetically, if you were to ask me out on a second date, I would hypothetically, possibly say yes."

"Great." He bops his own nose with his fork and then sets it down on the table. "Here goes." He looks serious; both his hands rest palm down on the table and his shoulders stiffen. Looking me dead in the eyes, he asks, "Bobbies and Rebels are in the World Series, what shirt do you wear?"

"Bobbies obviously."

He blinks. Sits back. "What?"

"Bobbies for life."

"But I'm on the Rebels."

"Yes, but are we dating, are we married? Are we just fooling around? There's going to have to be a huge commitment on my part in order to put a Rebels shirt on. Sorry."

"We're dating."

"Eh." I wave my hand.

"Fine. We're living together."

"Hmm, I don't know." I twist a strand of hair in my finger.

"Christ, we're married."

"Ugh." I wince. "I'm sorry, I just don't think it will ever happen."

"Not even if we're married, for fuck's sake?" he asks, dumbfounded. It's endearing, especially since he's pushing his hand through his hair in distress, tousling it.

"Do we have kids?" I ask.

"Six."

"Six?" Now it's time for my eyes to pop out of their sockets. "Do you really think I want to birth six children?"

"Hell, no." He shakes his head. "We adopted six kids from all around the world. We're going to have the most diverse and loving family you'll ever see."

Adopting six kids, now that's incredibly sweet. Or mad? No, it's sweet. In fact, it's extremely rare to meet a man who not only knows he wants to adopt kids, but is willing to look outside of the US, knowing how much he could offer that child. *Good God, this man is a unicorn.*

"We have the means for it, after all," he says, continuing. "You're taking over the city of Chicago, and I'll be raining home runs on every opposing team. We would be the power couple, the new king and queen of the city. *Excuse me, Oprah and Steadman, a new, hip couple is in town.* People would wear our faces on their shirts like the royals in England. We're the next Kate and William, the next Meghan and Harry. People will scream our name and then faint, only for us to give them mouth-to-mouth because even though we're super famous, we are also humanitarians."

"Wow." I sit back in my chair. "That's quite the picture you paint." I know what my mom will say about him already. *Don't lose him, Dorothy. He's gold. Gorgeous and selfless.*

"So . . . with all that said, our six children at your side, would you wear a Rebels shirt?"

I take some time to think about it, mulling over the idea of switching to black and red as my team colors. Could I do it?

With the way Jason is smiling at me, hope in his eyes, how could I ever deny him that joy—and I say that as if we've been married for ten years.

"I would wear halfsies. Half Bobbies, half Rebels, and that's the best I can do."

He lifts his finger to the sky. "I'll take it."

"**W**hat do you mean you've never been on a roller coaster?"

"Just never have been," I say, my hand looped through his as we walk through the park across from his apartment building. The night is chilly but Jason didn't want to head up to our apartments just yet, therefore I'm one of the luckiest girls alive as I'm wearing Jason's blazer.

Not only does it smell like heaven—like him—but its silk lining feels magnificent on my bare skin and it's warm, just like him.

Even though he's standing next to me, guiding me through the park, it still feels like by wearing his jacket, he's holding me. Not sure he's going to be able to get this back from me.

"But you grew up in Southern California, near Six Flags. You never visited the theme park?"

I shake my head. "Nope. Never went to Knott's Berry Farm either."

"Disneyland?" he asks, truly concerned.

"Obviously I went to Disneyland, but they don't really have roller coasters there, just mini ones, nothing like a drop that will make your stomach pop into your throat."

"True, okay. Well, we need to rectify this."

"What?" I shake my head. "No, that's okay. I'm good with never going on one."

"Nope, it's official, our second date will be at Six Flags Great America. We have to go during the week though, when everyone is in school. This Thursday, what do you say?"

"Are you insane? We are not—"

Jason stops us and spins me toward him where he grips my chin lightly and says, "Play hooky with me, Dottie. It will be fun. I won't even go for a run that morning. We can get up early, grab some donuts from Frankie Donuts, and then head over."

It's tempting, oh boy, it's tempting, but I have a huge meeting to prepare for that's taking place on Friday. I think about it for a second. If I spend the rest of this week focusing on the meeting and work Thursday night when we're done being kids, I could possibly fit it in . . .

"If you think about it, if we dated in college, going to Six Flags is something we totally would have done. But since you never came up to me, never made a move, we were deprived of that entertainment. Now we have to make up for lost time."

"Oh, you're really reaching now."

He rubs his thumb across my cheek. "Please, Dottie. Come scream your head off with me and eat tons and tons of junk food."

"When you put it like that, how could I possibly say no?"

"That a girl." He hooks his arm around my shoulder and kisses the side of my head. "Thursday it is. Should we wear matching shirts? Something that says, 'I'm with her. I'm with him' with arrows? Or we could wear shirts that say Future Mrs. and Mr."

"Now you're getting ahead of yourself. Matching shirts aren't necessary."

From the corner of my eye, I can see him bite down on his bottom lip, thinking, processing. "The more I put some thought into it, the more I truly believe we need matching shirts. Think of the endless photo opportunities."

"If you want me to skip work and go to Six Flags with you, we are not wearing matching shirts."

"That's what you think," he says with a smile.

Why do I feel like come Thursday, I'll be wearing the same damn shirt as Jason? Probably because it feels next to impossible to say no to this man, even when I'm trying to put my foot down. And yet somehow, I don't feel I'm losing control here. It feels . . . safe to allow him to take the lead. *Occasionally. I won't let him get too used to it.*

~

The elevator doors open and Jason unwraps his arms from around my waist. The entire ride up, he held me, my back to his chest. It was sweet and romantic, especially when he whispered in my ear how great I smell and how he loves my hair down.

Hand in hand, we walk down the hallway to our respective apartments and then stop at our doors. I shrug out of his jacket and hand it to him. He opens his apartment, tosses the jacket inside, and then turns back to me.

Sighing, he pushes a strand of hair out of my face. "God, you're fucking gorgeous."

I smile shyly, knowing his compliment is genuine, straight from the heart.

"I had a great time tonight. Thank you for asking me out."

"Was it everything you dreamed of?"

"Well, not everything," I say, licking my lips and letting him get the hint.

"Ah, I see what you're looking for, that kiss you denied me earlier. But I don't know now. I think I might want to save it."

Of course, he'd say that. I shouldn't expect anything less from him at this point.

So I shrug my shoulders and say, "Your loss."

I barely have a chance to turn around before he pulls me into his chest and captures my mouth with his. Light at first, he nibbles, testing the area, before he deepens the kiss, tightening his grip on my cheek while his other hand falls to the small of my back, pressing me into his hard body.

Desperation races through my veins as I light up from the inside out. I grip the back of his neck and pull myself closer, reaching up on my tiptoes to gain the best access possible. I open my mouth and swipe my tongue across his, pulling a groan deep from the pit of his chest.

Our breaths mix together, our limbs tangle, and our lips perform a seductive dance as we make out in the hallway.

He tastes so good, like cotton candy.

He feels like stone beneath my fingertips, strong and sturdy.

And the sounds he's making, the groans into my mouth, it's my undoing. I wrap a foot around his leg and pull him closer, needing more, wanting more, ready to disrobe right here, right now.

But before I can reach back for the zipper of my dress, Jason is separating us, putting much unwanted distance between us.

"Wh-what are you doing?"

He swipes his mouth, his chest rapidly rising and falling as he stares at me. "Fuck," he mutters, taking another step back. "Get in your apartment right now, Dottie."

"No, I don't want to. I want to make out some more. I want to—"

"Don't finish that sentence. We are done here. The date is over. Our date will not continue into extracurricular activities."

"Why the hell not?" I ask, hands on my hips.

"Because, after what you told me at dinner, how other men have taken from you, used you, I want you to be absolutely convinced that it's you I want. Make me prove myself to you, Dottie, because you deserve that. You deserve for this to be right." He lifts my hand, kisses the back of it, and then pushes through his apartment door. "Good night, sweet cheeks. Thanks for an amazing night."

I pout because . . . abs. I wanted to feel his abs. "You're making me sad."

"You will appreciate it in the morning, when you wake up wanting me even more." He winks and then shuts the door to his apartment, leaving me wanting him already.

CHAPTER TWENTY-ONE

JASON

"**W**elcome home, you beautiful, beautiful man," I shout, pressing a kiss directly on Knox's lips, who then in return punches me in the gut—well, barely punches me because I've gotten smart now and move away before he can make direct contact.

"What the fuck did I tell you about doing that?" Knox says, wiping his mouth with the back of his hand.

Emory laughs next to him and like one big happy family, we all enter their apartment.

I've been waiting all afternoon for these guys to return. Not only do I want to hear about their trip, but I need to tell them about the most recent development in my life.

I need to show them how there are floating hearts orbiting my head.

I need to gush and gab about the romance that's taken over every thought of my day.

Heart eyes.

Cupid arrow in my butt.

Call me a goner, because I'm in *like*.

Yes, like, not love quite yet, but I can see myself getting there.

The excitement is bursting out of me and before they can set their bags down and get settled, I let it out. "I'm going to be a father," I say, spreading my arms wide, chest heaving, eyes wildly open like saucers.

Knox pauses and spins toward me. "What the fuck are you talking about?" He gives me the *lowered brows consternation* look. It's pretty impressive really. "Please for the love of God tell me you didn't get some random girl knocked up."

"What? No. Why would you think that?"

With confusion in her brow, Emory says, "Because you said you're going to be a father."

"Yeah, someday." I walk over to their kitchen and pick an apple from their fruit bowl. I take a bite and lean against the counter. "How was your trip?"

Knox shakes his head, confusion clear in his eyes. "No, explain to us what the fuck you're talking about. What do you mean you're going to be a father? Is this one of those things where you think you're going to help parent our baby? Where you turn this into a sitcom in your head? Two men, a lady, and a baby?"

"No, but fuck, I'd watch that show so hard." I tap my wrist where a watch would be. "Come on, Netflix, let's get a move on it." I take another bite of my apple. "So . . . come on, what did your parents say?"

Emory takes a step forward, placing her hand on my forearm. "Jason, are you okay? You seem a little crazed."

"Crazed? I'm not crazed. I'm just . . ." God, I can't hold it in any further. "I'm in like!" I shout right before taking another bite of my apple. "I'm in like and I want everyone to know about it. This is only the beginning. Next, I'm going to be a father. Can you see it, little Orson babies running around, all from different countries, all proud to have a dad with the finest ass in baseball?"

Emory and Knox both stare at me, blankly, unmoving.

I snap my finger at them. "Are you two okay?"

"Are *you* okay?" Knox asks. "Dude, you're fucking losing it.

What the hell are you talking about? Does this have to do with Dottie?"

"Ohhh." Emory nods her head. "That makes sense. Uh, did something happen between you two?" She clasps her hands together.

"Oh, something happened. We had a date last night and it was fantastic. She's so cool and smart and then at the drop of a hat, her asshole closes up and she becomes the most uptight person I've ever seen. I love it."

"You love how she's uptight?" Knox asks.

"Oh yeah, gets me hot. Love seeing her in a tizzy. Or when she sticks her nose in the air, when something I say is completely beneath her . . . makes me want to say it all over again."

"Seems like Dottie's worst nightmare," Knox says, walking to the kitchen and filling two cups of water for him and Emory.

"Oh yeah, I'm pretty sure there are times where her fist itches to give me a fat lip with some of my antics, but then I just flash her my winning smile and all is forgiven."

"I doubt that's the case," Knox mumbles and takes Emory by the hand to sit on the couch. I follow closely behind. "Are you two dating now?"

"Yup," I say with finality. "We're a couple, so I'm sorry to inform you but your title of cutest couple is about to be stolen."

"You think we're cuter than Milly and Carson?" Emory asks.

"Of course. No competition. Milly is gorgeous but Carson is bringing down the team. I surpass them without even having a girlfriend, hell, if I were coupled up with my nightstand, I'd be a better couple."

"I'll be sure to spread the news on to Carson." Knox laughs to himself.

"Not the best idea, you know how sensitive he is."

"I think you're referring to yourself," Knox points out.

I chuckle. "True, I'm very sensitive and if he finds out and comes after my ass, I won't recover easily, which means I'll be over here at your place, begging you to nurse me back to health so my lady friend doesn't have to see me in such a weak state."

Knox scratches the side of his jaw and says, "Have I ever told you how much I really don't like you?"

"Almost every day." I wink at him.

"What does this all mean? Can we go on double dates?" Emory asks with excitement.

"I would LOVE that," I say just as there's a knock at the door. Knox gets up to welcome their visitor while I lean over the armchair and say to Emory, "We can take one of those couples cooking classes I hear people raving about."

"Yes, that would be so much—"

"Look who it is," Knox announces to the room as Dottie steps into view, and fuck, does she look good. She's wearing a tight red dress, nude heels, and her hair is pulled up into a well-polished bun on the top of her head.

Dottie smiles at Emory but when she sees me, her smile falters. I know why. She's probably wondering what I've said to our friends.

"There she is," I say, standing and walking to her. "You're out of work early."

"I . . . I'm going back—" I plant a giant kiss on her lips and when she doesn't kiss back, I grip the small of her back and plaster her against my chest. I lightly part her lips with my tongue and before I know it, her mouth opens to me and I give her a gentle, sweet kiss, loving the way she melts into my body. Fuck, I love kissing this woman.

Whispering, I say, "You look amazing."

"Thank you," she whispers back as Emory claps her hands and comes up to the both of us.

"Oh my God, this is so exciting. Look at you two. You're so cute."

"See, told you," I say to Knox, elbowing him in the stomach. We are cute.

~

After Dottie dropped the keys off and gave Emory a rundown on the plants, I snagged her by the hand and pulled her into my apartment.

"I have to get back to work if I'm going to go to the amusement park with you tomorrow."

"That's fine, just let me have a second with you."

She bites her bottom lip and the usual hard tone of her voice disappears when she says, "Okay. Just a second."

Smiling, I bring her to my living room where we both take a seat on my couch.

"What did you tell them?" Dottie asks, sitting next to me but keeping a distance.

"Just that you're my girl, that we're dating, and that I'm in like."

"In like?"

"Yeah, the stage before love. I also might have announced something about babies but that's neither here nor there."

"I really think you need help."

I chuckle and entwine our hands together. "Probably. So, you're going back to the office? Probably for the best, as I have to hit the cages this afternoon. One of the pitchers wants to meet with me, get to know me, maybe toss a ball around a little."

"Are you nervous about being on a new team?"

"Nah, I'm excited. Tampa was awesome, but Chicago is home. Even if I'm playing for the Rebels, I know they're a great group of guys and we have some amazing prospects in the farm system. I feel good about it."

"You're so positive, all the time. It's infectious."

"Yeah?" I tip her chin with my finger. "Find yourself smiling more often?"

"Maybe a little."

With the sun shining through my floor-to-ceiling windows, playing with the light and shadow on Dottie's beautiful face, I know these are moments I'll appreciate with her, where she drops her impenetrable shield and becomes vulnerable. She allows herself to enjoy the moment, to feel, to experience.

She isn't guarded, she isn't trying to put on a strong face, instead she's sitting here with me, hand in hand, taking a second to breathe.

"Kind of wish I didn't have to go to work."

"I know, but it will be worth it tomorrow." I tug on her hand, forcing her to fall into my chest. Her free hand lands on my pec and I lift her chin just enough that we're a breath away from connecting.

And I wait.

I don't close the distance. No, I wait for her to do it, giving her the green light to make the final move.

There isn't much waiting because she dives in, her mouth connecting with mine, her hand sliding up my chest to my neck where her fingers play with the short strands of my hair.

She shifts and I bring her closer with my hand directly on her ass, gripping the round globe just tight enough to let her know I will own her in the bedroom.

"God, I want you," she says, moving her lips to my cheek, to my jaw. "I want you so bad, Jason."

I suck in a harsh breath when she moves to my ear and plays with my lobe. "Don't you want me?"

"More than you'll ever know," I admit, getting lost in her touch. "But you have work, and I have batting practice. Our first time is going to be an all-night event."

She huffs in disappointment and pushes off me. That was painful. It's even more painful watching her stand and pressing her hand to her forehead as if she can't believe I'm actually turning her down . . . again.

I can't believe it either, but I meant what I said, I want a night with her, an entire night.

"I'm sor—"

Dottie faces me and from her side, slowly unzips her dress until it's a puddle of fabric on the floor. Standing before me in nothing but a matching black lace thong and bra is the most absurdly sexy woman. "Dottie . . ."

She lifts her heel-covered foot and presses it against my chest, forcing me to lean back into the couch and before I can protest, she works her hands to my thighs, slowly climbing with deep pressure until she reaches the button and fly of my pants.

"I want you too."

She undoes the button.

"Like really fucking bad."

There goes the zipper.

"But shouldn't we . . . oh fuck." My head falls to the back of the couch as she pulls my rock-hard cock out of my briefs and jeans. She shimmies my pants down along with my briefs with little help from me, and then grips my cock.

A look of awe and nerves scatter through her expression as she pumps my length up and down.

"Hey, Dottie, that feels— Ahhh fuck, that feels good," I say when she rubs her thumb over the head, playing with the tip. Jesus fuck, I nearly fly out of my jeans from the sensation. Just as I start to get comfortable, she stands up and straddles my legs before sitting down on my lap. She reaches behind her and undoes her bra, letting it fall to the ground with her dress.

There is no stopping me now, not when I get sight of the most perfect pair of breasts I've ever seen in my goddamn life.

Holy shit, Dottie.

Round and plump with dark nipples, they sway and bounce with her every move, perfect for her body size. I reach up and cup one, feeling the weight in my palm before I cup the other. She brings her thong-clad center to my dick and then leans back, placing her hands on my thighs.

And then, she rocks her hips and I just about blackout from the sensation, from the position, from the feel of her in my hands, from just how wet she is through her underwear.

"Shit," I grunt, taking hold of her hips and giving her a better angle on my cock.

She must like it because her mouth falls open, a silent moan floating into the air. Her hands grip tighter on my thighs as she undulates with my help. Up and down, up and down, the friction building and building between us, the heat in the room skyrocketing, this moment branded on my brain.

"Right there, right there," she says, her stomach hollowing out, her hips rocking faster. "Yes, Jason. Oh my God, yes." Her chest lifts. I hold her up with one hand while I keep pressing down on her hips, intensifying the experience for both of us. "Oh . . . fuck," she groans just as her pleasure takes over. I watch as she falls into bliss . . . from riding my cock. God, she's incredible. I love that she took exactly what she wanted, however she wanted. So fucking hot.

"Shit, that was—" Her hand falls to my erection and she starts pumping feverishly, her hold so tight that I need to focus on how to breathe as air escapes my lungs at a rapid succession.

Her breasts rest against my legs, and I wish I was free of my pants to feel her hard nipples rubbing against my skin. Not strong enough to even consider taking my pants all the way off, I go for the next best thing. I reach out and cup her breast, passing my thumb over her nipple. Hard, like a pebble, I relish in the contradiction between her soft breast to her erect nipple, the feeling so erotic I can already feel my impending orgasm.

It begins with her stroke, the tight hold she has on me.

It continues with the little passes of her tongue over the head of my cock. Flicks that travel around in a circle and then focus on the underneath.

She looks up at me with so much lust that it breaks my self-control.

And it all tumbles down when she reaches down and squeezes the base of my cock while her mouth takes me all the way in.

Fuck. I'm gone.

Like an out-of-body experience, I feel myself floating off the couch, the rest of my apartment turning black, leaving just me and Dottie, together, her swallowing my dick so hard, so fast, that I squeeze her shoulder. The voice that falls past my lips sounds nothing like me, as it's almost a squeak.

"Going to come."

She pops her mouth off my dick just long enough to say, "Good," before lowering her head again.

There's nothing to grip as pressure builds at the base of my spine. No hair to hold on to, no shirt. Fuck this couch and its sturdy fabric. I reach behind me, hold the edge of the couch, and as she sucks me one last time, hard and long, I come.

I come like a goddamn king, ferociously, and with a long groan so I don't realize Dottie is climbing back on top of me until her lips are passing over mine.

"I have to go."

"Wh-what?" I say breathlessly, unsure if I can even lift my head, let alone help her dress. "Just stay for a second."

"Can't. I have a lot to do."

I watch like a chump, sitting back on the couch, dick lying against my stomach, still reeling from what just happened as she dresses.

"You can't just leave me like this."

She laughs and slips her dress over her head. "I think I can. I don't predict you'll be getting up in the near future." She has that right. She zips up her dress and pats at her hair, not a strand out of place. "Thank you . . . for this."

"Uh, why are you thanking me? I don't think I did anything."

"You did more than you think." Her cheeks redden when she lowers to my lap and sits across it. Her hands fall to my chest as she places a soft kiss against my lips. "I will say this. I'm going to text Jessica, my assistant, because I don't think I have any Chap-Stick at the office and I'm going to need some."

"Ah, now I can do something for you." I reach into my pocket of my loose pants lying mid-thigh and hand her my Carmex. "Here, take it with you."

"Thank you." She pops off the cap and smooths the balm over the corners of her mouth, wincing for a second.

"Hey, you okay?"

She nods and puts the cap back on. "You were just a lot bigger than I've, uh, ever seen."

"Oh." I chuckle. "Sorry," I say awkwardly, not that I can change my dick size or anything.

"Don't be sorry. Just need to get used to it is all." She plays with the collar of my shirt. "I can't wait to have you inside me, especially after having you in my mouth."

Jesus Christ. This woman is like a gift sent from above.

"Keep saying things like that and you're never getting out of here."

With one more kiss and a pat to my chest, she lifts off my lap and heads for the door to my apartment. "I'll text you later. Can't wait for tomorrow."

"Can't wait either. Bye, sweet cheeks."

She waves her fingers at me and is out the door, leaving me spent with my dick and balls out. I think I might have to cancel batting practice. She just sucked all the energy out of me. Literally and figuratively. *Shit. How did I get so fucking lucky?*

~

Dottie: *I miss being across the hall from you.*
    Jason: *Words I never thought you'd say.*
    Dottie: *I know, I surprised myself, but despite your annoying tendencies and non-stop chattering, I miss it.*
    Jason: *You're making my heart soar like a fucking falcon. A goddamn FALCON, Dottie.*
    Dottie: *Falcon. That's pretty serious. Do you know what would have been more serious? An albatross.*
    Jason: *Pfft, no way. They might have a ten-foot wingspan, but they're seabirds, so they shit in the ocean. Where's the fun in that?*
    Dottie: *As opposed to . . .*
    Jason: *Shitting on people's heads, of course. If I was a bird, that would be my main purpose in life, shitting on unsuspecting people's heads. Think*

about it, being targeted by a bird bowel movement is detrimental as a human being. You're just going about your normal business when all of a sudden, WHACK, white goop drips from your forehead down your cheek. What is that, you think? You carefully touch it, your fingers immediately wet with semi-warm liquid. And when you realize it's an anal secretion from a flying vertebrate, all hell breaks loose. The horror! The disgust! The SHAME OF BEING SHIT ON. There's no coming back from that. #DayRuined And as the maniacal bird, there you are, floating around in the peaceful skies, watching idiot humans running around in circles, *trying to get rid of the poo-poo. With one flip of the feather—or the bird, hey-o—you're off to the bird feeder, filling up so you can drop turd once again. A vicious cycle of humans feeding birds only to get shit on unsuspectedly, I AM HERE FOR THAT!*

Dottie: *I was wrong. I don't have to be across the hall to be annoyed by you.*

CHAPTER TWENTY-TWO

DOTTIE

"**I**f you didn't want to bring attention to yourself, you shouldn't have forced me to wear matching shirts," I say as Jason ducks under a plain baseball hat and sunglasses. He's been spotted once already by a fan. He was very kind, signed the boy's shirt, took a picture, and then went on his way. But now he's hunkering behind me, trying to hide. Which is ridiculous, since he's six two with a chest the size of two of my bodies put together. There's no hiding him.

And then the matching shirts. I should have known he was serious. When he picked me up this morning, he handed me a neon-yellow shirt that says "His muscles are mine." That's when he unzipped his sweatshirt and puffed his chest with pride. His shirt of course said "Her nips are for my (finger) tips."

Mortified doesn't adequately describe how I've felt while walking around the amusement park, noticing people squinting to read our shirts . . . but needing sunglasses to avoid the glare.

But after a few laughs *and* many sneers from uppity parents, I'm feeling a little more comfortable.

"I guess I didn't think it was going to be this hard to go out."

He brings his arm around my shoulders. "I'm sorry, you must be sick of people stopping us."

"You didn't think it was going to be a big deal? Jason, you're a professional baseball player born and bred in Chicago. You went to Brentwood, so people have been following your career. Of course they're going to recognize you. Just because you played for Tampa doesn't mean they forgot about you, especially since you're back in Chicago, playing for the home team."

"One of the home teams." He lets out a deep breath. "That makes me feel a little better. To be honest, I was feeling a little apprehensive about winning over the city of Chicago again. I grew up a Bobbies fan, they all know that, so are they really going to accept me as a Rebel?"

We're walking along a path to one of the giant roller coasters Jason has been ecstatic to take me on. He wanted to start big—no working me into it—straight to the big guys.

I've been stalling by peering into the little shops, but he's done. He announced it was time, so now I'm walking as slowly as possible.

"You're worried if you're going to be accepted as a Rebel?" I laugh. "I didn't grow up here, but I've lived here long enough to know how serious baseball fans are. When they announced you were traded to the Rebels, every Bobbies fan out there wept themselves to sleep. Word around the street was, they wanted you to replace Walker."

"Oh, come on," Jason grumbles with an obvious eye-roll. "Walker is one hell of a catcher. He had the second-best batting average on the team last year too."

"But he has the worst attitude in baseball. Fans don't like that."

"Lady fans don't," he counters. "Men love it."

"Not true." I shake my head as we get in line for the death-defying roller coaster I can't seem to get myself to look at. I'd rather go in blind. "There are a few men at work who don't like Walker Rockwell. They think he's an asshole on the field and not a team player."

"He hasn't been painted in a good light, but he's actually a really nice guy. A quiet one, but nice."

"Do you know him well?"

"I'm working with him on my charity. His sister passed, not sure how, but she had some disabilities. I knew he was the guy I wanted to pair up with. Plus, I know his reputation is shitty and thought it could help him. Bringing the two catchers for Chicago together. It's going to be awesome. We have a celebrity softball game planned to include kids with disabilities in the area along with some of the biggest names in baseball. It's going to be the first weekend in December at the Rebels stadium, my first game there."

"Wow," I say, taken aback by what a great idea the celebrity softball game is. But not only that. Jason is just . . . so damn impressive. First, who looks out so honestly for kids with disabilities? But also, who thinks about trying to elevate a rival team member whose exit could pave the way for his own succession to the team he's loved forever? It's just ridiculous how generous and . . . selfless . . . this man is. I'm astonished. "That's a great idea. I'm floored by your attitude toward Rockwell, but it's an amazing concept on all fronts. Are you selling tickets to the game?"

"Yeah." We move forward in the line. "One of the stipulations about my trade to the Rebels was their support of The Lineup. They've kept their promise and have truly helped me put everything together. Natalie, my sister, has been in talks with them as well, organizing the local side, getting kids from around the area to participate and apply. It's going to be a pretty big event. We have some sponsors—"

"I'd like to be one," I say, not even having to think about it. "I'd love to be a silent sponsor, anything you need."

"Dottie." He smiles softly. "You already donated ten thousand dollars. That's more than enough." Leaning in, he places a sweet kiss to my forehead. "Don't forget, your donation or *accidental* donation is what brought us together."

"That was from me. I want this to be from the company."

"I mean, I'm not going to deny the kids more money for equipment, but you don't have to. I didn't tell you about the event to look for a donation."

"I know you would never do that." I see where he's going with this, cautious with my past and previous guys using me and my family. He has his arm around me, so I do the same, bringing my arm around his trim waist. I look up at him and say, "You're different, Jason. I know this. You wouldn't hurt me, you wouldn't use me. You're a genuine human being and because of that, I want to support The Lineup. Please."

He chuckles and cups my cheek. "How the fuck can I say no to that?" He bends down and places a sensual kiss to my lips just as an attendant asks us how many people in our party.

I hold up two fingers and say, "Two."

"Lane one," the college looking student says in a monotone voice, not at all happy to be at work today, especially while wearing one of the most ridiculous outfits I've ever seen. Why do amusement parks torture their employees with ill-fitting, retro-looking outfits? They're supposed to be happy, so give them something to wear to be happy in.

Together, we make it to lane one as the car pulls up. I glance at the seats and then back at Jason. "What the hell is that?"

"That's the X-Flight. The first wing coaster in North America. It's supposed to feel like you're sitting on the wing of an airplane," Jason says with pure excitement.

"But . . . we're hanging off the track."

"Which makes it fun. Come on, Dottie, you're not scared, are you?"

"Yeah, I am."

"Ma'am, you either need to get on or move to the other side and wait for your partner," one of the ride attendants says, annoyed.

Jason holds his hand out. "Don't go weak on me now, Domico."

Damn it, when he looks at me like that, assuring me with his kind eyes that he'd never let anything happen to me, I find myself getting strapped into a roller coaster and praying to the heavens above that everything is going to be okay.

~

"It's okay. Shh, yup, just let it out." I rub Jason's back as he hovers over a trash can, barfing his breakfast inside the canister as onlookers pass by. "Bad hot dog," I say to a couple who are staring us down. "He's not at all suffering from motion sickness. He's a tough guy."

"Fuck," he mumbles and sighs.

X-Flight was AMAZING. And since there hasn't really been any lines, we went on it three times in a row and then hit up Goliath, the largest wooden roller coaster, then Batman, and then Vertical Velocity, which was Jason's undoing. He was looking green around Batman, but he swore he was okay and when we were waiting for Vertical Velocity, he looked pale. I told him we should probably get something to drink and take a break, but being the "macho man" he is, he swore he was okay.

Guess what? He wasn't.

It's been ten minutes and we haven't moved from this trash can. Thankfully it's in an alcove, tucked away so we aren't dead center in the middle of the park for all viewing eyes.

"How are you doing? Do you want me to get you water?"

"No. Stay with me. I might need your breasts to rest upon."

"I want you to get better, but that's not happening in public."

He takes a deep breath and then lifts up, holding on to the trash can for support. I grip his side, letting him know that I'm here for him. My breasts can be there for him later.

"You okay?" I ask, loving how vulnerable he is right now and not even caring to hide it.

He nods. "Much better. Man, those donuts must have been off to bring on this bout of food poisoning."

"Yup." I chuckle. "It was totally the donuts. It wasn't the twisty turny—"

He brings his hand to his mouth and shakes his head. "Don't mention them. Please, for the love of God, don't mention them."

"Oh, Jason." I wrap my arms around him and rest my head on his chest. He immediately returns the embrace and sinks into it, resting his cheek on top of my head. "You're too cute. Seriously, sometimes you are too adorable."

"Adorable but sexy, right?"

"Really sexy."

"Even if I'm barfing in a trash can because Big Daddy Boo-Boo Bear can't handle roller coasters anymore?"

"Even if you call yourself Big Daddy Boo-Boo Bear."

"That means a lot to me." He squeezes me and says, "Maybe we should go play some carnival games."

"Oh, are you going to show off your ability to win me a giant stuffed animal?"

"Normally, I'd puff my chest and say, 'Yes, watch how amazing I am,' but I'm feeling exposed and raw right now. I'm not sure how well I might do so I'm just praying I don't make a fool of myself."

We start to head toward the carnival games, screams passing every few seconds as well as whooshes of the roller coasters speeding through the air. I'm more than happy taking it easy with Jason since puking on a ride is the last thing both of us want, but I will say this, I'm pretty sure Jason made me into a roller coaster junkie. I need to find another way to come back here, even if it's by myself.

"Just so you know, if you did make a fool of yourself, I'd still like you. I'd still go back to your apartment with you, and I'd still mount you."

That puts a full-on smile on his face. "I see what's happening here." He stops at a kiosk and gets a water for both of us. When he's finished his he says, "The tough girl from the boardroom, the ruthless vixen who makes men in suits cry . . . what she's really into are sensitive men, men who will pull out the emotions she usually has to hide when dealing in business. Am I right?"

"I mean, I wouldn't say that's how I am always, but I think I found someone who matches me nicely, who makes me escape my head, and shows me the fun in life, the beauty in everyday things."

I've only known Jason for a few weeks now, but even in those weeks, I've come to realize one thing: he does make me feel like a different person. He helps me see the positive, how to bottle it up and experience it. Not that I was a super negative person before he came around, but I'd forgotten it was okay to stop, take a breath, and *intentionally* live in the moment.

"That's a big compliment. Thank you, Dottie." He kisses the side of my head and chuckles.

"What?"

"That old lady back there. She read our shirts."

"Let me guess, a gasp with a cane shake?"

"You could not be more right. I think she'll be writing a hand-written letter to the park tonight before she hits the hay at five thirty. A perk of getting older, eating dinner at four, yelling at some children for being too rambunctious, and then flopping into bed before the nightly news."

"Why do I see that as a future reality for you?"

"You can see me as an old man?" We walk through an arch, indicating a new land, the carnival games up ahead. "Am I hot, bald? Bet my nutsac is super wrinkly."

"Isn't it already wrinkly? Scrotums aren't pretty."

"I beg your pardon?" Jason brings his hand to his chest in total shock, the color in his face coming back as his quirky personality starts to awaken. "Scrotums were carved by God and placed on a man as his own personal Baby Bjorn. Day in and day out, men are carrying the future of the world's children between their legs. It's a struggle every day, keeping them safe, making sure we don't zip them up after a pee, protecting their intelligence from incoming kicks and punches. Women bitch and complain about having to carry a baby for nine months in their belly. Try a lifetime of carrying a dangling sac between your legs with the fear of getting punctured every day by a pencil."

I don't . . .

I can't . . .

Why?

Why do these thoughts cross his mind? And why does he voice them in such an oddly charming way that I'm laughing but also funnily appalled at the same time?

Instead of defending the obvious and getting into an absurd debate that will only result in him going on a playful tirade of nursing his unborn children, I give him a simple answer.

"The sacrifices men make. Unbelievable. You should have your dicks sucked every night for your heroism."

"I could not agree more," he says, chest puffed, as if he won.

"Then again, sticking your dick into a woman's mouth is like shoving your children into the belly of the beast. Letting your unborn kin be swallowed whole while you welcome the all-consuming pleasure from it. Maybe you're not as heroic as you think you are."

There. Take that, Jason.

I smile coyly to myself.

"God created blow jobs for one reason: so men can dispense of the moronic sperm."

Did not hear that coming . . .

"Okay, so if that's your theory, how do you explain the people on this earth who stick their heads in microwaves and think it's funny?"

"Easy. Their dads didn't do a good enough job seeking out blow jobs. I'm not saying we're all perfect, but I'm sure as hell saying I am. Which by the way"—he stops and lifts my chin but *doesn't* kiss me—"thanks for swallowing my idiots yesterday. You did the world a service."

I'm starting to think Jason's dad didn't get enough blow jobs in his younger years . . .

~

"**Y**ou're totally crushing on me, aren't you?" Jason asks from the driver's side of his car. After we played quite a few carnival games, where Jason showed off his talents and earned a giant, stuffed Tweety Bird, we found a grateful little girl to take it off our hands.

There are a few things I need to make known.

I've never seen anything sexier than when Jason flipped his baseball hat backward, cocked his arm back, and demolished every throwing game available. His arm rippled, his shirt clung to every muscle in his back, and he wore a smile the entire time, genuinely having a grand time. He helped me win a few games, but all in all, I stood there and watched in awe the pure strength power through his body as he tackled every carnival game.

I don't think I've ever laughed as much as I have today. We didn't talk about anything too serious, just had a good time bantering back and forth. Most of the time, it was him going off on some weird tangent I had a hard time following, but the passion in his completely ridiculous tangents had me buckling over and sprouting giggles everywhere we went.

And finally, I don't think I've ever swooned as hard as I did when Jason found a little girl to give the giant Tweety Bird to. He carried it around under his arm, scanning the amusement park until he found a little girl with the cutest pigtails bouncing up and down out of pure joy that he was approaching with the stuffed animal. But that wasn't all he looked for. She had Down syndrome, and I don't think I'll ever forget the smile on her face. The total and unfiltered delight. And her parents? They were so grateful, but when they realized who was giving their sweet daughter the stuffed toy, they freaked out. Jason took his time talking to the dad about the upcoming season. He signed a napkin, and then took a few pictures. My favorite was the one of him holding the girl in one arm and in the other was Tweety. Adorable. The parents already tagged him, and Jason—because he's the greatest guy I know—is trending in Chicago from the kind gesture.

To say my ovaries ache is an understatement.

And to answer his question, am I "totally crushing" on him?

Yes, in fact I am.

I'm crushing really hard.

"Come on." He rattles my hand. "You can admit it. I can see it in your eyes, so even if you try to deny the crushing, I know it's there. I know it's how you're feeling. Might be nice to hear it from your beautiful lips."

"You want me to sit here and pump your ego?"

"Yes, that would be amazing. Thanks."

I shake my head in laughter and let out a long sigh. I lull my head to the side and say, "Yes, I'm crushing on you. Are you happy?"

"Very. Now, tell me in detail what exactly you're crushing on. Don't leave one stone unturned."

"Be happy I confessed to crushing on you."

"I'm always happy, but I want to feel giddy." He squeezes my hand. "Won't you make that happen for me? Make me feel a special tingle deep in my soul?"

"Why do I even choose to hang out with you?" I ask, chuckling. I can feel a deep tingle, but it's not in my soul, that's for damn sure.

"That's what I want to know. Let me hear it. Three things, and then I'll say three things about you."

He turns right after stopping at a traffic light and heads toward my apartment.

"You go first," I say, feeling almost shy.

"That's fair. Three things I like about you? How could I possibly narrow it down to just three? There are just so many things—"

"Okay, just get on with it."

"Bossy, I like that you're bossy. I really like it when you're trying to get your way with me and I don't follow your *orders*. The look of displeasure that crosses your face. God, so fucking cute."

No one has ever liked me for being bossy . . . ever. Jason really is in his own world, maybe universe.

"I think your intelligence and drive is really fucking sexy. It doesn't hurt that you look like a queen in a power suit."

"A queen, huh?"

"Total dynasty." He winks. "And the third thing I like about you is this. You might put up this tough front, a total boss bitch, but deep down, you're a softy just like me."

"Hmm, I don't know about that."

"Please. I saw the way you looked at that little girl today. You lit up when she started jumping up and down in excitement. And you comforted me while I was having a special moment with the trash can earlier. If you didn't have a kind heart, you would have gone off on more rides. There are other examples, but my point is, you're a softy, but you just don't show it off as much as I do."

I stare out the window, watching the familiar buildings pass by. "I wasn't always jaded, you know. There was a time where I was more easygoing, not so stiff all the time. But a few rough relationships will change your perspective."

"That's why you need to be in the right relationship."

"And let me guess, the right one is with you?" I chuckle, but he answers with a serious tone.

"You tell me."

"I think it is," I say, taking a second to observe his hard, carved jaw, and the smallest of dimples etched in the corners of his cheeks. You wouldn't see it head-on, but from this angle, I can faintly make it out. This man should have been made with permanent dimples, but then I guess that would be too easy. You have to be close to him to appreciate the simplicity but sexiness of his dimples, and that's one thing I really like about him. Everyone might get his entertaining personality, but not everyone gets to see this side of him, the way I get to see him. Even Emory and Lindsay probably have no idea just how incredible he is. They called him a good guy, but he's so much more. Genuine, thoughtful, self-absorbed in a selfless way, even though that sounds like an oxymoron. He's let me into his private sanctum, and I feel . . . *honored. Weird, but true.*

"Good answer. Now give me three things you like about me." He pulls into the parking garage of my apartment complex and parks in the visitor spot next to my car. "Don't think you're going to get out of it."

"As if you would let me." I turn toward him in my seat and rest my head against the headrest. "Three things, wow, how could I possibly narrow it down?" I say with humor, copying him.

He playfully pokes my side. "Get on with it."

Looking him in the eyes, I say, "Your infectious smile, it's hard to be around you and not be in a good mood and it starts with your smile." He delivers that smile. "Your caring heart. You're a giver in many ways when given your stature and celebrity, you could easily be a taker. It's sexy." He takes my hand in his and links our fingers. "And I would be remiss to leave out the most important attribute . . ." He waits on bated breath. "Your butt, it's just too good to leave out of the top three."

"Fuck." His smile grows bigger. "I think I might cry." He pretends to get choked up and waves his hand in front of his face. "You know how important my ass is to me. You get me, Dottie. You get me."

"Oddly, I do."

"Which is why"—he reaches behind my seat and lifts up a duffel bag—"I brought an overnight bag."

"You're spending the night?"

"Yup. I'm going to go upstairs to your place, brush my teeth, and then stick my tongue down your throat. Pizza for dinner?"

"Uh," I laugh, "sure."

He fist-pumps. "Pizza and making out. Best night ever."

I could think of other reasons why it's turning out to be not only the best night ever, but the best day ever, and they all start with the energetic man next to me.

CHAPTER TWENTY-THREE

JASON

Pizza and making out, wow, what a great night, right?
Wrong.

I was so wrong.

When we got to Dottie's apartment, she gave me a quick tour, let me set my bag down in her bedroom, and then she ordered some pizza while I brushed my teeth. I've avoided kissing her ever since I became acquainted with my new friend, trash can number 34298. I know this because this was the number I read over and over again when my head was stuffed inside.

I planned on making up for lost kissing time. Which is what we did while waiting for the pizza.

It started off casual, you know what I'm talking about. An innocent touch here, a purposeful caress there. She scooted onto my lap, sitting sideways, and we made out. It was sweet and innocent, nothing that spoke SEX SEX SEX in bright neon letters. And we kept our hands out of the private zones. It was perfect.

Pizza arrived. We ate. We talked. We laughed. It was a great dinner and then we decided on a movie to watch. She wanted action, I wanted romance—naturally—so we settled on *True Lies*, which is a little of both. Before the movie started, we both decided to change into our jam-jams and that was the turning point of our night.

I came out in a respectable pair of flannel pants and a plain white T-shirt. Yes, the shirt is purposefully tight just as a subtle reminder of what I have to offer.

Guess who didn't get the subtle memo? Our resident hottie . . . Dottie.

She strutted into the living room wearing another one of those godforsaken nightgowns—not that I'm really complaining, but I kind of am, because how the hell am I supposed to pay attention to the intricate plot of *True Lies* with Boobsy McGee sitting next to me with no bra on, acting as if everything is just casual, like I don't want to stick my penis in her cleavage?

Because I do. I want to dipstick her tits so bad it's all my mind can think about—dip, dip, dip, DIP—I can't think of anything else other than whipping my proud penis out of its confines and testing out the warmth of her boobs.

Oh, and don't you even think for a second that she chose her nighttime wear without thought. There was a lot of thought put into her choice. There was malicious thought, because I'm going to let you in on a little secret. When we were making out, I told her I didn't want to take it any further tonight than just kissing and I saw it, the look of disappointment cross her face right before it turned to calculating.

She avoided getting handsy and only using her mouth before pizza arrived but now that it's movie time, she threw down the gauntlet with that little number she's wearing.

Hell, I'm pretty sure I can see the outline of her nipples.

But what she didn't take into account is, even though I'm suffering inside, I have more willpower than it might seem. She might be taunting me with her spaghetti strap, silky nightgown that hits just above her thighs, but guess what, lady? I've had to pee on my hands many times to make them tough for catching, and letting pee sit on your hands for an obscene amount of time takes more willpower than one can imagine. And side note: peeing on your hands is an old catcher's trick; it's disgusting, but it works to toughen up the hands.

Despite currently living in a fiery hell of denying myself sweet release, I'm outwardly as casual as one can get. Hand draped over this girl's leg, one arm spanning along the back of the couch, slightly slouched, but still able to have a good view of the television. I'm acting like I'm watching the movie, perfectly content with where I am, but from the corner of my eye, I'm watching Dottie like a hawk. The small shifts that make her boobs pop, the tiny touches that graze my inner thigh . . . every move is full of intent.

She wants me.

But it's not going to happen. I'm holding strong. I will court this woman the right way, damn it.

"Love this scene," I say, my voice sounding surprisingly normal despite how tense and tight my balls feel right now.

"Jamie Lee Curtis was made for this movie. She does such a good job."

"Couldn't agree more."

Dottie shifts on the couch and leans into my body, her legs tucked under her, curling in the opposite direction than me. Her hand falls to my chest and her head rests on my shoulder. "That's better. More comfortable."

Yeah, maybe for you.

But I take advantage of the position and drape my arm over her, drawing lazy circles on her exposed clavicle.

"Do you think you could ever be in the secret service?" she asks, her finger casually working its way up and down my chest.

"No. I'm too much of a pussy," I answer honestly, hoping it deters her in her pursuit to touch me.

It doesn't.

"I could see you doing it. You're a protector."

"Yeah, when I'm put in a position I need to be. I will defend anyone in my life to the day I die, but that doesn't mean I want that as a job."

"True, but maybe an action hero." She pushes up so she can look down at me. "You have the body for it." She reaches down and pulls up the hem of my shirt. "You sure have the abs for it."

The cold air hits my stomach, causing my muscles to twitch.

"I'll be honest, I've never dated anyone with the kind of body you have." Her hand drags my shirt up higher until my stomach and chest is exposed. "How many hours do you spend in the gym?"

"Enough," I say on a gulp. With a wicked smile and an exploratory finger, she circles my nipple, sending a jolt of pleasure straight to my groin. "Dottie," I warn.

"Just exploring."

"Exploring can get you in trouble."

"What if I want trouble?" she asks, moving her hand down my stomach to the waistband of my flannel pants where she slips her hand underneath. Because I'm an idiot, I'm not wearing briefs. Therefore, her hand connects directly with my cock, her palm rubbing over the soft skin for a brief moment, feeling how I'm instantly hard in her hand.

"Dottie, come on, babe, I'm trying here."

"Trying what? To torture both of us?" she asks, moving her hand down to my balls where she massages them as well, and holy fuck does it feel good.

Really fucking good.

So good that a hiss escapes my lips as my head falls to the back of the couch.

"I want to court you, do it right."

"And I want to feel your dick inside me. Which do you think will bring us more pleasure?"

Valid point.

But still . . .

I reach down and take her hand out of my pants, my penis hating me. I look her in the eyes and say, "You deserve more."

"I deserve you," she says, her words so full of hidden meaning that I can feel her desperation in those three little words. "This isn't just fucking to me, Jason. This, us, it means something to me. I know it's been quick between us, but I feel something for you. I think I've felt it since college, since the first time I saw you. I don't want to wait. I want to enjoy you . . . us."

"I want that too," I say, cupping her cheek. "But I'm serious about this. I want our first time to be special and worth the wait."

Her face falls, the smile disappearing, the spark in her eyes evaporating as she turtles in on herself and nods. I've never seen her like this before. Vulnerable and disappointed, waving her white flag and letting someone else get their way.

I'll be honest, I don't like it.

Do you know what else I don't like? Dottie pulling away. Dottie not snuggling into my chest. Dottie staying silent during the movie. Dottie mentally removing herself from the night. I can't have that, nor do I want it.

And there seems to be only one way to take care of it.

"Fuck it," I say, standing from the couch and pulling my shirt off.

Dottie's eyes widen right before I pick her up from the couch and toss her over my shoulder.

"Jason," she says, concerned. "What are you doing?"

I don't answer her.

I don't speak a damn word.

I walk to her bedroom, shut the door, and then set her on the bed where I observe her. Excitement erupts in her eyes.

She's about to understand what it's like to be with Jason Orson.

"Take your tits out of your nightgown." She reaches for the hem, but I bark, "No. Leave it on. Just take your tits out." Her eyes widen . . . probably from my tone of voice. When it comes to the bedroom, I don't fuck around.

Unsure, she removes her breasts and I take a second to stare at them. When she goes to rub them, I snap at her again. "Don't fucking touch them. Just let me stare. I want to watch your breathing pick up, see how aroused you get from this."

In the silence of her large bedroom, I stare at her and watch every movement she makes. A little intake here, a slight shift there. How her eyes go hazy with lust, how her legs start to slowly part, and that's when I see it. She's wearing nothing underneath. The fucking vixen. She knew exactly what she was doing this whole time. I'm about to make sure she never regrets her decision tonight.

"Reach up with your right hand and play with your nipple. Massage it, pluck at it, pinch it, roll it; do everything and anything that makes you wet for me. Spread your legs wider, because I want to see that pussy glisten."

She bites her bottom lip and does as I say, playing with her nipple. There's something to be said about a powerful woman, one who runs her world every day, breaking down and giving in to the demands of her man in the bedroom. It's hot how responsive she is, how willing she is to listen. I love everything about it.

With my thumbs, I snag the waistband of my pants and push them down only to step out of the fabric and toss them to the side with a flick of my toe. Cock jutted out, I grip it with one hand and slowly start to stroke up and down, giving her an eyeful.

She licks her lips and her hips start to rock as she stares at me.

"Switch your hands. Make yourself moan. I won't be touching you until I think you're fully ready, so give me the goddamn show I deserve."

With that, she pulls on the fabric of her nightgown, exposing her lower half completely and then spreads her legs all the way, presenting me with one of the most gorgeous and erotic scenes I've ever seen.

"Pinch your nipple harder, I want to hear you moan."

She pinches, and her hips lift as a low moan falls past her precious lips.

"Again."

She pinches. *Groans.*

"Again."

This time her head falls to the side, her chest heaving.

"Again."

Her other hand roams up her body to her other breast and she applies the same pressure.

As she continues to work her nipples until she's dripping wet while small cries fall from her lips, I hold the base of my cock, keeping the pressure tight around the root and then slowly pulling the built-up pressure to the tip of my dick, only to repeat the stroke. Together we touch ourselves to the point that we're both breathing heavily. *Fuck. This is so fucking hot.*

"Are you ready for me, Dottie?"

"Yes," she moans, her pelvis rotating, seeking relief.

"Touch yourself. Let me see how wet you are on your fingers."

Without hesitation, she drags her fingers down her body to her pussy. With two fingers, she swipes over her slit and then holds them up to me. I walk over and closely examine them and then, I pull them into my mouth, sucking on the tips, making Dottie's eyes widen.

"Get on all fours."

"I want to see you when you fuck me."

"You will, but on your knees for now."

She does as I say, and I take my time to take in her pert ass, how the nightgown fabric barely skims her skin. Normally I like to be completely naked, but the nightgown has now become a part of this.

I step up behind her and slide my hand over the globe of her ass and then to her lower back, dragging her nightgown with it until it hits her shoulder blades. Circling my hand to the front, I find her breast and cup it, giving it a few squeezes as I line my rock-hard erection along her ass.

"Do you feel that, Dottie? Do you feel how fucking hard I am? That's because of you. Whenever you're around, you do this to me.

You entice me, intrigue me, make me so goddamn horny with need. That's why I'm about to fuck you into this mattress, because I can't take your teasing any longer. But if we're going to do this, we're going to do this on my terms."

I pinch her nipple and she rears back on a scream.

"Oh God, Jason."

With my free hand, I run my finger along the nub, testing how wet she is.

She's soaking, but I'm not about to give in. Instead, I stroke her lightly, pretending my finger is a feather, keeping the pressure as soft as a whisper so she knows I'm down there, but I'm down there for one purpose: to torture her.

With my dick still rubbing against her ass, I continue to pinch her nipples and stroke her until she lowers her head to the mattress and groans out in frustration.

"Jason," she cries out. "Please."

"Please what?"

"Please, fuck me."

Satisfied, I release my grip and flip her to her back. The shocked look soon subsides when I tear her nightgown over her head, and then place both my hands on her knees. I spread them wide and take a look at her, completely exposed. Smooth skin stretches over her body, skin I want my mouth all over.

"Are you on the pill?"

"Yes." She nods.

"Good, because I want nothing between us." I bring my aching cock to her entrance and move it up and down along her wetness, coating my dick in her arousal. "I love seeing your aroused pussy on my dick. I love seeing how wet you get from my touch, just from looking at me." I rub her again and she shifts, trying to get me to enter her. "How many times do you plan on coming tonight, Dottie?"

"As many as you'll allow me."

"Perfect answer." I slide my hands down to her inner thighs and drop to my knees. Keeping her spread, I bring my face down to her pussy and flick my tongue along her clit.

"Oh fuck," she cries out, her hands gripping the comforter. "I don't know how much I can take."

"Are you begging me to eat your pussy, Dottie?"

"Yes . . . please, Jason, yes."

"Fuck, I love hearing my name fall off your tongue like that, so desperate, so needy."

Not wasting any more time, I move my mouth to her pussy, open wide, and suck her in right before swirling my tongue over her clit over and over and over again.

I'm vibrating my tongue, flicking, swirling, pressing down on her clit and then of course, sucking on it.

She writhes on the mattress, her shoulders twisting and turning, her mouth falling open, her eyes squeezing shut. Her hands drop to my head, her fingers digging into my hair, pulling, tugging, trying to grip anything as I hold her hips to the mattress, not letting her set the pace, but letting me control when she comes.

"Fu-uck, Jason. Please. Jesus, please."

I pull away and lightly kiss the inside of her thighs, moving back to her mound, and above, then back. Flick my tongue, swirl. Pull back. Kiss her thigh and repeat.

Her arm flies over her eyes, and I'm almost positive she's about to cry from sweet torture. It's in that moment that I realize I have her right where I want her.

With my thumbs, I spread her lips and flatten my tongue against her clit, giving her long strokes with medium pressure, enough to make her come in seconds.

She screams out my name as she heaves up and down, her body twisting and turning until she calls out for me to slow down.

"I can't . . . take, oh God." I flick her clit again and her hips drive forward. So fucking responsive. It's sexy as shit.

When her body settles, I bring her legs up to her chest and say, "Hold on to your knees. Keep them wide."

Eyes still watery from her orgasm, her breath trying to catch up, her hands reach out, shaky and unsteady and she grips her knees, spreading herself wide.

"Perfect." I hover over her body and bring my mouth to hers where I very softly kiss her along her lips. I reach up and cup her cheek, allowing my thumb to stroke her cheek a few times. "You're gorgeous, Dottie. So fucking beautiful." She presses her cheek into my hand and for a second, we share an intimate moment as my dick lines up against her wet pussy. Tempting me, begging me to thrust deep inside her. I wait a few more seconds, marveling in the way her soft lips play with mine.

"Are you ready for me?"

She nods.

"Good, because I need to be inside you like I need my next breath." I grip the base of my aching cock and position it at her entrance. Slowly, I start to enter her, taking it one painstakingly inch at a time.

"Shit, Jason," she says, her mouth falling open and her eyes widening. "Slow, I need"—she swallows hard—"I need you to go slow."

And I need to go fucking fast or my dick might just break off, but I understand. I'm larger than most, so I grin down and bear the sweet torture.

"Relax, Dottie."

"I know." She nods, taking another deep breath. "Feels so good, but unlike anything"—she moans when I push forward another inch—"unlike anything I've ever felt."

I can say the same about her. Warm and tight, like I'm dipping myself into heaven.

Wanting her to relax, I drop my mouth to hers and take one of her breasts in my hand. I massage and pinch her nipple while I trail kisses over her mouth, to her jaw, down her neck and back up.

I slip in another inch, and then another as I feel her relax with each pass of my mouth, until I'm fully inside her and fuck, does it feel good.

"Christ," I whisper in her ear. "Dottie, I need to pump my hips."

She nods. "I need that too."

Thank fuck.

Lifting up with my arms pressed to the mattress, I start to piston my hips in and out, but keeping it relatively slow, drawing my attention to our connection. So hot.

Watching my dick slide in and out of her—claiming her—sends a jolt of lust through my veins, causing my hips to move even faster.

Then she moans, her hands falling to my shoulders where she pierces me with her nails. The sensation of her pussy squeezing my cock and her nails digging into my skin sends me into overdrive. My toes start to go numb and my impending orgasm is just out of reach.

"Fuck," I grunt, pumping harder and harder. "Ahh, fuck, Dottie."

She pulls my head down to hers and drives her tongue into my mouth. I match her intensity, each thrust, each lick, until we're both tensing together. My head falls to her shoulder as she cries out my name, her pussy clenching around me, her hips erratically flying with mine.

That's all it takes. My body seizes and I spill inside her, my pelvis stilling as euphoria shoots through me, touching every limb, every nerve ending, every goddamn part of my body until I collapse on top of her.

"Jesus fucking Christ," I mumble, reeling from what just happened between us.

"I . . . never . . . Jason." I get what she's *trying* to say, because I'm feeling the same damn way.

I've never felt anything like that before.

I've had sex, plenty of it, but the connection we share, the way she listened, relinquished herself to me, fully trusting her body into my hands, it was a combination of so many untapped sensations that I'm not sure I'll fall off this high easily. Nor am I going to be able to let go of this woman.

Tough as stone on the outside, soft and sweet on the inside, with a need to be taken care of . . . she's fucking perfect.

I press a kiss to her cheek and rest there with her wrapped around me. Together we catch our breath, and then we spend the rest of the night snuggling. *Fuck, this is almost too good to be true. I found her. My woman. My future.*

CHAPTER TWENTY-FOUR

DOTTIE

"There she is," Lindsay says, clapping obnoxiously loud as I make my way through the restaurant to the table where Emory, Milly, and Lindsay are sitting, waiting for me.

It's been a hectic week, or last two weeks I guess. The Carltons have put their decision on hold and extended their vacation instead, leaving me in the balance. They haven't been super responsive, but they said when they get back—not sure when—they'll let me know. They'll set up a time to have dinner.

Their email seemed short, almost like they might not be going with our proposal, which has made me unattainable as a friend and desperately neurotic.

The only good thing about the situation right now is Jason has been over to my place almost every night. I've come home to homecooked dinners—I gave my chef some much-needed time off —and then we've spent the rest of our nights talking . . . naked.

We've been on a few other dates, not many though given my schedule, which terrifies me because I'm already busy. What happens if we continue to date and he begins his season? We're barely going to see each other. When I brought that up, he kissed me on the nose and said it's a bridge we'll cross when we get there.

Must be easy for him to not worry about it, just sweep it under the rug, but uncertainty isn't easy for me. I like to have a plan. I like to know what's ahead. I like to be able to prepare myself for what's to come.

But lately, it seems like my entire life is full of uncertainty, and it's driving me crazy.

"Sorry," I say, pulling out my chair and taking a seat, letting my entire body flop into the chair. Emory set up brunch a few days ago and begged me to come since they haven't seen me in well . . . two weeks. "I ran into the office quickly this morning to pull some numbers. But I'm here."

"Yes, you are, and what a glow you have about you, don't you think, ladies?"

Milly, the shy one of the group, nods over her mimosa, but Emory has a giant smile on her face . . . a knowing one.

"It's so strange that we haven't seen you around lately," Emory says, lifting her plain orange juice to her mouth. "I wonder why that is."

"Have you seen Jason?" Lindsay asks, looking like a doofus with the way she won't stop wiggling her eyebrows. My girls know me well enough that I was going to order a mimosa, so they had one already brought to me. Thankful for the refreshment, I down half of it.

"No, he hasn't been around to annoy us lately." Emory taps her chin. "I wonder where he could be."

"You guys are so immature." I shake my head. "Why don't you two be more like Milly? She's sweet and doesn't pester."

"I don't, but I like *their* pestering," Milly replies with ease.

Ugh damn it, Milly. She's supposed to be on my side.

"When have we ever been mature?" Lindsay asks, plopping a piece of fruit from the plate in the middle of the table in her mouth. "Just tell us what's going on with you and Jason. We've given you space, now it's time to dish."

"I'm surprised you guys don't already know," I say, picking up a piece of pineapple. "Jason has zero ability to keep anything to himself. I assumed he'd told Knox and Carson, who in return told Emory and Milly and of course, relayed the information to you, Lindsay."

"He's said nothing," Emory says, looking disappointed. "And I even forced Knox to ask, but he said Jason has been dead silent. Believe me, we are just as shocked as the guys."

It's because I told him if he said anything to Knox and Carson, I wouldn't be sucking his dick anytime soon. In the last two weeks, I've sucked it at least six times. I finally figured out the way to keep Jason Orson quiet—just stick his dick in my mouth.

"It's why we called for brunch today, because we need to know what's going on." Lindsay pokes me. "Spill."

Smiling, I lean back and cross one leg over the other. "I'm not going to go into detail, so don't ask for it. Got it?" I specifically look at Lindsay, who rolls her eyes and agrees. Good. Unable to contain how giddy I am, I say, "Jason and I are dating. He's been at my house almost every night for the past two weeks." Emory claps her hands. "He's unlike any man I've ever been with. He annoys me to no end, but at the drop of a hat, has me begging for his atten-tion. He can make me laugh and swoon all in the same moment and"—I clear my throat and lean forward so the people around us can't hear—"he's the best sex I've ever had. Like surpasses any and all men."

"Seriously?" Emory asks. "I thought he'd be a gentle lover given his personality."

"Very gentle," Lindsay says. "Probably asks you for consent before every coupling, right?" Lindsay jokes. Little does she know.

"He's an animal," I say, shocking them, even poor Milly, whose face turns bright red. Carson told us a while back she didn't have many girlfriends growing up or even in recent years, so when they got married, we took her in as our own. She's slowly opening up, but I can tell every time she hangs out with us, she's out of her element. And when we have gatherings at Knox and Emory's apartment, she always drifts over to the guys, not because she needs to be by Carson all the time, but because she wants to talk baseball. She's sweet, we love her, and she's about to get a small eye-opener.

"He's what?" Lindsay asks, setting her drink down in shock. "No way. Jason?"

Now I know I said I wouldn't go into detail, but I feel the need to prove to them that his personality doesn't quite match his actions in bed.

"First of all"—I point to all of them—"none of this leaves this table. You hear me? If Carson and Knox tell Jason what I'm about to tell you, he'll never let me live it down. So, keep your mouths shut."

"That's easy for me since I'm not dating a hunky baseball player," Lindsay says, crossing her arms over her chest.

"I won't say anything," Milly says, looking distraught over the idea of not telling Carson.

"You know me, I keep everything from Knox," Emory says flippantly, but that is a boldfaced lie. She tells that man everything.

"I'm especially talking to you, Emory. You and Knox are gossip gatherers, and your apartment is an infestation of gossip."

"No, it's not. I won't tell him. Promise."

Satisfied, I say, "First of all, Jason has the biggest penis I've ever seen. Girth, length . . . THE towel picture is all that and then some."

"Shut up. Guh," Lindsay groans. "You lucky, lucky girl."

"Have you seen the towel pic?" Emory asks Milly, who pushes up her glasses and brings her mimosa to her mouth.

"Um, I think Carson showed it to me once. He wanted to compare himself."

We all chuckle, because that's definitely something Carson would do.

"Let's just say the picture doesn't do him justice. And if you think he's docile and meek in bed, you'd be wrong." I flip my hair over my shoulder and say, "He's all alpha. It's like he flips this switch and turns on this side of him I never expected. He's controlling, demanding, and . . . adventurous."

"Stahp." Lindsay fans herself. "God, I can see it. All those muscles, all that testosterone." Lindsay sets her hand on the table and leans forward. "Oh God, you've seen his bare ass. Is it everything you've ever dreamed of?"

"It's like a freaking juicy shelf attached to his back." The girls laugh. "And it's tight, really freaking tight. And I'm going to tell you this, watching him shower should be a sin. He's such a specimen. Rippled abs, thick pecs, and ass that pops like Jennifer Lopez. I can't keep my hands off him."

"And let me guess," Lindsay says, sounding jealous but also happy for me at the same time—if that makes sense, "he cuddles you afterwards, strokes your hair, and continuously whispers in your ear how beautiful you are."

A slow smile perks up on my face.

"Every. Time."

"Ugh, I need a Jason."

Emory smiles gently and places her hand on mine. "So what does this mean? You really like him?"

I nod. "I do, I like him a lot. And not only for the great sex, but because he appreciates me and doesn't want me to change. He likes how I can get angry at the drop of a hat. He enjoys watching me work until the late hours of the night because he understands drive and goals. He's there for me, even if I come home late and all he gets to do is hold me. And on those off days, when we get to spend time together, he makes me forget about everything stressful happening in my life, every last taxing piece of it, and helps me relax. I know it's been quick, but I honestly can say this without hesitation, I'm falling for the man."

"Oh my God," Emory squeals.

"I think I might cry," Lindsay says.

Clearing her throat, Milly says, "He's a really good man, and has one of the prettiest swings in baseball."

We all pause and then laugh together, because Milly is so . . . Milly, and it's why we love her.

~

"There's my girl," Jason says as I walk through the door. Like every other day, he swoops into the entryway of my apartment and brings me into his embrace.

He grips the back of my head and places a searing kiss on my lips before pulling me into a hug and kissing the side of my head. Sweet and demanding simultaneously. I haven't even set my purse down before he already has me wired up and ready to go.

"How was work?"

"The same," I answer, taking my heels off and setting my purse down. I leave them in the entryway. I'll take care of them later. I untuck my merlot-colored blouse and then unzip my skirt, letting that fall to the floor as well. In seconds, I'm like the father from *The Goldbergs* the minute he walks through the door.

"It's so hot when you do that." Jason's eyes fill with lust as he takes his hand in mine and leads me to the couch. "Dinner is still in the oven."

"Smells amazing."

He takes a seat on the couch and then pulls me on top of him. He's in nothing but a pair of athletic shorts, just the way I like him, his chest exposed for my staring and touching purposes.

I get comfortable, and his hands immediately go to my bare ass. He gingerly strokes each globe before his fingers start toying with my thong.

"I missed you today. You weren't a very good texter."

"I was not about to sext with you while having a meeting with our board of directors."

"But where's the fun in that? That's what being adventurous is all about. Getting wet and turned on when you shouldn't be."

"And then what?" I ask him, drawing circles on his chest. "I'm horny for the rest of the day?"

"No, that's when you call your man to your office so he can take care of your needs."

"Ohhh, I see. You want office sex."

"Doesn't everyone?" He grips my sides and shifts me so I can feel his already hardening erection. This man's virility is unbelievable. "Think about it. You bent over your desk, me behind you." He rubs me up and down and I let him, because even though we had shower sex this morning, I still want him. I don't think I'll ever stop wanting him. "Making you beg for my cock until you fall apart with desperation." Yup, I want this. I pick up the pace, letting my arousal lead the way as I dry-hump his cock. "And even when you're on the verge of tears, begging me to fuck you, I'd still wait. I'd wait until I felt like you'd completely break, and then I'd fuck you from behind."

"Jesus, Jason." That's one thing I overlooked with the girls. The dirty talk. The man drives me wild with every word that leaves his sensual lips. I reach up and undo the buttons of my shirt, letting it fall to the side, and then I undo my bra, watching as Jason's green eyes turn a shade darker. His hands fall to my breasts where he brings them to his mouth and starts sucking. My head falls back, my hair dancing across my back, as this passionate man begins to own my body once again.

I slow down my hips to a torturous pace, and it doesn't take Jason long to get sick of it because he tosses me to the side of the couch, shucks his shorts, and tears my thong off me. Determination and heat build right before he descends on me. He lifts one of my legs to the back of the couch and then spreads the other to the floor—thank God, I'm flexible.

Hands on my hips, he presses his cock to my entrance and then fully inserts himself. He slides in with ease from how turned on I am.

He grumbles something to himself and then starts rocking his hips, holding me down so firmly I have nothing to do but give in to the sheer force behind his body.

I grip the arm of the couch and hold on as Jason takes over.

"You're so fucking tight, so fucking perfect." Sweat beads at his brow from his exertion, from his controlled movements. I know he wants it harder—and he's given it to me harder before, shaking my bed around on the floor—but when we have sex first thing after work, he seems to hold back, as if to give me a second to breathe. I appreciate it, but not this time. I want all of him.

"Harder," I say, causing his brows to narrow and his hips to still. "Wh-what are you doing?" I ask, looking up at him.

"Let's get one thing straight, Dottie. You might be the boss in the boardroom, but you're sure as hell not the boss in the bedroom. Got it?"

I should be startled, shocked even, but I'm not, because this is Jason, this is his kingdom and I've given over to it. I trust him enough to rule our lives in the bedroom, to take over and be in charge of our pleasure. I never knew that choosing submission could be so freeing. Allowing him to use and tantalize my body to his heart's content. Lindsay was right. I'm a lucky, lucky girl.

Nodding, I say, "Yes, got it."

"Good." He starts moving his hips again, but this time, he goes at a snail's pace. "Trust that I know what you need, Dottie. Trust that in the moment, I can not only feel your desire, but I can read it as well." He starts to pump a little harder. "Know that I don't just fuck you, but I read your body, I watch how tight your nipples get, I wait for the moment you bite down on your lips right before your pussy clenches around my thick cock. I know the pattern of your breathing, the arch of your back before you come, and the sounds you make right before you hit that precipice."

My body climbs toward my orgasm with his every word, his every stroke.

"Trust that I know how to not only fuck you but pleasure you so every other man is worthless to you."

Already there.

"What's that?" Jason asks.

Did I say that out loud? Oh crap.

He slams into me now. Moving my hips with his hands, pulling me onto his cock. "What did you just say?"

Crying out his name, my orgasm toying with me, I breathe out a heavy breath and say, "Already there."

"Already there, what?" he says through clenched teeth, both of us rocking to the point of no return.

"You're . . . ahhh." I cry out when he pinches my nipple. Pleasure shoots through my legs, to my stomach and before I can stop it, my orgasm crashes into me like a tidal wave, rocking me harder than I've ever felt.

"Mother . . . fucker," Jason says, as I feel him tense and spill inside me. "Fuck," he groans, rocking his hips slowly. He opens his eyes and stares at me. Leaning down, he captures my lips and kisses them sensually and sweetly. I bring my hands to the back of his head and entwine my fingers. Keeping him close, never wanting to let him go as the emotions and feelings for this man overwhelm me.

Tears threaten to fall. I realize what I'm about to say holds such impact on our relationship that once I put it out there, I won't be able to take it back. But I'm not sure I can hold it in either. He needs to know how much he means to me, how desperate I am for him.

I place my hand on his cheek and put a small distance between our lips so I have his full attention.

His brow creases as he takes in my expression. "What's wrong, baby?"

God, when he calls me that, when his voice is so full of concern right after he took every last piece of me, how could I ever be without this man?

"I'm already there." His brow creases even more. "When you said you're going to pleasure me until every other man is worthless to me." I pause. "I'm already there. And not just because you rock my world in the bedroom . . . or on the couch"—we both smile—"but because you treat me unlike anyone has ever treated me before, like I'm the most precious thing that's ever come into your life."

"Because you are." His thumb caresses my cheek. "You're so goddamn precious to me, Dottie."

He gently kisses me as the timer goes off.

"That would be dinner." He gives me one more of his delicious kisses and then hops up from the couch, bare ass and all.

While he's getting dinner ready, I quickly clean up and return to the kitchen wearing one of his baseball shirts. I bring him his shorts. Dinner is set on the table, our chairs next to each other rather than across, because he's cute like that.

When I hand him the shorts, he asks, "No naked dinner tonight?"

"That was last night. We can be somewhat civilized tonight."

"Civilized, huh?" He slips his shorts on, covering up his perfectly sculpted ass . . . and his incredible cock. Let's not forget that wonderful appendage. "Then how on earth will you be able to stare at my juicy shelf?"

He works his way around the kitchen as I pause. Did he just say what I thought he said?

"Why did you call it that?"

Smiling, he pours us both a glass of wine. "No reason. But I suggest next time you tell our friends about our sex life, you go into detail about the length and girth of my dick. I'd appreciate that."

I am going to kill them.

Lips pursed to the side, hands clenching at my hips, I ask, "What did they say?"

Casually, he hands me my wine and leans his hip against the counter. "Oh, you know, just that I'm an alpha in the bedroom, a complete animal." Oh, sweet Jesus, my cheeks flame. "The best you've ever had."

Yup, I am going to kill them.

Through clenched teeth, I ask, "Who told you? No, I don't even have to ask. I know it was Knox."

"Nope." Jason shakes his head and I take a step back.

"Did Lindsay seriously call you or something? I mean, I know she—"

"Wasn't Lindsay." He smiles over his wine glass as I bring my hand to my chest.

On a whisper, I say "Was it . . . Milly?"

"Yep."

"No."

He nods, looking so pleased with himself. "Yup."

"I don't believe it. She would never. That's not how she is."

"Looks like she needs to learn girl code because she spoke to Carson in the shower like they were spilling the deets in the locker room. She, of course, afterward told him not to say anything to me, but you know how we ladies can be." He pretends to fluff his hair. "Always gabbing."

And just like that, he turns me from wanting to shove his cock down my mouth to wanting to chop it off with my own teeth.

"So . . . an animal, huh?" He wiggles his eyebrows and I know this is just the beginning of long and torturous teasing for many, many, many nights to come.

Hand on my hip, I say, "If you ever want to stick your penis inside me again, I suggest you don't bring this up anymore."

"You know"—he taps his chin—"I distinctively remember you threatening me with no more blow jobs if I spoke of our coupling to my friends and then . . . one brunch . . . you completely destroy the trust between a man and a woman." He snaps his fingers. "Just like that."

"You're being dramatic."

"I'm being dramatic?" he asks—in a dramatic tone—as he points to his chest. "I'm not dramatic. I'm searching for the truth and it will be told tonight." He shakes his fist to the sky.

"What are you even talking about? The truth is out. I told my friends. There, it's done."

"That's not the truth I'm looking for."

Okay, I bite.

"What's the truth you're looking for?"

"That you're more loose-lipped than I am."

I laugh out loud. Straight-up chortle. I wipe at my eyes and say, "Oh yeah, okay. Suuuuure, Jason."

"You are. I didn't tell my boys what's going on out of respect of you. I never told them about your amazing tits, or tried to impersonate your O face to them or"—he leans forward and lifts a brow —"told them how you like *me* to call *you* daddy."

I push at his chest, my laugh echoing through the room. "I do not like that, you fucking weirdo."

I really don't. I never said that. He joked about it the other night, him calling *me* Daddy, and now it's all he does to annoy me when I'm being demanding. He's such an idiot.

But he's my idiot.

Chuckling, he says, "But then you, out of all people, go to a brunch, and let it all out on the table. Our deepest and darkest secrets." He looks to the ceiling in a dream-like state, painting a picture for me. "I can see it now. There you were, legs crossed, your pussy sore from our last fucking." Jesus, this man. "You can feel me between your legs as the girls beg you for details. Your intentions were good. Eat some pastries, drink some mimosas, satisfy your need for girl time, but then the inquisition starts. You try to ignore them, brush them off, but the entire time all you can think about is how moments before you arrived, I was fucking you against the door, my aftershave branding your body. It's all so overwhelming. You're giddy, you're turned on just thinking about me, you're bursting at the seams, needing to tell someone about the giant, massive, oversized, and gargantuan cock that's entered your life and claimed your sweet, tight, greedy pussy."

I can't even . . .

How am I supposed to date this guy—easily, I know—but seriously, he's so over the top.

"You're out of your mind."

"Am I?" he asks, pulling out my chair for me and helping me take a seat. "Or am I scarily accurate?"

"Insane."

"Nah." He shakes his head. "I'm one hundred percent accurate."

Maybe just a little . . . especially about the greedy part.

CHAPTER TWENTY-FIVE

JASON

*J*ason: *Can't stop thinking about the way you squirted all over my face this morning.*

    Dottie: *One, I did not squirt all over your face. Jesus Christ, Jason. Two, I didn't squirt. I just came. . . hard.*

    Jason: *Babe, that was a straight-up squirt. You scored air on it, at least a few inches.*

    Dottie: *Why do you insist upon making my face turn bright red at work?*

    Jason: *Because it's fun for me. Send me a picture and while you're at it, send a picture of your naked tits too. Mommy misses her daddy's boobies.*

    Dottie: *Please, for the love of God, pause and read that last sentence. YOU ARE DERANGED. This is over between us. I can't possibly see someone who says shit like that.*

    Jason: *Too far?*

    Dottie: *You think? We're on a timeout. Do you hear me? A timeout.*

    Jason: *I'd prefer a spanking as punishment. You know, like the spanking I gave you last night? Fuck, babe. You screamed so loud when you came, I have partial ear damage.*

    Dottie: *Bye, Jason.*

Jason: Wait, don't you want to talk about the scream that ended all screams?

Jason: Hello?

Jason: Dottie?

Jason: . . . Daddy?

Dottie: I hate you.

Jason: There's my girl. Have a good rest of your day. See you tonight. Xoxoxxxxx *My penis and your vagina 4ever*

I stuff my phone away in my pocket, satisfied with my midday conversation with my girl and tap my foot on the turf floor. Where the hell is he?

I glance at my watch; two minutes past the time we were supposed to meet. That's unlike him. I stand from the bench, walk out of the private batting cages and spot Walker, kneeling on the ground and talking to a kid. I watch carefully the way he interacts with the young boy. Giving him pointers, speaking softly. It's unlike any side I've seen of Walker, but then again, most of the time, the media only shows his moments of outbursts and rage because when there's drama, media outlets tend to show that.

After a few more minutes, Walker stands, ruffles the kid's head, gives the father a quick handshake, and then heads in my direction. I was right. He does have exactly what I thought he has. Heart. Kindness. When he reaches me, I say, "Looks like you do have a heart in that barrel of a chest."

Walker pushes past me and into the cages, and I follow him. "If we're going to do this, don't say stupid shit."

"I don't ever say stupid—" He gives me a look. "Fine, I might say stupid shit on occasion, but I can't help it, it's in my nature. Just like it's in your nature to be a big grumpus."

"Grumpus equals stupid shit."

"What? No way. That can be a term of endearment."

"Listen." He holds his hand out to stop me. His brows narrow and his eyes sharpen. Man, this guy is intimidating. I'm a big dude, but he might be able to plow through my intestines with one fist to the gut. "We're here to talk about the event and hit some balls, not to become friends."

"Whoa, hey now, let's not get hasty," I say, wiping my hands from his statement. "Why don't we take it slow and see where things go? You never know, we might become the best of friends."

"We won't."

"We might."

"No."

"Never say never."

"Never."

Fuck, he's infuriating.

"Let's just say we agree to disagree at the moment and leave the friendship card on the table where it's easy to reach in case we want to flash it at each other."

He drags his hand down his face.

"You hitting first, or am I?"

"You, because it seems like you need to get some tension out of your shoulders."

We set up the tee, and I grab a bucket of balls while Walker warms up his back with a bat in hand. He shifts side to side, bat behind his neck.

"Is this weird? To practice together? We're opposing catchers."

Walker shrugs and takes a few practice swings. "It's whatever we make it." He steps up to the tee and whacks the ball I placed, sending it all the way to the far net.

Milly hooked us up with a private cage in the Division One Athletics facilities she owns with her brothers, since it felt weird taking the opponent to either one of our team facilities. Not to mention, I've never worked out in my new team facilities, so to do it with a Bobbie doesn't feel right.

"I spoke with my sister and we're ready to announce the celebrity game in a week or so, just waiting on a few confirmations. Knox, Carson, and you are jumping on board from the Bobbies. I have a few guys from the Rebels, and then we have Jessica Gomez and Maria Mendez from the former Olympic team who will school us as well."

He swings, his bat a powerful weapon in his hands as he pushes through the ball. From the tension in his grip, I can tell this man has a lot of pent-up anger inside and with every swing, it seems to loosen a fraction.

"What about celebrities for entertainment?"

"Yup, we have Harrison Done, Brandon Woelfel, Yakim Trent, and a few others."

"Harrison Done, huh?" Walker asks. "Didn't know the fucker cared about anything other than his face on the screen."

"This will be televised. He's from Chicago, so his face will be on the screen."

Walker barely smiles, but I see it, the humor in his features. "Makes sense then."

"We're setting up VIP tickets. Should I set any aside for your family?"

He shakes his head. "No."

"No?" I place a ball on the tee and his swing nearly whips my hand off before I can pull away. "But this is to help honor your sister, my brother. Can they not make it?"

"We don't talk," he answers curtly, tapping the ground for another ball. "No need to send an invite."

"Oh, sorry, man. I didn't mean to—"

"It's fine." He taps the tee with his bat. "Load me up."

Feeling bad I made him uncomfortable, I continue placing balls on the tee, watching as he takes his aggression out on each and every unsuspecting ball.

We spend the next hour going back and forth between hitting and loading. We do a soft toss, but nothing too extreme and the whole time, we barely talk. A few words here and there about the event and how it should help the surrounding schools with inclusion in sports, and hopefully as time goes on, we can grow nationwide. Before we left, Walker pledged to gather a few more players from around the league. He assured me he's all in when it comes to the foundation, but doesn't want his name on anything other than appearances. When I asked him why, he said because it wasn't necessary to be recognized. He just wants to do good.

As I drove back to Dottie's apartment afterward, I thought about how misunderstood Walker is, how the media portrays him as the monster behind the plate when in fact, he's a genuinely respectable guy. He might be short-tempered and have a lot of anger, but he's still a decent man. I see his heart, and I hope I can help others see it too.

~

"What the fuck do you think you're doing?" I boom, turning around to see a wooden spoon in Dottie's hand, hovering over my tortellini soup that I've been nursing to perfection since I got home.

"It was bubbling, I was going to stir it."

Hands held out to stop her, I say, "Don't. Touch. It."

She props her hand on her hip and points the spoon at me. "You know, I don't appreciate your yelling. I'm being helpful."

"Like you were helpful two nights ago where you burned the garlic bread to an unrecognizable state?"

"Who knew a broil setting could fry it?" She shrugs.

I point to my chest. "I knew. I KNEW. But you insisted upon taking care of it and then guess what happened? We had lasagna with no garlic bread." I press my hand to my forehead, trying to calm myself. "No garlic bread."

"Oh my God, get over it. I sucked you off as an apology."

"And that apology was accepted, but that doesn't mean it still doesn't hurt to think about it."

"Why am I with you?" Dottie asks, setting down the spoon, causing me to relax.

She tries to walk past me but I snag her by the waist and press her against the counter. "Because you really like me, despite my neurosis. I honestly think you really like them. You live for them.

If you don't roll your eyes at least five times a day, you feel uneasy, dizzy, like you might not be able to get up the next morning."

"How did you know?" she asks deadpanned, but with a tip of her lips, letting me know she's just as humored as me.

Do you know what I live for right now? Seeing my girl try to hold back her laughter when I'm teasing her. She's so guarded and uptight most of the time that I love seeing peeks of her beautiful personality.

"I just know you, babe." I press a kiss to her nose and keep her held tight against me. I've been wanting to ask her something for a while now but I've been holding off, wanting to make sure we were pretty solid before I asked. I couldn't ask for a more solid foundation at this point. "Hey, can I talk to you about something serious?"

"Serious? Do you even know that word?"

"On occasion." I smile.

"Okay, should I be sitting down?"

"Nah, just stay here in my arms." I reach up and push her hair behind her ear and then cup her cheek. I place a gentle kiss across her lips and when I pull away, I see the edge in her eyes disappear as they soften. I'm pretty sure they only soften for me, which makes me feel really goddamn special.

"You have my attention; what do you want to talk about?"

I entwine our fingers together and say, "So you know I've been working on that charity game, right?"

"Oh no, do you want me to play in it?"

"No." I laugh. "Unless, are you good?"

"Not even a little. You would ask me to leave the minute I stepped onto the field."

"Good to know. Glad you're honest, but no, that's not what I was going to ask. We're going to have a celebration dinner after. Walker and I are funding the whole thing and we'll announce the amount raised as well as present the checks to some of the local high schools." I bring her hand to my mouth and kiss her knuckles. "It's about a month away, but things feel pretty solid between us so

I was wondering if you wanted to be my date to the dinner? I'm telling you now so you can check your schedule. If you can't make it, that's—"

"Jason," she says, her voice compassionate and sweet. "I'll be there. No matter what, I'll be there."

"Yeah?" I ask, excitement blooming in my chest. "You'll be my date, even a month out?"

She nods while linking her fingers around my neck. "I might be annoyed by you on a day-to-day basis and there are moments I want to strangle you, but you make me happy, Jason. I'm not going anywhere. You're stuck with me."

"God, that just made my dick hard." *It made my heart burst too, but I won't be sharing that tidbit.* I do know when to shut up. *Sometimes.*

She reaches down between us and cups me, causing my eyes to roll back. "Looks like we need to do something about that then." She presses a quick kiss against my mouth and then drops to her knees, pulling my shorts with her.

God, this woman . . .

CHAPTER TWENTY-SIX

DOTTIE

M s. Domico,

  We hope you're fairing well. We're sorry about the delay in our plans, but we wanted a few more weeks in peace and quiet before we made such a significant decision.

  We talked it over and we're hoping to have dinner with you, your dad, and hopefully, Jason. We understand Jason is a celebrity and we respect his privacy, but we're not looking to have dinner with him because of his status on the baseball field, but because he's the man who's stolen your heart.

  We understand this is a big ask, but we're hoping you'll say yes.

  We'd love to set up dinner this Friday night? Let us know if that works for you.

  Thank you and hope to see you soon.

  Sincerely,

  Mr. and Mrs. Carlton

~

F riday. They chose Friday. They couldn't have picked another day to give me more time to prepare? No, they chose Friday. Two days from now.

When I got the email, I panicked, because the subject line read dinner date, and then I read it and panicked even more. They want Jason there, and I know he'll do it, but at this point, I can't remember a damn thing I said to the Carltons about Jason. Will *they* remember every detail? I sure hope not, because that could be a disaster.

All I know is that I'm standing outside Jason's apartment, trying to work up the courage to ask him to a business dinner. I know he asked me to be his date to his fundraiser, but this feels different. It feels like I'm using him to show the Carltons that I'm the right person for the job. And maybe that's what propelled me to give in to the temptation of seeing what Jason and I could be, but it isn't what's kept me around.

I'm falling for the man and hard . . . that's if I haven't fallen already. Every day, every minute, I can feel myself growing closer and closer to him to the point that it feels like a piece of me is missing when he's not around.

Which means this dinner should be easy, because there's no faking the feelings I have for him.

Feeling like I gained some confidence back, I raise my hand to knock on the door when Knox and Emory's apartment door opens.

"Oh," Emory says, bringing her hand to her chest while nervously chuckling. "I wasn't expecting to see you there." She wiggles her eyebrows. "Going to visit with Jason?"

"Nope, I just like standing outside his door."

"Aren't you charming? But while I have you here, I want to extend—"

Jason's door opens and his sexy smile appears when he spots me. "I heard voices. I didn't know you were coming over, babe." He pulls me in by the waist and keeps his hand protectively around me while talking to Emory. "Unless . . . was she coming to visit you?"

Emory shakes her head. "No, we were both actually coming to see you."

"Lucky me." He kisses the side of my neck. "I know why this little sex-crazed harlot is here." Whispering he says, "She wants the dick." I shouldn't be shocked at this point from his ability to make me blush in seconds . . .

Emory laughs. "Giving her the good dick, huh, Jason?"

"Only the best of the best. Told you I would take care of your friend."

"That you are, but while I have you both here, I wanted to invite you to our Friends-Giving we're having. Not sure who's going home for Thanksgiving, but we thought we would host a little get together at our place. Knox's mom will be visiting and she plans on making a turkey. We'll pitch in with the sides—"

"Calling the yams," Jason says, raising his hand with excitement. "I have a killer recipe that will blow everyone's dicks off, including Dottie's. We all know she has the hardest dick of us all."

"What is wrong with you?" I ask, laughing while Emory gives us a strange look.

"You two are odd," she finally says.

"Us? Uh, no." I shake my head. "He's the weird one, I just deal with it."

"Because of the good dick," Jason says, leaning forward as if to put an exclamation point on the end of his sentence.

"Ah yes, it all makes sense." Emory chuckles and even though she thinks we're weird—well, Jason is weird—she still loves us together. She's said as much when we've talked. She loves Jason, thinks he's a sweetheart—obnoxious, but a sweetheart—and she couldn't pick a better guy for me.

I agree completely.

"We will be there," I say, holding on to Jason's arm that's wrapped around me.

"Perfect. Dottie, just bring crescent rolls; we don't need you cooking."

"I'll have my chef make us something."

"Ah," Jason cries out in insult. "How dare you mention that chef again. I told you, cheat on me with another penis, but do not cheat on me in the kitchen." Addressing Emory, he says, "I'll make two things: Yams and homemade stuffing from homemade bread because if anything, I'm a fancy fuck."

"So fancy." Emory heads back to her apartment. "Thank you. Now you two go do your thing."

We say our goodbyes and Jason quickly pulls me into his apartment and pushes me against his closed door. His hands fall to my waist while his mouth finds mine. I melt against the wood as he takes over, moving his hand up my body to cup my cheek, his body adding pressure as he kisses me unlike any man has ever before. *Passionately*.

"Jason," I murmur when his mouth finds my jaw.

"Missed you today, sweet cheeks." He moves to my neck and my hand falls to his chest. "I'm so happy you came over."

"I . . ." Oh God his mouth feels so good. "I need to talk to you."

He stills, his head lifting. When he looks me in the eyes, his face falls. "What's wrong?"

"Nothing. I just need to talk to you."

He stands tall, looking concerned. "Okay." He takes me by the hand and takes me to the couch where he pulls me down on his lap. Hands still connected, he asks, "What's up?"

And just like that, a wave of nerves hit me. This is ridiculous. I don't get nervous. I'm rock solid, take no prisoners, show no emotions, but here I am, sitting on the lap of the man who owns my heart, and all I can think about is how nervous I am about a simple question.

Maybe because it isn't a simple question, not where relationships are concerned. I've never really had a man in my life to invite to a business dinner, or a dinner with my parents for that matter.

Every relationship I've had has been surface level; I've never gone deep like I have with Jason. Therefore, this feels so much more real and the stakes are higher if he says no.

"Dottie." He squeezes my side. "What's wrong, babe? You look . . . different."

Wanting to be honest with him, I say, "Just nervous."

"Nervous?" His brow creases. "But it's me. You can tell me anything."

"I know." I take a deep breath and say, "So you know I've been working hard on the Carlton project?"

"Yeah, breaking your back over it. Are they finally coming back from vacation?"

I nod. "They are and they requested to have dinner Friday night to talk."

"That's great. Did they sound positive?"

"It was an email so I couldn't really tell, but they did have a request."

"What was it? We'll make it happen." The tension eases in my shoulders when he says that. He's eager to help. I should have known this wouldn't be as big a deal as it was in my head.

"They, uh, know we're dating and since they're all about family, they wanted to meet the man who I'm seeing. I know it's asking a lot but—"

"Babe." He smiles at me. "I'm in." His hand snakes up my neck. "I'm all in with you, you know that, right?"

"I . . . I do now."

"I thought I made that clear. I like you, Dottie, a lot. I have no plans to go anywhere."

"I know, but this is a business thing."

"So, that's what I'm here for. That includes every aspect of your life." He brings my mouth to his and presses a gentle kiss across my lips. When he pulls away, he says, "Why don't you have them over to your place? I'll cook a ham—I have a great recipe— and we can put on a noteworthy dinner for them, show them the kind of give and take we have with our relationship."

"No, I don't want you to go to all that trouble."

"It's not trouble if it's for you. Plus, if you use that chef of yours for this dinner, I'm going to be pissed."

I chuckle and nod. "Okay, you can make dinner, but let me help?"

"Do you want the contract?"

"Yes."

He pats my leg. "Then leave the cooking to me."

"I'm not that bad."

"And you're not great either."

"You know, you were so close to getting a blow job, but after that comment, I don't think that's going to happen."

"Good," he says matter-of-factly. "Because I planned on doing other things with you and the first item on my to-do list is eat your pussy."

He flips me on my back on the carpet of his living room and pushes my skirt up to my waist while dragging my thong down at the same time. In seconds, I'm bare and spread to him, my heart racing a mile a minute.

"Hold your legs open. I need to use my hands for other things."

I do as he says and before I can catch my next breath, his tongue is swirling over my clit, his fingers spreading me wide.

"Oh Jason," I moan, feeling a wave of arousal hit me, igniting my body into a fiery inferno.

He wastes no time in swirling his tongue over and over, flattening it and then flicking it until my body is so wound up, I'm seconds from coming.

He must see the tension coiling inside me because right when I'm a moment from finding euphoria, he stops and removes his pants. He brings his cock to my entrance and says, "I need to be inside you. Now."

He pushes himself in until he bottoms out, both of us groaning together at the sensation.

"Fuck, Dottie . . . Do you feel this? This connection we have?"

"Yes," I whisper, barely able to get my voice to work as he

starts pumping his hips, filling me up so much that I feel like he's sucking the breath right from my lungs.

"This isn't going anywhere. I'm not going anywhere. Are you?"

I shake my head.

"Say it," he barks out through his teeth, the pressure building between us.

"I'm . . . oh God—" He thrusts hard, his balls slapping against me, his hand falling to my clit where he rubs it, bringing me to the edge. "Jason . . . yes."

"Say it, Dottie."

"I'm, fuck . . . I'm not going . . . anywhere."

"Damn right you're not." He plows into me, and I can feel us inching up the carpet with each thrust, but I don't care about the rug burn, or how twisted my clothes are at this point, because all I care about is being with this man.

Loving this man.

He's everything I could have ever dreamed of and so much more.

When I say I'm never leaving, I'm not. He's it for me.

My man.

My Jason.

CHAPTER TWENTY-SEVEN

JASON

I glance around the apartment.

Coast is clear.

I lift up the apron Dottie got me that says "Eat my food, Lick my dick" and hold the freshly polished spoon in front of my junk.

Clear as day I see my rod and nuggets dangling upside down, happy to be attached to this machine of a body.

"What are you doing?"

"Shhhh-it," I say, scrambling to drop my apron, the spoon clattering to the floor. Great. Now I'm going to have to polish it again.

"Were you checking out your penis in the spoon reflection?" Dottie asks, appearing from her bedroom in a robe and nothing else. Her hair is down and in waves, her makeup subtle but highlighting her gorgeous eyes, and she smells like a goddamn field of flowers.

"I was." I take the spoon in hand and start polishing it again. "The only way to tell if your silverware has been properly polished is if you can see the reflection of your junk in it."

Pause.

Blink.

"Charming." She bites her bottom lip and looks around the apartment. "I should have had those cleaners come back to the apartment. It doesn't look clean enough. Does it look clean enough?"

"Dottie, the apartment looks phenomenal. Stop stressing and try to relax."

"I don't think I'll relax until this is over."

"Hey"—I point the spoon at her—"you said if I cooked naked, you wouldn't be so tense."

She smiles shamefully at me and says, "I lied."

"You're telling me my ass has been hanging out this entire time for no reason? Do you realize how unsanitary that is?"

"Are you stirring with your butt muscles?"

"No . . . but that seems like a party trick I'm willing to dedicate some time to in order to master."

"Please don't." She chuckles and then lets out a long breath. "Maybe I just need to get my mind off things."

"I can do that for you." I wiggle my eyebrows at her.

She looks down at my crotch and then back up at me. "You literally came an hour ago. And this morning—twice—before I left for work. How could you possibly want sex again?"

"Dottie, I will always want sex with you," I say. "Always." She's the reason I'm perpetually horny. Her body, her mind, her sass, her mouth . . . every part of her calls to me. *It always will.*

She smiles and walks over to me, her robe shifting back and forth, giving me peeks of her cleavage. When she stands a few inches from me, she lowers her hands to my bare ass and gives it a small squeeze while placing a kiss on my jaw.

"You are the best man I know. Do you realize that?"

"Tell me more."

One hand falls to the front of my apron and slips under the canvas fabric to my growing erection. She casually strokes my length while bringing her mouth to mine.

"You are so good to me." Her finger swirls around the head of my cock. "Take care of me." She brushes down and then back up to swirl. Teeth nip my jaw. "Make me laugh." Pushes my apron to the side and with the hand that's squeezing my ass, she holds the loose fabric out of the way so my dick is hanging out in the open. "Make me swoon." Slowly she moves her body south until her mouth is directly in front of my already aching arousal. "And you always make me horny."

That's something I can't hear enough. She opens her mouth and is about to take me in when I lift her up and spin her around instead. Not even needing to be told what to do, she undoes her robe, lets it fall to the floor, and then braces both her hands on the counter while sticking her ass in the air.

"Jesus Christ, Dottie," I mutter while dragging my hand over my mouth. I push her long black hair to the side so I can see her elegant neck, lean forward, and insert my cock inside her while placing kisses along her shoulder blade.

Reaching around, I grab both her tits and play with her nipples, rolling them and squeezing them, loving how a simple touch can spur her on even more. She backs into me, moving her pelvis, riding my cock to her own pleasure. I let her find her pleasure, let her take control, or at least, let her think she's in control.

"God, Jason, you make me so hot." She's swiveling her hips now and lowers her hand to her clit where she plays with it, her cries of pleasure reverberating against the cabinets in the kitchen. "Yes, yes," she breathes out. "Oh my God, Jason."

My balls ache as my stomach bottoms out, my orgasm coming out of nowhere. I grab her hips and pump hard a few times before she cries out my name, her pussy spasming around my cock, forcing my own orgasm.

I roar against her back, my hips stilling as I come inside her, moving her hips until I've completely spilled every last ounce of my passion.

"Christ," I breathe against her back, laughing at the same time. "That was unexpected."

She chuckles. "And unsanitary."

I kiss between her shoulder blades and spin her around. "All the food is on the other side of the kitchen or in the oven. We're good." I cup her cheeks and kiss her on the lips. "Are you feeling better?"

"Yes. Thank you." With another kiss, she turns and opens her computer that's on the counter and says, "I'm going to clean up and then answer some emails. Is dinner almost—"

Ding.

"Ready?" she finishes on a laugh.

"Yup. Now we're in the important phase."

"What phase is that?"

"The crisping." I give her one last kiss, don the pink oven mitts that match the ones she gave me, and check the oven. A wave of yummy ham caramelized in brown sugar and pineapple hits me. "Oh babe, this is going to be amazing. The Carltons are going to pick your proposal based on this meal alone."

She's hovered over her computer as she says, "They would be crazy not to."

"Now we're going to turn this on broil and let it crisp the edges so we get that perfect texture."

"I'm going to do a quick rinse off and avoid my hair and makeup as best as possible."

"Why?" I ask, spinning around as she starts to walk away. "Don't want sex smell on you?"

"Can you not?" She shivers with revulsion. "God, Jason."

"What?" I laugh. "Bottle that up in a candle for me, especially if it's a special-edition Dottie scent."

"That's right," she says, walking away, "Get out all the pervy comments now. Let them fly so you're on your best behavior when they get here."

"I'm an ace at these things," I call out as she disappears. "A fucking ace."

Keeping the oven door open so I have a trained eye on the ham, I rehearse in my head all the thoughtful questions I came up with to ask Mr. and Mrs. Carlton.

How did you two meet?

Was it love at first sight?

Did you—

Ding.

"What was that?" I ask myself, looking around the kitchen. Am I missing a timer?

Ding.

I check the oven, then the counter . . .

Ding.

My eyes fly to Dottie's computer. Oh, okay. I chuckle to myself, letting the short panic fade. I have everything timed out, and at this point in preparation there should be no extra—hey, why does that email have my name as the subject line?

I glance at the ham and then turn back to the computer, leaning a little closer.

Does it say Jason?

I squint.

Yup, that says Jason.

Maybe it's a different Jason . . . or maybe it's about me and the dinner tonight. Should I look at it?

No.

That's Dottie's email. She'll read it and tell me what it says. Right?

What if she doesn't? What if she's too nervous to tell me what it says? I don't want to disappoint her tonight.

I bite my bottom lip and look toward her bedroom.

Maybe a quick glance, just to get the gist of it.

I step away from the oven but then catch myself.

"No," I mutter, turning away. "That's her work email. It's private. If I need to know the information, she'll tell me."

Keeping my eye on the ham, I watch the juices spark inside the oven while the email bores a hole in the back of my head.

It's calling out to me, tapping me on the shoulder, encouraging me to read it, look at it, practically smell it for information.

"Ah," I groan, pulling on my hair with my oven mitts.

Just a quick once-over.

I glance at the ham one more time. I look down the hallway—the coast is clear—and then I read the email.

Dottie,

I'm assuming everything is set for tonight. I have all the confidence in the world that you can close the deal.

As for Jason, how did he take the news about your fake relationship? I'm assuming okay if he's willing to go along with tonight. I still feel uncomfortable about you using him for the dinner, but as long as he's in the know, that's all that matters.

Knock them dead. Love you, kid.

Dad.

My eyes swim over the words, rereading the same sentence as if it's not registering in my brain.

I still feel uncomfortable about you using him for the dinner, but as long as he's in the know, that's all that matters.

Using me?

Fake relationship?

What?

I shift on my feet, reading the email again. He must be mistaken. What we have isn't fake. There's nothing fake about our relationship. I've never felt something so real in my life.

But . . . what if . . .

No. I shake my head and step away from my computer, my mind reeling with every conversation I've had with Dottie.

This is real. Real for me, real for her.

Then again . . .

When did she talk to the Carltons about me? They've been on vacation for a while, so she must have told them before they left. When was that though? Shit, either way the timing doesn't seem to work. Why would she tell her dad this was fake unless . . . it started that way?

Shit.

I wrack my brain, trying to figure out the timeline, tempted to go through her emails to help me but think better of it. I'm sure they aren't ones she'd keep.

What about the enchilada fiasco night? She went to work that day pissed as shit at me. I didn't think she'd come to dinner, and yet she showed up. But . . . she more than just showed up; she came on to me and hard. It was weird at the time, still fucking weird now that I think about it, but if she was desperate to seal the deal, I wouldn't put it past her to do anything it takes.

Holy.

Fuck.

I step back again, both oven mitt hands on top of my head as I try to understand the implications of this.

Does she actually like me? Or has this all been a fucking game to her? Have I been a pawn in her life? Using me for sex and career gain?

I don't want to believe it, but then again, I know the drive that hides behind those seductive eyes of hers.

I still feel uncomfortable about you using him.

Why would her dad say those specific words? "Using him." He would only use that precise term if that's what she told him.

My heart plummets to the floor, shattering right there on the spot as my breathing starts to pick up.

All the late-night conversations, the flirty smiles, the serious talk about belonging to one another . . . it was all a farce, a goddamn lie for her gain.

Fuck. It's like Melissa all over again. I'd thought she was into me as well, but she'd been all over other guys at the same time. Why can women lie so easily? What do they really gain from being so . . . false?

"Fuck," I say to myself just as a burning smell hits my nose.

I spin around only to find the oven bursting with a flaming ham.

"Ahh," I scream as if my body was replaced with a ten-year-old girl's. Flames crawl out of the oven and tickle the kitchen air as I dance around the tiled floor, arms flailing, trying to locate a fire extinguisher. "I'm going to die," I say in the most dramatic voice ever heard. "Fire. It's a fucking fire." I jog in place, my cock and balls bouncing against my apron. "Charred to death naked. Ahhhhh."

I bounce.

I dance.

I flail every limb of my body.

I pray to Jesus for indoor rain.

"It's a goddamn inferno in here. This is how I die, naked, and —" I spot a red canister in the corner and quickly run to it.

Praise you, praise you!

I pull the metal clip, take the hose, and point it at the oven. Using my most efficient twinkle toes, I waltz around the kitchen, a fire extinguisher as my partner, hand and hose, and together we douse the fire until it's completely out.

On a deep sigh, I relax my shoulders and stare at the charred ham.

Completely ruined.

All that hard work. All that prep. All that tasty, crispy smell.

Gone.

The email, the uncertainty, the ruined ham—the fact that I almost burned up in flames naked as the day I was born—it all comes crashing down on me, leaving me to sink to the floor into a pile of sodden emotions.

And even though the ham is the final kick to the crotch, that's not what's slowly draining the life from my body. That's not what's causing this ill feeling to bubble up inside me.

It's the email.

The words "using him" flashing, making me feel like a complete idiot.

A lone tear falls down my cheek.

What's bringing me the most grief? What I thought Dottie felt for me wasn't really true.

I feel like a goddamn fool.

An idiot for thinking that this high-powered woman with work on her mind constantly could genuinely open her heart to me.

"Fuck," I mutter, rubbing my eye with my mitt-covered palm.

I take calming breaths and as air fills my lungs, anger filters into my veins. How many times has she told me I'm ridiculous? How often has she told me she should hate me but then said words to buffer the truth? I'm competitive by nature, but I'm not sticking around to attempt to win this. Win her. *Because she doesn't want to be won. At least, not by me.*

Fuck this and fuck her.

I can't be here any longer, and I sure as shit can't be here when the Carltons arrive. No fucking way. Unlike a certain woman, I'm not a talented actor.

Standing, I toss the oven mitts to the ground and tear off my apron. Naked, I walk to Dottie's bedroom and quickly put on my jeans and shirt. Without a word, I head to the living room and grab my shoes.

That's when Dottie pops out of the bedroom in her robe, a confused look on her face. "Is something burning?"

I ignore her and finish tying my shoes. When I stand, she's coming toward me, and even though it looks like she's concerned, I honestly can't tell if it's real or not at this point.

"Jason, what's wrong? Your eyes are bloodshot." She glances over my shoulder. "Did something happen to the ham?"

"Yeah, it's fucking charred. I wouldn't serve it if I were you."

I move past her and walk toward the door.

"Where are you going?"

"Anywhere but here."

She pads across the hardwood floors and steps in front of me. "Wait, what's going on? Is everything okay?" Her hand crawls up my chest and I grip her wrist, stopping her. Her eyes widen, and I slowly remove her touch from my body.

"No, it's not okay." I push my hand through my hair. "Care to tell me why I'm really here?"

"Wh-what are you talking about?"

"Don't act like you don't fucking know."

"Jason." Her voice goes weak, scared. "I really don't."

"No?" I twist to the side and then back at her, distraught and so fucking angry that I'm about to lose my goddamn cool. "Then why the fuck is your dad emailing you about me, and saying he feels uncomfortable about you using me for your career?"

She stills, her breath catching in her throat as she looks toward her open computer.

"Yeah, that's what I fucking thought." I go to move past her again, but she stops me with her hand to my chest. "I suggest you don't fucking touch me right now, Dottie."

"Jason, it's not what you think."

That's what they always say.

"It's not?" My brows shoot up to my hairline. "So you didn't tell the Carltons we were dating before we actually were?"

She twists her hands together and looks off to the side. "I mean—"

"Get out of my fucking way."

"Wait, please let me explain."

"Why? So you can lie to me like you've been lying during our entire relationship?" My breath catches in my chest as a wave of pain hits me. "I really fucking liked you, Dottie, and all this, that email . . . you've crushed me." Whispering and staring at the ground, I say, "You broke my heart."

"I haven't been lying to you," she says, her voice full of sorrow. I glance up to see tears streaming down her face and for a brief second, I wonder if she's telling the truth. "Everything we've felt between us, that's been real. I was just in a tough spot a while ago. The Carltons weren't going to consider my proposal because I wasn't in a relationship. It was really stupid, and I panicked. I told them I was in one and dropped your name like an idiot."

"And that's why you came over to my apartment that night, to make a move, to try to make what you said a reality. Great. So glad I could be a part of your game."

"I liked you before that," she says. "I had such a bad crush on you in college and then seeing you again, years later, it all came flooding back. This wasn't an overnight thing. This has been brewing inside me for a long time."

"Yeah, that's evident from the way you had security remove me from your office." I drag my hand over my mouth and say, "Fuck, Dottie. Has this all been a goddamn joke to you?"

"No," she sobs, trying to take my hand, but I whip it away. "This has been"—she wipes at her face, completely falling apart in front of me—"this has been so much more than I ever expected."

"But how did it start?" I ask, wanting the truth.

"It . . ." Her lip trembles. "It started . . ."

"Fucking say it, Dottie."

She reels back, as if my voice is venom splashing her face. Her face blanches, her tears roll down like a waterfall, and her hands shake as the clutches them to her chest. "It was—"

I put my hand up, unable to look at her anymore. "You know what? Save it. I'm done."

"Wh-what?" she asks, her voice rocking with pain. "What do you mean, you're done?"

"It's exactly what it means. I'm done. We're done," I say with such finality that I convince myself of the words. "And you know what the real fucking kicker is? Out of everyone, you should know what it feels like to be used." I point at her. "You should know the anguish, the heartache, the unfiltered pain it causes to find out you aren't loved, you aren't cared for . . . you're just a pawn in someone's game." I look her up and down, disgust filling me. "I expected so much more from you, Dottie."

I head to her door, opening it as she cries out in a sob. "Jason, please. Let me explain. I'm sorry."

"Sorry isn't going to cut it, Dottie. You just broke my trust and there's no coming back from that."

Before she can say another word, I exit her apartment and head to mine. The entire drive, I fucking cry like an asshole. When I reach my door, I consider knocking on Knox and Emory's door, but instead, I head inside my dark apartment and slide to the ground against my bed. *Fuck.* How did she fool me? How did she fucking fool her friends? They've known her for years. *Years.* I know they weren't in on it.

This wasn't an overnight thing. This has been brewing inside me for a long time.

I'm so fucking stupid. It was an overnight thing.

My mom once said that when I give my heart away to someone, it will be theirs for life. That they'll take care of it because they'll know how lucky they are. "Well, Mom, apparently that's utter bullshit. I gave my heart to Dottie Domico, and she trampled on it. Destroyed it. Broke it.

Broke me.

CHAPTER TWENTY-EIGHT

DOTTIE

The minute the door clicks shut, I fall to the ground in a heap of tears.

My hands cover my eyes as regret assails me, stabbing me in the chest with every image of Jason's heartbroken face that crosses my mind.

Like a steel weight resting heavily on my lungs, my actions, my dishonesty, it's impossible to breathe.

We're done.

Those two words dig deep into my soul as realization smacks me in the face. He didn't just leave, he didn't just storm off . . . he broke up with me.

He actually broke up with me.

He's gone, and from the finality in his voice, he's never coming back.

"I'm so stupid," I mutter, shaking my head. "So fucking stupid."

How did I not tell him? How did I drag this out for so long and not say anything?

Because I was terrified I'd lose him . . . but I lost him anyway.

From my seated position, I glance toward the kitchen and

dining room. The table is elegantly set using my finest dishes and silverware that I know he spent time polishing. Cream cloth napkins are folded into a swan shape, and the wine we picked out specifically to pair well with the ham is on the table, ready to be opened.

He did this for me, and I didn't even have the decency to tell him the truth about the Carltons.

What did that email say? What words caused such agony for the man I love?

Standing on shaky legs, I walk to my computer and there it is, clear as day, an email from my dad. Subject line: Jason. Probably the reason Jason opened it.

I can't be mad at him for invading my privacy, because if I was in his shoes, I'd probably have done the same thing.

On a deep breath, I read through it quickly, my eyes swimming with regret as they wash over the words 'fake relationship . . . using him.'

Shit . . . I bury my head in my hands again, more sobs wracking my body. What he must be feeling right now. It was never fake, not for me. My first attempt at trying to win him over might have been forced, but the rest of it wasn't. Nothing about my pursuit for him was fake. Nothing about our relationship was unreal. I can still taste him in my mouth, feel him between my legs, smell his scent all over my body, hear the deep baritone of his voice over my skin as he demands more from me.

I shake my head in disgust. This is such a mess. I am such a mess.

I glance at the stove, the charred ham, a symbol of my dead relationship. The time he spent on it, the time he spent on *us*, up in flames in the matter of seconds.

And I only have myself to blame.

I need to talk to him. I need to make this right. He needs to know it was him and only thoughts of him that made our relationship real.

Picking up my phone from the counter, I type out a quick text to Jason, knowing fully well he'll ignore it.

Dottie: *I'm so sorry, Jason. Please hear me when I say you deserve so much better than how I treated you. If I were a better person, I'd leave you alone, but I'm not, and I'm selfish, because I want you in my life. What we had was real. It was so real. I'm sorry I made you doubt that.*

Tears cascading down my cheeks, I scroll through my contacts and press call while bringing the phone to my ear. I don't want to make this phone call, but at this point, there's no other option.

I wipe the tears off my face and brace myself as the phone is picked up.

"Miss Domico, how can I help you?"

I suck in a sharp breath. There is no way they can help me. In fact, I wouldn't deserve it if they tried. I know I've ruined any chance of Domico Industries securing the contract, but at this point, why give a shit? *He's gone.* "Hi, Mr. Carlton I'm afraid I'm going to have to cancel . . ."

∽

E **mory:** *Dottie . . .*
    Lindsay: *Oh girl, Emory just told me everything.*
Emory: *Knox spoke with Jason last night. Why didn't you tell him?*
Dottie: *Because I'm an idiot. I really don't want to talk about this.*
Emory: *I don't think that's how this friend thing goes. We're here for you, even when you're a complete dumbass.*
Lindsay: *I thought you told him. Why did I think you told him? Ugh, Dottie, Knox said Jason looked terrible.*
Emory: *You weren't supposed to tell her that.*
Lindsay: *She needs to know. Jason is a good guy and she really hurt him.*
Dottie: *I know I hurt him. He made that quite clear when he was leaving my apartment. I don't think I've ever felt this sick, this awful, this unbelievably sorry in my entire life.*
Emory: *He cried with Knox . . .*

I suck in a breath reading Emory's text as I rest my head against my tear-soaked pillow. It's been two days since he left, and I've yet to get out of bed after cancelling the dinner. I've sent Jason countless texts and I even tried calling him a few times but as expected, he's been radio silent. I've considered going to his apartment but have thought better of it. I'm the last person he wants knocking on his door right now.

Lindsay: *That tears my heart out. He's such a sweet, amazing guy.*

Dottie: *I know. Okay, I KNOW! I fucked up and if I could, I'd take everything back. I don't need you two rubbing it in my face.*

Emory: *We're not rubbing it in your face, we're making sure you drop that shield of yours and allow yourself to feel the pain you caused him.*

Lindsay: *You're so guarded all the time. It's important to allow yourself to feel, to know that there are people out there who you hurt with your actions.*

Dottie: *Are you trying to say I'm heartless?*

Emory: *No. But you are clueless. Please don't be clueless about this. Jason was perfect for you. Everything you needed and so much more. You need to find a way to make this right.*

Dottie: *And how would you suggest that?*

Lindsay: *That's for you to figure out. But we've known each other for a long time and this is the first time I'm not taking your side. #TeamJason*

Dottie: *You don't have to be an asshole, Lindsay.*

Emory: *Lindsay is right. You truly messed up. You can't blame anyone but yourself. I love you, but I'm afraid I'm Team Jason too.*

Dottie: *So I lost my man and my best friends. Great.*

Lindsay: *Your man . . . see? You couldn't even say boyfriend. I know you've been burned in the past, but that doesn't mean you close yourself off to everyone. You might have thought you were giving yourself over to Jason but you still held him at arm's length. All he wanted was for you to be honest with him and accept him for who he is.*

Dottie: *I do accept him.*

Emory: *But accepting him means that you know he needs a deeper connection where you're concerned. You kept it surface level with him. And it led to this, never fully trusting him with your truth, with your heart.*

Dottie: *Because I was hurt.*

Lindsay: *By other men. Other men hurt you, Dottie. Not Jason. That was your mistake, by sticking Jason in the same group as the men you once dated, you never gave him a chance.*

Dottie: *I only didn't tell him about the Carltons. I gave him my entire self.*

Emory: *Don't you see it? If you gave him all of you, then you would have told him, but you were still holding back in case he hurt you. He never had a chance.*

Lindsay: *I love you, but she's right.*

I toss my phone to the side, annoyed with the conversation, and try to shut my eyes, but even shut they burn from all the tears I've shed the past two days.

Are they right? Did I not truly give myself to Jason?

I was scared of losing him. Or was I scared of him seeing my true colors, the determined businesswoman I am? Because what if after he saw my true self he wouldn't want to be with me anymore?

That seems more accurate than being scared, because I've been scared before, and it's never truly affected my decisions. But with Jason, it was different.

Because he was different.

Rolling to my back, I stare at the ceiling and suck in a large breath.

I fucked up my relationship with Jason.

I fucked over this deal with the Carltons by cancelling with them.

I am slowly killing my career with my terrible choices.

And lastly, once again, I've let my dad down. Caused him more discomfort and embarrassment.

All because of what? A man in my past who mistreated me? *Tarnished my reputation.*

A man who I trusted, who lied to me, and broke me . . . just like I did to Jason.

And that realization strikes me harder than any other thought as Jason's words return.

You should know the anguish, the heartache, the unfiltered pain it causes to find out you aren't loved, you aren't cared for . . . you're just a pawn in someone's game.

Deep in my soul, I know that's not how I treated things with Jason, but from the outside looking in, from his perspective, dealing with a woman who unintentionally kept him at arm's length emotionally, yeah . . . I can see where he'd wholeheartedly believe I lied for my own gain.

I pick up my phone again and scroll through Emory and Lindsay's texts, feeling less defensive and more responsive to what they're saying. It's time I take responsibility for my actions, or lack thereof, and it starts with telling the truth because the lies have done enough damage.

~

"Mr. and Mrs. Carlton are here to see you," Jessica says, stepping into my doorway with a knock.

Being in the high-powered position I am in my dad's company, I've always prided myself on never being nervous, of being able to stay cool and calm through any business deal or interaction, but right now, I'm sweating.

I woke up this morning not wanting to get out of bed. I wanted to continue wallowing in my pain by looking through the pictures we took at the amusement park, something I did all weekend. But I knew I had responsibilities and it started with talking to the Carltons.

Wiping my hand on my dress pants, I stand from my chair. "Please show them in."

Clouded with uneasiness, I stiffen my back and face the music. This moment is going to cost me the biggest deal of my career, possibly my job, damage my relationship with my dad, but I know it's the right thing to do.

Hands linked in front of me, I give Mr. and Mrs. Carlton a soft smile as they enter my office. We exchange greetings with handshakes, and I set them up with some drinks as we take a seat in my office that overlooks the Chicago skyline.

When I decided on telling them the truth, I knew it would be hard. I'm putting not only my name on the line, but my dad's, and it's why I asked him to meet us here as well.

Right on time, my dad knocks on the door and is surprised to see Mr. and Mrs. Carlton already seated. I have yet to tell him everything that went down on Friday because frankly, I wasn't only embarrassed, but heartbroken. I didn't have it in me to disappoint another man in my life, so I sent him a quick email to meet me on Monday in my office.

I can only imagine what's running through his head. He's probably thinking I closed on the deal from the bright smile on his face.

Shit, I hate this. Facing the consequences of my actions.

Once he greets the Carltons, he takes a seat as well.

With a deep breath, I say, "Thank you all for meeting me here today and adjusting your schedules. I really appreciate it." I scoot forward on my chair, trying not to fidget like my dad taught me. Fidgeting shows weakness and if anything, I need to be as strong as I can possibly be in this moment. "I'm really sorry about canceling dinner on Friday." From the corner of my eye, I see my dad pull on his cufflink, an indication that he's not entirely happy to not be briefed before this meeting.

"That's quite all right, Miss Domico. We are understanding people."

Let's see just how understanding.

"I told you I had to cancel because of an emergency, which in fact, was true. The dinner we prepared caught up in flames."

"Oh dear," says Mrs. Carlton. "Is your home okay?"

"Yes, it was contained in the oven, but it happened because of me. You see, I've been dating Jason Orson, but not for as long as I told you." Mr. Carlton's eyebrows sharpen. "I've only been seeing him for a little over a month."

"I see," Mr. Carlton says, his usual jovial self, angry.

Controlling my breath and not letting it escape me, I say, "I was desperate to show you that even though I might not have been the family person you were looking for, we still were a family operated company. I wanted to keep you interested to grant me more time to prove that to you. I went about it the wrong way, and . . . I'm so sorry I deceived you."

"I see," Mrs. Carlton says looking out the window.

"I never meant to deceive you or make you feel like you'd been fooled. I can tell you from the heart, right now, that Jason Orson is everything I ever asked for in a man and I really—"

Mr. Carlton clears his throat and grips the edges of his armrest. "Yes, well, I don't need to hear you prattle on. I think our time here is done." He stands, lending his hand to his wife who takes it and lifts from her chair. "We'll see ourselves out."

Fuck. Panic constricts my throat, desperate pleas at the tip of my tongue that can't seem to find a voice. *No.*

"Mr. and Mrs. Carlton," my dad says, standing as well. "Please know this isn't how we conduct business."

"No?" Mr. Carlton asks, a sturdiness to his question. "She's your daughter is she not? She must have learned how to be untrustworthy somewhere."

My dad reels back, as if he's been slapped. Shit . . . shit, shit, shit.

The crashing down of the moment drowns me as I try to float to the top, try to find the courage to stand on two legs as I realize this is just like the last time I disappointed my dad. The disappointment in his face, but the need to protect me as well.

I step in, placing a hand on my dad's forearm. "I assure you, Mr. Carlton, my dad had nothing to do with this. He didn't condone what I did. This was all on me and I will forever regret this decision."

"Yes, you will," he says, heading toward the door. He takes his wife's hand and says, "What you learn quickly in this business, Miss Domico, is even though it's a take-no-prisoners atmosphere, the businesses and executives who finish in a golden light and live a fruitful life are the ones who take the honest path in business. I hope this lesson serves you well."

They vacate my office, disappointment written all over their features, and that's when I realize, I'm pretty sure they were ready to pick the Domicos. Had I not come clean, we'd be popping champagne and celebrating.

It wouldn't have felt right though, especially with the way things ended with Jason.

God, I miss him so much it hurts.

When they're out of earshot, my dad turns on me, anger etched in his eyes. "What the hell was that, Dorothy?"

And here's the moment I've been dreading the most about today. "It was the truth. They deserved it."

"They deserved it from the very beginning." He drags his hand over his face. "You just cost us millions over that deal."

"I know, Dad—"

"No, I don't think you do. You not only cost us money, but you cost us our reputation." He tosses his hand in the air. "What the hell am I supposed to do with this now?"

"Nothing," I say, as an acute sense of loss builds inside me.

In my dream of dreams, I pictured everything going right, that the Carltons would congratulate me on being truthful, and my dad would think it was a risk but proud of me for not hiding behind deception.

That was the dream. Somewhat misguided.

Reality? This is the end of everything I've built over the last few years, everything I thought I wanted and worked for since college. I wasn't sure if I was going to do this or not, but I feel as though I don't have a choice. I pick up a letter off my desk and hand it to him. "Here's my resignation. Please consider this my two weeks' notice or until you can find a replacement."

"Dorothy . . ." my dad says, resigned. He can barely look at me.

"Don't, Dad. I know this is necessary, and I'm saving you the trouble of having to do it yourself. I'd hoped the Carltons would have appreciated my sincerity—my choice to come clean—and maybe still go with us, but I knew that was a long shot. I screwed this up big time, even with your warning. If this were anyone else, you'd have fired them on the spot. I should have listened to you, I never should have dragged Jason into this mess and because of my immature decisions, I hurt the company. This needs to be done."

"But this is my legacy. I've built this business from the ground up; it was supposed to be passed on to you," he says, looking weak and disheartened.

I hate this. That I've done this to him.

"I know, but I'll be honest, Dad. This job, even though it's fun working for you, it's been stressful, and I've made choices I'll always regret. It's turned me into a person I'm not exactly proud of, and it's made me jaded and closed off, a trait that didn't emerge until I sat at this desk. I admire everything you've built and done for our family—for me. And I'm heartbroken over how I've treated that gift and the responsibilities you entrusted to me. I can see I've lost sight of who *I* am. What I should be doing."

"Is this about Nick?" he asks, walking toward me and taking my hand in his.

I shake my head, but maybe some of it is. "It stems from Nick, from the distrust his betrayal created. I worked extra hard after he hurt me to prove I'm more than the family name, that I'm my own entity. I can see I did anything to make myself feel empowered. To feel *powerful*." I shake my head. "The drive blinded me, made my actions unacceptable, and I ruined the best thing that's ever happened to me . . . Jason."

"Sweetie," he says softly, pulling me into a hug. "You need that kind of drive for this business."

"It's not the person I am. I thought it was, but it's not."

He kisses the top of my head and says, "You were always more of your mother's daughter with the soft soul and kind heart. It's why you donate so generously. *That's* who you are. That's the woman I'm incredibly proud of."

I try to digest his words, but they don't feel right at this moment. They don't quite fit with how I feel about myself.

Sighing, my dad asks, "So if you're not working for me, what are you going to do?"

"I have some ideas. Some ideas that will help me feel more fulfilled. At least I hope."

He exhales, pulling on his tie before he lowers his head in defeat. "Shit, Dorothy."

"I know." Tears well up in my eyes. "I'm so sorry, Dad. So, so sorry."

"Oh, sweetie." He squeezes me tighter, and that's when I break down against his pristine Tom Ford suit. "Shh," he says, rubbing the back of my head. But it's impossible for me to stop crying now the waterworks have taken over. I clutch his suit jacket and sob. "Sweetie, all these tears, there not just for the job . . ."

I shake my head. "No."

"It's about the boy."

I nod.

"What happened?"

"He . . . he . . ." I catch my breath. "He saw your email. He was so upset, so heartbroken. He broke things off with me and left. I don't think I've ever seen someone so devastated than I did in that moment." I don't think I've ever caused anyone so much pain before or felt so . . . ashamed.

"I don't know, right now you're giving him a run for his money."

I pull away and wipe away my tears. "I love him, Dad, and before I could even say it, I lost him."

"Who's to say you still can't say it?"

"He'll push me away." I shake my head.

"You never know until you try, sweetie, and now that you've resigned, looks like you have some time on your hands. Make it up to him."

"I don't know how," I say, feeling vulnerable and exposed, but I guess that's what being in love is all about, shedding a layer of skin so the other person can see your true self, your soul. "What if he turns me away?"

"Then at least you'll know you gave it your all, like everything else in your life."

~

I'm going to puke.

Yup, right here, in the hallway, puke is happening.

It took me a few days to gain the nerve, but once I grabbed enough courage, I didn't let myself turn back.

A VP from the California office has been wanting to move to Chicago within the company, but there haven't been any positions open. Now I'm leaving, the transition is seamless and the guy, Kent, is unsurprisingly an intelligent and a trusted employee. I feel comfortable with him taking over and my dad feels safe with his company.

He flew out immediately, and I've been helping him with the transition.

We gave Jessica a raise, because of everything that's gone on, and she'll take on some new responsibilities. She was teary when I told her I was resigning, and we both got emotional after that. I'll miss her, as she's a very competent assistant. I know this is for the best though.

Even what I'm about to do.

I raise my hand to the door I've grown quite familiar with and before I can chicken out, I give it a few knocks.

This is going to be simple. I'm going to lay it on the line for him and what he does with the information is up to him.

I hear him approach and hold my breath as he opens the door. Wearing nothing but a pair of sweatpants and a shocked face, he grips the side of the door and asks, "What the hell are you doing here?"

Hostile. It's the only way I can describe his voice. There's no hurt, there's no confusion, just pure hostility.

"I wanted to talk to you."

"We're done talking. Did you not get that last Friday?"

"No, I did." My throat tightens, making it hard to squeeze out my words. "But"—I swallow hard—"I wanted to tell you something, before you shut the door on me."

He doesn't say anything, but stands there, waiting. I guess that means I continue. "My intention wasn't to use you, Jason, nor was it to make you feel that what we had wasn't true. Before you knew who I was, I felt something for you, this strong force pulling me toward you, a force I wanted to ignore for as long as I could because I was scared." I clear my throat. "When I made a slip-up in my business meeting, claiming you as my boyfriend, I knew it was stupid, and the minute the words fell past my lips I instantly regretted them. After the meeting, I convinced myself that because you were trying to get me to go out with you, I could give in to my feelings and take you up on a date."

His jaw clenches and I know he's seconds from slamming that door in my face.

"I met with the Carltons this week and told them the truth. Like I expected, it was a deal-breaker, but I wanted to be honest anyway—"

"I'm glad your conscience finally kicked in." His hand grips tighter on the door. "I don't have time for this shit."

He starts to close the door, but I shout, "Jason, wait. Please let me finish."

"No, Dottie, I've heard everything I want to hear. Nothing you say is going to change how I feel. We're done." Shocking me, he slams the door, the sound of a steel lock clicking into place, and I know. Opening it will never be possible . . . ever again.

I haven't seen this side of Jason before, so angry, so unforgiving, which only means one thing: I hurt him to his core, and it seems there's no recovering from that.

Heart heavy, I gulp hard as hot tears slip down my cheeks. I knew it wouldn't be easy, but I didn't expect it to be this hard, this painful . . . this devastating.

Then again, I'm sure this is exactly how Jason felt when he read that email.

I wish I could challenge Jason for doubting the truth of my feelings rather than simply believing the initial lie that set things in motion. But maybe Lindsay was right. Maybe I hadn't given him enough of me, I had held back parts of me.

This overwhelming misery is on me.

On a choking cry, I cover my mouth and tear away from Jason's door. I once thought that Nick destroyed me. He didn't. He never touched my heart.

Unlike Jason Orson.

He *owns my heart*.

Even in its shattered form.

CHAPTER TWENTY-NINE

JASON

Ten years later . . .

"Dude, you look like shit," Carson says, clapping me on the shoulder.

"This is my best sweater, and it's supposed to make me look devastatingly handsome."

"It's olive green," Carson says with a question in his raised eyebrow.

"Leave me alone." I rest my head on the counter. "It's been ten years since my heart was broken and it still aches."

"Ten years?" Carson laughs. "It's been ten fucking days."

Ten days later (That's right, sorry about that) . . .

"I know, but ten days has felt like ten years. And I *thought* wearing my green sweater to Friendsgiving would be a nice pick-me-up but you just peed all over that idea."

"Does anyone like this sweater besides you?"

"I get a lot of once-overs whenever I wear it. I think it's how the color brings out my delicate green eyes."

"Or it's the cross-stitched mountain range on the front."

I glance at my sweater and then rub my fingers over the cross-stitch. "I used to pretend it was brail and it would read, 'You're handsome, always have been, always will be.'"

"I don't understand how we're friends." Carson shakes his head.

"Running pole-to-pole suicides at Brentwood together formed an unbreakable bond."

"God, you're right." Carson takes a seat next to me at the bar and picks up a bacon-wrapped scallop from the appetizer platter. This is no ordinary appetizer platter; this shit is fancy. Emory, Knox, and his mom went all out and when I said I wasn't coming, they told me Dottie went to California to have Thanksgiving with her family, so I had no choice but to come for a while before I went to my childhood home to spend time with my family.

As promised, I brought the yams, but to hell if I was going to bring homemade stuffing on Dottie's behalf. Ohhh, no. I wasn't about to slave over the stove for her. Not again.

If I'm being entirely honest, sometimes I think about the charred ham and what it would have tasted like if it didn't get set on fire by an inferno of lies. I think about how the wine would have paired perfectly with the rich flavors I infused into that meat. I'm clearly upset over what Dottie did, but there's also a piece of me that's upset that I let the ham catch on fire. Rookie mistake, leaving the watched-over broiler for a second.

I think we all know what happens when you take your eyes off the broiler; it eats your meal alive and then laughs at you when you're crying into your burnt and unrecognizable dish.

Can you tell I'm trying to think about anything but the heart-splitting reality that the girl I was falling for obliterated my heart?

And fuck, what was she thinking coming over the other day? I know she wanted to apologize, but seeing her, wrecked like that . . . fuck, it's only made things worse. I never want to see my girl with red-rimmed eyes and tear-stained cheeks. It just about did me in, but even though seeing her pained me, I couldn't quite feel the pain. I knew it was there, harboring deep in my bones for later, but in that moment, all I saw was red.

Anger boiled over, and I didn't want to hear one word she had to say.

Because in all honesty, it doesn't matter. She broke my trust and that isn't something we can recover from. Not when she's been in the same position, not when she's been used before, not when she made me believe what we shared, the bond I clung to every second of every goddamn day was real . . . when it wasn't.

Fuck, just thinking about it again has my stomach hollowing out in nausea.

"Hey, what are you two doing?" Milly asks, saddling up next to Carson and placing a sweet kiss on the side of his cheek.

Glad they're in love. Sense the sarcasm?

What I wouldn't give to have that kind of affection right now. I almost ask Carson if he'll kiss my temple and lovingly stroke my pec but think better of it. I'm pretty sure I know what the answer would be, even in my vulnerable state. Maybe ten days ago, right after everything went down, he might have petted my head for a brief moment, but now, he's probably thinking I should have gotten over everything.

The heart doesn't work that fast unfortunately.

"Carson is making fun of my sweater," I say, popping a black olive in my mouth.

Milly leans over to look at it. "Is that cross-stitch?"

I rub my palm over the intricate stitching. "It is."

"It's . . . nice."

"Why, thank—"

"She's being polite, dude," Carson says, eating another scallop. "There was a pause in her sentence. She hates it."

"I don't hate it," Milly says, but then doesn't continue. She doesn't love it, that's for damn sure.

"Fine." I reach behind me, pull my sweater over my head, drop it on the floor, and then bury my hands in my hair. "Happy? Now my nipples are going to get hard from being cold."

"Why is your shirt off?" Knox asks, standing on the other side of the countertop to indulge in some appetizers.

321

"Everyone hates it, so I'd rather be naked."

"I liked it," Knox says casually.

"Really?" I perk up.

"No." He laughs and shakes his head. "Hideous, man."

Growing angry, I say, "Don't you see I'm suffering here? My heart is broken, and you assholes are being jerks. Don't kick a man when he's down."

"He's right," Emory says, rubbing my back and reaching over to grab an olive. "Jason needs our love right now, not our jokes."

I thumb toward Emory. "She gets it."

"How are you doing, Jason?"

"Not great," I admit. "I can't even look at her without getting angry. She came over the other day to talk to me."

"What did she say?" Knox asks.

"Just that she told the Carltons the truth. Like, good for you, thumbs up, you still fucked me over."

"That's all she said?" Emory asks, looking confused.

"It's all I let her say before I closed the door. Honestly, there's nothing she can say that will make me feel better. When I read the email from her dad, I was stunned. I've never felt so embarrassed, so humiliated. I was cooking for her business meeting, bare-ass naked, and she was only using me for her own personal gain."

"Why were you naked?" Carson asks. Of course, that's what he focuses on.

"Because cooking naked is sexy. Try it, it will spice up your marriage," I say, waving my hand in his direction.

"Our marriage doesn't need spicing up, isn't that right, Milly? Just this morning the turkey wasn't the only thing that was stuffed."

Everyone turns to her as her face immediately lights up in a bright shade of red.

"Don't torture the poor girl," Lindsay says from the living room where she's playing Candy Land with her son and Mama G.

"I think we need to forget about the whole Dottie thing, okay? I've moved on."

"What?" Emory asks. "Are you dating someone else?"

"No." I shake my head while picking up a pickle. Sweet, of course, because Carson brought the pickles. "But I heard if you say things into the universe, they come true. Setting intentions."

"I think Dottie is a lovely young lady who got caught up in trying to prove herself and said the wrong thing," Mama G says. Together we all spin around to look at her. No one messes with Mama G, so when she says something, we pay attention. "Haven't you ever wanted something so badly that you'll do anything to get it?" She pointedly looks at the three professional baseball players in the apartment. "Pretty sure you have. What makes it any different for Dottie?"

"Because she lied; she could have told me the truth."

"If that's what you're going to base this all off, what she *could* have done, then you, my sweet boy, are a fool."

Silence falls over the apartment, Mama G's words stinging . . . hard.

"Oh shit," Knox mutters. "She called you a fool."

"I don't think I can breathe," Carson says, looking scared shitless.

I'm right there with him. Mama G was our designated cheer squad when Knox was at Brentwood. Our mother hen, always bringing us treats and acting as if we were her own. There is no denying it. Her comment drives a stake right to my heart. How can she call me a fool? Dottie lied. End of story. Yes, we all understand that yearning and drive we've experienced getting to the level of baseball we're at. But we didn't do that by lying to those we cared about. I mean, Emory did withhold from Knox that she was still living in Chicago. *But that wasn't to use him* . . . Carson did run from Milly and then encourage business her way, even though he didn't contact her . . . *But that wasn't really lying to her* . . .

All four of them hurt each other before they got together. All four were devastated . . . *for a time*. But then they found love—

No, it's not the same. I refuse to be called a fool over someone else's deceit.

"Now." She claps her hands together. "Let's all hold hands and say what we're grateful for," she says in a cheery disposition, as if she didn't just insult me.

"I'll be grateful if Jason puts his shirt back on," Knox says, but I don't laugh.

I feel a haze fall over me.

Am I really being a fool?

She hurt me. She used me. How is that *me* being a fool?

"**W**ow, it's beautiful in here," Emory says, taking in the old warehouse turned banquet hall we rented for the after-event party.

We decorated the space with an old-fashioned baseball theme. Pennants stream across the rafters, cracker jacks, peanuts, and popcorn are centerpieces at each table, along with pinstripe table-cloths. We used old crates for display and made table flags with The Lineup logo on them. Natalie did an amazing job and since the food is baseball-park themed, I can't wait to dig in.

My team won the game of course, because I stacked my side, leaving Walker with a few good players. He didn't mind. All he cared about was connecting with the athletes who came to represent their disability. I saw him stay close to one girl in particular with pigtails, and I wondered if she reminds him of his sister? Most likely.

Joseph clung to my side the whole time, enamored with the big names we had on the field. He scored two runs—we had endless substitution—and like in high school, I hit him in both times. It felt good being out there on the field with him, seeing that infectious smile again. I wish someone else was there to see it.

Yeah, okay, so Dottie was supposed to be here today and clearly, she isn't. Which is fine, whatever, I told her to go suck it and for good reason. I don't need to remind you what happened. You remember, so try to tell me I was wrong. I wasn't, right?

With each day that passes, I think about what Mama G said, what she called me. And now that I'm at this event with the closest people in my life, I still feel empty. *She's* supposed to be here, holding my hand, meeting my family, hanging out with my friends, being a part of this charity that's one of the proudest things I've ever created.

But she's not.

And that makes me sad.

"Natalie did a good job with the event planning," I say, trying to put on a good smile. Even though this event isn't what I hoped for, with Dottie at my side, there are still a lot of people here for me, for Joseph, and I need to give them my all. "She's been working her butt off."

"I like Natalie," Emory says, leaning into Knox. "Such a shame she's already taken; she and Walker could be a good couple. Or Cory."

"Nice try," I say. "She's happily married, so don't stir the pot."

"I would never, but is there another Natalie we could find for Walker? He's so angry all the time, and maybe if he had a Natalie, he would change."

"Maybe you should stick to your job as a librarian and skip the matchmaking," Knox says, drawing an appalled sound from Emory.

Hormonal and insulted, not a good combination. Even I know that, and I'm an idiot most of the time.

Emory drags him away just as Carson and Milly walk up to me. "Thank fuck we won. I think I would have screamed if we didn't bring home the W."

"You know it was for fun, right?" Natalie asks, joining our little circle.

"Competition is never just for fun," Milly says, answering for all three of us.

Natalie laughs. "I forgot who I was talking to. Yes, of course, good thing you guys won."

Milly joined in on the game and had the time of her life. She's a

325

genius when it comes to baseball. She can fix anyone's swing—who's willing to listen to her—and she's the reason why my boy, Carson, makes the All-Star team. I should give him credit for the practice he puts in as well. But growing up, she studied, she never played, because she wanted to play baseball, not softball, and she was never given the chance. So when I handed her a jersey for our team, she looked up at me with the most grateful eyes I've ever seen.

The event is all about inclusion, and that means the girls who want to play with the boys can.

Plus, she was a total ringer and having her on my team was the icing on top of the cake.

"Thank you again for letting me play," Milly says, looking shy.

"Yeah, thank you, man," Carson says with so much sincerity it makes me want to cry.

"I love you guys."

Because I know Carson loves it so much, I grab him by the cheeks and pull him in tight, planting a giant kiss on his lips before releasing him.

"Motherfucker," he growls, swiping at his mouth. "What did I tell you about that shit? No, just no."

"You're so afraid you're going to fall in love with me. Just let it happen, bro. Just let it happen."

"I'm not going to punch you in the gut right now because this is a charity event, and because you just made some dreams come true for my wife today, but if this was any other time, know that my fist would be tickling your intestines."

"Noted," I say on a smile, that feels entirely too fake.

"As much fun as this is, I need to borrow you for a second." Natalie pulls on my arm and I follow her to the small stage we have set up. She drags me behind the curtain.

"What are you—?"

My voice falls when I see Dottie standing there, an envelope in her hand, wearing a Bobbies baseball hat, jeans, and a Rebels T-shirt.

Shit . . . the shirt.

She looks really fucking good, especially with those colors displayed across her chest.

"Miss Domico wanted to hand you a donation before she goes." Natalie gives me a knowing look and then leaves.

Trying to gain my bearings, I say, "Uh, what are you doing here?"

"Well, I watched the game and wanted to keep my donation promise. I know I said I'd be here for the dinner, but I don't think it's appropriate for me to stay. I bought a table and had Lindsay invite some of her third graders and their parents to join. But before I leave, I wanted to deliver this to you."

She gives me the envelope and nods at me to open it.

Cautious, I tip open the flap and peek inside. A check written to The Lineup for . . . holy shit, one million dollars.

What the actual fuck?

I snap the envelope shut and say, "What the hell is this?"

"My donation."

"One million dollars?"

"Well, we have a very generous non-profit section. We always donate at the end of the year. I convinced my dad to make a substantial donation to The Lineup."

"With one million dollars?"

"Yes."

I try to keep my brain focused on the girl in front of me, but it keeps running away, thinking of all the kids we can help with one million dollars. This is huge.

Bigger than huge . . . it's phenomenal.

With the contribution from the Rebels, from this event, and from Dottie, there's so much—

I pause and stare at the check, and then back into Dottie's hopeful eyes.

Wait . . .

"Are you trying to buy me?"

"What?"

"Trying to buy yourself back into my life." I hold up the envelope. "Is that what this is all about?"

"Jason." She shakes her head, tears immediately forming in her eyes. "If that's what you think, I didn't do a good enough job letting you get to know me."

"No, you didn't," I say before I can stop myself. "We spent so much time together and yet, it always felt like you never fully let me in."

"I was trying," she says. "Trying to form trust—"

"Well, you broke our trust the minute you neglected to tell me about the Carlton meeting. Did you ever think that maybe, just maybe, I would have laughed it off and said, why don't we give it a try then? The dating?"

My anger starts to take over again.

"I . . . I didn't—"

"You didn't, because you were too chickenshit to let me be the man I am. You didn't give me a goddamn chance, Dottie. If you did, you would have been surprised at how understanding I am."

"I see." She frowns and takes a step back. "You'll always think the worst of me." She turns halfway around but pauses. "For what it's worth, this was how much I'd always planned on donating." She takes a hiccupped breath. "I believe in what you're trying to do, your mission. I believe in *you*, Jason."

I stare at the envelope and then back at her, the word "Stop" on the tip of my tongue, but I'm unable to pull the trigger. Because even though I'd love to take her into my arms, there's still hurt billowing deep inside me. So, maybe I am a fool. A miserable, disconsolate fool. *Fuck.*

～

K*nock. Knock.*

The door opens and Knox waltzes in looking like he just pulled himself out of a dumpster, wearing holey sweats and a Brentwood Baseball shirt that must be at least a decade old.

"Come on in," I say, my head resting against the back of my couch. I'm watching football, not giving two shits who wins, and drowning myself in potato skins.

Piles and piles of potato skins.

I'll need to run at least ten miles a day until spring training to wear off all the fat in these things. Here's hoping they go straight to my ass and make it even juicier than before.

Knox grabs a beer from my fridge for the both of us and then flops on my couch next to me. Before he leans all the way back, he picks up a potato skin and shoves the whole thing in his mouth. "These are cold," he says with a mouthful.

"Yeah, I made them two hours ago."

"Great." Knox quickly chews and swallows. "We haven't seen you since the fundraiser. That's strange for you."

"Are you saying I'm an annoying neighbor?"

"A little." He chuckles and then nudges my shoulder. "Seriously, dude, what's up? Still bummed about Dottie?"

"Bummed? More like confused." I drag my hand down my face, pausing to rub my eyes for a few seconds. "I don't know, dude, am I being a fool here?"

"Want some honesty?"

"Yeah, I need something, because I'm drowning right now."

"Okay." He sits up and props one leg on the couch so he's facing me. "What if I told you Dottie is moving back to California?"

"What?" I sit up, and potato skin flakes fly off my chest. "What do you mean she's moving to California?"

"She's leaving. She popped over to our apartment yesterday and told us the news. She resigned from her job at her dad's company and is starting a company where she trains women to be their own boss. She's excited about it, but she said it might be best to have a fresh start, so she's going back to California."

"But . . . what about you guys? The baby?"

Knox shrugs. "I honestly think it's too painful for her to stay, be around everyone, around you."

"That's her own damn fault," I say, even though it feels bitter passing by my lips.

"Yeah, I get where you're coming from, man. When Emory broke up with me in college, I was fucking pissed. And then she left without saying bye. It was a tough pill to swallow. I didn't want to talk to her even though I promised we'd always be friends. Every text I sent her was like swallowing a basketful of knives. I harbored that anger, held on to it for so long, and I punished *her* because of how angry I was. I said stupid shit, did stupid shit, because I wanted her to hurt as bad as I hurt, and do you know where that got me?"

"Where?"

"Eight years of being without my girl because of my stubborn ass. I still don't agree with what she did, I still think she stole years from our lives of being together. But it forced me to sit back and reflect: did I want to be right? Or did I want to be happy?" He points to his chest and says, "I wanted to be happy. So I chose to forgive and forget, to move on, because we're humans and we all make mistakes, even if there was intention behind those mistakes."

"You think I'm being a fool?" I ask, Knox's words sinking in with each breath I take.

"I think you're a fool if you let her move back to California." He sips his beer. "What do you want, Jason? Do you want to be happy? Or do you want to be right?"

Well . . . fuck. When he puts it like that?

I bite my bottom lip and groan. "I want to be happy . . . and I love her," I answer wearily.

"Then be the great man I know you are; go to her and be happy. Be happy for the both of you."

The thought of seeing her again turns my nerves inside out and in all honesty, I do want to be happy, but I'm also fucking terrified I'll get hurt again.

CHAPTER THIRTY

DOTTIE

On a deep breath, I take in my office one last time. Security took my belongings to my car already, but I wanted to spend a few more moments in the office where I became my own.

This is where I held my first interview as the boss, searching for the right employee.

This is where I secured one of the biggest deals of my life, proving I belonged in this position.

This is where my dad held me tight and told me he was proud of the woman I'd become.

And this is where the love of my life walked in, flowers in hand, with a date in his back pocket.

This is where it all started, and it's sad to say goodbye to it, but it's for the best. I know my new venture will be more satisfying and less stressful. The money obviously won't be as great, but that's never been a big deal to me. I want to feel fulfilled. I don't feel fulfilled in Chicago anymore. Yes, my friends are here and I'll miss them dearly, but it's too painful knowing Jason is right across the hall and can pop in anytime when I'm visiting them. And even worse, when the wisest woman on the planet makes Jason her man . . . I wouldn't survive seeing that.

I'm the one who messed up, so I'm the one who should leave.

I give my desk a final once-over and then stand from my chair, just as a tall figure walks into my office.

I stumble back for a second, startled, until I realize it's Jason. My heart sinks to my stomach, and my breath escapes me from the mere sight of him.

He's so incredibly handsome.

Not sure if he did it on purpose, but he's wearing the same thing he wore the first time he waltzed into my office, but this time, the smile he once had has disappeared and in its place is a blank stare, almost as if he doesn't quite believe that he's here.

Why is he here?

Hope blooms briefly, wondering if he's here to make up, if he's here to listen to my pleas again, or if he's willing to give me one more chance.

"Hey," he says gruffly, staring at the floor. "I uh, I heard you were leaving town."

Cautiously, I walk toward him and stop a few feet away. With a nervous shake, I say, "Yeah, I leave in a few days."

He nods and looks out toward the skyline. "You resigned?"

I can't read him and it's bothering me. Is he happy? Sad? Angry? It almost seems like his emotions were knocked loose from his heart and he's just a shell of the man I used to know. I could use a hint to why he's here, anything to ease my building anxiety, anything to help ease the excitement fighting to overtake that anxiety.

"Yes." I link my hands together, forcing myself to avoid reaching out and touch him. "For many reasons, but happiness in my job being one of them."

His lips twist to the side. "Knox told me."

"I assumed. News seems to travel fast between our friends," I say with an awkward chuckle. He doesn't say anything. "How did the rest of the event go? Did you raise a lot of money?"

"Yeah." He finally looks up at me. "Thank you. Not sure if I actually said that or not. But thank you for the donation. It's going to make a giant difference . . . take us to the next level."

"It was our pleasure," I reply robotically.

He takes a step forward and my heart lurches in my throat. His gaze lifts, connects with mine, and I swear, in that moment I don't breathe. Not for a second. Lungs stilled, heartbeat pounding in my ears, I hang in the balance as he takes one more step forward.

Skin tingling, emotions taut, I sway, despite trying to remain steady as my body trembles with anticipation of why he's—

"Here," he says, holding out a bag I didn't see when he walked in. Then again, I was distracted by his eyes and the lack of expression on his face.

"What's this?" I ask, taking the reusable bag from him. He sticks his hands in his pockets and rocks on his heels while his gaze returns to the floor.

Is he . . . retreating?

"Some of your things you left at my place." My heart tumbles past my ribs and straight to the floor, taking on every cut and scrape along the way. He grips the back of his neck and takes another step back. "I uh . . . didn't want you to leave without it."

I didn't want you to leave without it. Not, I don't want *you* to leave.

He's done.

I swallow the biggest lump in my throat, trying to hold it together in front of him. "Thank you," I say, my voice a mere whisper . . . choked.

He takes another step back and as if my heart is attached to a string being dragged by his foot, it follows along.

"Sure. If I missed anything, I'll, uh, mail it."

I shake my head, trying to plaster on a fake smile, but it comes out weak and ineffective. "No need." I stare down into the bag, seeing a shampoo bottle, my body lotion . . . and a shirt. He could have thrown this out. He could have done anything with it, other than bring it here where I got my hopes up. Where I thought his presence meant forgiveness. "If I, uh," I swallow hard again, "haven't noticed it's missing in a few weeks . . . probably don't need it."

"Yeah. Sure." He scratches the top of his head and takes one more step back. "I should go."

My teeth chatter, my lips tremble and before he can leave, I call out, "Wait, Jason." A stray tear falls onto my cheek and I quickly swipe it away as I try to gather myself. When he looks at me, I take a deep breath and say, "I want you to know—"

Shaking his head, he says, "Let's not say anything, okay?" I suck in a breath. *Right. Say nothing.*

Devoid of emotion, he turns his back toward me and walks out of the office door . . . but not before knocking on the doorframe as what? A final parting goodbye?

Then he leaves.

Just like that.

Out of my world.

I collapse into a chair and bury my head into my hands as anguish trickles up my spine, sending a wave of heat and humiliation through my veins.

Burning embarrassment and regret consume me.

Shame and self-hatred eat me alive.

And as I sob into my hands, I realize the one thing I cared about the most in this world, just walked out of my door without a care that I'll be moving away from him.

It's over.

~

"A re you sure you want to drive this to California yourself?" Emory asks, looking at my small moving truck. I only packed the things that mattered to me. Furniture was donated. No need to be reminded of all the surfaces Jason and I had fun on.

"Yes." I nod, eyes burning from all the tears I've shed over the past few days while finishing my packing. It seemed Jason's impromptu visit not only unleashed a dam of emotions, but it burned a hole deep inside me, one that I don't think will ever be repaired.

Foolish me. I can say I tried. I can also say his passion when things are great translates to exuberance, which turns to desolation when things are bad . . . and that *I did that to him*. And maybe, he gave me some of his passion, his experience of emotions, because I haven't stopped aching within.

Taking a deep breath, I say, "It will give me some nice alone time to think."

Emory bites her bottom lip and says, "I'm worried about you, Dottie."

"Don't be." I give her the best smile I can muster. "I'll be fine."

"Then why are you crying?"

Am I?

I wipe at my eyes and feel wetness on my fingers. Clearing my throat, I say, "Sad that I won't see this baby grow inside of you." I glance over her shoulder, at the entrance to her building for any familiar figures.

I said goodbye to Lindsay at her place, then drove to Knox and Emory's to have one final goodbye. Did I wish I'd see Jason and a miracle would occur and he'd tell me not to go? Tell me to stay because he loves me? Yep. That would be me. The desperate fool.

"I'll send you so many pictures," Emory says, pulling me into a hug. Knox stands silently behind her, hands in his pockets, staring at the sidewalk. He hasn't said much since they came down from their apartment, but I guess he wouldn't since I hurt his friend.

When we pull away, I glance at the entrance again, willing for him to pop out of the doors.

I then turn my attention to Knox and say, "I'm sorry about everything."

He shakes his head. "No need to apologize, Dottie. We're cool." He doesn't hug me, he doesn't even look at me, and I'm not sure if he's angry at me, at the situation, or at his friend.

I look toward the doors, hope falling with every second that passes. I want to delay this parting, wait outside all day, just to see him one more time in person, to hear his voice, take in his fresh smell, to—

"Sweetie." Emory takes my hand and forces me to look her in the eyes. "He's not here."

"Oh, I wasn't—"

"He's in the Bahamas. He left a couple days ago." Emory nibbles on her lip and looks like she's about to cry.

Once again, disappointment plummets through me and smashes to the ground.

"Oh," I say as more tears fall from my eyes. "Okay, yeah, sure." I suck in a deep breath as snot starts to drip from my nose. Very unladylike, I dab at it with my long-sleeved T-shirt. "I wasn't you know, looking for him or anything."

"Dottie, your eyes were glued to the door," Emory points out wearily.

"I know." I nod and wipe at my eyes again. "I was just being foolish." On a deep breath, I say, "Okay, I need to get a move on. Thank you for everything." I give them both a chaste hug and then step toward my truck. "Send me lots of pictures. Love you guys."

I hurtle myself into my truck and fasten my seatbelt. With my hands at ten and two on the steering wheel, I take one more deep breath and then give them a parting wave right before starting the truck.

It's time to start a new chapter, even if it feels like this one is unfinished. Even if this one means I'll be very, very alone.

CHAPTER THIRTY-ONE

JASON

K *nox: I can't believe you let her fucking leave.*

I stare at the text and then set my phone to the side.

I can't believe I let her leave either but the moment I stepped into her office, with the intention of possibly making things right between us, something stopped me. I don't know what it was but seeing her standing there—in the office where she threw me out—it brought back memories of how she deceived me. And I froze.

I fucking froze.

Natalie walks over with a pineapple drink for both of us and sits in her lounge chair. I should be enjoying our gorgeous surroundings and the hot sun beating down on my naked chest. *Should. Be.*

Taking the drink from her, I resume staring out at the crystal blue ocean and say, "When is Ansel getting here?"

"About that." Natalie leans back on her lounger and says, "We're separated."

"What?" I ask, shooting up from my lounge chair to stare at my sister.

MEGHAN QUINN

When we rescheduled this trip, Natalie told me Ansel was coming later, I didn't think he wasn't coming at all.

"What do you mean you're separated? For how long?"

"Six months," she answers, avoiding eye contact.

"Six months?" I shout. "You've been separated from your husband for six months and you're just telling me now? What the fuck, Natalie? Do Mom and Dad know? Joseph?"

She shakes her head. "You're the first to know."

"What? Why?" Our family has always been close, so this makes no sense at all.

She removes her sunglasses and swipes at her teary eyes. "Embarrassed. I thought I could make it work. Everyone saw us as the couple that would be together forever and I wanted to prove them right, but Ansel had other ideas."

"What do you mean?" I ask through clenched teeth.

"He said he wasn't happy. Thought I spent too much time taking care of Joseph, helping you, never giving him attention . . . so he found it some other way."

"That son of a bitch," I say, my jaw clenched so tight I might crack a molar. "He fucking cheated on you?"

She shrugs as if it's nothing, but I can see right through her glassy eyes. This is more than nothing. This is devastating. Ansel was her middle school sweetheart, the man she told me after her eighth-grade dance she was going to marry one day. They went to college together, spent every waking moment together. They were the couple to strive to be. She put everything into their marriage, and I remember thinking, I'm going to do the same one day.

What the fuck?

"I wasn't enough," she says, stirring her drink.

"Bullshit," I say, taking her hand in mine. "You are enough, Nat. You are more than enough."

She shakes her head. "Not for him."

"Fuck him." I set my drink down, the glass ready to break in my hand if I hold on to it anymore. "He's going to fucking regret this." I crack my neck to the side, steam breathing into me.

Natalie presses her hand to my forearm. "Don't hurt him, Jase."

I laugh. "Yeah, okay, Nat."

"I'm serious. He's not worth it."

"He sure as shit isn't worth it. But *you* are. No one, and I mean no one, hurts my sister and gets away with it. Do you understand that? No one."

"I know. But Ansel is pissed that I filed for divorce, and I'm asking for the apartment and took away his season tickets you gave him. If you attack him, I'm sure he'll press charges."

"Damn right you took away his season tickets. He's fucking high if he thinks he's keeping those." Needing to pace, I stand in front of Natalie and walk back and forth. "Is that why you made these last-minute plans for us? To get away?"

She nods. "I thought we both needed it. I had to legitimately move your initial dates because of the photo shoot—which went so well, don't you think?—but I needed to get away too." She shrugs. "I wanted this time with you." Fuck. I hate that this dipshit treated my sister like this. And I hate the sadness and . . . *resignation* in her expression. But then she lowers her glasses and looks me in the eyes. "Jason, why didn't you go after her?"

I shake my head. "This isn't about me. We're talking about Ansel and your divorce apparently. I need time to wrap my head around this."

"No, you want a distraction and you're using me as one. How about we fix one problem at a time, one that can actually be solved. Last I spoke with you, you were going to Dottie's office to ask her to stay. What happened?"

Fuming from Natalie's news and her persistence of changing the subject, I stuff my hand through my hair and pull on the short strands. "I don't know, okay? I got there, her betrayal hit me again hard, and I froze."

"And you let her leave?"

"Yeah. I handed her shit from my apartment and left."

"Jason . . . that's awful."

MEGHAN QUINN

I whip toward her. "That's awful? What about everything she did to me? What about—?"

"You told me you love her. You said you want to be happy. You were going to go make up, so every excuse you're about to lay down is invalid, because you were moments away from making your life better again."

Exhausted, I flop on the lounge chair and drape my arm over my eyes. "It's just . . . fuck, Nat, it's scary, okay? I've never had feelings for someone like this. I let her into my heart, into my world, and she hurt me."

"She didn't tell you the full truth. But everyone, even her friends, know what you two had was real. Just seeing you together, I knew there was something special, and then seeing her at the event, after everything went down . . . I don't think I've ever seen a more remorseful, love-struck person in my life, Jason. And I can assure you, I know what a look *without* remorse looks like." At that, she stumbles, and I want to punch Ansel in the face so hard. "Dottie loves you, and she's hurting because she hurt you. If she was truly malicious, she wouldn't care. But she does, she cares so much. It's obvious in her actions, her attempts to win you back, her ability to look at herself, find truth and honesty within her and tell the people around her about her mistakes. That's the kind of woman you want to be with, as that's the kind of woman who will always care for you."

"Then why didn't she take care of my heart in the first place?"

Natalie shrugs. "Maybe that's a question you need to ask her? But from the outside and what you've told me, I will tell you right now, Mama G was right in what she said, you're a fool."

Shit . . .

"How can you say that, be so positive about love when you're going through what you're going through?"

She fixes her sunglasses over her eyes and sips from her drink. "I'm heavily medicated."

"Seriously?"

She lightly chuckles. "No. But just because my love life is bleak, that doesn't mean I should project my problems onto you. I know when I see love, and you two were made to love each other."

"And if she hurts me again?"

"Then you talk it through. It's when she stops wanting to talk that you need to worry." She pauses, takes a sip of her cocktail. "Trust me."

~

Five days in the Bahamas with my sister should have been relaxing, but it was anything but.

Not only did the resort staff keep calling us Mr. and Mrs. Orson and sending champagne to our two-bedroom suite—awkward—but every second of my vacation was spent worrying over Dottie and whether or not I should fly straight to California from the Bahamas.

If you're wondering . . . I didn't.

So when I showed up at Knox's door, looking for a chat and he told me to get lost, I knew I fucked up.

I don't blame the dismissal.

I told him I loved her. I told him I wanted to be happy, *not right,* but when it came down to it, I chickened out.

That was until last night.

Last night, when I was lying in my bed alone, staring at the ceiling, I replayed my entire relationship with Dottie.

I thought about how I wish I'd known her in college and wondered about the feelings she had for me back then. Were they purely physical, or was there more substance to those feelings?

I thought about our first date, how she looked so strong and confident, but there were little moments where I caught wariness in her eyes, nervousness, almost disbelief that I'd brought dinner to her for no other reason than to honor a promise. Now, knowing how she'd been treated before—dishonestly—I understand why she had me dragged out by security. *I hadn't earned her trust.* I saw something in her and as I thought about it, I knew it was interest, maybe infatuation. I knew there was more to this woman and I was determined to find out what it was.

Throughout our relationship, I was always peeling back more layers to her. And even though there were rare moments where I saw how vulnerable she was, I witnessed her caring side, her beautifully intelligent side, and of course her sassy side. If she was faking our relationship, just using me, I never would have seen so many parts of her. I would have barely broken the surface, if that.

But Dottie, even though it was slow, showed me who she was, a strong-willed but also reticent woman. Her heart *was* jaded, and I should have realized it would take time to soften her rough edges. No, I should have listened more, because it was there. I had gotten close to her, and from what I know about Dottie, that was rare. It was about time I finished what I started.

It's why I'm standing outside her parents' Malibu house, the ocean crashing into the shore in the distance, and the bright sun shining down on me. Even though this might be terrifying, it's going to be a good day.

Stepping up to the door, I give it a few loud knocks and then wait.

I sent a text to Knox this morning telling him was I was going to make everything right and he said it was about damn time and to not fuck it up, because apparently he's never seen me as happy as I am when Dottie is around.

I have to admit, he's right.

The door opens and a woman in a white leisure suit answers. There are qualities about her that look just like Dottie, which causes me to assume this is her mom.

"Oh," she says, looking startled. Hand to her chest, she asks, "Are you Jason?"

I nod. "Yes, ma'am. Am I right to assume you're Mrs. Domico?"

"Why, yes." She lends out her hand and I give it a shake. "Are you looking for Dottie?"

"I am." I glance past her. "Is she here?"

She nods and parts the door open. "She's out on the balcony with her coffee. Would you like a cup?"

"Uh, it will make me too jittery. I'm good."

"Okay." She steps to the side, her eyes giving me a full once-over. Not in a leery, old-woman way, just a *are you good enough for my daughter* way. Totally understand that one. "Please, come in. She's right back there." She gestures to the giant sliding glass doors that take up an entire wall.

Damn, this house is nice.

I give her a curt nod and make my way across the concrete floors, past the ostentatious fireplace—when you have money, you have money—and to the parted sliding glass door where I find Dottie sitting in a lounge chair, feet tucked into her body, blanket over her shoulders, a cup of coffee in hand. Her raven hair is stacked on top of her head and her feet are covered in white slippers.

In that moment, observing her, I realize I want nothing more than to push my need to hold a grudge to the side and bury my head into her sweet scent, to have her arms wrap around me and hold me close. I want every inch of her, every piece, even if it takes years to earn.

I take a step forward and say, "Good morning."

Her head whips to the side in surprise, her eyes widening when she spots me. And that's when I see her tear-streaked cheeks. She quickly wipes at her face and straightens up.

"J-Jason," she stumbles. "What are you doing here?"

Once again, I feel tongue-tied and unsure of what to say. I scratch the side of my jaw and say, "I, uh . . . shit," I mutter, looking at my feet.

She reaches out and takes my hand, pulling me to the edge of her lounge chair. When I glance at her, she says, "Now that you're here, please don't leave." Tears fall down her cheek. "Please don't leave, Jason." Eyes bloodshot, absolute sorrow in her voice. I did this. I hate that I caused this pain.

"I'm not leaving," I say, the words hoarse as they fall past my lips. "Not now"—I look up at her—"not ever."

Her lip trembles, and I reach out and brush my thumb over it, which only makes more tears fall as her shaky hand comes up to mine. I move my hand to her cheek and she pushes into it, her eyes briefly closing.

"Jason," she says on a choked sob. "Will you please listen to me?"

I nod. "Yes."

Opening her eyes, she takes a deep breath but keeps her hand gripping mine tightly, as if silently willing me to not move. "I try to find a positive with all the regrets I make in my life." She shifts and moves closer. "I try to put a spin on them to show that maybe they're not regrets, more like steppingstones to get me to where I'm supposed to be. I never regret anything with that way of thinking, but I do have one, one that I will never let myself spin or turn into a steppingstone. I know what I did—or *didn't* do—wasn't a steppingstone, but more like a roadblock to happiness." She slowly takes another steady breath. "I don't regret telling the Carltons that you were my boyfriend, because it gave me the nudge I needed to give in to my feelings for you, but I'll always regret not telling you, not being honest, not giving you the benefit of the doubt of being the great and understanding man that you are." She lifts my palm and kisses it gently. "I'm sorry, Jason. I'm sorry for hurting you, for making you feel anything less than a perfect and beautiful man. I'm sorry for putting us through this pain, and I'm sorry I never told you how much I admire you, how much I care for you, and how much I love you."

Those three little words . . . they whisk the breath from my lungs as my eyes tear up as well. I wondered, I questioned, were her feelings anything like mine? I just got my confirmation.

She loves me.

All this pain, this hurt deep in my chest, it eases and lets my heart beat again, beat wildly for the woman in front of me.

"Christ." I clear my throat, feeling an overwhelming sense of joy that I try to voice, but it comes out garbled. "That . . . fuck, Dottie." Without giving it a second thought, I pull her into my chest and wrap my arms around her delicate frame. When she returns the embrace, my heart nearly flies out of my chest. Lifting her chin, I force her to look me in the eyes. "I won't lie and say you didn't hurt me, because you did, but I also can't stay away from you, not when I have this undying love for you that shows up at any hour of the day. I can't suppress it, I can't forget about it, and I can't just drop it like it never happened. I won't. I wanted to stay mad at you, I wanted to hurt you, I wanted to punish you, but in the end, it would only be punishing myself." I tilt her chin up a little more and bring her lips inches from mine. "I love you, Dottie. I love you so fucking much, and I'd forever regret not telling you that." A soft sob escapes her. She tries to pull away, to wipe her face, but I hold her still and close the space between us, pressing a soft kiss across her mouth. My lips spread in a smile while my eyes shed with joyful tears now. "I know this is a lot to ask of you, but please don't stay here, please don't start a new life here. Stay in Chicago with your friends . . . with me. Be my partner in crime, my best friend, my lover, my girlfriend."

Her eyes wearily search mine. "Are you sure?"

What I need. *What I suspect she needs too.* "Positive."

"But do you forgive me?"

Smiling, I say, "Might have to suck some of my idiots out of me —you know, with those magical lips of yours—but I think all will be forgiven."

She laughs, snot bubbling out of her cute, little nose. She's a mess, a beautiful mess, but I don't care and press my lips against hers. I love this woman so much. She's a kind, genuine soul, someone I thought I'd never find, with her sassy mouth, ball-busting personality, but incredibly softness as well. She can't cook for shit, but there are so many other ways her character complements mine. She's loyal.

Strong.

True.

Funny.

Adorably testy.

Dottie Domico is my woman—yes, I'm a roaring caveman—and I'll make sure to spend the rest of my life making sure I'm the man she needs and can rely on too.

EPILOGUE

JASON

"Are you boys ready?" Cory Potter asks, standing from his chair in the locker room, looking like a magnificent piece of man meat. This is his second season on the team, and he's already taken on a leadership role. I still can't believe I get to play next to him, wear the same jersey as him . . . see him naked in the locker room showers.

Any single ladies out there? Telling you right now, the man rivals my own dick, and I think we all know how giant the wildebeest between my legs is. If you've forgotten, I'll have my girlfriend remind you. She has a fresh memory, since I plowed her into our bed before reporting to the stadium for our opening day game.

Yeah, I said our bed.

Look out, Jason Orson is domesticated. I have a girlfriend that I share an apartment with. We are living in sin and loving it. Once we made up, we *romantically* fucked on her childhood bed—and were caught by her mom. To say it was awkward is an understatement, but thankfully all she saw was my ass and swinging balls that slapped Dottie like a pendulum. She said it sounded like a fish out of water, flopping around. I couldn't stop laughing all through breakfast. Dottie didn't think it was very funny, but she wouldn't be Dottie if she did.

"You ready, Orson?" Cory asks, gripping my shoulder. "Nervous?"

"Pfft, never."

Over spring training, I grew close with Cory, not just because his brother-in-law is one of my best friends, but because we both grew up Bobbies fans and now play for the rival team. It's easy to sit under his leadership, seeing the work he puts in every day, and I understand why he's as great as he is. He never gets too big for his head. He never thinks he's the greatest, but that *he* needs to be catching up, putting in extra time, waking up early, hitting the weight room one last time before going to bed. His work ethic is impeccable and something I've started to replicate.

Thankfully Dottie can work anywhere, so when I went to Florida for spring training, she came with me. I spend as much time with her as possible when I'm not on the ball field, and she's understanding because we both get it. Having drive, goals . . . it's what makes us both thrive.

And one of the best things that's happened since we got back together is that she's helped run Natalie through her Boss Babe program, giving Natalie much more confidence to make the decisions she needs to make for The Lineup and confidence in life. They've grown pretty close, and I'm happy about that. She needs someone more than ever right now, someone that will help lift her up, rather than drag her down like Ansel. The fuckhead.

"I'm not talking about the game," Cory says. "I'm talking about the proposal."

"Oh." I chuckle and shake my head. "Nah, my girl loves me, she's going to say yes."

I stand and stick the ring box in my back pocket. We organized for her to throw out the first pitch to me as an inauguration for my first season as a Rebel. When I told the front office that I wanted to propose to my girlfriend on the field, they couldn't have been more ecstatic. Feel-good stories like these go viral and any leg up they can have on the Bobbies is something they're interested in.

They orchestrated the entire proposal, setting up a false inauguration day for me.

We head out to the field where I spot Dottie in the dugout wearing one of my jerseys and looking so goddamn adorable, that when I gravitate toward her, I pull her into a hug. I press a kiss to her ear and say, "Just like we practiced. Focus on me and throw."

"I know. I know," she says, sounding nervous.

We've been practicing for the last week and she's really got it down, but you never know what's going to happen when she throws the ball while a packed stadium watches. I assured her no matter what happens, the fans will love her because she's mine, and everyone loves Jason Orson. Can you imagine the epic eye-roll and "you're ridiculous" I received from that?

Yes, it's true, the Rebel fans have taken a liking to me.

I think it's from THE towel picture . . .

"Just don't short-hop me like you did on Monday."

She chuckles. "Wouldn't dream of catching you in your 'nuggets' again."

"Thank you, witty wench." I press one more kiss to her lips and then take off toward my spot behind the plate. The announcer introduces me to the Rebels as the new starting catcher, and the crowd erupts. God, I'm so popular. It was definitely THE towel picture.

Then the announcer introduces Dottie, who receives a warm reception as well. The field assistant walks her out to the designated spot in front of the mound and hands her a ball.

I make the most important squat of my life and watch as my girl cutely lifts her leg like a pitcher and delivers a strike straight into my glove. The fans cheer loudly for her, and now it's my time.

Ball and glove in hand, I jog up to her, and then kneel down on one knee. Very comfortable in this position, and I bet there are many lenses focused in on my juicy shelf. Her eyes go wide as I set my glove down with the ball and then reach into my back pocket. The stadium cheers louder than before, as all my guys line up on the foul line, whopping it up for one of their own.

Taking a deep breath, I bring her hand to mine and hold the ring box open to her. Her free hand falls to her mouth, and I try to make her hear me over the stadium noise.

"Dorothy Domico, I couldn't imagine another day without officially calling you mine. You're the girl meant for me. Rough around the edges, makes me work for a smile, but has the sweetest, kindest soul I've ever met. You're a classic contradiction of love and hate, loving me every day with your beautiful heart, hating on me with the rolling of your eyes at my jokes. I don't want to take another breath without you by my side. Be mine forever. Will you marry me?"

She nods, tears spilling from her eyes. I slip the ring on her shaking hand and then scoop her up. Her legs wrap around my waist and she grips my cheeks. "Oh my God," she cries. "Jason . . . oh my God."

I laugh and kiss her as the crowd yells. The announcer congratulates me, fireworks are shot off, and Bruno Mars's *"Marry You"* plays on the speakers as I twirl my girl on my new turf, starting the season off right.

My team joins us on the field along with Dottie's parents, Lindsay, and Emory. They give us hugs, congratulations, and a montage of our relationship is played on the mega-tron.

It's a goddamn romantic comedy out here and guess what? I'M. HERE. FOR. IT!

I'm so fucking here for it.

In the midst of the chaos, Dottie brings her lips to my ear and says, "You're ridiculous. But I love you so much, Jason. Forever and always."

Cue the camera spinning around us.

Cue the mushy music.

Cue the tears.

Because this story might have started with a burnt ham, but it's sure as hell ending with one hell of a happily ever after.

THE END

Made in the USA
Middletown, DE
17 August 2024

59354050R00197